Generation Z

The Queen Enslaved
Book 5

Peter Meredith

Fictional works by Peter Meredith:

A Perfect America
Infinite Reality: Daggerland Online Novel 1
Infinite Assassins: Daggerland Online Novel 2
Generation Z
Generation Z: The Queen of the Dead
Generation Z: The Queen of War
Generation Z: The Queen Unthroned
Generation Z: The Queen Enslaved
The Sacrificial Daughter
The Apocalypse Crusade War of the Undead: Day One
The Apocalypse Crusade War of the Undead: Day Two
The Apocalypse Crusade War of the Undead Day Three
The Apocalypse Crusade War of the Undead Day Four
The Horror of the Shade: Trilogy of the Void 1
An Illusion of Hell: Trilogy of the Void 2
Hell Blade: Trilogy of the Void 3
The Punished
Sprite
The Blood Lure The Hidden Land Novel 1
The King's Trap The Hidden Land Novel 2
To Ensnare a Queen The Hidden Land Novel 3
The Apocalypse: The Undead World Novel 1
The Apocalypse Survivors: The Undead World Novel 2
The Apocalypse Outcasts: The Undead World Novel 3
The Apocalypse Fugitives: The Undead World Novel 4
The Apocalypse Renegades: The Undead World Novel 5
The Apocalypse Exile: The Undead World Novel 6
The Apocalypse War: The Undead World Novel 7
The Apocalypse Executioner: The Undead World Novel 8
The Apocalypse Revenge: The Undead World Novel 9
The Apocalypse Sacrifice: The Undead World 10
The Edge of Hell: Gods of the Undead Book One
The Edge of Temptation: Gods of the Undead Book Two
The Witch: Jillybean in the Undead World
Jillybean's First Adventure: An Undead World Expansion
Tales from the Butcher's Block

3

Chapter 1
Prologue—Three Days Earlier

A morgue-like chill permeated the labyrinth of rooms beneath the Governor's mansion and, as Deanna Grey walked along the dim corridor, she wrapped her shawl more tightly around her bare shoulders. She was a tall, golden-haired beauty who hid her pain and fear behind a carefully arranged and artfully painted mask.

A close inspection would have revealed cracks in her appearance that hadn't been there a week before. Her blue eyes, for instance, once radiated a soft warmth; now they were hard as ice. Her lips, always so quick to smile, were now pressed firmly together to hold in the snarl that wanted to explode out of her.

Had someone been using the seven stages of grief as a measurement of her mental state, they would have been surprised at how quickly she had blown right through both shock and denial, and how deeply rooted she was in the stage of anger.

Deanna was furious. She was angry enough to kill. Had Joslyn Reynolds been there, Deanna wouldn't have been able to stop herself from beating her to death with her bare hands. A gun or a knife would be too easy, much too quick and far too painless.

The Governor, using sheer will, forced her fists to unclench so she could simply open the door to the very back room where a gruesome spectacle confronted her. It was bloody and sickeningly horrible, and her only reaction to the shocking nature of the scene was that her perfectly tweezed brows knit together and her normally soft hands crimped back into uncompromising fists.

This wasn't the first partially eaten corpse she had seen. It lay huddled against the far wall in a wide red pool, somewhat like a bit of castoff stew meat lying in a bowl. Around the red pool were splatters and sprays of clotting blood, and around these were hundreds of circular red drops, as if it had rained blood in the room.

And in all this gore were footprints. The smallest were her Emily's. Although her legs just seemed to grow and grow, her feet were still dainty.

"Like a dancer's," Deanna said, drawing out the "S" slightly. Her teeth would not unclench even to speak, so everything came out with a reptilian hiss. She stepped over these dainty prints, afraid to mar anything that had once been her daughter's. Everything else was fair game. Nothing mattered to Deanna except getting her daughter back.

She strode through the room, uncaring that it was a crime scene. She knew who the victim was, and it wasn't Eddie Sanders. He was the villain in all this and had gotten everything he deserved.

"One of the villains," Deanna whispered, again with the hiss. She had a long list of people who would pay if she ever brought them to justice. The list started with Joslyn Reynolds. Deanna's fingernails dug crescents into her palm as she pictured the backstabbing bitch. It was expected that the Black Captain was next on the list, but what might not have been expected was that Jillybean was third. She had started all of this, after all.

"What did you say?" Deberha Perkins asked. The Island's lone sheriff stood in the doorway, a green sheen to her usually friendly face. For years, hers had been something of a ceremonial position and now that she was faced with an actual crime, her stress level could be graphed by the number and depth of the lines crossing her forehead. There had been five before she saw the corpse; now there were six and they were quickly becoming crags.

"Nothing," Deanna answered, sharply. She hunkered down next to the body, her long hair flowing from one shoulder to hang like a golden curtain. Even squatting over a decrepit corpse, she had the knack of looking perpetually ready to be photographed.

The body was a different story. Few things looked as appalling to Deberha as Eddie Sanders' stinking cadaver. Meek and mild Neil Martin had torn out Eddie's throat, although whether he had done it with his teeth or his black-clawed fingers, she didn't know. Eddie's eyes had been gouged out by hand, there was no question about that. The only question concerning his eyes was: where were they?

Deberha looked around, a lump growing in her throat. The eyes were nowhere to be found, and she could only hope that Neil had pocketed them for some reason, though she really doubted it. Against her will, her own eyes were constantly being dragged to the gaping black sockets where Eddie's had once been. The lump in her throat grew larger with each glance.

She tore her gaze away only to end up staring at the sickeningly large hole in the corpse's torso. Eddie had been horridly violated. His intestines had been pulled out and pawed through as if Neil had been looking for a lost bit of jewelry. Even worse, his heart had been ripped from its proper place and was now leaning against a dusty baseboard.

The sheriff had never seen a heart out of the body like that and it was nothing like she could've ever imagined. There were ugly red tubes jutting from the top of it, each dribbling blood, and there was something of a membranous skein clinging to it like a ghastly veil. And there was a big chunk missing. Deberha took a deep, shaky breath.

"Almost done?" she begged. The lump in her throat had reached a point where swallowing was no longer an option, and she knew that if she stayed in the room much longer, the lump would have to come up.

Deanna only grunted as she dug through Eddie's pockets, searching for clues or evidence, or anything that would help make sense of what had happened. First, they had come for Neil, hoping to kill him. Then they had taken Emily. But why? Going after Neil made sense since he was the one thing keeping Jillybean sane.

But what did Emily do? Why had she been taken?

Eddie's pockets were empty and, if there had been any clues about him, they were hidden by the blood.

Frustrated, she stood and glared around the room. This was her second stop. Her first, Joslyn's home, had been equally frustrating, and she had given in to the desire to wreak some measure of vengeance by completely ransacking the house. Walls were torn down, mirrors were smashed, and drawers were emptied and thrown into heaps.

Deberha had to stop her from setting the place on fire.

Deanna didn't know what she had expected to find that would point to anyone other than the Black Captain. Jillybean's war was coming north, spilling over to include innocent people —and no one was more innocent than Emily.

Eddie Sanders was a literal dead end. Gina Sanders was not. "Do you have your cuffs on you, Deberha?"

"My cuffs?" Deberha shrunk inward. She had once played high school volleyball and had been something of a strapping woman. That had been thirty years before and now she had a sagging quality to her from her breasts to her hips, and walked with a bit of a waddle. She hadn't cuffed anyone in years. "Oh, Governor. It won't come to that. I know Gina and she…"

"Do you really know her?" Deanna said, through her clenched teeth. "I bet you thought you knew Eddie, too. Hmm? Did you? Did you know he was going to take my Emily?"

"God, no!" Deberha answered, with a nervous twitch of her shoulders.

Deanna pushed past her, saying, "Then you don't know Gina, either. None of us do." She marched out of what had been her house, thinking she wouldn't be coming back. What was there to come back to? A dead body and Emily's screams etched into the walls? No. Coming back would drive her as insane as Jillybean. She would lie in bed, stare uselessly at the ceiling, and discover a thousand previously missed clues, or she would imagine the terror Emily was feeling, or she would picture the torture she would suffer at the hand of the Corsairs.

"No," Deanna whispered, stopping in the doorway. "That's not going to happen." Her other option was far preferable: she would take one of the small sailboats and follow after Neil Martin and Stu Currans. Chances were she would die in some horrible manner out in the wilderness, and that was okay. First, she had to look Gina Sanders in the eye, and she wasn't going to do that unarmed and wearing an off-the-shoulder black dress and a pumpkin pendant.

In the back of her closet was a cardboard box that hadn't been opened for ten years. Stripping off the dress, she pulled on musty-smelling camouflage. Over it, she slid on a shredded grey blanket that would hide her from the zombies once she made it to the mainland. Next to the cardboard box was a gun safe that was covered in dust. Inside was her nine-millimeter, an M4 and four magazines for each.

The weight of it all was comforting, and the soft whiff of oil and spent gunpowder shimmering up from the weapons was strangely natural. It brought a snarling grin to her face. "I need a knife," she said, speaking to the M4 as she pulled back the charging handle.

"No, you really don't," Deberha said from the doorway, the closest her modest bravery would allow. "You told me to send some of the guys over to keep an eye on her place. Remember? Norris said he'd…"

Deanna wasn't listening. She slung the rifle and once more pushed past the dumpy woman, hurrying down to the kitchen; she knew the knife she wanted and when she pulled it from the drawer, the light played along its razor-sharp length invitingly. She thumbed its edge, losing the grin as she did. It could have been sharper.

"It's not like you're going to be doing surgery," she told herself. She didn't know exactly what she was going to be doing with the knife other than perhaps releasing some of her fury with it. "No, it doesn't need to be sharp."

"Governor," Deberha begged, following Deanna as she marched out the front door without looking back. "You can't do this, she rasped almost in Deanna's ear. There was a surprising number of people standing in the driveway and on the lawn. More sat along the low stone wall that bordered her property, looking like over-grown ravens in the pre-dawn light.

Or vultures, Deanna thought. *Will they finish eating Eddie once I'm out of sight?* It was a terrible thought made worse by the fact that she didn't care. The body had to be gotten rid of somehow.

Deanna didn't bother whispering. "I can do whatever I want, I'm Governor."

"Yeah, yeah, that's sort of true, but you know she has rights," Deberha said, trying to pluck at Deanna's sleeve. "We don't torture our citizens."

"Who said anything about torture?" Deanna asked, shrugging off the hand. "I'm just going to stab her until she tells me what she knows. Then I'm going to kill her." Deberha tried again to explain their laws, but Deanna was too enraged and brought the carving knife up, separating them with a flick of her wrist, as if it were a magic wand. "What about Emily, damn it? What about her? What about her rights? You want to talk about torture then let's talk about what the Corsairs are going to do to her!"

Deberha's mouth opened very wide as if she had a great deal to say on the subject, yet not even a squeak came out.

"That's what I thought," Deanna scoffed, before marching on.

It took Deberha a few gulps of air before she could find the courage to speak again. By then Deanna was at the end of her driveway. The crowd of shadowy, faceless people parted as she drew near as if Deanna were an angry pulsing ball of fire thrusting back the darkness.

"Stop! You can't do this. Not even as governor."

"Then I quit. Tell Norris that he finally got his wish. Let him deal with all this crap."

"I'll arrest you!" Deberha's voice had never been so girlishly high.

This brought on a collective, "ooooh," from the crowd. It also stopped Deanna. The knife *clanked* onto the black asphalt as she took her rifle in both hands. Deberha swallowed loudly without swallowing her fear. "W-we have laws and our people… our *citizens* have rights."

"*She* is not a citizen. *She* is a traitor. And in case you haven't realized it, we are at war! Abduction. Assassination. These are acts of war, Deberha. So no, Gina doesn't have rights. I can do what I want to her." That they were at war should have been obvious hours before and yet the crowd seemed startled by the thought. The dark rustled with their coarse whispers.

"No. *Norris* can, can, can maybe do what he wants to her. Remember, you just said you quit? If he's governor, he's in charge and you're just a citizen. Is that what you want?" Deberha was a strangely effective sheriff. They both knew that Norris Barnes would be a catastrophe as a wartime governor. He excelled at good 'ol boy back-slapping, political grips and grins, and "speech-ifying" as he liked to say. Where he lacked was in the ability to make a true decision when it really counted. If there were any consequences to a choice, he always chose not to decide. Instead, he would "study" the issue, or convene commissions, anything to keep a choice at arm's length.

Deanna paused, trying to picture what a Norris Barnes governorship would look like with a Corsair threat hanging over their head. She found she couldn't and just a slight bit of air went out of her rage. The weight of the gun in her hands seemed to gather.

Deberha could sense her softening. "We need you, Deanna. And Emily needs you. She needs you to keep your head screwed on right. If you went out there in the wilderness, what good would you do? You're not a Valkyrie anymore. And you're not a slave, either. You're not even a sailor. You'd have to walk and that would take days and days. If you throw your life away just trying to get there, what good will Emily be to them? She'd be worthless, and you know how they treat worthless girls."

"I know." In fact, no one knew better than Deanna. She too had been a slave once, forced to do horrible, degrading things to stay alive. That couldn't be Emily and the truth was, it would be if Deanna didn't make exact, perfect decisions. She knew there was very little chance of making it to Grays Harbor alive, and there was even less of one to get into the Hoquiam unseen. Her chance of finding Emily in a town crawling with Corsairs, and freeing her, was microscopic.

There was no chance of getting her daughter out alive, not alone, not without some sort of help, and there'd be no help coming from Bainbridge. Deanna was stuck, and Emily was doomed.

"Unless Neil can come through…or Jillybean," she said under her breath. If they couldn't, the Black Captain would be coming to Deanna with some sort of deal. There was only one reason to take Emily and that was to use her as a hostage; the Captain was going to try to keep Bainbridge out of his war. This realization had an immediate calming effect on her.

Her bag of a stomach still ached, and her shrunken heart still hurt, but her mind was clear. She could think without wanting to scream her lungs out.

The Captain feared Bainbridge, which told her that he either had an inflated view of her army, or he was weaker than she could have guessed. "He's weak," she decided. "Which means we have to get stronger. First things first." She needed to make sure it was indeed the Captain who had taken her daughter and to find that out, she needed authority.

"Screw Norris," she said to Deberha. "I am still governor." Stooping, she picked up the carving knife and began heading north, while the sky turned pink off to her right. She gave it a glance and never saw such a hateful sunrise.

Deberha trailed after her, squeaking, "Governor. Governor." Behind her rumbled the mass of shadowy people. They followed in an endless whisper. Deanna ignored them as well. There was only one person on her mind: Gina Sanders.

"She in there?" Deanna asked one of the men Deberha had sent to keep an eye on Eddie's home. The island had never witnessed a murder or a kidnapping, and no one had known precisely what to do. There were vague notions that warrants, and arrest orders had to be prepared and so Gina had been left to stew alone with her toddler all night long.

Deanna didn't knock and neither did she expect the front door to be locked because no one on Bainbridge locked their front door. She walked in, the knife in her hand.

Gina sat on the couch across the room, the bright dawn light warming the side of her face through the cream filter of her curtains. In her arm was her baby, a perfect mixture of ginger Eddie and caramel Gina.

"I'd put the baby down, if I were you," Deanna said, shutting the door behind her. She made a point of locking it. "You don't want him to get hurt."

Chapter 2

Mike Gunter was able to truly enjoy the *Queen's Revenge* for exactly seventy-eight seconds. With the night wind gently ruffling back his shoulder-length blonde hair, he walked the sixty-foot length of her sparkling deck with one hand trailing on the rail, the other caressing the larger of the two booms. *Two booms!* It was the grandest, most wonderfully magnificent ship he'd ever been on, and it was all his.

He was captain of the finest sailing ship in existence, so it was no wonder that a huge smile kept trying to creep over his face. He couldn't allow it, however.

A glance at the stern showed Jenn Lockhart staring back toward the muddy little island where they had left Jillybean to a horrible fate. Even though the dark hid Jenn's face, it couldn't hide her misery. Or Emily Grey's for that matter, or Neil Martin's or Stu Curran's. In their own way, each of them loved Jillybean.

Just at that moment, Mike was the closest he had ever come to loving Jillybean. He had always respected her, but now that she had traded her life for his, that respect had grown. It was the gift of the *Queen's Revenge* that really warmed his heart. He patted the ship's rail—he was already in love with *her*—and went to Jenn. Taking the flag from her, he said, "We'll get her back. Remember, Jillybean thinks five steps ahead. She knows we're going to win this fight."

The words were not a second from his mouth when lights began to emerge in the darkness. Jillybean's immense hundred and thirty boat fleet was beginning to set flames to kettles and hang them from the mast the way the Corsairs did.

"You want us to light up too, Cap?" Deaf Mick asked. With his awful six-toothed mouth, his scraggly beard, and his undeniable lack of hygiene, he had more than a passing resemblance to a goat and Mike jerked a bit at the sight of him before looking around for a more palatable sailor. For as large as it was, the *Queen's Revenge* was sparsely crewed. It was so empty that it had an abandoned feel to it. Other than the one ex-Corsair, there were two thin and sickly Santas, Knights Sergeant Troy Holt, Stu Currans and Gerry "the Greek" Xydis.

Deaf Mick was the closest of them. "Run the Queen's flag up first," Mike answered, handing over the last white and gold banner.

The dark hid Deaf Mick's sour, gap-toothed sneer as he handled the flag. He was the only one on board who knew the trap that had been set. It would happen at any moment and as he ran up the flag and saw the golden crown unfurl, he was busy plotting. His job was to keep the *Queen's Revenge* from escaping, although he hadn't been told how.

He wasn't all that worried. In spite of his troll-ish IQ, Deaf Mick had a sinister mind; he knew which ropes could be frayed so that when they "suddenly" snapped he wouldn't be looked at as the culprit. All he had to do was "Wait for the lights." That had been Mark Leney's whispered instructions. That was all the knowledge of the secret plan that Deaf Mick possessed.

He knew they were going to go back to being Corsairs, but *how* was a mystery that he hadn't even considered solving. Some things were best not thought about. He hadn't even been asked if he wanted to go back to being a Corsair, at least not in any verbal manner. The Corsairs didn't really need to blab things to get their point across. A raised eyebrow, a soft tsk, or a cleared throat was all that was needed to let people know you were ready for a change.

Leney was in charge of the revolt and that was enough for Deaf Mick. He had proven himself when they had started digging that great big river in the hills above Highton. There had been a tsunami of grumbling which he both stoked and pacified; he had been walking the proverbial tightrope with death on either side of him. If he swayed too far towards the Queen, the Corsairs would poison him along with her. If he swung too far towards the Corsairs, she would string him up by his ballsack.

Somehow, he had managed to set things up using only sly hints and the occasional hidden message. There had only been the *when* of it that had been up in the air. It seemed as though they had all been waiting for the Queen to finally take a drink out of the wrong cup, only the days kept slipping by and she refused to die. Then they got to Grays Harbor only to find the Captain had buttoned up Hoquiam and sent his fleet into hiding.

This wasn't much of a strategy and Deaf Mick had worried the Queen would somehow win again. He was sure that she would roll over the Captain as she had rolled over everyone else. The furtive winks had ceased and the knowing looks became nervous ones. Then, completely out of the blue, she had thrown away everything she had worked so hard to achieve by trading herself for three complete nobodies—and expecting hardened,

13

blood-thirsty pirates like Deaf Mick to follow them? A fifteen-year-old girl? Mick would have said the idea was contemptuous if he knew what the word meant.

Just like that, the secret plan was back in place. The Queen even helped the revolt by landing the most doubtful elements on shore. Gone were the traitorous Coos Bay Clan and the backstabbing Magnum Killers, as well as the near useless Santas. What was better, Leney had managed to keep the "true" Corsairs back, manning the ships. To top it all off, Leney was now the fleet commander!

Deaf Mick could barely contain his mirth as he ran up the insipid white and gold flag to the top of the main mast. He had to clamp his greasy lips shut to keep from laughing. Not that it mattered, much. He could have danced a jig in the middle of the deck for all that anyone was paying attention to him.

Most of the tiny crew were at the stern commiserating with the new Queen, who looked strangely familiar to Mick. Moping beside her was some ragged-looking bushman, the strange little zombie creature that seemed partially human, and a little blonde girl who was even younger than the new queen. Deaf Mick had secretly called dibs on her and had leered at her tight little rear as she came aboard. The fact that she was probably not even in high school was a plus in his eyes.

The wet-eared boy of a captain hung close by, as did a beefy, black-bearded man who looked to be at least three-quarters Corsair.

At the bow were two wispy and timid Santas who were arguing over what it "meant" that they had been assigned to the *Queen's Revenge*. The only person who was paying any attention to what was important was the annoying boy-scout of a Guardian. He was staring out across the dark water as the fleet lit its kettles.

"Who gave the order to light up the fleet?" he asked, looking back as Deaf Mick slid out his belt knife.

The Corsair froze. "Hmm?" He couldn't exactly say that it was Mark Leney, signaling the beginning of a revolt, so he gestured, somewhat ambiguously, toward the stern where the new Queen was fighting to pull herself together. With everyone looking at her, no one saw Mick give the main shroud a quick flick with his knife, scoring it deeply.

"I really don't know," Jenn answered in complete honesty. She was in a perfect state of befuddlement. An hour before, she had been a prisoner of the Corsairs and wondering if she'd be allowed to pee before they started gang-raping her. Now her mind was balanced precariously as it tried to come to grips with zombie Neil Martin weeping on her arm—Jillybean giving up her crown when right on the verge of victory—being saved from the Black Captain—and suddenly being thrust back into a leadership role she had never asked for.

Mike finally took his eyes off the beautiful lines of the *Queen's Revenge* and began to ask, "Does this ship have a signal book or a…" His mouth ceased working as he gazed in confusion at the ship closest to them. Three hundred yards off their starboard beam lay the forty-foot *Blood Belle*. She was lit by four kettles and in the flickering light, he could see her crew yanking down Jillybean's black and silver flag.

There was a cheer as it was tossed overboard, and an even bigger one as up ran the Corsair flag of jet black.

"What the ever-lovin' hell?" Mike demanded. "You!" He pointed at Deaf Mick. "Get the main up. They can't do…" Another cheer had him choking on his words. The thirty-eight-foot *Slaughter Wagon* had just run up its own Corsair flag. After this, more and more ships followed suit until half the fleet was flying the black flag.

Because no one knew exactly where loyalties lay, not every captain had been told of the revolt and now Deaf Mick held his breath. If half the fleet remained loyal to the Queen, Grays Harbor was only seconds away from being the sight of the largest naval battle since Leyte Gulf.

Everyone from the new Queen on down knew it as well and a heavy silence followed the last cheer. It lasted until Bangle Bob of the *Falling Axe* roared out, "Take her down!" The Queen's flag was torn down with such violence that the halyard at the top of the mast broke off and dropped down to smack Bangle Bob square on the crown of his bald head, denting it so deeply that Bob was out before he hit the deck and shortly after his body was rolled overboard by his eager first mate.

The cry of "Take her down!" echoed across the bucking waters of the harbor and soon every ship but one was flying the black flag.

"Get the main up!" Mike ordered, racing to the secondary mast as Deaf Mick fiddled, pretending to be stymied by a knot. Mike had the second sail flying in seconds and the two Santas had a jib up before Deaf Mick even began hauling on a line.

Troy elbowed him to the side. "New guy, get the wheel, hard to port." By "new guy" he meant Stu, who was all set to spin the wheel all the way to the left.

"Belay that order!" Mike barked. "A half-turn to starboard, Stu. We're already gathering more air on the right." The *Queen's Revenge*, the biggest and now the only boat in Jenn's fleet, heeled to starboard as the wind filled the second sail and jib. The deck took on a list that a kid could sled on as she danced on the building waves and raced for the mouth of the harbor.

Despite everything going on, Mike grinned. She was a fast, stiff boat and was quickly drawing away from the Corsair fleet.

"We're just going to leave her?" Neil asked, still looking back at the little muck of an island. He was talking about Jillybean—she was the reason he had risked his disgusting excuse of a life for in the first place. The reason why was lost in the soft grey mud of his dying brain.

"If you have any better ideas," Mike said, "I'd love to hear them."

Neil didn't have a single idea about anything. All he had inside were desires. He wanted Jillybean back. He was hungry. He thought that maybe he was sleepy. It was hard to tell. "Ideas? No, I don't think so."

Not a surprise, Mike thought. The one surprise was that Neil had any thoughts at all. It was hard to tell with the dark night, but Neil looked a hell of a lot like a zombie. It seemed rude to ask or stare.

"We have to get out of here," Emily stated, unequivocally, trying not to panic. "Jillybean sacrificed herself specifically for us to escape. She wanted us to get away." She was the only one who wore their fear so openly. She had great big eyes for the black fleet, some of which were plowing north, others speeding south on the wind, while the great majority were coming straight after them.

"We should go to Alaska," Jenn murmured under her breath. Twenty minutes before she had been a hostage, then she had been queen, leading a great invasion, and now she was fleeing for her life, once again. Yes, Alaska sounded perfect. Rumor had it there were no Corsairs, only a few mostly frozen zombies, and a cuisine that ran the gamut from fried walrus to stuffed penguin. It sounded perfect.

Stu heard the suggestion and grunted his approval. He would never go, however. He had come back to save Jenn, Mike and Emily. Once he got them to safety, he would then try to save Jillybean.

But first. "We should get you and Emily below deck. They'll probably start shooting once they realize they're not going to catch us."

"All unnecessary people should go below," Troy ordered, much to Mike's annoyance.

Mike stepped in front of him. "Yes, let's get everyone down in the front cabin, except..." Deaf Mick was already heading for the stairs, pushing past Stu. Mike glared. "Right. We don't need cowards. Jenn, Emily, you two." He meant the Santas and hoped that Neil would follow along as part of the herd. Of course, he didn't and for the next five minutes, he stumbled around on deck until the first ranging shot zinged through the dark.

The bullet didn't even come close to them. They were, after all, nothing but a blur that was growing blurrier with each passing second. Still, Mike's shoulders twitched and his entire body tensed. Fearless as always, Stu stood like granite. Troy Holt yawned as if getting shot at was perfectly dull.

Neil glanced around. "Did you guys hear something?"

"That's just great," Mike grumbled, under his breath. Louder, he called out, "Cutting to port."

The *Queen's Revenge* now leaned to the left as she picked up speed. Mike grinned again feeling the tension of the moment drain from him. It was replaced by a different tension. He could feel the wind strike the sails, run through the mast, down the hull and into the keel. From there the strength of the wind ran up the rudder to the wheel and into his hands. Mike was like a child on Christmas morning. He was one with the ship and in his heart, he was sure they would get away. They were just too fast, and if the Corsairs wanted to stop them, they'd have to rattle off hundreds and hundreds of bullets.

No, they would turn back soon.

"Coming to Starboard." He announced with all the confidence in the world. It was then that the main halyard broke.

The mainsail abruptly tore free and began lashing the starboard side of the boat like a great canvas whip as the nose of the ship went far over to windward and then died in the water, spinning gently around until they were facing the oncoming ships.

Troy leapt on the sail, trying to hold the thrashing canvas down with wide spread arms, while Mike screamed orders at Stu to swing the boom just so, and to haul down the top jib which was pressing them down by the bow and keeping them from picking up speed.

None of it mattered now. The lead Corsairs were doing ten knots. It was only a matter of time before they were caught, once more.

Chapter 3

Tommy Conrad stood at the bow of the *Blood Belle* as it gained on the *Queen's Revenge,* his wide, homely face lit by a great yellow smile. His men joked that when he smiled he resembled a softly rotting jack-o-lantern two weeks after Halloween. He didn't care one bit, not then at least. He was going to claim the big boat for his own and kill any man who even considered looking at her with anything but proper admiration.

That included the Black Captain. Yes, the Captain wasn't quite the alpha dog he'd always pretended to be. There was no getting past the fact that he had been bested by an insane-in-the-membrane bit of tail, and if he hadn't been saved by Mark Leney of all people, he'd probably be dead by then.

And not only would Conrad claim the boat, he'd claim at least one of the girls he had seen on deck earlier. While details had been lacking in his telescope, they hadn't been in his mind. "Look at them," he muttered, spewing the aroma of rotting teeth over wet lips. "Lost the main and now they're flopping around trying to squeeze every ounce of speed out of that secondary sail."

Next to him, his first mate, Jake Annarino pursed his lips. "He ain't doing bad for all that. Better than a lot of ours woulda done. He's got much of his wind on the front third." Mike Gunter was fighting like mad to keep the bow from lurching to the south where there was nothing but shallows and mud shoals.

"Yeah, ain't bad. Maybe worth keeping around. The Captain's got a lot of people to replace." *And I can throw him a bone since I'll be taking the best ship for my own.* "Go get that kid," he told Jake. "Let's see if he knows anything about this sailor of theirs."

In the captain's cabin, ten-year-old Aaron Altman sat on the edge of the bed, his knobby knees tucked up to his pointy chin, a ball of simmering rancid grease in the pit of his stomach and his face battered into a mishmash of ugly lumps, each a separate color representing time along the bruise spectrum. Some were so purple that they were black while others were the green-yellow of a sunrise in hell.

He had his ears pricked, ready to hop up at the first sound of a step on the other side of the door. He wasn't allowed on the bed.

His place for the last four days was in the corner of the cabin where Captain Conrad, in his "generosity," had given him a towel to be used as a combination pillow, blanket and mattress —one of the bluest of his bruises was due to Aaron's lack of gratitude for the gift.

During the voyage north from Highton, Aaron had lived in a state of indescribable fear, deathly afraid in a way he'd never felt before. Conrad was a monster. He was cruel and evil. He enjoyed hurting people and seemed happiest when Aaron was crying. Conrad was a real Corsair. This was how they really were when the Queen wasn't looking.

The Queen thought she could change them or use them, or something, but in this one thing, she was blind. Mostly, that is. She had given Aaron a bomb, "Just in case things go wrong," she had whispered to him in her tent on the hill above Highton.

"What could go wrong?"

He could not remember her answer precisely. She had fed him with little bits of imagery so that he saw himself as the linchpin, holding the fate of his people in his little hand. When all was said and done, he was pretty sure that the Hill-people would throw a parade for him, and the Queen would name a holiday after him, and his picture would hang on walls and banners, and people would name their children after him.

Looking back, he realized that in not so many words, the Queen had actually asked him to kill himself and, in the heat of the moment, with his heart bursting for her, he had agreed.

She had given him a bomb and instructions: where, when, and how to use it. The idea had seemed so heroic at the time. Then reality set in. The target for his bomb was supposed to be Captain Steinmeyer. "He's not the worst of them," she had said. "He might even treat you with some respect; don't let that allow you to falter."

But Aaron had never made it to Steinmeyer's boat. During the utter chaos of loading the fleet, he'd been sent to the wrong ship, where he'd been quickly grabbed by a bony-faced sailor who had taken him below deck to "Stow his gear."

The creepy sailor had followed him down into the dark galley and into a cramped back cabin which was crowded with stained sleeping bags and piles of reeking clothes. The room wasn't just unhealthy, it felt seedy, as if *bad* things happened in it.

He hesitated in the door for just a second too long. The sailor suddenly pushed him inside and then threw himself onto Aaron.

"Wait, I…" A nasty tar-smelling hand was slammed onto Aaron's mouth by the sailor, who leered over him and pawed at his privates, his hot sticky breath coming faster and faster. Captain Conrad had "rescued" him, kicking the sailor away. Before Aaron could thank him, the Captain slapped the young boy hard enough to spin his eyeballs in his head.

"If I catch you in here again, boy, I'll toss you in the blue and see how well you can swim one-handed."

Aaron tried to explain that he'd been forced into the room and that it wasn't his fault and that all of this was a big misunderstanding since he was supposed to be on Captain Steinmeyer's boat. He barely got a word out of his mouth before Conrad hit him again.

From that moment on, he was the Captain's cabin boy, which sounded a lot like what the scary sailor had wanted to make him. Thankfully, the position was eighty percent cleaning, ten percent getting threatened with beatings, and only ten percent actual beatings.

If things did not "sparkle," Conrad smashed Aaron across the face. The blows were like thunderclaps and afterwards, he'd find himself splayed on the floor, his head spinning and his legs too wobbly to hold himself upright. At night his ears would throb with a pulsating wah, wah, wah. He had begun to shake like a nervous, in-bred poodle whenever he heard anyone come near the cabin.

And this was no exception.

Aaron heard the steps and jumped up, his shoulders hunched in, his spine bent in a permanent cringe. It was only Jake. "Yes sir?"

"Get your ass up on deck. The Captain wants you." He knew better than to ask why. Asking anything was a sure-fire way to get smacked.

Jake turned on his heel and Aaron dutifully followed him up into the cold night. If anything, he was more afraid when he was on deck than anywhere else. The sailors all joked about giving him a "bath," and more than one had given him a hard shove toward the low railing. No one really knew if the Captain would even care if he went over. Aaron guessed he'd only be mad because he wasn't the one doing the pushing.

The thrashing black water scared Aaron to death. He had not tried swimming since he had lost his arm and had no desire to, guessing it would be a slow, painful death, unless one of the water zombies got to him first.

He edged as far from the rail as he could as he came up on deck. Right away, he saw the Captain at the front of the ship staring at the *Queen's Revenge*, which was a half a mile or so ahead of them. Aaron only knew her because she was a white ship while all the rest were black. It looked to him like they were chasing her, causing his fear to double. He was sure the only thing keeping him alive was the Queen. If the revolt she had worried about was actually happening, his life wouldn't be worth a nickel.

Above his head, the snapping flag drew his attention. It was blacker than the night and unblemished. The silver crown was gone. He began to shake worse than ever. He was so frightened that he chanced a look back to see how close they were to shore. They weren't close at all.

The *Blood Belle* was leading a phalanx of about forty ships and as Aaron watched, the pilot gave the wheel a turn to cut off what looked like a slightly faster ship. There was a good deal of cursing and jawing back and forth. Further back, were more ships, lights blazing all around, black flags strung from the top of masts. The entire fleet had gone over.

"What the hell, boy?" Jake barked, grabbing him by his stump. "You got a death wish lollygagging on deck like this." He dragged Aaron right up to the Captain who was still turned away. "You wanted the boy."

Conrad pulled his eyes from the prize and glanced at Aaron before shoving the binoculars into his one hand. "Who they got captaining that ship? You know him?"

Working binoculars one handed was almost impossible. The view was terribly blurry and yet Aaron was so afraid he'd drop the glasses in the ocean that he didn't try to adjust them.

"That's Mike Gunter," Aaron said of the blonde blur at the wheel. He could see six people. Four were scrambling around on deck doing something to their big sail, which had come loose from its boom. The last person, he incorrectly identified as the Queen, though in a way he was right, only it was Queen Jennifer and not Queen Jillian. She was staring back at the *Blood Belle*, almost as if she were looking right at Aaron.

He couldn't know it, but she was contemplating running down her flag and jumping into the harbor with it. The ships might stop for her which would allow the rest to escape.

"And?" the Captain demanded, impatiently. "What about him? Is he good?"

"Yes sir," Aaron said, handing back the binoculars. "He captained the *Saber* during the first battle on the bay. That was our only ship and they said he burned down four Corsair ships and caused the Santas and you guys to fight each other…"

The Captain's brutish lips twisted into a sneer. He remembered the *Saber* all right, and he would remember that battle if he lived to a hundred. Nothing he'd ever experienced had been so intense; the clouds of smoke that hung on the water like black fog, the roaring fires as ships went up in flames, and the rain of bullets washing across the decks. The chaos had been fantastic, with black ships going every which way and no one entirely sure who was friend and who was foe.

The *Saber* had been in the thick of the fighting, yet it had never engaged. Instead, it had ghosted among the ships like a phantom.

"I remember, he's a tricky one," Conrad said, nodding in satisfaction. He turned and barked at the man at the wheel. "Swing a touch starboard. Let's get a little upwind of him. Signal the squadron to do the same. He's going to send out some smokers soon, not that it'll do him any good."

The crew went about the simple tasks with a touch less bravado. They too remembered the sea battles and the defeats. The string of losses hung like heavy chains around their necks. They were a superstitious lot and trusted nothing that smacked of bad luck, and what was unluckier than a sniveling, cringing one-armed boy?

"There's trash stinking up the deck," one sailor muttered loud enough for the captain to hear. "Clean up on aisle one." A bit of snickering followed this. Trash was always thrown overboard, and the mutterer was hinting that Aaron should be tossed away like yesterday's fish heads.

Conrad had been staring at the *Queen's Revenge*; now he turned and saw Aaron was still hanging around, looking sad and useless, and unlucky. His first thought was to swat the kid over the rail himself, then he reconsidered. Wasn't this kid a favorite of the Queen? If so, the Black Captain would almost certainly want to use him to get at her. Conrad decided to keep the kid, to help sweeten the tripe he was going to force down the Captain's throat.

"I'll give him Gunter, too and everyone will be happy. Jake! I want our best rifleman up here. I doubt they'll shoot off any torpedoes, but if they do I want to know right away, and I want the lot of them blasted out of the water. And someone other than Rick get this kid out of my sight. I don't want him touched. He's going to be a gift for the Captain."

A filthy hand came down on Aaron's shoulder and he was thrust back toward the stairs. He tripped over an outstretched leg and thumped onto the deck. The same hand closed on his good arm and hauled him to his feet. Hot, foul words were whispered into his ear, "The Captain is going to open his gift with a knife. He's gonna unzip your belly with a razor so that you can see your guts in a little bag…"

"They're lighting off smoke!" someone cried. Every head turned to stare as Mike let the first of his floating smoke generators go.

"What did I say about the smoke?" Conrad laughed. "It's all he's got. It'll take them at least twenty minutes to get the sail up and we'll be on 'em in ten." His laughter was infectious, especially as they were upwind of the smoke and had a perfect view of the *Queen's Revenge* as it lumbered along desperately trying to make it out of the harbor where a howling storm was beginning to rage.

It was their only chance and Conrad wasn't going to give them the opportunity. Mike Gunter lit off a second smoker, cut it loose and then sent the great ship in among the acrid clouds, her mast a white beacon above. Now the entire crew was laughing and pointing; they knew exactly where the ship was.

"Make straight for the harbor entrance," Conrad ordered, a smile lifting the corners of his mask of a beard. "And why is this dumb kid still on deck?"

Aaron had stopped to watch the chase. Now, he scurried below. He didn't go to the captain's cabin, however. Instead he crouched at the base of the stairs where the shadows collected. He was deathly afraid. He was afraid to act and more afraid not to. He huddled, shaking violently, knowing that his short life was over, one way or the other.

Even if the Black Captain didn't unzip his belly, he would have no use for a skinny one-armed boy. They would drown him, or burn him alive, or force him to do terrible things. Aaron had heard the stories about what the Corsairs did to people they didn't need. Around the campfire at night, the stories had been chilling. Now, he felt as though he was about to pee his pants.

There was really only one thing he could do: die a hero. Only, he was just a kid. He was ten-years-old and a small ten-year-old at that. Small and weak…

His heart jumped crazily in his chest and a squirt of urine shot from his penis as a black cloud rushed silently down the stairs. Making a pathetic mewling sound in his throat, he cringed away and watched as the cloud swirled and undulated before dissipating, leaving only the familiar stench of burnt barley behind.

The cloud had come from one of the Queen's smoke bombs. *Are we close?* Aaron wondered. He pictured himself jumping across to the *Queen's Revenge* just as her mainsail was raised and she shot away like lightning. It was a good dream, and he was about to climb the stairs to see how close to reality it really was, when he remembered the bomb Jillybean had given him.

Turning, he hurried along the heaving galley floor to the back cabin. It was just as rank and seedy as ever. He had hidden the bomb under one of the flung about backpacks the day he had come aboard, and until that moment he had been too afraid to go back and check on it.

The pack was still there, sitting against one wall, looking like a squatting toad. The bomb hadn't been touched. It was the size of a small loaf of bread and even in the dark it looked exactly like a bomb. Gently, he picked it up as if he were picking up a baby made from cotton candy. His grip was so nonexistent that when he stood, and the boat lurched over a swell, he dropped the thing. Another squirt of urine added to the damp of his pants and he had to clench his legs together to keep his bladder from letting go altogether.

With his lungs pumping erratically, he once more picked up the bomb and looked it over, seeing why it hadn't exploded right away.

"I forgot to turn it on." A simple switch was all it took and once it was armed, Aaron's full-body tremble became even more acute. Instead of walking around with a bomb in his shaking hand, he put it into the open pack. The detonator, which had been taped to its side, he kept in his pee-smelling pants pocket, thinking that no one would touch it there.

The "where" of planting the bomb had already been decided for him by Jillybean. *Among the torpedoes*, she had told him with a soft pat of his only hand. The *Blood Belle* had three, all of which were kept in the Captain's cabin. Aaron had lived in constant terror of them going off accidentally since coming on board. Now, he gently tucked the bomb beneath one and hurried from the room.

Just as he did, there was a gunshot from almost directly overhead. He froze, expecting more, or maybe even a return shot. There was only the steady crash of the boat as it dropped after each swell.

Aaron put one foot on the stairs leading to the deck, and to his death, when the boat shifted hard to port. As he frequently did, he reached out to brace himself with his left hand, only to realize a second too late that he didn't have a left hand anymore. He slammed heavily into the hull. Before he could recover, the ship hauled back to the right.

Someone above screamed, "We got 'em now!"

No one noticed Aaron as he came on deck. It seemed to him that in the last few minutes, they had sailed straight into hell. Pressing down from above was an immense ceiling of swirling horrible, wet darkness that was lit every few seconds by stabs of lightning, while below the *Blood Belle*, the water was like ink. All around them were clouds of smoke that seemed to throttle the light from the swaying kettles.

The clouds were now so thick that they made the black Corsair boat riding just off their beam look like a phantom. Parts of the ship, the bow, a bit of sail and a length of its deck, would solidify for a brief second before dissolving back into the nothing of the night.

Not more than seventy yards ahead, the *Queen's Revenge* looked like a true ghost ship. Her white sails and hull had an eerie, spectral glow about them. She faded in and out, and Aaron was sure that if he blinked, she would be gone forever.

Instead, as he watched, her lines grew more and more firm. The Corsairs were catching up quickly. Captain Conrad seemed more concerned with his rivals. "Get your ass back, Hayashi! You know I'm the ranking man here."

Jared Hayashi of the *Black Dream* yelled something back, but all Aaron heard were useless curse words. The ships were neck and neck, while crowding close behind were another fifteen or so, the better part of two squadrons.

"That greedy son of a bitch!" Conrad groused, his beard drenched with rain, seawater and spittle. "Jake give him a brush. Hell, give him more than a brush. What's a little paint?"

"You do see the *Revenge* is about to get her main back in action?"

"And do you see that Hayashi has us by a knot?" the Captain raged, pointing at the phantom ship off their beam. "That's who I'm worried about. Even with her main, the *Revenge* won't be able to get up to speed in a blink. Not in this mess. She'll carry away her main mast if she tries."

The very thought of losing a mast in the middle of a storm caused every eye to look up at their own. The mast was bowing with the strain of the wind, and the backstay was letting out a quivering, frightened sound and was a stray gust away from snapping.

"Turn the damned wheel," Conrad ordered, wearing a madman's grin. Aaron thought everyone's attention was on the coming collision, but the same sailor who had ran his grubby hands over his body when he first came on board suddenly grabbed him by his collar.

"Look who came to join us," he yelled over the wind.

Aaron didn't struggle. He couldn't, actually. His one good hand was stuffed down into the pocket of his now skintight jeans.

Conrad barely gave him a glance. "Get him below and teach him a lesson. It's going to be lessons all around. You hear that, Hayashi? It's time you learned who's top dog!"

Finally, Aaron was able to get the detonator out of his pocket. He thumbed the arming button and felt a single moment of lightness, almost as if he were floating just above the deck and not standing on it. He should have pressed the red button right then; however the feeling was too perfect. "Wait," he told the sailor. And just like that, the feeling of lightness ended and in the next breath all of his fears came screaming back, doubling in strength.

"Wait? I'm not going to…What is that?" The sailor's eyes bulged out of his bony face.

"It's a bomb," the boy said, backing out of the man's now slack grip. Aaron kept backing away as the two ships neared one another and the *Queen's Revenge* loomed, her main running up the mast. He tried to press the button. He really wanted to as the two ships came together with a scream of wood and a thunder of hoarse curses. Aaron wanted to more than anything, but the little boy in him failed. His courage was not up to the test.

"He's got a bomb!" the bony-faced sailor cried. He turned to run, though where on a forty-foot ship would be safe, he didn't know. Nor did he consider that a bomb the size of Aaron's detonator wouldn't do much more than blow his other arm off.

Pure chaos erupted with no one really understanding the situation, especially the first mate who was also the first person to react. He made a leap for the detonator in Aaron's hand, hoping to grab it while the boy was turned away. His hand closed on Aaron's just an inch too high, landing right on the boy's thumb, forcing it down.

The searing white fireball that erupted took out both Corsair ships and lit up the sky for miles, and the thundering echo could be heard all the way to Hoquiam.

Chapter 4

Emily Grey was on an adventure alright and there wasn't a single thing romantic or fun about it. It was exciting, there was no denying that. It was so exciting that at times she wondered if an almost twelve-year-old could have a heart attack.

Before this her adventure had been mostly dreary and awful. The trip to Hoquiam had been an exhausting grind, and she had never been this tired in her short life. Three days on the *Calypso* had left her hating the ocean. She'd been violently seasick, and when she wasn't throwing up her meager meals, she had been endlessly cold. The boat was cramped and terribly uncomfortable.

Because she'd been throwing up so much, Joslyn wouldn't let her sleep in the single bed on board, instead she had to make do with the stiff, convertible galley table. The cushions were soft in the same way tree trunks were soft, and she woke every morning feeling as though she had transformed during the night into a ninety-year-old woman with a bad back.

The cruise south along the Pacific coast was so bad that she wanted to get to Hoquiam as fast as possible. Except there was nothing fast about the *Calypso*. Even with the wind racing at their backs she was a pokey little ship and they never seemed to actually get anywhere. According to Mike Gunter, the "current" was against them.

Joslyn had believed that only to a point. On the morning of the third day, she had made very believable threats against both Jenn Lockhart and Emily. The "current" became a non-issue and they made it to Grays Harbor just ahead of the Queen's fleet.

It had been an awesome sight seeing so many ships and for a moment Emily thought her long nightmare was over. Then Joslyn, who was red-eyed and raggedy at that point, had told Mike that she would kill them all if they were taken by the Queen. With the crazy pulsing from her stark-white face, she was very believable and Mike suddenly discovered that the *Calypso* had another gear.

They had escaped from the Queen only to become prisoners of the Corsairs. Even compared to being kidnapped, that had been a holy terror. She had never been in a more frightening place. Hoquiam was a city of screams. They had been there only a few hours and a minute hadn't gone by when there wasn't a high, rending scream cutting the air and causing the hairs on the back of Emily's neck to lift.

The Corsair's lair was a dirty, stinking, rat-infested prison, where barbed-wire topped walls were there to keep the wretched slaves in. There were slaves of all sorts: rickety old slaves, and vacant-eyed women slaves in filthy grey lingerie, and male slaves with new whip-scars layered over old whip-scars. There were even little kid slaves with clunky black collars on their skinny necks. All the slaves wore collars. Some were big, weighty things the size of toilet seats, while others were delicate and silver. These last were always strung on the prettier slaves. Some slaves had chains hanging from their collars and dragged around heavy barbells wherever they went.

Hoquiam was bustling with a great deal of energy. The prison-city was being transformed into a fortress. Trenches had been dug and small brick, two-person mini-forts were popping up everywhere. The river on one side of the town had been dammed up, so they had been forced to cross a deep, muddy bog on a bridge of flat boards. On the other side of the town, the river had doubled in size and was fast moving.

Escape from Hoquiam would be impossible, and any attack would be doomed to failure.

Emily had figured she would be a slave until she could work out some way to kill herself. With the collars, she guessed that hanging would be the best option and she began to plot exactly how to do it. She would want to pad the collar first. That was a given. After all, no one wanted an uncomfortable suicide. Then she'd need a rope of some sort. She knew she'd likely have to fashion one.

She had just worked out most of the kinks in her plan when she found out that they were being traded for Jillybean. When she heard the news, she had to keep the smile from her face. It was like trading a Barbie Doll for a live scorpion.

But the Black Captain had turned out to be just as poisonous.

Emily stood with one foot hooked on the rail of the *Queen's Revenge*, staring back at Grays Harbor. The fastest Corsair ships were hot after them, while the rest were forming into squadrons and dropping anchor along the riverfront of Hoquiam.

"This is the last smoker," Jenn said, as she and Neil hauled a strange looking mash of life-preservers, duct tape, aluminum foil and cardboard out from the hold. "Do you want us to light it?"

Mike Gunter had to hold his shoulders in check to keep them from shrugging. The other smokers had been all but useless and he couldn't see why this one would be any different. But that wasn't something you said as captain.

He made a show of squinting back at the ships bearing down on them, as if judging the exact right moment. He then turned, gave a look at the sail that was only seconds from being raised, and sighed, knowing full well that it was being raised five minutes too late. The *Queen's Revenge* was too large of a ship to burst into sudden speed. It would take time for the sail to make any difference, and that was time they didn't have.

He smiled thinly. "Let's get the main up first." The eight people and one semi-zombie on board held their collective breath as Troy and Stu hauled on the halyard. From below, it looked like an acre of white canvas was being drawn up and tied off. Instead of filling, the sail sagged as the wind seemed to be holding its breath as well.

"Well, this sucks," Neil grouched. "We might as well light the stupid smoker. We can't get any more unlucky."

"Don't be too sure about that," Mike replied. The sailor in him knew that luck was extremely fickle. The lull could turn into a hurricane in a blink if they mocked things they didn't understand. "What do the signs say, Jenn?"

What signs? she didn't ask. Where would she look for signs? The stars were gone, obliterated by the menacing storm they were sliding straight into, while behind them were black ships hell bent on capturing them and sending them back to the Black Captain. As far as signs went, those ships told a pretty bleak story of how…

Her heart stopped as the lead ship erupted in an immense fireball that lit up the night.

"The signs are pretty good right now," she remarked after the sound of the blast roared over them and she could hear again.

Mike thought the exact opposite. They were outgunned and out-torpedoed, and the only thing that was keeping them from being shredded by a thousand bullets or blown to smithereens was the situational detente they found themselves in. The Corsairs wanted them alive but would resort to deadly force if the *Queen's Revenge* upped the ante.

"That wasn't us!" Mike screamed at the top of his lungs. Quieter, he hissed, "Light the smoker and let her go. Stu, get one of the Santas and get a torpedo ready. Everyone else, hold on, we're going to run with the wind." The twin booms swung overhead and the boat took a gentle turn so that they were aiming at the southern peninsula that made up half the "mouth" of the harbor. Tall rollers were crashing on shore with thunderous, angry bellows.

Mike couldn't run too far with the wind or he'd run them right to their deaths. He gave it only a minute before trying to cut due west again, only the wind had shifted and was now right in their faces. The big boat began to wallow.

"Back south!" Troy cried.

It seemed like the right direction. The remaining Corsairs were all bending in that direction as the fastest point of sailing. Yet they were all faster than the *Queen's Revenge* in this slop, so it made no sense to let them pin her to the shore.

"We will go north," he ordered and swung them along the opposite tack of his enemies, knowing they would pass dangerously close to each other. "Everyone get down!"

The move was unexpected and as they came about, a torpedo sped past. The bomb's pilot tried to make the turn as well but lost sight of it as the heavy waves increased. He detonated it fifty yards behind them. It was a waste of a torpedo and yet there was a great deal of cheering from the other side.

Mike chanced a look over the rail and saw the fifty-foot *Buzzsaw*. She had been Captain McCartt's ship before he led his troops ashore. Now, a proper Corsair was at the helm. *Buzzsaw* was not a fast ship, though she did have a wide beam and a deep keel. She was at her best when the ocean turned to soup. She shouldered aside the waves, dashed through the wreckage of the *Blood Belle* and the *Black Dream*, and bore down on the *Queen's Revenge*, looking to cut her off.

"Now what?" Troy asked.

Their only real option was to turn east; however, there was a solid wall of black ships in that direction. Their choices were terrible.

The only person with a worse choice was William Trafney. He was handcuffed to the kitchenette table, sitting almost in the exact middle of the *Buzzsaw*. Although he had been tolerated, no one had actually liked him since he had set foot on board a week before. The moment the crew of the *Buzzsaw* had passed into open revolt, he had been arrested and handcuffed. His bomb and detonator had been quickly discovered by men looking for loot.

He had been beaten as a matter of course, but the captain had decided not to hang him just yet, not while there was a chase on.

He'd assigned an ugly, tobacco chewing Corsair to watch over him, only just then the sailor was on the last step up to the deck, busy watching the action, and no one saw William furiously working the nuts loose from the bottom of the table. Unlike Aaron Altman who had hesitated, William was utterly at peace with his decision to destroy the *Buzzsaw*. The Queen had foreseen this exact moment and who was he to second guess her?

Detonating the bomb would mean his own death, and that was okay with him since he was living on borrowed time any way. Jillybean had saved him, quite possibly for this one purpose. It was a good purpose.

The top of the table came off just as Mike sent the *Queen's Revenge* tacking north. William didn't have time to go hunting around for his bomb. He'd been following the course of the pursuit easily enough and knew he was down to seconds left to make a difference. Luckily, he knew exactly where he could get all the ordnance needed to sink the ship.

Right beneath the stairs was a cubby where the ship's three torpedoes were kept. He had even seen one of the sailors looking over the controllers, so he knew they were stored there, as well. "Piece of cake," he whispered and hurried for the cubby. In seconds, he had armed the three devices and one of the detonators. Since he wasn't keen on dying for nothing, he planned on rushing up the stairs and leaping from the rail, detonating the bombs as he jumped.

With everyone's attention on the chase, he felt he had a good chance of making it. He didn't count on his guard finally looking back at the exact wrong moment. The scrawny man ran down the stairs in a jumble of feet; in his hand was a drawn pistol and on his face was a wicked grin. The man couldn't see the little box in William's hand. "Shot trying to escape," the Corsair whispered. "I'll be a hero." The gun began to orient on William.

"One of us will be a hero," William said, and pressed the detonator.

Unlike the *Blood Belle,* which saw the front third of the ship disintegrate in the blast, the *Buzzsaw* seemed to evaporate in a massive mushroom cloud.

Mike had been staring right at the ship when it exploded and could now see nothing but a piercing glare of white. He had no idea how much of the *Buzzsaw* was still floating and in fear of ramming her, he swung the wheel hard to the left.

As he did, another torpedo buzzed harmlessly by. A wave pushed it east where, a minute later, it fetched up against the side of the *Dark Gull*. It might have gone unnoticed had it not been for a stray fork of lightning, which cracked and boomed like another explosion.

Jillybean had hoped that her seven bombers would do more than just take out seven ships. She had hoped to spread confusion and perhaps even start a civil war among the hateful Corsairs, and she was on the verge of getting her wish. When a sailor on board the *Dark Gull* saw the torpedo, he screamed that they were being attacked and, before anyone could question the idea, the panicked man rattled off an entire magazine into the missile.

A shipmate at the stern thought he was shooting at the next closest ship and, without thinking, fired a long burst at it, hitting three men. In seconds, the two ships were ripping bullets into each other with no thought as to where any of their missed shots happened to go.

Fifty yards beyond the *Dark Gull*, the *Basilisk* had her deck swept by a rain of bullets. Her captain screamed for someone to douse the kettles as he swung hard to the east. The ship spun so quickly that when one of the wounded soldiers managed to get to his feet, he found himself facing an entirely different ship. He set his M16 to full auto and blasted away, starting off another battle.

Chaos spread through the fleet. More guns rattled away. Captains bawled for their fires to be doused as they swung their ships wildly left and right, afraid of torpedoes in the water. Four ships were set on fire as their panicked crews cut away their flaming kettles instead of lowering them.

With ships going every which way on a heaving sea, a like number of ships collided in two separate instances. The first involved only a volley of curses, but the second touched off a raging fight that would last half an hour and only ended when both ships slipped beneath the black water and sank straight to the bottom.

Most of the battles were short-lived. Two ships would appear suddenly out of the dark; there'd be a brief burst of shooting and then they'd be gone again. Or they would fire into the shadows of the smoke that hung over the water; sometimes there'd be return fire, sometimes they would get a torpedo streaking their way.

All totaled, the Black Captain's fleet lost thirteen of his boats, including a forty-footer that simply got too close to shore and couldn't get away as the wind sent them smashing onto the rocks.

The *Queen's Revenge* might have gotten away scot-free except that the first hard turn Mike made after the *Buzzsaw* blew up, pitched the ship well over. The deck had a sideways list like a sledding hill and Neil Martin went right over the side with an astonished look on his greying face.

With everything going on, the only people who saw him go over were Jenn and Emily.

"Neil!" Emily screamed, throwing one leg over the railing. Jenn tried to haul her back, but Emily was surprisingly strong and threw Jenn off with a twist of her shoulder.

"You'll drown," Jenn cried, as gunfire erupted out in the storm once more.

"I don't care." Emily ripped off her coat and tore off her shoes.

When she was at the rail, about to dive in, Jenn tried once more to stop her. "They'll catch you."

This stopped Emily. Even a petulant, headstrong teen wouldn't pretend not to care about that. She had already seen a glimpse of the criminal horror that the Corsairs perpetrated on their fellow man.

"Maybe," Emily admitted and then dove in.

Jenn rushed to the rail and saw just a streak of blonde of Emily's hair before she too was swallowed up by a wave.

Chapter 5

From the bridge of the fifty-foot *Courageous*, Jillybean watched the first of the flares—her flares—being launched. Instead of sending it on a high, arcing trajectory, Mark Leney had aimed it nearly straight up. Five hundred feet above the town it burst into eminence, dangling beneath a small parachute. Much to the Black Captain's annoyance, the wind floated it across the boggy eastern boundary of Hoquiam where it landed among the thousands of milling zombies.

Jillybean snorted at the attempt, enjoying the way the Captain's jaw muscles clenched. It was the only part of him that showed the least bit of emotion. Like her, he was clad in black from head to toe. He even had on a three-quarter length black leather trench coat. There, the similarities between them ended.

He was a tall, powerfully built man with rich coffee-colored skin, while she was the pale white of cream, not even five and a half feet tall and svelte. His hair was a tight afro, while hers was a blizzard of chestnut brown. Her eyes were huge, blue and luminous; his were dark, moist and usually hooded as if he had some great secret kept penned-up behind them. He kept a pair of revolvers strapped across his slim hips; her only weapon was her mind.

They both waited in intense silence until the next flare went up. It fizzled out just as its chute opened.

"You are trying my patience, Leney," the Black Captain growled into the radio.

"May I?" Jillybean asked, holding out a hand for the radio. He considered, his dark, evil eyes judging her, trying to fathom her intentions. A small shrug followed and he tossed her the radio. She caught it, deftly and thumbed the talk button. "Leney, this is your queen. You do know you have to light the flares before you send them up, right?"

In answer he told her screw herself. "Careful, Leney," she warned. "You don't want to get on my bad side, especially since you're in such deep trouble with your boss. You know that, right? You know he's going to kill you as soon as things have settled down a bit. Leney? Leney? Why aren't you answering?"

Another half a minute went by before Leney replied, "I'm not worried. I have always been faithful to the Captain. You were just a blip. No, you were just an illusion that we *all* fell for. It wasn't just me. But I was the one who came back. I was the one who brought us all back."

Jillybean winked at the Captain before saying, "Are you sure that was you? Are you sure I didn't set this up just so I could be alone with the Captain, so I could poison him?"

"Yeah, I-I'm sure."

"You don't sound too sure. And you know what, neither does the Captain. He's looking at his coffee mug and he's getting pale." She released the send button and grinned, picturing Leney going through mental gymnastics, trying to figure out if he was being tricked.

"Are you done yet?" the Captain asked. He knew better than to let the girl get anywhere near him or his food.

"Let's see what he says." She keyed the send button. "He's going faster than I thought, Leney. Any last words for him?"

Another silence. "I don't believe it and even if it's true, you are done. The Corsairs are done listening to you. I will kill you myself. And if you…"

She cut him off by popping off the back cover of the radio to inspect the batteries. They weren't hers as she had expected, instead they were a cheap knock off, poorly done. "Eh," she mumbled, putting them back in. "It's only a so-so job."

"It sounds like sour grapes to me." He turned the radio back on. "Leney, why aren't there flares in the damned sky? If I don't see them up there in ten seconds, it'll be you drinking the coffee."

Leney had one up in eight seconds. It too was poorly aimed. She said nothing this time, she only smiled, placidly.

"You're not what I expected," the Captain remarked. "You're playing it so cool that I have to ask, are you Jillybean? Or are you Eve? Not that it'll matter all that much. I still plan break you."

"And I still plan to kill you," she shot back. "But to answer your question, I am Jillybean. Eve is, well she's on hiatus at the moment." Jillybean's head was blessedly quiet. She had enough medicine pumping through her veins to keep her sane for some time, if her liver didn't fail first.

He murmured an, "I see," as he took up his binoculars and gazed across the harbor where a third of his fleet was chasing down the *Queen's Revenge*. It was three minutes from escaping, but just then, it looked as though it was about to be swallowed by his ships. "So, once I've cleaned up this riff-raff, which way should I turn? North to Bainbridge or south to sweep up the Guardians? Oh, I forgot to thank you for taking down their wall for me. That's going to make everything so much easier."

"If you really want my advice, I want something first. Who else do you have on Bainbridge spying for you?"

"An interesting question. By asking it, I have to assume that you think the answer will have actual meaning to you. Do you honestly think you might escape? In ten years, no one has ever escaped Hoquiam. They've tried. Oh yes, many have tried even though the penalty is, well let's just say it's sadistically cruel even by Corsair standards. And of course, it's carried out where everyone can…"

The first explosion jolted him into silence. He spun and stared in disbelief as the thunder rolled across the bay. When the violent wave of air shook the glass windows on the catamaran, he started yelling into the radio, "What's going on? What's going on?" No one knew and no one had time to find out. More explosions followed and soon gun blasts and horrendous fires were added to the mix. Jillybean watched with a pain in her chest, wondering how many of her most loyal followers were blowing themselves up.

The Captain suddenly turned on her and she had to swallow her pain. "Oh my, it looks serious," she said, her eyes overly wide with faux-innocence. "I certainly hope no one's been hurt."

His right hand dropped to one of his pistols. "What did you do?"

Her answer began with a casual shrug. "Me? Nothing. I swear. I can't believe you'd accuse me of doing anything so horrible as all that." She let a smile slip out. "Okay, maybe I did a little something. I might have strung some mines across the harbor entrance. How was I to know people were going to be driving boats all helter-skelter through there?"

"You don't have mines," he said, watching her closely. "I would have known."

"Then I don't know what I was building. Maybe you're right. Maybe they weren't mines. Maybe they were just floating explosives."

A snarl twisted his dark lips as he drew one of his twin .44 caliber Colt Anaconda revolvers from its holster. She only raised an eyebrow at it as if to say: *Really? A gun?* He slammed it back in its holster and turned back to the chaos of a night battle in a storm where the only real enemy the Corsairs were fighting was fear itself.

The running skirmish was so engrossing that Leney forgot to fire off his flares. It was almost twenty minutes before the Captain screamed him back into action. He then turned his anger on Jillybean, calling in a brute of a Corsair. The man had the complexion of a toadstool and big, filthy hands.

"Search her," the Captain ordered, "Search *all* of her."

Had she been carrying a knife or a gun anywhere on her, he would have found them easily, but otherwise, the man did a poor job of searching her. On the other hand, he violated her with great gusto, tearing off her clothes and "investigating" her almost to the point of raping her. All the while the Black Captain watched, a smarmy smile on his face.

She took it all without comment or expression. Even when the thug's callused fingers slipped inside of her most private parts, she remained cool, telling herself that it was *Just another body part.*

The hulking Corsair was disappointed in her lack of reaction; the Captain was not. "I love a good challenge and so far you've been my biggest challenge to date." He walked over and picked up one of her discarded boots. As he checked the heel and ran his hand inside, he added, "Too bad for you your threat has ended."

Although the *Queen's Revenge* had got away, the fleet was slowly, cautiously coming back together, everyone on the lookout for anything suspicious or strange. Even Leney was beginning to get the hang of the rockets and slowly, half of the Captain's zombie army was swinging north, just as the second half came south. The traitors, which is how he thought of the Coos Bay Clan and the Magnum Killers, would soon find themselves trapped between the two undead hordes.

The only question the Black Captain had, was whether or not he'd grant any sort of surrender. His gut told him it would be a bad idea.

He tossed the boot at Jillybean as she knelt, naked but undaunted. "Yes, it'll be fun breaking you. I'm going to enjoy watching that haughty look melt away with every passing day.

It's going to be a slow burn for you." He stepped up and touched her wild hair and acted as though he were going to run his hands through it.

Quickly, she stood. The brute hadn't taken much time inspecting her crazy mass of hair and she couldn't allow the Captain to start.

"I would advise against that," she told him, speaking as if the two were sitting across a desk from each other. "If sadistic torture is the reward for surrender, you'll only encourage your enemies to resist to an even greater degree."

"Experience contradicts you. Fear is far more powerful than common sense. Why do you think the old politicians stoked fear of their opponents more than they talked about what they planned on doing if elected? Yes, some people will fight harder, perhaps even to the death, but in the end it will be those that cower, those that run or give up who will make the difference. All I have to do is find those weak ones, those soft spots in the defense, and then, even a fortress like Bainbridge will fall."

She picked up her panties and stepped into them. "I just can't see that happening. Not any time soon at least, and not with the soldiers and equipment you have at your disposal. I'm sorry, but your men are wretched excuses for soldiers."

"Did I give you permission to get dressed?" he demanded.

"Do you really think being naked will cow me in anyway? If anything, it empowers me while at the same time it desensitizes you. Nudity is boring. That's why the purpose behind lingerie is not to reveal the female form but to add to it by giving it a hint of mystique."

His answer was a slap across the face. She fell in a heap onto the floor, her eyes crossing for a moment.

The Captain squatted down next to her. He grinned, seeing his red handprint on her cheek. "Yes, it's going to be fun breaking you. Now, I'm going to tell you to get dressed, and if your response is anything other than 'yes master' I'm going to hit you again. Get dressed."

"Yes, master," she answered, without hesitation, much to his surprise and enjoyment. He knew she didn't mean it and that was what made it fun. Smiling, he struck her again, harder this time. She faced the carpet for almost a full minute before she started nodding. "Would master like me to pretend I don't understand the concept behind learned helplessness?"

"What did they used to say? Fake it until you make it. So sure, pretend all you want. Lying to yourself is the first step in accepting your position as my slave."

"Yes master," she answered, and started to get dressed. There was only one thing about the situation that she hadn't expected. Where was Eve? Normally, a slap like that would have brought her roaring out of whatever dank hole in Jillybean's brain she hung out in.

There wasn't a peep from her and that was more unnerving than anything the Black Captain had done to her.

Once she was dressed, the Captain dismissed her and the thug, telling him, coincidentally enough, to find the darkest, dankest hole in his dungeon for her. She smirked at the wording, unafraid of being hit again.

A little aluminum boat transferred her and the brutish Corsair across to the horror that was Hoquiam. She sat at the prow of the little boat, her delicate hands cuffed in front of her. The brute sat right behind her, holding what looked like a harpoon in the same grubby hands that had been inside her.

"Go ahead and make a swim for it, *your Highness*," he mocked. His name was David Eustace and Jillybean decided she would kill him and sleep better at night for it. "You know you want to. Come on. If you had any real brains you'd jump in now and head right for the bottom. Drowning is an easy way to go compared to what you got coming."

She ignored him completely and gazed ahead. Although it looked as though she was just sitting there, in reality, her mind was whirring along at a prodigious rate. She was picking out and memorizing landmarks; she was searching for weaknesses in the guard posts; she was making a list of possible blindspots; and she mapped out the town's rain drainage system by calculating the changes in elevation within the town itself. These things were always laid out in a logical manner...usually.

Things would go ill for her if they weren't.

She was going to escape and the sooner the better. There would be a good deal of chaos over the next day or so which she would need to slip out of a town that had been altered over the last ten years to keep prisoners in. She also wanted to catch up to her own army. Although she had full confidence in Captain Grey's tactical ability to lead men in battle, she knew she outclassed him in regards to strategic awareness.

With her ability to outthink her opponents, she frequently saw the progression of battles hours in advance. Sometimes she saw the battle from start to finish before it began, though usually, she saw seven or eight versions of the same battle.

First, she had to escape. The boat eased up to a shoal that was guarded by a forest of sharpened logs and shafts of wood, all set in the soft earth at a variety of angles. The belt of spears was fifty yards deep and ran the entire length of the waterfront. Jillybean guessed that there were at least twenty-thousand spears all told. Beyond these was a triple-row of concertina wire. Then came widely spaced watchtowers. Unlike the ones on Bainbridge, these did not have searchlights.

"Can they see us?" she asked, meekly, indicating the dark towers. They were zigzagging along a very narrow path among the spears. She only half-expected him to answer.

"They do one better. They smell you."

He thought he was being cagey; however a low growl of a dog gave him away. She saw the shadowy little thing standing on the other side of the rolls of wire. It began racing back and forth, its growl growing more and more excited. It followed them to a break in the wire where another Corsair snapped a leash on him.

"Will he bite?" Jillybean asked. She was quite willing to risk being smacked by Eustace in order to pet the "guard" dog. She was almost certain it was a cocker spaniel, although it was hard to tell in the dark.

"Of course she'll bite," the handler snarled. "She's trained to. She'll take a finger off." The guard dog was now panting and wagging its little stump of a tail. Jillybean decided to risk it and let the cocker sniff the back of her cuffed hands. She was immediately licked. "Back off!" cried the handler. "Who is this bitch?"

Eustace chuckled as he pulled Jillybean away from the dog. "It's that crazy queen. We just got her in a trade."

"No way!" the Corsair stepped close to get a good look and as he did, the pungent aroma of old cabbage and sweat washed over her. "She's cute."

"Yeah, and guess who got to give her a very thorough cavity search?" He jabbed a thumb at his own chest. "Talk about tight, if you know what I mean."

"No way! You lucky bastard. Maybe I can get…"

He reached out a hand to grab her breast; Eustace knocked it away. "Hands off, Jack. She's the Captain's. No one touches what's his." The man started to apologize, but Eustace pushed him aside. "Can you believe that guy?" he asked Jillybean.

She snorted, "I know, right? He thinks he can just touch anyone with his sleazy, disgusting, perverted hands. Only a complete ass would do something like that. Am I right? Oh, of course you know. You were just doing that very thing to me, so you clearly know all about being a sleazy pervert."

He glared and she smiled. "What are you going to do? Punch me? Or do you want to molest me some more? Too bad you can't. Like you said, no one touches what's *his*."

"I aughta…"

Jillybean had very little experience with spitting, so it was something of a surprise that she was able to hawk something weighty into Eustace's face. His fists clenched and his teeth ground together. She tut-tutted him. "Careful now. You don't want to lose your temper, because I have a mouth on me and a vivid imagination. You don't want the Captain thinking you got a little extra frisky on the way over."

He grabbed her arm in a vice-like grip. "He'd never believe you." Despite saying that, he didn't touch her except for the painful grip. They walked in silence into the rat-infested town of Hoquiam. It was a place of utter squalor. Trash and feces were everywhere, as was the stench of urine and old, congealing blood.

Many towns were dying a slow death due to erosion from the elements or being taken over by the thrusting green hand of nature. Hoquiam was already dead. It was a fly-blown corpse and the people who lived there, were its maggots.

The streets were overflowing with refuse and the sidewalks were buckled or washed away altogether. It seemed that every other house was a burned-out hulk with only a wall or two left standing.

It was an empty town. The only people they passed were a few men loitering on rickety, leaning porches, and a handful of collared women hurrying by without daring to look up. Jillybean expected to be taken to the Captain's residence. Instead, she was taken to the town's three-cell police station.

There were two men cooking a pot of thin fish stew over a little fire set directly on the linoleum. The fire was the only light in the station.

43

One of the men was thin-faced and had a narrow, slightly elongated head. He had a perpetual backward lean to him, so his flint of an Adam's apple stuck out further than his pointy chin. "Well, well, what do we have here?" he asked, getting to his feet.

His friend was very tall and had to stand using a series of articulated, robotic moves. He rubbed large dirty hands together as his eyes wandered over Jillybean's black-garbed form. "What'd she do?"

"This is that whacky queen from San Francisco," Eustace said as he had before. This time he warned them quickly. "She's the Captain's so don't even think about touching her. He says to put her in the darkest dungeon."

They were obviously disappointed, which made her nervous. As far as she could see, there were only three cells, and none of them looked all that dark or dungeon-like. The very tall man led them past these cells and into a back area where there were a few offices and a couple of windowless storerooms. They went to the last storeroom.

It was empty except for a black, rectangular hole that had been carved through the linoleum in the middle of the room. Set over it was a heavy metal grate with a fat padlock going through a hasp drilled down into the floor.

Jillybean leaned back into the narrow-headed man as his friend keyed the lock and raised the grate with a grunt. "There's nothing to be afraid of. Get on in." He gestured to the pit. In the dark it seemed to go on forever. It could have been a hundred feet deep for all she knew.

"Can I get any light? Or something to drink? What about these cuffs? You'll take them off, right?"

Eustace shook his ugly bearded head. "The Captain didn't say nothing about taking off the cuffs. Now get in there or I'll throw you in."

"Slow down," the thin-headed man said. "That's not how things are done 'round here. We have our own rules." He looked like he was trying to swallow a smile that kept coming up the back of his throat. "No one goes in the pit looking like that. All dressed up I mean."

"I told you she's the Captain's," Eustace growled.

"An' she's gonna stay that way. Me an' Mitch won't touch her. But these are the rules the Captain put in place, an' who am I to argue with the rules?"

Jillybean hoped that Eustace would make a scene, but he only shrugged. Her cuffs were taken off and then all three men stepped back to watch. As much as she didn't want to get into the pit any quicker, she also didn't want to give the men a show. She stripped down, making sure to fold her clothes, and gave them to the rat-faced man.

Hoping the cuffs would be forgotten, she went to the edge of the pit where the barred hatch was fixed right to the subfloor.

"Hold on," Eustace said. "My orders haven't changed." He had the cuffs at the ready. Obediently, she turned to face him, offering her hands, and making sure to stare directly into his muddy brown eyes. Standing over the foul-smelling pit, her alabaster skin tented up with gooseflesh, she felt skinny and small, and knew there was little that was magical about her, but what there was, could be found in her large eyes. Better men than this had lost themselves in them.

The corner of his bearded mouth turned up. "No one touches her," he said, "or they'll answer to me." She nodded because this was what she wanted to hear.

He pushed her to her knees. The tall guard then took her by her cuffed hands and lowered her down into the pit, further and further. Like a frightened cat, she clung to his hands as she kept reaching with her toes. "Wait! How deep is this?" she cried.

"Very," he answered, with an evil grin, and dropped her into the darkness.

Chapter 6

Eleven-year-old Emily Grey had always thought she was a good swimmer. It was a skill that both her mother and Jillybean had insisted that she possess, and for as long as she could remember, she had spent the nicest summer days at the island's pool learning to swim and dive.

She was a natural with her long lanky limbs and slightly broader than average shoulders. Her only complaint when it came to her lessons, and swimming in general, was the cold. Seattle was grey and wet even during July, and her first leaps into the pool were always accompanied by a shriek.

The island pool was nothing compared to the numbing cold of the harbor. It was a shock to her system and she came up with a gasp, her teeth chattering and every joint in her body seizing up. She had to will her body into motion, but in what direction?

Behind her, the *Queen's Revenge* looked like it was jetting away, while in front of her were sinister sails that were blacker than black. She opened her mouth to scream Neil's name, only to have a wave dash itself squarely into her face. Foul-tasting seawater went right down into her lungs.

Before she could cough it all out, another wave broke over her head. The sea was raging and foaming like some wild beast. Panic gripped her heart and shut down her mind. She was so overwhelmed by this sudden fear of drowning that it robbed her of her ability to swim. Like someone who had never even seen water before, she began flailing around, desperately fighting to stay above the churning waves.

Her terror was so entirely pervasive that she grabbed the first thing in reach to cling to, despite the fact it was making a bubbly, whirling noise. It was a strange mechanical creature with something like a scuba tank for a body and a plastic wrapped box taped to the...

"It's a torpedo!"

Again, panic froze her and she could only cling desperately to the deadly bomb as it began to swing to the right, her weight changing its course. She wanted to let go. It would have been smart to let go. But she couldn't let go.

It was going to blow up. She knew it and she knew she had to get away, yet, all she could think about was how much the explosion would hurt. She was face to face with the bomb. It was all of nine inches away and when it exploded, her eyeballs would explode right along with it, her teeth would shoot through the back of her head, and her flesh would tear off in burnt...

In the midst of her terror she saw through the plastic covering and read the clearly printed words: Arm/Disarm on either side of a switch. Quickly, she shot out dainty fingers and flicked the switch to Disarm. She didn't trust the switch one bit and eyed the bomb with a tick working nervously at the corner of her mouth.

Only when the torpedo started to turn back towards the retreating *Queen's Revenge* did Emily snap out of it and come to her senses, remembering that she was only in the water to save Neil, and if she didn't get moving she was going to drown or freeze to death.

Steering the torpedo was as simple as adjusting the fins at the back. She quickly turned it back towards the Corsair ships, which were even then battling each other or racing away in all directions.

"Neil!" she cried. She zigzagged through the mouth of the bay until her torpedo began to sputter. This didn't stop her. She began to kick her legs, moving slowly through the rolling water. Once, a huge black ship cut her way and she ducked under the freezing surface; she came up blue-lipped with her teeth chattering.

Her only option was to keep kicking through the rain and the bucking sea.

Ten minutes later, she saw a body floating face down. She had seen many bodies, but this one was oddly small, just like her Uncle Neil. It was a desperate struggle to get to it. The body wasn't Neil's, it was a boy, a poor abused little child. His face was purple and swollen, he was missing an arm, and there was a foot-long spear of wood planted in his back.

She pushed it away, not realizing she was crying icy tears.

From there, she drifted along with the remains of a dozen people and four ships. The action of the choppy water brought them all together in a terrible soup. She called out Neil's name, though never very loudly. Too many times, Corsair ships would suddenly materialize out of the storm, looking dark and deadly.

At some point, she decided that it was important to have the bomb part of the torpedo, to possess it, so she worried at the duct tape until it came free. It was the size of a shoebox and she carried it stuffed down her shirt as if it were a baby.

47

"I should get rid of it. This is stupid!" She didn't get rid of it, however. She had no other weapon, not even a knife. Though what she would need a weapon for, she didn't rightly know. What she needed was some way to get warm. An icy feeling had settled deep inside her, and now her joints were growing stiffer, and her fingers and toes were starting to burn with the cold.

Her best chance was to get to shore, though that was problematic since the nearest land was a mile away and she had to swim into the face of the wind and waves. After five minutes of paddling, she had made it less than forty feet.

Still, she was outside the floating wreckage when another Corsair ship came gliding up, its kettle lights blazing. It was *The Hammer*, a gorgeous forty-seven footer. At the wheel was one of Mark Leney's handpicked men named Tam. He was a big, thick-armed Corsair with two chipped front teeth and a habit of tonguing them constantly.

Tam dropped sail fifty yards out and drifted through the waves toward the floating mess. A half-dozen sailors leaned over the rail and gazed about at the dead. One had a boat hook which he used to stir the rotting stew and snag different corpses.

"Who that?" he'd ask. Most of the time the body was too mangled to be identified, which didn't stop the Corsairs from arguing back and forth. It gave Emily time to screw up her courage. She knew she couldn't stay in the water all night and this might be her only chance to get a ride closer to shore. *The Hammer* had a small diving platform jutting from the stern. It was little more than a step, but since it sat a foot or so over the water, she hoped she'd be able to hide beneath it while the boat was on the move.

She took a breath and dove a few feet beneath the surging waves and swam in the boat's direction. It was too far to make it in one breath, especially with the hypothermia setting in. Her limbs felt like hunks of dead wood. She surfaced again after only a few seconds; she sucked in a lungful of air, got her bearings in a flash, and went down again, kicking as hard as she could. Another gulp of air and more slow underwater swimming until she saw the shadow rising over her.

Up close, the boat thrashed and banged as the waves bounced it up and down. There was no way she'd be able to hide beneath the platform; she'd have to cling to the edge of the boat and hope that no one looked back. That scenario didn't seem likely, which left her with another dilemma.

Did she risk a slow, painful death by freezing or did she risk a slower, far more painful life as a Corsair slave girl?

The idea of being used by everyone on board a dozen times before they even made landfall had Emily pulling herself up as far as she could to see if there was any possible way she could make it back to the torpedo she had abandoned. Her arms shook after only seconds and in her heart, she knew she wouldn't be able to make it. It was already lost in the darkness and if she couldn't find it...well, she didn't want to think about that.

She would hold on, there was no other choice. There was a rope dangling off the side of the boat. It was so inviting that paranoia came bubbling up out of her frozen chest. It had to be a trap, or it was hooked to something light and she would pull it over the side with her, or someone would notice how taut it was and follow it and find her splashing along, half-drowned in their wake.

Her heart quailed and she abandoned the idea of the rope. Still, she didn't give up all hope. There was a chance that the weather would keep most of the sailors below deck. And, the wheel of the boat was midship and not at the stern like so many other boats; if she could hang on somehow until they were underway, there was a chance that no one would even look back.

She might even be able to crawl onto the little platform and lie on it. Her main problem in all of this was that she would have to leave Neil to his fate. She didn't think he could swim even before becoming a zombie and now that he was one, she didn't hold out much hope that he was still alive...or undead, or whatever he was. One way or another, she was no good to him now.

The crew of *The Hammer* finished poking through the remains a minute later. The sail was hauled up and, just as she guessed, all but two of them went below. As the boat began to move again, Emily held onto the edge of the platform for as long as she could, which was less than three minutes. Her grip began to fail and she feared that she lacked the strength to get on board if she waited any longer.

Just getting onto the tiny platform took everything out of her and she lay there uselessly for another five minutes before she chanced a look over the back rail. The two Corsairs left on deck were huddled in a covered cockpit. The clear plastic kept out the rain, but it also retained a good deal of moisture, and was already fogging over.

If she wanted to, Emily saw that she could crawl over the back rail and slip down into the galley without being seen. If she wanted to get caught, that is. She had no idea what was down there or where the other Corsairs had gone. Judging by the flickering light and the wood smoke in the air, they had a fire going. It called to her.

She was still half-way to frozen. Her flesh had the consistency of wrinkled plastic and her limbs were beginning to crimp inwardly so that she was hunched like a sour, old crone.

The cold made her desperate and more than a little stupid. She slid over the rail, squirmed down on deck, and was just slithering toward the stairs when she heard the *zzzwip* of a zipper being drawn. Right out in the middle of everything, she froze and stared with unblinking eyes as one of the Corsairs stepped out of the cockpit.

He turned and headed for the bow, where he fiddled with one of the many ropes that did something concerning the sail.

Emily had no idea what to do. There was no doubt in her quivering heart that he would see her when he came back.

She cast about, seeing empty decking, ropes, a boathook tied to the gunwale and a few sun-faded, cushioned benches. The benches! During her miserable introduction to boating aboard the *Calypso,* she had discovered that to make the most of the limited space on board, the benches doubled as lockers.

Quickly, she heaved up on the cushion of the closest one and saw a cramped dark space that immediately reminded her of a coffin made for a child—it was perfect—except that it was mostly filled. In the dark, she couldn't tell what she was looking at, but by feel she discovered that they were life-jackets.

Time was against her and she only dared to pull out two. Tossing them aside, she slipped inside and tried to haul the lid of the locker closed. The top of the lid came down on her knees, the little nubs of her preteen breasts and the side of her face. She tried to shift her body and meld with the remaining life-jackets, but an inch-wide gap remained.

Through it, she could see the lower third of the Corsair as he turned. He took a few steps to his left and then turned side-on to her.

She couldn't see his face but in her heart, she knew he was looking at the life-jackets that she had tossed to the side, and the cushion that was canted back more than normal, and the locker with its glaring gap.

There was a pause of a second where he was likely piecing things together before he started walking towards her hiding place. Had she not been once again frozen by panic, she would have leapt up and dived over the side. She silently cursed herself and then began to cry in shame and fear, knowing that she had no chance of escaping the approaching Corsair.

His name was Jeff Blowers and he eyed the life-jackets, indeed realizing that they hadn't been there earlier. He had served onboard *The Hammer* for years under pitiless, sadistic Captain Trevor Waldron. The man had loved only two things in his life: gin and *The Hammer*. He had been a living terror to his crew, demanding that every teeny-tiny, stupid detail about the ship had to be absolutely perfect.

They polished the brass after every storm, they washed the deck twice a day, they cleaned the bathroom after each use until it sparkled, and they painted the hull whenever it got the tiniest nick on it. Had he still been alive, he would have stripped the flesh off of whoever had left the life-jackets on deck like that.

But he wasn't alive thanks to Blowers. When they had been fighting that hellacious mud-battle along the hills of the Marin Headland, ol' Captain Waldron had made the mistake of actually leading his crew into the fight. Blowers had waited until the firing was hot and heavy before he shot Waldron in the back, and as he fell in disbelief, choking on his own black blood, Blowers had whispered to him, "Hey, Trevor, when I get back, I'm gonna take a wicked pissah right on the deck of *The Hammer*. What do you think about that?"

Waldron had only gargled on his blood and Blowers had kept his word. Now, he gazed down at the life-jackets and shrugged. Things were different now, and if a couple of life-jackets weren't immediately stowed away, it was no sweat off his back.

All he cared about was shortening the sails. The wind was really picking up and if they didn't make adjustments, the boat could broach. This is what it meant to be a real sailor in Blowers's mind.

Only when he finally went back into the cockpit and zipped it up tight, did Emily allow herself to breathe again. She'd been holding her breath for almost a minute and now she was gasping. For reasons she couldn't understand, the harsh gasps wouldn't stop. She had never heard of someone hyperventilating before and needless to say, her fear redlined.

51

It felt like she was drowning in air, as if her lungs were so filled with oxygen that she couldn't take any more in and very little wanted to get out. She threw open the lid of her child-sized coffin and tried to scramble out, only her right foot became snagged in one of the life-jackets, causing her to get stuck halfway out of the locker.

Somehow, the simple fact of being twisted and turned, and pummeled by the wind and rain helped her. Her lungs began to act like lungs should and, as her breathing returned to normal, her fear ratcheted down by degrees. Eventually she was able to free herself. She crawled to the life-jackets and poked them through the rail. They disappeared in seconds and then she was back in her box, curled up with the remaining life-jackets.

Once they were better situated, there was more than enough room for the girl, and much to her amazement, she found that the locker was dry and comfortable. It was also warmer than she would have ever expected. Heat from the fire in the galley baked up into her, and with the now familiar rocking of the waves, she was soon asleep.

It was midnight before she woke to cursing, stomping feet, and the shrill cry of, "Move that dinghy of yours outta the way, Rat-face, you dumb bastard!"

"Dinghy, ha-ha, good one, Tam."

"How on earth did Rat-face get a boat? I mean really. He gets a boat and I don't. It's messed up."

"Stop your bellyaching, Walt and release some of that line. It's not even high tide. You want us to swamp? Some captain you'd be."

More of this banter followed until Emily started to grow sleepy again. She didn't fight it. Being kidnapped had taken a lot out of her and she slept two more hours until a kink in her neck woke her.

Very slowly, she cracked the lid to her little coffin and looked around. The rain had gone and the wind had abated some. There was more of a bite to the breeze now and cold fingers crawled across her damp skin as she eased herself up into a crouch. *The Hammer* was anchored a hundred yards off the dark town of Hoquiam. It sat among a fleet of about ninety black boats, strung out in three rows. Without their sails set, they seemed very small and not nearly as frightening as before.

By happy circumstance, *The Hammer* was on the outer row and Emily saw that there was nothing between it and the harbor.

She was sure she could escape. Although she had never actually sailed, she had watched Mike Gunter work his magic, when she wasn't puking, that is, and she had heard him rattle on and on about deflection angles and sail pitch until she thought her brain had turned to mush.

Mike had made it look easy.

First, she had to make sure there was no one left on board— then she had to get dry clothes or she would freeze to death. Mouse-like, she crept down into the galley and found that the ship was indeed empty.

"Now, I just need clean clothes," she whispered, going through the drawers in one of the cabins. Growing a third elbow was more likely. *The Hammer* had been away from Hoquiam for nine days and everything stank. It was an indescribable stink, too. A combination of every disgusting smell she could think of.

Still, stinking to high heaven was better than freezing to death, and she threw on a mishmash of filthy layers before she headed up on deck, where she poked around, trying to figure out what rope went to what sail. She was smart and she soon had her sails matched to the right ropes.

Using a steak knife from the galley, she cut away from the mooring line and from there everything went right to hell.

She tried to haul up the anchor, but she was too weak and while she struggled with it, *The Hammer* swung around and crashed right into another boat before she could do anything.

It wasn't a big crash or even a very loud one, still her heart was in her throat as she expected someone to come racing out on deck. Luckily, that boat was empty as well. Emily tried to kick the two boats apart, but they simply floated into each other again with the same echoing thump that had the downy hair on the back of her neck rising up.

"Forget it," she hissed and went back to the anchor. Bracing her long cricket legs, she pulled back on the anchor winch and slowly, ever so slowly, hauled up the anchor. As she drew up the rope, she pulled *The Hammer* away from the boat she'd hit, but then the anchor tugged free of the harbor floor and sure enough the boats came together again!

"What the hell are you doing?" someone grouched from somewhere up the line of boats. "Some of us are trying to sleep, damn it."

Emily didn't know whether to say anything and after a few seconds decided it was best to keep her mouth shut. She stuck the knife in among the chain-links of the anchor and hurried to the mainsail. It went up in a jiffy and quickly filled, and even quicker, it sent *The Hammer* running along the edge of the other boat making a high-pitched squeal.

"Jesus H. Christ!" the same man from up the line of boats cried. "Cut to starboard, you twat!"

This froze Emily. She knew starboard was a direction and guessed it meant to the right, since going left would only mean ramming more boats. Leaping into the cockpit, she spun the wheel to the right and for a good thirty seconds, the boat moved to the right, freeing itself.

Then the boom swung to the left and the boat heeled over again, moving almost in a straight line, which would have been just perfect if the harbor didn't curve and the long string of boats didn't curve along with it. *The Hammer* was aimed right for the second boat in the front of the line and picking up speed.

"Oh, God no," Emily whispered as she frantically tried to turn the wheel, but it was already all the way over. For a brief moment between indecision and action, she wondered if she had been wrong about what direction starboard was. She spun the wheel to the left and the boat fairly leapt forward with the cold wind right on her stern.

Now she was aimed at the fourth boat in line and she knew that no force on earth would keep her from crashing into it. She stood, paralyzed with uncertainty, her hands white-knuckling the wheel as the 35,000 pound, forty-seven foot *Hammer* struck the forty-four foot *Red Death* squarely amidships and sank her in less than a minute.

The collision didn't come with a thundering crash, but with a terrible, high scream that woke the entire harbor. A bell began clanging, kettles were being lit and sails were yanked up.

Emily could think of nothing better to do than hiding, and even had the lid to the locker pulled up when a harsh voice yelled, "Who the hell is that?" The man was on a little boat which was bouncing up and down in the rough water. He reached out and grabbed the rail of *The Hammer*. She was caught. Her life was over. Everyone knew it didn't matter to Corsairs if a girl was eleven or even five. They would use her, beat her and torture her and…her eyes fell on the bomb she had taken from the torpedo.

Without really understanding why, she flicked it to *armed* and then stepped back as if two feet would make any difference whatsoever when it blew up.

"Tie me off, boy!" the man growled. "And you better have a damned good excuse for all of this. A real damned good excuse."

Boy? In her over-sized clothes, surrounded by the gloomy shadows of the night, he thought she was a boy. For her entire life she had been very happy being born a girl, but just then she realized it would be far, far better being a boy among the Corsairs. Yes, it was true that they beat boys and were cruel, and sometimes they tortured them to death; it was also true that they frequently used them as little servants and groomed them to grow up to be Corsairs.

If she could be a boy, she might escape someday. It seemed like the only chance she had and she grabbed it with both hands. Slamming the lid, she darted for the galley stairs, only to trip over a length of rope. The heavy line tangled around one ankle and she spilled clumsily down the stairs. Landing in a heap, she kicked the rope away, and sped down into the unlit galley.

It was so dark that tables and chairs and tossed aside backpacks were only hinted at. She tripped over something, banged into something else, and began running her hands over an unfamiliar wall.

"Where's the kitchen?" she whispered to herself as she swung her left arm around like a girl who'd been suddenly struck blind. She had an idea how to hide her "girlness," by becoming the opposite of what she was. Instead of being stylish, pretty, clean and articulate, she'd hack off her hair with a steak knife, dirty her face with ash from the fire and do her best to mumble like an imbecile.

Being a boy was easy.

But finding the drawer where the knives were kept seemed impossible. She was completely turned around and was searching the wrong side of the galley when she heard the sound of boots tromping down the stairs.

Spinning, she saw the ghostly outlines of a bulky Corsair, and when he struck a match to his lantern, she was pinned to the hull by its light.

Chapter 7

Captain Grey's warped and hunched shoulders slumped when he saw the fleet lighting their kettle lights. While the ex-Corsairs around him broke out in a confusion of fearful babble, he knew right away what the lights meant: Jillybean had bitten off more than she could chew.

By dint of her unparalleled intelligence and her unsettling insanity, she had kept twenty-five hundred of the most vile and violent men cowering before her. And, had she remained queen, she would have easily swept away the meager remains of the Corsairs.

But she had gone and traded herself for three people and now thousands would die. In a way, it had been an unjustifiably selfish move and although Grey knew the danger and the risk, he had been all for it. His daughter, Emily, had been one of those being traded and he would have sent ten-thousand people to their deaths to keep her safe.

Incorrectly thinking that she was out of harm's way, he turned his calculating mind to the new variable presented.

When the fleet had been the Queen's to command, he had planned on using it to keep his men resupplied. Unburdened by days of rations, quarts of fresh water, extra gear and pounds and pounds of ammo, they would've been quick and nimble, hitting here and there, probing for weak points. Smoke and explosives would be used to their maximum effectiveness, causing mass confusion and stark fear among the defenders. Then, when the time was right, he would use his mobility to quickly concentrate his forces and attack, bringing overwhelming firepower to the point of assault.

Now, they were screwed six ways from Sunday.

With the addition of the fleet's crews, the number of enemies he faced had tripled. And that didn't count the army of zombies.

Grey had planned on using Jillybean's flares to draw the zombies into attacking the Eastern flank of Hoquiam while he attacked from the north and west. Caught between the two forces, the battle would've been over quickly.

He sighed as the first flare shot into the sky and had to remind himself that there was still a chance to win.

"Someone find McCartt and Steinmeyer!" he roared in that harsh way of his. "And who's that chick leading the Santas? Someone get her, too."

"I'm right here. Hi. We met back on the ship. I-it's Lexi May. M-m-my name, that is. It's Lexi May." She'd been around a lot of frightening men in her seventeen years, but Grey was, hands down, the scariest person she had ever seen. She had to force her size six sneakers to plant themselves in the weeds or she knew they would carry her right out into the night.

He shot her a look over the stained black rag he wore to cover the hideous nature of his ruined face. He saw the fear in her deep brown eyes—and the determination not to give in to it. "Good," he growled, and said nothing more until McCartt and Steinmeyer hurried over, both glancing up at the flare with every other step.

"Leney just gave it to us up the ass," Grey said without the least attempt to soften his tone because of Lexi May. If she couldn't handle a bit of coarseness then she shouldn't be leading soldiers into battle. "What's obvious is that the fleet has flipped for the Black Captain, which puts us in a terrible spot, a *nearly* impossible spot. Nearly, but not completely."

"Why the hell did she give the entire fleet to Leney?" McCartt demanded. "That made no sense at all. Was it even her or one of those kooks she keeps stored in her head? That's what I want to know."

"Shut your pie-hole," Grey growled. "What's done is done. If you want to live, you'll listen to me and do what I say when I say it." Both McCartt and Steinmeyer glared and Grey glared right back; his glare was impossible to match because it came with the unmistakable implied threat of decapitation.

When they looked away, Grey went on, "First off, I'm not trying to muscle in on your commands. Jillybean put me in charge because I have previous wartime experience. She trusted me to lead this attack and so should you."

"She also trusted Leney," Steinmeyer replied. "So, I don't think that recommendation carries any weight."

Grey's eyes narrowed to tiny angry slits but before he could say anything, McCartt jerked. "Hold on. You don't think we're still going to attack, do you? I mean, I mean, we don't have the ammo. Not for a slugging match, at least. And we've barely done any recon. You made it seem like it would be a few days before we attacked."

"Right now, attacking is our best chance," Grey told him, smacking his steel capped stump into the palm of his right hand. "Chances are they're as confused as we are. If we hit them now, they might cave before they can off-load the fleet. I need each of you to come up with sixty good men to lead the assault. We'll hit in three different places."

"Hit?" Steinmeyer asked. "Hit, as in crossing that river? Under fire? I doubt I could give you ten."

McCartt shrugged, indicating the same thing, though he secretly didn't think he could find anyone to lead an assault. Not right then, not with everything so up in the air. After all, what if the Black Captain offered some sort of amnesty? His only real dog in the fight was doing right by his people, which meant that allegiances were subject to change.

Grey read exactly this in his shadowed eyes. "Okay, now I'm starting to see why Jillybean did what she did. She couldn't use the Corsairs because they'd just switch sides. But by using you Magnum-morons, she's forcing you to fight. No matter what happens to your men, if the Captain catches you, he's going to use you three as an example. He's going to use you three to break the will of your people."

They stood in silence, looking back and forth from one to another until McCartt said, "Yeah, well, maybe, but that doesn't change much. I know my captains. They're sailors, not soldiers. I doubt we'll get them rushing headlong into a machine-gun nest. The plan you had of waiting until we got the zombies moving and laying down cover smoke was one thing. That would've worked, but this...no."

Steinmeyer agreed, while Lexi May said nothing.

McCartt was right; the plan would never work if the leaders didn't believe in it. Grey turned and gimped away for a few steps, staring out into the storm. The bay was shrouded by heavy clouds, hiding most of the fleet. He stormed inwardly: *We still have time to fight and win!*

They did; however that wouldn't change the truth of their situation. He turned back and growled, "Here's the deal: I'm in charge. You'll listen to me until we're out of danger. After that, you guys can go whichever way you want, but know this, the only safety available within a hundred miles of us is Bainbridge, and you're not getting on the island unless I vouch for you, so I better see some fight from your men. Weaklings will be left behind."

Once more the three glanced around at each other. Everything was happening so fast. They each needed time to figure out what was best for them, except there was no time. They knew about the zombie army and what the flares meant. They had to cut around to the north as fast as possible or they'd be trapped—but what then? Bainbridge? Could they really expect to be taken in by them?

Lexi May felt confident that the Santas would be. They were mostly known as traders and gamblers, and though they did their share of slaving, it was never warlike. The Magnum Killers and the Coos Bay Clan couldn't say the same. They'd been active Corsairs for years and were well known for their murderous ways.

Grey didn't give them time to think. "I'm going to need half of all the ammo you have. Don't look at me like that, McCartt. We need a reserve of men and ammo. This is how armies operate. If you want to be a bunch of individuals, tell me now and I'll leave you to your fate."

"No," McCartt said, hollow-voiced. "We're listening."

"Good. Steinmeyer, I want your clan to be in the van with me. I will be pressing the pace, so if anyone falls out, they fall out. The Magnum-morons will be next and then the Santas." Lexi May looked disappointed and Grey scoffed. "I've seen the Santas. I've never seen a bigger bunch of slugs in my life. If they were in the middle, it would slow us to a crawl. At least this way they'll be fighting to keep up. Speaking of fighting, if you have any good fighters, I want them in the very back acting as a rear guard."

She nodded with a small, thin smile, worried that she would be stuck in the very back all by herself. The Santas were a fractious bunch; more of an amalgam of thinly aligned groups than an actual "people," and how she was suddenly thrust into the role of leader, she didn't know. Before Jillybean had arrived to completely upset the entire world, Lexi May had "spoken" for a group that had only seventy people in it. Now, she was in charge of ten times that number, every last one of whom was happy as hell it wasn't them.

"We're heading straight north, across country to Highway 101," Grey said. "I want every last man in marching formation in ten minutes. We'll collect the ammo and work out any details as we go."

Exactly ten minutes later, he was barking orders so loudly that they could be heard across the swollen west branch of the Hoquiam River. It didn't matter. North was the only direction left to them. Three miles to the west was the Pacific; to the south was the harbor and to the east was Hoquiam itself.

For the next five miles, north was their only choice and, unfortunately, their options didn't get much better after that.

Twenty miles to the north was the lofty, snow-covered peak of Mount Olympus, the tallest in a range of mountains that dominated the area. There'd be no going through the treacherous mountains at this time of year, which left the little army only two choices. They could take the most direct route, marching sixty miles along a relatively narrow and, very predictable, route to the northwest.

It was also the most dangerous route to Bainbridge Island. With Puget Sound breaking up the land with its long watery fingers, they'd be forced to cross a land bridge that was only a mile wide. With bandits under the control of the Black Captain operating in the area, things could get hairy very quickly.

Their only other option was to angle off to the north and then curve around the Olympic Mountain range. It would almost triple the distance to Bainbridge and, at the end of an eight to eleven day march, they would have to cross an easily defended bridge just to get near the island.

He didn't even want to think how they planned to get to Bainbridge itself. Without any sort of navy, Bainbridge could be cut off by a dozen ships. Grey's thousand men would be left to starve in sight of the island.

"Luckily, it's perfect Washington weather for a walk," he said with a chuckle, drawing his ugly fur and feather cloak around him. In predictable fashion, it was five degrees above freezing, so instead of a soft snow that could be dusted off, his men were soaked to the bone and miserable. They looked at him from beneath their dripping brows as if he were to blame for all of this.

He didn't care about their looks or about them. He only knew that Jillybean, the only person who loved him, the only person who had shown him any kindness during the last ten years, had asked him to lead these men in war. Retreats were a valuable part of war and, if handled correctly, they could be as important as an actual victory in the field.

"Let's stop standing around, Steinmeyer," he said, and began marching north through a scrubby pine forest. Within a few minutes, he came across the first of many zombies. It was passing across his path, heading northeast, staring stupidly up at the latest flare.

Grey had an M4 strapped across his back, which he'd be a fool to use. Instead, he used a four-foot long black battleaxe that had a heavy, razor-sharp blade on one side and a spike on the other. Using it meant coming within arm's reach of a terrible ugly death.

Then again, death was always within arm's reach for Grey. He lived in the wild where a wrong step or an ill-timed cough could mean a fight for his life.

Unless something went utterly wrong, this wasn't going to be a fight for his life. It probably wasn't even going to be a fight he'd remember in a week. The behemoth was only about seven and a half feet tall and couldn't have weighed more than a quarter of a ton. Up close, he saw it was a shaggy-headed female with breasts as flat as pancakes. It smelled as if it had been wallowing in a cesspool.

With a grunting, overhand swing, he buried the spike of his axe a foot deep into the back of the creature's head, and for a few seconds, it seemed confused by the fact that it was dead. It kept on walking with the axe in its head, much to Grey's annoyance.

"Give me that," he muttered, and pulled the beast down by the axe handle. It tried to grab him, but he stomped down on its wrist and began to work the handle back and forth until the spike came free. The zombie gave only a twitch in acknowledgment of its death as steam billowed out of the gaping hole in its head.

Grey marched on without looking back, his sharp eyes shifting back and forth, his ears pricked for the least sound—and heard Steinmeyer's clansmen whispering back and forth to each other. "Like a bunch of hens clucking," he grumbled. "For God's sake, shut them up, Steinmeyer." Under his breath he added, "And what kind of name is Steinmeyer?"

As Steinmeyer hurried down the line, Grey went on in his odd crab-like walk. Despite his deformities, he could cover a lot of ground, apparently without tiring. Three miles swept under his feet before he heard the first of the explosions drifting on the wind from the harbor.

A grin stretched the scarred and mutilated flesh around his mouth. Anyone seeing it would've blanched at the hideous sight and called it an evil grin. Perhaps they would've been right in this case. Grey did receive quite a bit of sadistic joy knowing that Jillybean was behind whatever mischief was afoot. With every blast, his grin widened until it was a nasty smile that showed the roots of his teeth, what teeth he had left. He was down to twenty-two.

The smile vanished as gunfire blasted out in the middle of his column. "Keep them moving, Steinmeyer," he ordered before running, hunched over, back down the trail he had blazed. As he went, he grabbed men and turned them back to the north. "Don't look back! Keep up! What's with this gap? Dress-up this damned formation." And so on, until he came to a human corpse and one actually dead zombie.

"Strip the dead and get moving. Come on, it's a job for two people. The rest better run to catch up!"

He shoved anyone who wasn't running. For good measure, he let his mask fall so that they could see his hideous face. Many of them ran simply out of fear of him. He marched to the end of the line just as a flare went off a hundred yards overhead.

"Lexi! You better get them running or you'll get half your command eaten."

She implored them to run, but many were out of shape and more were insolent to the point of rebelling. Grey knew how to take care of rebels; he swatted one upside the head with the flat of his axe. The man staggered around much like the zombie had.

"The next one of you who steps out of line will get the smart end. Now go!"

They ran as best as they could. He watched with a shake of his head, as they began to falter after only half a minute. Many of them were going to die. He took the axe by the neck and started after in his crabbing, gallop of a run and as he passed the Santas dragging ass at the back end of the formation, he remarked, "Try to save some energy for when the zombies tear you to pieces. The more you scream the more lives you'll save."

Another flare shot up over head. Leney's aim was becoming dangerously accurate, and was accompanied by a new batch of shouts and more gunfire from ahead. "Don't slow down!" he roared to the Santas as he passed them. "It's only a few zombies."

It was more than a few. Twenty-eight of the beasts in a ragged wave had appeared out of the rain. More gun blasts were added to the shouts and screams. In the dark, the monsters seemed unstoppable, as bullets winged left and right, blasting away ears and scalp and bone, none of which did anything except enrage the beasts even more.

A bullet had to hit working brain matter to destroy one of them and even then it wasn't always a hundred percent effective. Grey preferred his axe. Being so close made aiming easy. It was also far more satisfying. Nothing compared to the thrill of matching his hobbled, broken body against the planet's greatest killing machines.

Of course, he wasn't stupid about it. The first one he took from the side, striking at the neck. As they frequently were, the beast stood in a hunch, the ridges of its vertebrae a perfect target. The blade sheared seven inches deep, severing the creature's spinal cord. It dropped in its tracks and Grey used its own weight and momentum to free the axe and was on to the next.

In the night, his black cloak and deadly blade made him only a flying shadow whisking close to the ground, and compared to McCartt's Magnum Killers firing away, he was easily overlooked. He spiked a rotted head the size of a beachball and hewed a leg from a ghastly naked body.

By then, the giants were in among his column and sending men flying, screaming like children.

Wiping black blood from his brow, he shook his head, wondering how these were the same men that had everyone so afraid. Hefting the axe, he waded back into the battle, killing three more before the last was shot dead.

"Strip the dead and let's move!" he bellowed.

"Do you want us to keep going in this direction?" Steinmeyer asked. He had slunk back to the middle of the formation to see what was happening and now he regretted it, thinking that he could've gotten his men clean away.

Grey turned his skeletal head upward as a new flare burst into light. "Yes. It's two more miles to the highway. Get there as fast as you can."

The zombies were moving far faster than the men. And what was more, their strength wasn't robbed by fear, their legs didn't tire as they plodded through the mud, and they weren't weighed down with weapons and ammo or even sopping wet clothes.

After barely a mile, Grey knew they would never make it to the highway. The zombies were pressing in too close. He would have to change tactics if he wanted his army to survive. Pulling Lexi May, McCartt and Steinmeyer aside, he told them his new plan.

"You know this falls into the category of: it's just so stupid it might work," McCartt noted.

"It'll work if everyone does what they're told," Grey shot back. "Besides, yours is the easy part. All you gotta do is sit tight and pray."

Grey had the tough part. Five minutes later, he had Lexi May light the cobbled together torch. "No shooting!" he ordered in a voice that could be heard by the men huddled around the trees. "No moving, no talking, and no screaming even if one of them figures it out. Take it like a man or it'll be all of you."

They had been only an hour on their own and already his little army...his pathetic little army, was in need of saving. He strode out from the edge of the wood, walking north, waving the torch high over his mottled head. It didn't take even a minute before the zombies had caught sight of him.

"Come on, boys. Come to papa," he yelled and then laughed like the madman he was.

Chapter 8

The darkness was *almost* complete. When Jillybean first landed on the dirt floor of her cell, she didn't think a single mote of light had ever managed to find its way into this particular hellhole. It felt as though she was in the bowels of the earth, and it smelled that way as well. Gradually, she discovered that a very few transient beams were slipping beneath the door and through its cracks.

She could just make out the ghostly impression of her cuffed hands when she held them in front of her face.

The meager light was better than nothing, and with it she explored the extent of her cell. It was five feet wide by eight feet long. Its furnishings were as scant as the light. There was a piss-smelling blanket of wool, a piss-smelling pillow and a piss-smelling piss-bucket.

The one thing she had expected to find in the cell, but didn't, was Eve or Ernest, or even Sadie. Because of the pee, she hadn't expected Ipes. He had a large sensitive nose, and had he been around, he would have used that as an excuse to leave, when really, he had a "dislike" for the dark, which he claimed was far different than being afraid of the dark, though what the differences were he had never attempted to articulate. He relied on the circular logic of: *It just is.*

"You guys are missing out," Jillybean said, feeling a strange touch of loneliness. She wasn't used to being this companionless. Even though she had mostly kept to herself on Bainbridge, she hadn't been completely friendless. She had Neil, and Deanna, and Emily—all three of whom were in terrible danger.

Neil could be a full-fledged zombie before she found him again. Emily would almost certainly be on her way to San Francisco just then, with who knew how many Corsair boats would be chasing after her. Deanna was in the most danger. If the Black Captain had managed to recruit a sweet man like Eddie Sanders and had turned Joslyn Reynolds, one of Deanna's closest friends, into a kidnapper, who else had he managed to recruit? How many spies or assassins were there on Bainbridge?

Jillybean had every intention of escaping from the Corsair's lair. "But who's going to be around when I get out?"

The words fell flat against the dirt walls, making her wonder if anyone would hear her if she screamed. "And would they care?" She knew the answer to that.

To stave off the feeling of isolation, she made a more thorough inspection of the cell. In one dark corner was something that looked like a burrowed hole. Naked, she squatted and reached into the hole. It only went a few feet back. Someone had begun excavating an escape tunnel, digging bare-handed through hard-packed, rocky earth.

It was obviously a waste of time. Any tunnel would require that same volume of earth excavated from said tunnel to be moved somewhere. A ten-foot long tunnel would fill half the cell and would be patently obvious.

"Especially as there would be a slope to keep the tunnel open and..." Her words twisted in her throat—something had moved in the hole. She wanted to pretend it was just a rat, but she had a distinct feeling of being watched, like there was someone or something in it.

"It's just my imagination," she told herself and then paused to let her imagination answer her disquiet. The intense silence went on without let up.

Determined not to let the dark get to her, she stood, running her hand up the dirt wall. There were strange grooves etched in it. Squinting, she saw that the walls of her cell were scarred over with scratchings from fingernails. They were words, though it was too dark to make out what was written. She was tempted to trace them to find out what they said. "You know it won't be anything good," she told herself. "How could it be? I don't think I've ever been in such a depressing place."

She fully expected a voice in her head to remind her of one of the many dismal prisons she'd been in, but they were still quiet. "The River King's holding cells were bad," she said, feeling the weight of the silence, "but only because they were so crowded. Now that was a real stink. Then again, it did have plenty of light and lots of company." Too much company, she remembered as she pressed her thumb into the wall, feeling the dirt crumble away. "Ugh. The prison of the Azael was like a hotel compared to this place."

Clapping her hands together, as much as the cuffs would allow, she tried to rid them of the dirt, the jingling metal giving her ears something to drink. For ears they felt very thirsty. "But, hands down, the worst was the witch's dungeon."

A shiver ran across her bare shoulders at the memory. Of all the enemies she had ever faced, no one could match the witch's evil. She had been attempting to manufacture semi-thinking zombies to use as slaves and had hoped that six-year-old Jillybean, with her exceptionally high IQ, would be the perfect test subject.

The little girl had found herself handcuffed to a post, the only way in or out guarded by one of the most ferocious zombies she had ever seen. She'd been captured completely unprepared for the situation and had managed to escape by the skin of her teeth.

"That had been a pickle to get out of," she mumbled, somewhat absently, peering intently at one corner of her cell where someone had tried to dig hand and foot holds. "A woman, judging by the depth. A man would need to get his foot a good deal deeper to hold his weight. A waste of time, either way."

Getting to the bars set in the ceiling overhead wasn't the real hurdle. She estimated that the heavy gate-like bars were eight or nine feet overhead. A tall man could easily jump up and catch the bars, but what would he do then? How would he pick the lock while dangling? He certainly wouldn't be able to do it one-handed. And if he could get the lock out of the hasp, how would he manage to lift the very gate he was dangling from? It was a physical impossibility—at least for most people.

Jillybean gazed upward and saw only a challenge. It was a challenge made a hundred times more difficult by the fact that she was naked. Although her clothes had been pawed at, they hadn't been searched by a true professional.

Someone who knew what they were doing would have found a key to a common set of handcuffs, a razor blade, two paperclips and a long filament of copper wire sewn into her belt. Along the hem of her long leather coat was sewn a double-wrapped ounce of Fluorosulfuric acid in powder form, and in the left sleeve was another double bag of powder, this one a formula of her own making. More wire and straightened paperclips were sewn into the cuffs of her black jeans.

It was everything a girl would need to escape the average dungeon.

"At least my clothes are keeping clean," she said, finding the thinnest of silver-linings in the predicament she was in.

As if she couldn't be allowed one good thought, she heard the key rattle in the door. There were only a few reasons why her guards would come back. One of those was to bring her something to eat or drink. All the other reasons were far more nefarious.

Light flared in the room, allowing her to see the dirt cage more clearly. Her eyes immediately shifted to the hole at the base of the wall; it was, of course still empty and yet her back twitched, ominously. Forcing her mind away from the hole, she gazed around the tiny room. As she had suspected, there were depressing, desperate things etched on the walls. She ignored them and concentrated on the important details of her cell: the few rocks, the area of dark earth in one corner, the blanket, the pillow, the bucket...

"Yummy, yummy." The narrow-headed man came and stood on her bars, peering down between his splayed feet.

She didn't bother looking up; she stood defiantly, her chained arms across her chest. "You heard what's-his-name," she said. "Hands off the merchandise."

"Oh, yeah. You're looky-no-touchy, we get it." He stared hungrily down at her, licking his lips; yet she didn't move a muscle. He had an excellent view of the top of her head and little else. "Aw-right," he eventually said and turned to go.

The moment the door shut, she hurried to the corner and began digging at the earth; it was full dark now. Barely an inch below the surface, she found a rusty, pee-smelling fork with a bent tine. A childlike grin spread across her face. "You'll do just fine," she said to the fork, and like a magician, with a flick of her wrist, she was out of the cuffs in under a minute.

She went right to work on the blanket, worrying it with her teeth before tearing the worn material into long strips from it. She was light and figured that three entwined strips would hold her weight. Nine strips gave her three, five-foot lengths of rope, which she loosely knotted around her neck.

Taking the stained case off the pillow, she filled it with the remains of the blanket, all the rocks she could find, and the fork. Using one more strip from the blanket, she cinched it tight and tied it across her shoulder.

"Now for the tough part."

Because of the world she lived in, Jillybean exercised as a matter of necessity. She derived no joy in it and would never describe herself as either athletic or sporty. She preferred the idea of dying at seventy with a book in her hand to dying at ninety with sweat on her upper lip.

It was why she looked at the leap to the bars with the same trepidation the average person reserves when considering the task of cracking a physics textbook.

She gave the jump an abortive first try and realized she would never make it. Grimacing at the smell, she poured out the piss-bucket into the little hole against the wall. She then set the bucket upside down beneath the window-sized grate. With a grunt, she launched herself at the bars.

In the dark, the bars seemed to be more like a shadow version of reality and it looked as though they were retreating from her grasping fingers. She only managed to get a grip with a single pinky and came down painfully, smashing onto the piss-bucket.

She groaned from the landing, then groaned louder when she sniffed the piss-smelling dirt that now covered her. "At least Eve wasn't here to see that. I'd never live it down." Brushing herself off, she set the plastic bucket back into place, arranged her ropes for a second try. She jumped higher this time and her hands found their grip. She walked her hands back to one end of the grate before swinging her feet upward and hooking the bars with her ankles.

"If the guard comes in now, he's going to get an eyeful," she said to herself as she wiggled her calves through the bars until she had a bar hooked beneath each knee. She could then release her hands and go to work. The position was agonizingly painful and she had to grab for the bars after tying every one of the six knots.

Tying the ends of each of her twined ropes made something that resembled a poor man's hammock. Once she had tested each knot, she unhooked her legs and eased onto the ropes, settling one beneath her shoulders, another across her buttocks and the last beneath her thighs.

It was a strange position. She was basically lying inches from the ceiling of her cell. It was odd, but comfortable. Reaching through the bars, she inspected the lock with just her fingers. For its purpose, it was an unnecessarily large lock. She tried the fork and the tine went in a third of an inch.

"Good enough." Next, she reached down into her crazy mass of hair and found the two tiny metal pieces that she kept tied there for exactly situations like this. They seemed to happen with more frequency than she would have ever thought possible when the apocalypse first occurred. Since then, she had worked hard to make herself more valuable so that capturing her was preferable to killing her.

Holding her breath and closing her eyes, she ran one of the tiny pieces of metal into the lock, feeling the tumblers. They were disagreeably stiff. She spat on the metal, something that wasn't easy with her nose pointed at the bars. Once it was wet, she tried again, working it around and then repeating the process until the tumblers moved easily.

Then she crooked one of the pieces of metal, wound the other around it like a tiny handle and began to *rake* the tumblers, giving the fork a gentle twist every second or so. Before becoming queen, Jillybean never had any actual spare time. When she wasn't studying or experimenting, she was practicing. Sometimes she practiced throwing knives; other times it was surgery, and sometimes it was opening locks. This was the first time she had opened one while lying suspended from a ceiling with her hands working upside down.

Otherwise, it was routine stuff and she had to keep herself from whistling while she worked. After a few minutes, the lock clicked and she slid it out of the hasp.

Now, all she had to do was the impossible: lift the very grate she was hanging from. It was impossible because any upward force applied to the bars was perfectly countered by the downward needed to supply the upward force with a fulcrum. The strongest man in the world couldn't have done it.

A smart girl could find a way around the problem, however.

First, she pushed the pillowcase through the bars and set it aside. Next, she snapped the cuffs onto the now free hasp. She then untied the rope that held her thighs up, once again hooking her legs. After tying this rope to the free end of the handcuffs, she used the fork to poke and slide the other end of the rope under the edge of the bars.

Taking the free end, she made a little hitch in the rope three feet down where she could place one foot. Slowly, she unhooked her legs and settled her weight into the hitch. The entwined wool rope stretched with the strain and made a noise that had her heart in her throat. The knots seemed to lengthen and grow thinner and thinner, and then they stopped. She was in a slowly spinning half-crouch; awkward but useful.

Now, she had only to lift the weight of the metal grate that sat against her shoulders; again the wool rope stretched and made a noise suggesting it was on the verge of snapping.

Thankfully, it held and Jillybean was able to push the bars up high enough to scramble under.

"Free at last. Free at last. Thank God, almighty I'm free at last," she whispered, getting to her feet and squinting around the dark room. It was an empty, windowless rectangle; its only features were the door that led out and the grate that led back to the pit.

Her first action was to ready a weapon. The rocks she had collected as well as the heavy lock went into the shabby pillowcase. She twisted it and tied it off; it was crude, but it would work.

Next, she shoved everything else into the corner before going to the door and tested her little bits of metal and the fork in the door's lock. The fork wouldn't fit, but the others went in easily enough. She held off making the attempt. It was still relatively early. Besides, she was safer in her little room. Inside the room, she controlled more variables. She had the advantage of surprise.

She expected another visit from the guard at any time. If both came at once, she would slip out and slam the door shut behind her. Shoving her metal bits into the lock would keep them from using their key and since the door opened outward, she'd be able to brace it quickly enough to keep them locked inside. Threatening to burn down the building would keep them quiet long enough for her to get dressed and make her escape. It was the best scenario and the least likely.

"There'll be just one," she told herself and then paused for a response. Still nothing. "I should be happy. And maybe if I wasn't sitting bare-naked on this freezing floor with my nipples poking out a mile, I would be." Being thirsty, hungry and sleepy wasn't helping either.

The wait made it all worse. She sat there for three hours before the first solid rays of light began to shimmer under the door.

Jillybean was up in a flash, her back to the wall, the pillowcase cocked and ready to swing. It was the taller of the two guards who came through the door with his lantern held casually in one hand and a small pail in the other. After so much time in the dark, the light seared into her retinas. She didn't dare attempt to whack him with the weighted pillowcase until she could see more than strange dark blobs set against the background of the sun.

The room wasn't large and in five strides the guard was at the grate. "It's dinner time and it's not the usual slop. The Captain sent over a…" He had just set down the pail when he saw the lock was missing from the hasp. His name was Jorgensen and his mind wasn't exactly spring-loaded. Since he "knew" escape from the pit was impossible, he figured that his partner had forgotten to put the lock back on the hasp the last time he'd been in to check on his prisoner.

"But why would he take it off?" he mumbled as he started gazing around at the floor. "Up to no good. He's gonna get us in dutch with the Captain, I just know it." Jillybean swung the pillowcase, punctuating the end of Jorgensen's sentence with a hearty crash.

The mean end of the pillowcase connected with the corner of his squarish head and glanced off, taking a palm-sized chunk of scalp along with it. Although it wasn't a perfect strike, it was enough to make his right leg buckle. He fell onto the grating, his left hand and arm sliding through the bars up to his shoulder. Pain was just beginning to register when Jillybean pinwheeled the pillowcase up and around again.

Its bloody end struck with a meaty thump and Jorgensen made a sound like he had swallowed his tongue. He twitched and jerked and gagged until a last crashing blow from the girl put an end to it. Immediately, she knelt next to the body, her head cocked as she ran her hands around in his clothes.

He carried a huge .44 that was just simply too big for her small hands. She took it anyway. She also grabbed his jacket, pulling it from his still warm corpse. There was a jackknife with a four-inch blade tucked inside one of the pockets. "That'll do," she whispered, knowing that eyewitnesses couldn't be allowed to live, no matter what she promised them.

The narrow-headed guard was taken easily enough. He came whistling out of the bathroom to find Jillybean holding his friend's hand-cannon pointed at his chest. Wisely, he believed her when she told him she would shoot if he made a sound. Foolishly, he believed her when she said she wouldn't hurt him if he cooperated.

When he was on his knees, she brained him with the gun and slit his throat as he slumped on the tile—and not a peep from Eve cheering her on, or from Sadie telling Jillybean how worried she was about the path she was taking, or anything from

Ipes telling her not to touch other people's blood because of germs and ickyness.

She tried not to let it bother her and forced the thought of her missing voices out of her head as she went to a barrel of clean water; she drank heavily and washed thoroughly. Since the rain was still coming down in sheets, she didn't bother drying off before putting on her black clothes.

With her pockets heavy with weapons and ammo, she went to the door and glanced out: it was dark, cold and miserably wet, all of which added up to the perfect time to make an escape. She knew the way out of Hoquiam. A half mile to the east were the remains of the Riverside Bridge. It had been dropped into the river years before, but now with the water no longer flowing, its broken concrete slabs were sitting out of the mud like toppled tombstones.

She could scramble from one to the next with little fear that any of the Corsairs would chance a shot in the dark. No, not with thousands of zombies on the move. Getting there was the only problem since the streets were filled with scurrying men and slaves. A steady stream of them had been coming up from the harbor for the last few hours as the fleet disgorged its sailors.

Of course, Jillybean had a plan. She had noted the storm drains on the way to the police station, which sat on the top of a little rise. Across the street, the land sloped down to the river; the drains on that side would logically funnel in that direction and should empty just north of the now defunct bridge.

Heading into a sewer during a mammoth rainstorm was dangerous and intolerably stupid, unless the only other choice was hanging around Hoquiam as a wanted fugitive; then it was the next best thing to genius.

It wouldn't be the first time that she had gone down into a sewer in the middle of a storm. This time she'd go in prepared. Dodging groups of Corsairs, she crossed the street to a run-down shack of a home. Its door had been kicked in and instead of window panes, it sported only jagged pieces of glass like knives; few places looked so utterly abandoned as this one. It had an attached garage which almost always meant there were tools to be had.

She wasn't disappointed and came away with a hacksaw, an extra blade for it, a five-foot length of rubber hose, and four wire coat hangers. A football helmet would've been nice, but she wasn't that lucky.

73

"I just have to get down in there," she said, kneeling next to a torched Subaru that looked as though it had partially melted into the cracked pavement. A few feet away, a geyser of water poured down into a hole in the street that had once been a proper storm drain. It now looked like the Earth had grown a mouth. "First things first."

With quick motions, she straightened the coat hangers, twisted the ends together and ran it up into the hose to form a sort of snorkel. She made sure all her odds and ends were in their places and began to ease toward the hole, feet first. Just as her knee-high leather boots got damp, a group of three men and what looked like a boy came up the hill.

They were heading to the police station—they had come from the harbor. Those two facts stopped Jillybean on the precipice of the hole.

DON'T!!!

The scream came from somewhere deep and exploded in her mind. She fell back into the rushing water and struggled to get back into a sitting position, her blue eyes batting wildly as the echoes receded. The group was at the doors now where the light from inside spilled onto them. It wasn't a boy after all. It was a girl. A blonde girl.

It was Emily.

Jillybean tossed aside the hose and the saw and pulled the two handguns she had taken off the guards. She started marching across the street...

DON'T!!!

The screamed word staggered her like a punch to the temple. "Crawl back into your hole, Eve. I'm doing this."

Chapter 9

The girl in black staggered through the rain. The storm that was finally taming her wild hair and drenching her to the bone was slacking some, while the storm in her mind had grown in strength. The screams were enough for her to want to tear her hair out by the roots and stuff it all in her ears.

"Go back to wherever you were, Eve. This is Emily, damn it."

I don't care if it was Mom, you're not going in there! Your one job is to get us out of here. Jillybean! I said STOP!

Her head rattled with the scream, but Jillybean didn't stop, though the stagger did become a drunken lurch, which carried her off to the right a little. "And I said, shut up," she snarled, yanking her shoulder around as if pulling a hand from it.

But it's three to one. We'll die. Jillybean, this is not what we do.

Jillybean took another step and as she did, Eve sent a quick image into her head. She saw herself pulling back the door; she didn't look like some avenging demon in black, but rather like a small, skinny woman holding guns too large for her hands. And when she started blasting away, the bullets didn't run true into the Corsairs' hearts. They hit bellies and arms or missed altogether. Then bullets were flying back at her, causing her to flinch so that her aim grew worse and she began to hit the wall behind them.

A bullet glanced off her hip, turning her sideways, then another cut a groove into her flesh along the run of her outstretched right arm.

"Stop it!"

No. I'm not going to let you kill us, especially for her. She's a threat, Jillybean. She's the daughter of a governor and in a few years she'll be a full woman and beautiful. She'll be dangerous to us then. She'll undermine you and take what's yours. The image of tall and lean Stu Currans flashed into her mind; Emily was draped all over him. *You're a queen, act like it.*

"Your jealousy is embarrassing." Jillybean said. "And it sounds like Ernest is using you like a ventriloquist's dummy. Tell him to shut up, too." Her right shoulder suddenly jerked.

Ernest isn't here anymore. None of them are. Listen. She went silent for a few seconds, and in that short time, everything around Jillybean went utterly silent as well. It reminded her of when she was in the pit. It was as though she were buried miles beneath the surface of the earth. Tendrils of unforgiving darkness began to wrap themselves around her.

"Stop it!" She gave another shrug of her shoulders. "I'm glad they're gone," she lied. She was glad Ernest was gone, but not Ipes. She loved Ipes and Sadie, too. On a good day, she could tell herself that they weren't real and that they were only manifestations of her basic, primal need for security and love. But she didn't have many good days. Too many of her days, even back on Bainbridge, were ragged, exhausting struggles to hold her mind together. She used crutches to keep the madness back: her drugs, her books, her experiments...her imaginary friends. The truth was, she needed them.

"And I'll be glad when you're gone as well." Even this felt like a lie. Eve was horrible and terrible and...

You need me, she hissed. *You need me because you know there's something worse inside you. Something that gets out every once in a while. Do you remember all those sick kids in Sacramento? The ones that weren't going to make it? I didn't kill them.*

Jillybean's body began to stiffen as her muscles fought against her. Gritting her teeth, she tried to struggle on. It was as if she were pushing against hurricane-force winds. They fought her to a standstill. "Then who did? It wasn't me and Ernest wasn't around yet. And don't even try to pin this on Jenn."

You know who it was, Eve said, her voice only a ghostly whisper. She was fading into the quiet darkness and Jillybean should've been glad; however, the darkness seemed endless, and the quiet was the quiet of death.

"I don't know, which is why I asked. Tell me. Eve?" The girl was gone and Jillybean was free again. Free and empty. Free and weak. She looked around and only just realized she was standing in the very middle of a street in the middle of Corsair territory.

The sheets of rain had turned to a patter and her boots squished as she hurried across the street to the police station's thick glass doors. The fire was still burning merrily, the smoke climbing up a makeshift chimney that had once been an oven hood. Jillybean could see inside easily enough. The three Corsairs were standing at the front counter and looking around. They had already called out twice and didn't know what to do next.

Two of them wanted to take the girl into one of the back rooms and rape her, while the last was the man who had nabbed her on the *The Hammer*. His name was Lou McCulloch and he was the third officer of the *Midnight Raven*. He was not a pleasant fellow even by Corsair standards and was ready to crack some skulls. In his mind, the girl was his by rights and he wasn't going to share any part of her.

"*We* are not raping her," he said, glaring so furiously that his beady black eyes almost wholly disappeared into the pouches under his eyes. "I'm taking her to the Captain."

"That wasn't our orders," one of the other men reminded him. "We were to bring her here and nowhere else."

Lou's fists balled; if the kid said one more word, he was going to feed him his teeth. "I know the orders. I was there same as you when the 'acting' fleet commander said what he said. And that was all well and good then, but there's no one here."

"That's lucky is what that is," the other one said. "You know Mailbox would get after her the moment we leave. Here's what I say; I say it makes no sense to let this chance go to waste." He looked Emily over, licking his cracked lips. She forced herself not to react.

"I said no." Lou wanted nothing more than to rape her, as well. She was young, beautiful, and best of all, clean. He would have ripped her clothes off her right there in the galley of *The Hammer*, except a strange and amazing bout of clarity had softened his manhood. It occurred to him that finding the girl was the equivalent of finding a goldmine.

Right away he knew that she wasn't a stow away Corsair whore, and he had been around the Queen enough to know she wasn't one of her tagalongs from Alcatraz. This meant she had to be one of the three people who'd been traded for the Queen, and that meant she was valuable.

The girl was his only chance of getting his own boat. He would be *Captain* Lou, and in his mind's eye, he saw himself at the wheel of *The Hammer* as it scudded along under full sail. For the last ten years, he had wanted nothing else, but he had been placed on unlucky boat after unlucky boat. In fact, he had still been on board the *Midnight Raven* because her main had begun to tear along the clew and he'd been sulkily adding a reinforcing patch when he saw *The Hammer* banging along.

Unfortunately, he'd had to bring the girl before the acting fleet commander, who was none other than Stinky Jim. He hadn't ever been a captain and yet because of his connections, he was the damned fleet commander now that Mark Leney was on shore shooting his flares.

Taking orders from Stinky Jim was almost the straw that broke Lou's back, and he had been close to pulling his piece and plugging the ripe-smelling bastard.

"Mailbox ain't here and we don't have the keys to the cells, so we don't have a choice." Lou reached out to take Emily's hand to drag her out of there, but stopped as he saw the figure on the other side of the door. It was small, hunched and garbed head-to-toe in black. Lou mistook Jillybean for the narrow-headed guard everyone called Mailbox.

He turned away, cursing his luck, and wondering if a bit of gang-rape would decrease the girl's value.

"Where the hell have you been, Mail…" one of the Corsairs started to ask, only to stop when he saw that it wasn't Mailbox. Unbelievably, he found himself staring at the Queen. "Weren't you captured or something?"

"Or something," she agreed, bringing her guns up. She had wanted to go in guns blazing; however, Emily was standing in the middle of the little group. "Let's get those hands in the air. I don't want to have to kill any of you." Except a small part of her did. That part wanted to start blasting and was just looking for an excuse. It found it in Lou McCulloch.

Forget the girl, he thought, here was his big opportunity. Somehow the Queen was free. He had no idea how she had managed it and he really didn't care. His mind was focused on the fact that if he could capture her, the Captain would almost certainly give him *The Hammer* or maybe even a bigger ship.

Without giving himself a moment to consider the wisdom of his actions, he whirled, grabbed for Emily's hand, and tried to pull his pistol all in one move.

Emily was quicker than he expected and shied back, yanking her hands to her chest. Lou found himself half-turned, a gun in his hand. The other two Corsairs were stock-still, frozen by the suddenness of the situation.

Lou was on his own. With no better idea, he turned and fired at the Queen and as he did he saw flames blasting from the pistols in her hands, and above the fire, he saw her alabaster face, unflinching even as a bullet swished by her cheek. His first shot missed an inch to the left and his second three to the right.

Behind her, the glass door splintered into a thousand pieces before raining down in seeming silence.

The air overflowed with the thunder of guns as her second shot crashed into his collarbone, torquing him so that when he fired again, he missed by three feet, his bullet zipping out into the rain. He fell and tried to put out a hand to stop himself, only his arm was no longer his to command. It dangled limply as blood ran down from the ragged hole high up in his chest.

His face connected with the linoleum chin first and a chunk of his tongue was snipped right off as his teeth came together. The pain was searing and yet nothing compared to the outrage of his collarbone, the pieces of which ground together like so much kindling.

The pain was short-lived as Jillybean shot him twice more.

As she pulled the trigger, she wore a dispassionate look; the same sort one would wear while reading the back of a cereal box. And for her, the room was unnervingly quiet. She could see the flashes and the blood, and Emily trying to scramble out of the way, and the one Corsair pulling a .40 caliber Smith & Wesson from his jacket pocket.

He had long ago filed down the front sight for just such an emergency and had practiced pulling the piece, but that had been too long ago. Worse for him, he had never practiced pulling and firing the weapon, and now when it mattered, his hand was charged as if with electricity and he fired as he was still bringing the weapon up.

The bullet whined off the linoleum between Jillybean's feet. She had ice in her veins and again didn't flinch as she brought up her two guns. She missed with the big cannon but not with the 9mm Beretta, which drove a neat, bloodless hole into his chest and dropped him on the spot.

This left only one Corsair. Everything had happened so quickly that he felt like a spectator, his head wagging back and forth. Now his mouth fell open as he stared at the smoking guns in her hands.

"I didn't do anything," he said.

Jillybean had to read his lips because she was still engulfed in that awful silence. She read the words and didn't believe them. He was a Corsair and that meant he was evil, yet a hundred reasons why she should let him live roiled up inside her. They were a hundred reasons for pity and mercy. They were a hundred reasons that fell on deaf ears. She pulled both triggers and sent him stumbling back. He fell into the fire and twitched as his jacket smoldered and hissed.

"We don't have time for trials," she whispered, finally hearing her own words, which sounded a great deal like a hollow rationalization. Her eyes sought out Emily who wore a flat blank look as if she had been smacked in the face—all except the eyes. She had steel blue eyes and they held a touch of judgement in them.

"You are the last person who should look at me like that," she told Emily. "You should know that if I kill a man it's because there really wasn't a choice."

Emily's soft girlish lips popped open. "Aunt Jillybean? I didn't think that was you. You, you, you looked so terrible. I thought it was Eve."

Jillybean knelt over Lou and took his weapons and ammo, saying, "No, this was all me." A second later, Emily did the same with the Corsair with the tiny hole in his chest. He looked asleep to her and she tried to pretend that he was, not knowing if she could touch him otherwise. She had absolutely no intention of going anywhere near the body in the fire. It was beginning to sizzle and the smell was a special kind of nasty. It made her head feel light and her throat tighten.

"But I'm not sorry," Jillybean went on. "We don't have time for second-guessing anything. Half the town had to have heard that shooting. Come on." She too ignored the fire-roasted body. She had enough weapons and fairly clanked as she went to the shattered door and peeked out into the drizzle.

Right away, she caught sight of someone ducking behind a junked-out old car up the block. The person let out a hissing whisper, which was answered by another whisper from around the side of the building. Beyond that was the sound of feet slapping as they ran in their direction. Everywhere, the shadows were moving.

"Out the back!" Jillybean whispered and raced through the station for the back door. The knob clicked back and forth uselessly. "That doesn't make any sense." The door wasn't going to open, it had been locked from the outside.

There was only one way out of the prison and that was going to be through a hail of bullets.

"It's locked," Jillybean said, grabbing Emily by the hand, and running back the way they had come. As she ran, she cried over her shoulder, "We can do this, Emily. Across the street is a sewer opening. Get down into it and follow the water. It's going to empty in a bog that's east of the town. It used to be a river; now the only way to make it across is by using the remains of a bridge that you'll see just to the…"

Emily pulled back. "What about you?"

"I'll be right behind you. I'll lay down some cover fire to get you across the street. Right by the sewer you'll find…"

"And I'll lay down some to get you across," she interrupted, obstinately.

This made Jillybean smile sadly. "That's not how cover fire works. Yes, part of its purpose is to get your enemy to hunker down, but it's also used to draw their attention away from the real objective. If you shoot, they'll shoot at you, which would mean I'll be running into their line of fire. No, your only objective is to escape. I left a saw and hose right by the sewer. Take those when you go in."

Emily looked like she was about to interrupt, again. Jillybean glared her into silence. "Don't worry about me. I've escaped from tougher places than this. The only thing you need to worry about is getting back home. You know the way?"

"Northeast, but…"

"But nothing. Stay away from the fighting. Be smart and be brave." Jillybean grabbed her in a crushing hug and then thrust her back. "The moment I start shooting, count to three and run." There was no more time for words. Every second brought more Corsairs running.

With a deep breath, Jillybean stepped halfway out the shattered door and began shooting at the shadows, the car, and the edge of the building. The flashes from her two guns were bright like mini-sunbursts and even before Emily shot away from the station, Jillybean was almost completely night blind. It didn't stop her from pulling the triggers of both guns and spraying bullets indiscriminately, hoping to get lucky.

She had her own count going and when she hit six-Mississippi, she ducked back inside, leaving only her left arm extended, firing until the gun went dry. Once she had switched pistols, she was about to stick her arm out again when thunder seemed to erupt from every direction.

Glass and chips of brick sprayed over her as bullets screamed by. There was a high, piercing cry, and Jillybean felt her heart seize until she realized that it hadn't come from across the street, but had come from around the corner of the building.

Suddenly, the angle of the shooting changed. The bullets were no longer tearing up the door of the police station, they were flying back and forth from one side of the building to the other.

The Corsairs were shooting each other!

Jillybean felt a surge of hope and yelled, "Don't let up boys!" In response, the firing from both sides picked up. More men came and joined the fight, which spread to the next block. The screams and rattle of small arms fire were music to Jillybean's ears. "You're missing out, Eve. You normally like chaos."

There was no response and again she felt that senseless moment of disquiet.

"It'll just take some getting used to. But, I am healing. That's the good news." Again, it felt like a lie. "No, it's not. No more voices is a good thing. I only have to figure out a way to live long enough to enjoy it."

Escape wasn't out of the question. The Fluorosulfuric acid she carried was powerful enough to dissolve metal. All she had to do was add water. She hurried for one of the offices she had seen. It had windows with heavy metal screens covering them. The screens themselves were too large and thick for the small amount of acid she possessed; however, the screws holding them in place were perfect. The acid would eat down into the cement and she could be free in minutes.

What was also perfect was the evil-smelling haze filling the front room. There was almost nothing worse than the stink of burning human hair, and anyone entering the station would have to take a serious gut-check before going on.

In her mind's eye, she had already escaped and was tracking Emily through the hills east of them when she entered the office. It was not just dark, it was other-worldly dark—dark enough to stop her in her tracks. The dark was even deeper than what she had experienced in the pit.

Tentatively, she put out a questing hand and pawed into the darkness and quickly withdrew it. The darkness wasn't just deep, it was also icy cold and there was a silky texture to the air. Jillybean took a step back, her hand cradled to her chest. Air shouldn't have any texture.

"It-it's my mind playing tricks again," she stuttered. "That's fine. A little darkness never hurt anyone...then why is my heart hammering like this? Eve? Ernest? Is that you cooking up something? If so, you're barking up the wrong tree. I have to get out of here. E-Emily needs me."

The gunfire was starting to wane behind her and she knew she had to move. "The windows are straight ahead. Ten feet no more." She pushed forward with her left hand outstretched, her right holding the Smith&Wesson at the ready. Not even three steps in, her hand hit something wet and sticky. Its shape was that of a partially crushed cantaloupe with strands...of hair.

Suddenly it struck her that this was no cantaloupe, this was a human head that had been beaten in—a vision of herself bashing in the taller guard came and she tried to step back, only to trip over something else. She landed in more wetness—blood, she knew.

With her free hand, she poked at what she had tripped over: cloth over something stiffening in the cold. Her fingers traced a shoulder and a neck and the handle of a jackknife, her jackknife. It was the man they called Mailbox.

"But I left him in the room with the pit." Her words fell dead as if she were in the pit again, a hundred feet straight down into the dirt. "I'm not in the pit or the room or..." The jackknife moved under her hands, as did Mailbox. He was rolling over.

Jillybean fired the Smith&Wesson, and in the flash of light she saw that it was Mailbox coming back to life, though not as a zombie. His eyes were black pits with red glints of fire deep in them and his mouth was larger, his teeth the size of a donkey's. His lips were stretched back to reveal all of his hideous teeth, black gums and all. She shot the gun again, blasting through those ghastly inhuman teeth.

Then she was in the sinister darkness again. But she was still not alone. Mailbox laughed like a donkey braying and gnashed his teeth. She heard one tooth fall onto the linoleum with a *tink*.

She fled then, running into walls and a desk and then the side of the door, before she found herself in the hall. In one direction, the hall dead-ended at the locked back door and in the other was certain capture at the hands of the Corsairs.

She ran for the Corsairs. Anything was better than being trapped by the demon possessing Mailbox and his bloody-headed friend.

Chapter 10

Grey couldn't believe he was risking his life for a bunch of cutthroat slavers, degenerate pimps, lazy, mouth-breathing gamblers, and ex-Corsairs who were all wishing they could go back to being full-time Corsairs so that they could resume their raping and murdering. They were villainous scum that didn't deserve a drop of his blood. They were jackals and he was a lion.

Still, a lion was flesh and blood, a natural creature. The things that chased after him were not. They were more akin to demons than to men. They did not tire and they did not know fear. They did not feel pain.

Captain James Grey knew pain intimately. Frequently, it was the only thing he could feel. Happiness? He hadn't had a moment of happiness in ten years. Same with joy. Anger was fleeting; it took too much work. Sadness was for wimps. Grey was too busy surviving to take the time to mope around. Jealousy? Please. Despite being hideously ugly, he wasn't the least bit jealous of rugged, sharp-eyed Stu Currans or boyishly cute Mike Gunter. No one knew better than he did that looks were fleeting. Even when a person's face wasn't melted off in an explosion, a man's looks faded until one day, if he was lucky, he would look in the mirror and see a wrinkled old goat staring back.

For Grey, pain was the only constant in his life. He lived with pain every moment of every day. It was his only companion. Even sitting still, it hurt to breathe. His teeth ached when he drank water. His joints cried out when he tried to wash his hair. Putting his boots on made him wince and he woke himself up at night as he tried to roll from his left side to his right. Of course, rolling from his right to his left also made him gasp.

But here he was waving a damned torch and letting an army of zombies chase him down. Moreover, he was not at all certain he was doing the right thing. It seemed unlikely, but Jillybean might have been outthought by the Black Captain. She had known about the spies and the assassins, but had she known that Leney would turn on her so completely?

If so, why had she walked straight into a gigantic trap? If not, then she had made the biggest blunder in her life. "And we're all going to pay," he whispered in that harsh way of his. He paused at the top of a small rise, his chest billowing, rain running off him in rivers. Without his cape and his armor, he felt naked. Without his mask, he felt like some sort of hobgoblin escaped from a book. Without his axe, he felt weak. And without the cap on his mangled, stunted left arm, he felt like half a man.

Mask, cape, armor, it was all useless weight. He was in the middle of a chase that combined the worst aspects of both a marathon and a sprint. He hadn't been jogging. No, he had been running full-out, going up and down hills, splashing through bogs and wading through swamps, and dodging through forests.

His axe and armor would only slow him down and tire him out. And they wouldn't do him a lick of good. There were too many to fight. Behind him, shambling along with terrifying speed, were hundreds of howling, screaming-mad creatures, practically tearing down the hill to get at him.

Rocks and boulders used for leverage were heaved up out of the ground and sent thoughtlessly bounding away, and when heavy trees were in their way, the largest of the beasts would simply uproot them and fling them aside, while the smaller six-hundred pound creatures tore down limbs. Already an entire swath of forest was destroyed. The trees were about the only barrier that would slow them in the least. A few minutes before, he had passed through a small farm and monkeyed over a security fence. The zombies had gone through it without thought, as if it wasn't even there.

It might as well have been made of paper plates and tampons.

His pause on the top of the hill couldn't even be described as a "breather." He had only stopped to add another layer of cloth to his homemade torch. There was a hiss as he spun an old shirt on the two tines. The rain was soaking through the bag he had tied at his waist and the flame sputtered momentarily. Waving it helped to fan the flames. The roars below him doubled and he laughed manically, "You like that, don't you?"

When the closest of them was ten yards away, Grey turned and began leaping sideways down the hill, more like a chimpanzee than a man. Because his left leg was four inches shorter than his right, he could zip down a hill better than when he was young and healthy.

Still, the zombies were faster. Their speed increased as gravity sucked them down. Grey wasn't at all worried. The beasts had little in the way of dexterity. They could not control their gross motor skills or their momentum, or their direction.

85

They could only go down, running faster and faster until they inevitably tripped and went tumbling and crashing like hideous, fleshy boulders.

Waving the torch, Grey cut to the left, letting them blunder and bounce on by. It was like an avalanche of corpses, and more trees were destroyed. Branches tore out eyes and rocks smashed in skulls and broke bones. Grey would have laughed out loud if he'd had the energy.

All he could do was wave his torch and race on, cutting across the face of the hill at a diagonal. Now there were zombies both above and below. The break-neck tumble was already forgotten and the beasts were getting to their feet and taking up the chase once more, this time in a position to cut him off. He wasn't all that worried since there was another belt of forest up ahead that he could duck into. And after that was a stream with steep banks, where they'd find themselves trapped until enough of them piled up to allow the rest to scramble up the other bank.

He knew this land even better than the Corsairs. When they weren't raiding, they were fishermen, since it demanded so little in the way of actual work.

For ten years, Grey had not just been hunting across this stretch of Washington, he had been fighting wars here. He and Jillybean had long believed that their next fight would be with the ever-encroaching Corsairs. Both had studied the land; her through maps while he had crossed the terrain on foot, picking out details and fighting battles in his mind. It was why he'd been so confident to land his forces even with Jillybean being traded away.

Now, it would be a struggle to save his wretched force from destruction without ever coming to blows with his true enemy.

But not that much of a struggle. His destination: the old gas station/motel combo, was now visible. It sat like a shadowed, grey jumble of blocks high up on a hill. He had sheltered there a number of times and knew that the rotting timbers barely keeping the buildings standing, would go up in a snap, and once all three buildings were burning, the flares being shot into the sky would be meaningless to the zombies.

He just had to make it there before his lungs burned themselves out completely. In spite of his deformities, he trained harder than any man, and he could run for miles. However, he couldn't sprint for miles and his lungs felt like they were on fire.

Through the forest he ran in a gentle zig-zag, using the trees to scrape the nearest zombies off of him. Then he was at the stream. There was no time to climb down; he could only fling himself off the ten-foot bank and trust that he wouldn't break an ankle when he landed. The water was normally little more than a foot deep. On that night, it was over three-feet deep and he landed with a splash that nearly put out his torch.

Desperately, he waved it overhead as around him the stream surged and foamed as hundreds of zombies fell from the bank. Before he could turn, the dead were piling up, damming the stream. Grey hurried to the other bank and went up like a goat.

His last few rags were ruined, too wet to use, so he angled toward the road that led to the gas station where a number of cars had died almost within reach of it. Like most cars found on these desolate highways, they were crammed with someone's worldly possessions.

What had once been considered too valuable to leave behind was all junk now and among the useless TVs and computers were suitcases, flung open like so many mouths. Inside the closest was a mound of moldy clothes. The top layers were damp. Deeper down, amid rat droppings, he found a wool sweater and set that alight, thrusting the torch right into the suitcase.

Smoke churned slowly for a few seconds before the clothes caught. The suitcase went up readily enough and maybe the car would as well, but he was running again and couldn't spare a second to look back. The smell of corruption and death washed over him as he ran; one of the beasts was closing on him quickly. Leaping the guardrail, he was back in the forest with the sound of breaking branches right behind him.

He darted and dodged in and around the trees until there was a tremendous crash and a howl of anger behind him—just in time, too. The strength in Grey's warped legs was fading. He stumbled on through the trees, the torch burning more brightly than ever as the rain ceased coming down in sheets and began to fall in something only slightly heavier than a drizzle.

The torch was so bright now that it cast a flickering golden ball of light around Grey as he ran; everything outside that globe lay in deep shadow. From out of the shadow, not far to his front, came a frenzied, frothing inhuman cry followed by the sound of more branches breaking and trees crashing down and the ground beneath his feet trembled, until it seemed as though he was the center of a moving earthquake.

Somehow, he had managed to drag the two halves of the Captain's zombie army together—without even knowing there were two halves.

There'd be no dodging this time. The entire forest was coming apart as the howling beasts converged on him, drawn by the torch. There was only one thing he could do. Cocking his arm, he hurled the torch as high and as far as he could. In the flickering light, he saw a thousand hideous upturned faces...and one hoary old Hemlock standing eighty feet tall and looking like an unyielding sentinel.

With the torch still flying, Grey stole to the Hemlock and put his back to the trunk knowing that when it hit the ground, all hell was going to break loose. It was worse than he expected. The torch actually got caught up in the bushy branches of a two-hundred-year old pine with a trunk two-feet in diameter. It wasn't going to come down as easily as many of the other trees, but that didn't stop the zombies from trying.

The largest of the beasts attacked the pine, tearing off the bark and lower branches in their rage. Although the tree shook, the torch was good and wedged in there, and what was more, a branch with a matted wedge of old needles caught on fire. Grey's thumping heart leapt in his chest; if the entire tree went up in flames, he could skip away and none of the undead would notice.

He didn't trust his luck and while there was a fire to distract them, he began to slink away. Not a moment too soon, it seemed. A nine-footer stretched up a long arm and caught hold of a thick branch and began pulling, tipping the entire tree. More of them latched onto the branch, though most did so with the "idea" they'd be able to climb up it. The dead were terrible at both climbing and coming up with workable ideas, and soon the large bough snapped, spilling the zombies into a seething mass of arms and legs and hellish snapping mouths onto the muddy forest floor.

The tree sprung back upright and the torch tumbled down where it was smothered as seven of the closest zombies threw themselves on it.

Grey saw none of this, he was too busy dodging a mess of gargantuan undead freaks who were suddenly without a flame to chase or a reason to be running around in the rain. As they usually did at night, they slunk next to the largest trees and huddled together for warmth, making it a tricky walk for Grey, who couldn't tell what was a tree and what was a zombie.

He brushed up against one and had to freeze in place as huge, wet eyes suddenly blinked open. A minute went by before the milky eyes closed again and Grey could move on. He didn't have time to waste. When Mark Leney realized that his zombie army had been drawn off, he would certainly begin shooting his flares higher, hoping to pull them back.

Grey had to get back to his forces and move them east as fast as he could. He just had to keep the zombies in place for a little while longer. The gas station/motel combo would be the way to go. Once it was burning, the zombies would no longer be a threat.

The toughest part was yet to come. The forest ended a few hundred yards from the gas station and from its murky edge, he could easily see thirty zombies wandering about. Most of these were the very lame, but some were simply late for the party or had been distracted.

There had been a time when a man could adopt the zombie shamble and if he was careful and lucky, he could move right through an entire company of the beasts. Now that the creatures were all giants, they tended to look on any smaller zombie as a possible meal and attack without warning.

"I have the dark on my side," he told himself, as if it would be some sort of shield.

Right off, a few of the lame ones pivoted his way and began to drag or limp toward him. He picked up the pace slightly, eyeing the closing space. One was going to cut him off, so he was forced to suddenly sprint for twenty yards and then settle back down into a slouching ramble.

The sound of a heavy footfall was his only warning that one of the big brutes had seen him. Grey went from awkward lurch to sprint in a single step. With their long legs and the unholy energy found in their boundless rage, some of the beasts were terrifyingly fast. But only in a straight line. He had no intention of running in a straight line.

Nature had given him plenty of examples of a slower creature escaping a speedier one, and none were so prescient than the bunny. These rodents were irredeemably stupid and survived only by mass producing themselves and being able to turn on a dime.

Grey ran twenty yards and then juked hard to the right and watched as a huge naked man-shaped creature went sprawling. Grey was nowhere near being safe. Already two others were rushing over and the first was getting up.

Except for two more violent cuts, he made straight for the main doors of the gas station. The door on the left had lost one of the lower glass panels; Grey ducked right through it at almost full speed, sliding on slick linoleum and dusty glass. Like an ugly warped bowling ball, he slammed into an empty display case with a crash.

It was a loud crash, but nothing compared to the explosion as seven-hundred and fifty pounds of undead meat crashed into the locked double doors. Glass and metal went flying in a merry jingle. Grey was up in a heartbeat and racing down the empty aisles, while behind him two more zombies rushed in, both falling over the first.

At the end of the aisle was a second set of doors which led to the cafe that had once served both the attached motel and the infrequent truckers who made their way through the interior of the state. A sign above the counter read: *Best Burger from Walla-Walla to West Palm Beach!*

Grey had read that sign twice before and each time his stomach had growled. This time was no different. He launched himself over the cafe's counter and hunkered down in the waitress well between the counter and the kitchen and, just as one of the brutes came stomping in, its size twenty-eight feet bleeding from the glass, Grey's stomach let loose with a hungry growl.

There was a fifty-fifty chance the beast had heard and, trapped as he was, Grey did not like those odds. Quick as a cat, he grabbed a plastic cup from beneath the counter and flung it across the far end of the counter. It bounced around among the booths and Grey was able to breathe a sigh of relief as the monsters went after the sound.

He thought he'd be able to sit there for a few minutes and then move on once the dead lost interest in poking around the empty restaurant, but fate had another idea in mind for him. The three zombies made only a half-hearted attempt at finding him. They pushed at some tables and upended a booth, and finally one knocked over a tray that had more of the thick red cups perched on it. These were tough cups and made to take a licking. And they could bounce.

One did just that, bipping and bopping across the floor until it bounced behind the counter and rolled up to Grey's feet. A huge shaggy head had followed its course and now its wet black eyes ran up Grey's leg, along his lean belly, his bulging chest and into his eyes. For a second, the two stared at each other, then the beast went berserk.

It lunged along the counter, spilling dusty old plates and dull silverware with a crash and a clatter. Grey was too quick. He hopped up and dove through the narrow window that led to the kitchens in a blink, slowed only by the mangled hump on his back. Once through, he fell ungracefully among the metal bins of the service station before upending the entire thing and falling to the slimy tiles with a crash that seemed to go on and on as the bins bounded and clanged away.

Behind him, the zombies were going mad. They tore the counter completely off its foundation and threw it down. Then they attacked the wall; stainless steel sinks were pulled up and tossed aside. The soda fountain went next. A hundred neatly stacked plates were reduced to an uncountable number of ceramic shards, which were sent flying everywhere.

The noise was shocking. The screams and the crashes could be heard out on the highway and far into the woods. Hundreds of zombies turned and began to hurry towards the restaurant. Grey knew they were coming, just as he knew they would tear the building down to get at him.

Already the three on the other side of the wall were ripping at the long open "window" that led to the kitchens, trying to make the opening big enough to climb through. He turned to get up and when his good hand slid in decade-old grease and he nearly smashed his cheek against the tile floor. In the dark he saw something that made him pause; it was the cover to the grease trap.

It gave off a nasty rancid odor; it gave Grey an idea. Grease would burn. He threw off the cover and dipped his hand into the opening. On top, the grease had gelled into a solid crust-like mass which he plunged his hand through. Beneath this plug, the rotted fat was still semi-liquid and stank to unholy hell.

He began to pull out great handfuls of the glop which he tossed here and there. Thirty seconds was all the time he gave himself before he took a lighter to the mess. He had expected it to catch right away, but the lighter burnt his thumb before he caught the first tiny flicker of blue flame. It gave off a sooty black smoke which was even worse smelling than the ancient oil itself.

Slowly, the tiny flame began to spread and in its light, he saw one of the huge zombies half-in and half-out of the gaping wound it had created in the wall.

"Time to scoot," he told himself and ran for the back exit. The door opened onto a crumbling cement loading dock. To the right was the back of the gas station and across from him at an angle was the rear of the motel which looked out over a parking lot—and of course, there were zombies here as well. The night moved and moaned with shadows of monstrous size.

Grey ran for the motel with the shadows converging. A ground floor window was smashed in; he headed for that, leaping through just ahead of a strangely fleshy monster. It wasn't fat exactly it just seemed to have too much skin for its body.

With another crash, it came through the window, knocking down part of the wall. This seemed to have knocked the monster senseless and it was still lying mostly in the opening when more zombies trampled over it to gain access to the room. By then, Grey was racing up pitch-black stairs to the second floor where he found the place in a complete shambles. Every door had been bashed open and the contents of the rooms strewn in the hall.

It was perfect. He ducked into the first room on the right and began lighting the drapes and sheets. Overturning a mattress, he lit that as well. Smoke was already filling the room when he went to the next and did the same, the only difference this time was that he grabbed a long floor lamp, smashed off the shade, wrapped it with a fleece towel and used it as a torch.

This made lighting the next two rooms on fire a breeze. He was just going onto the fifth when he stumbled to a stop. Thirty feet down the hall was a hag-like creature just shy of seven feet tall and oddly thin for a zombie. Grey guessed that it had somehow trapped itself in the hotel and couldn't find its way out again.

Although small compared to most, it carried a deadly disease in its mouth and claws. Regardless, Grey charged. The fire from the first two rooms had spilled out into the corridor and was eating up the carpet and the walls just as he had hoped it would. He was trapped.

Raising his torch almost to the ceiling, he rushed forward and rammed the flaming lamp into the hag's face. There was an explosion of sparks and then the lamp was swatted out of his grip. Grey dodged low and to the right as raking claws swished over his head. He snaked past the beast and was up, running in his crab-like manner, heading for the main stairs, the half-blind crone hot on his tail.

The door pushed open and with the fiend so close, he had to trust his luck. He took a flying leap into the dark stairwell, sailed completely down the first flight, and smashed into the wall. His stunted left arm took the brunt of the blow and a zing of pain went up to his shoulder, but he was in one piece. The zombie fell down the stairs face-first and thumped to a halt at his feet.

Had this been another time, he might have stomped the thing to death, but he didn't have time. The entire undead army would be ringing the motel in no time. He went down the next flight in a normal manner and was out in the lobby in seconds.

More zombies ranged up and down the halls. He tucked his chin down and limped for the front doors, stopping only long enough to snatch a curtain from the long front window. He wrapped the tattered material around his misshapen body so that not even his head stuck out, he slipped right through the front doors.

Just as he had suspected, zombies were flocking in towards the gas station/motel combo. They stared upward as the flames licked the sky. The grease fire had set the restaurant ablaze and the roof was already beginning to go up. The motel would soon follow. It would be a hellacious blaze, visible for miles, exactly what he needed.

Grey didn't dare look back as he shuffled along under the curtain. The only defense he had against the horde was a thin bit of fraying polyester. If a head or even an eye peeked out, he would be swarmed in seconds.

It took ten minutes to get clear of the beasts, and then he was off and running again. He had to get back before the fire burned low and the Black Captain figured out what he had done.

Chapter 11

Emily Grey was terrifyingly alone. The bravery she had shown diving into the harbor after her Uncle Neil had been instinctive as well as perfectly idiotic. She had pictured herself grabbing her uncle and somehow holding him up above the water while the *Queen's Revenge* looped around and picked them up. Foolishly, she figured she would have to tread water for only five minutes or so, something she could do back in the pool on Bainbridge without a problem.

Instead, Neil disappeared in a blink and the boat had raced away, chased by torpedoes, leaving her stuck miles from land. Everything else that might have been seen as brave had been forced on her, but now she had to make a real decision. She could pick up the saw and the hose, and climb down into the black sewer where the water roared with a voice like a lion and where she was sure she would drown, or she could try to slip away in the middle of a gunfight.

Slipping away seemed like the smart move. It was dark and with the rain she might be able to slink along in the underbrush and *maybe* find her way out to the river and *perhaps* find the broken bridge Jillybean had spoken of. Maybe and perhaps sounded like weak sauce, then again, the hole in the earth was *certain* death—except that was the way Jillybean had told her to go.

Emily fretted at the edge of the hole as the gunfire picked up and men screamed back and forth. Even when someone came and threw themselves against the back of the junked-out Subaru, she hesitated. Drowning held a certain terror for her. It made capture, rape and torture seem not so bad, and she would have surrendered to the man firing his gun only four feet away if Jillybean wasn't in the process of risking her life, even then to give her a chance to get away.

"She would never let me get hurt," Emily whispered, her heart thudding more heavily with every beat as she edged to the drain. For a month now, she had told everyone she was *almost* twelve, but she had never felt closer to ten than at the moment. She was just a kid, not a warrior.

Bullets began kicking off the street near the front of the car. A few skipped across the hood and passed over her head. They felt very close, too close. She scrunched down and began to think that she was going to get shot if she didn't get down into that hole. She eased closer, her hands full, her ragged Corsair clothes weighed down by rainwater and guns.

If I go in there, I'm going to sink, she thought. "Except it's a sewer and not a giant pit." A bullet whipped under the car this time and sent up a spark right next to her hand.

She whimpered as she slunk down into the hole, discovering an entirely new fear that was greater than drowning: the sewer was pitch black. She'd be drowning in utter darkness and was there anything worse than that? Getting shot in the head seemed like an easier way to go out.

"Or, I could hide part-way and escape later!" This was a fantastic compromise and she edged into the broken sewer pipe. At over two-feet across, the pipe was plenty big enough for her skinny body; perhaps even too big. Had it been a tighter fit, she would've been able to brace herself more easily. As it was, she had to stick her legs out at a diagonal and grip with her toes.

When she started to slip the first time, she dropped both the saw and the hose, which were gone in a blink. The next time her feet slipped, she made a frantic grab for the edge of the sewer and held on for dear life. Her feet scrambled for purchase on the slick surface, but there was no grip and soon she was left dangling.

Finally, her hands lost their strength and she dropped, her hands and feet frantically scraping the sides of the cylinder, certain that it was going to be a fall of thirty or forty feet. She didn't even have time to scream. The entire length of the pipe was only ten feet and she technically only dropped five feet, landing in such intense, inky darkness that she couldn't see her hand in front of her face and was forced to quest about with outstretched arms to discover that she wasn't dead and probably wasn't going to die anytime soon.

She found herself in a squat rectangular cement box with water rushing through it, moving from south to north. Kneeling, she splashed around in the water searching for the hose, which had disappeared, and the saw which was under her right foot along with a pile of broken asphalt and tree branches.

The short drop, combined with her lack of drowning, had boosted her courage somewhat and she ducked down to inspect the outflow tunnel with her hands. All she could feel was cement and water, and maybe a gap between the two of about five inches. It wasn't much.

"And what happens if it gets deeper?" Her voice was a register higher than normal; she knew the answer. She would drown. "But the rain was getting lighter, and I can always turn back." With that she crawled down into the blackness, her head turned sideways, her scalp scraping the top of the tunnel. She tried to tell herself that a half-mile wasn't all that far.

On hands and knees with her head twisted at a painful angle so she could breathe, it was very far. The rough black dungarees she wore protected her knees to a degree, but her hands suffered badly. She eventually took off her jacket and wrapped her hands in the sleeves. Just then, the saw seemed like a waste and she considered leaving it behind.

If anyone else had suggested she carry it, she might have dropped it, but because it was Jillybean, she looped her belt through the handle and dragged it along.

The water did rise but the dark was so complete that she only began to notice when her cheek was scraping the top of the tunnel. Panic surged in her at the exact same moment she felt a touch of hope. There was light up ahead...well, something that resembled light. There was a fuzzy nebulousness marring the perfection of the complete dark.

Emily took a deep breath and half-swam, half-floated along the current. At some point, she lifted a hand to check the water level; it went almost to the top! *Go Back!* a part of her screamed and she tried to stop her momentum, however the rushing water was pushing too hard and she realized that going back had never been an option. She was going forward even if only as a slowly rotting corpse.

The level of panic rose to a scream and suddenly she *had* to take a breath of air. It was all she could think about. Her lungs burned and her throat felt weak, as if it was about to give in and suck in a lungful of rainwater. She scrabbled forward until her hand thrust into something dark and *gishy*.

Something was blocking the tunnel. The panic was complete now. Like a sprinter, she dug the tips of her sneakers into the concrete and drove as hard as she could into the mushy mass until it began to slide along the tube. The grey light seemed to expand and as it did, the need to take a breath became overpowering. Bubbles erupted from her nose and her mind was shrieking as the tunnel suddenly enlarged and she shot upward into one of the box-like little compartments and was struck by a torrent of falling water.

She ducked away and, without any thought to her situation, she gasped noisily, her head tilted back and her mouth wide. Even away from the geyser, water poured down on her, washing away a nasty greasy slime she hadn't known she was covered in. She smelled it before she saw it. All around her was a horrid, gut-churning stench that didn't just permeate her nostrils, it coated her tongue, making her gag. She turned away from the very meager light and gazed down, looking for the source and saw that what she had been pushing through the tunnel was a dead body, bloated and corrupt. It had been in the sewer for so long that it was falling apart, its skin blistering and erupting pus.

Burning vomit surged up her throat and erupted from her mouth, jetting in a brown foam against the wall of the little box. A second wave followed the first, while the third was little more than a chunky, croaking burp. She didn't wait for a fourth and attacked the wall, clawing her way upwards, once more in a mindless panic. Her nails tore and peeled back, but she didn't even notice; the only thing she cared about was the desperate need to get away from the corpse.

She didn't even know why. It wasn't a zombie. It wasn't going to suddenly sit up and attack her flailing feet. Her ability to reason had left her completely and had been replaced by madness.

Fortunately, the climb was short. Unfortunately, the tunnel led to a gutter opening that, unlike the last, was fully intact and all of seven inches high. Had she been thinking straight, she would never have tried to crawl through, but her mind had gone over to horror and she tried anyway, managing to get stuck with her head and one arm poking out into the night.

A river of rain water poured over her and tried to drown her, or so it seemed as the panic took on a different form: intense *cleithrophobia*, which is the fear of being trapped, only in this case she was afraid of being trapped forever, unable to move while rats gnawed her face off and the corpse below her came alive and started to eat her from the toes on up.

Unable to help herself, she squirmed and shimmied, and had she been able to draw a breath, she would've screamed herself hoarse. And she would've been recaptured.

The blocks around the police station were swarming with Corsairs and just then she couldn't have cared less. Nothing mattered to the girl except getting out from the constricting cement crushing down on her. With a grunt, she pushed herself back, fell down the tunnel, and landed on the decrepit body, which let out a cloud of green gas in a long, groaning burp.

Emily backed away, clapping a hand to her mouth. She knew she had to get out of the tiny box of a room, and slowly she eased around the body, standing on her tiptoes to keep from touching it.

To pull it back from the next tunnel, she used a long stick that floated on the black water. More of the foul gas escaped from the body and then a thick worm of intestine slid out from beneath it, making her whimper and retch simultaneously. The hunk of intestine was, in fact, the hose that Jillybean had left for her and when Emily realized it, she grabbed frantically for it before it floated away.

Her hand just caught the edge and she reeled it back in, holding it as far from her body as she could. The rubber had a thick coating of slime on it that smelled like spoiled meat. The cascade of falling water washed the gunk away, most of the smell and she had to hope, most of the taste.

There was only one way she was going to get through the next tunnel and that was to use the hose to breathe through. Why she needed it so long, she didn't know and decided to use the hacksaw to cut away a portion, seven inches long. The remainder, she looped around her thin waist.

This minor bit of crafting settled her down amazingly. She was even able to bring herself to kick aside the body and stab the stick into it to keep it from floating down the tunnel after her.

After one last rinse of the tube, she stuck the horrible smelling rubber in her mouth, gagged around the end, and swam into the tunnel, this time on her back. The rushing current pushed her into the impenetrable darkness. With her left hand plugging her nose, and her right holding the free end of the tube out of the water, she floated swiftly down the sewer, practically scraping the top of the tunnel.

It took only three minutes to get to the next cement box; she didn't even try to climb up this one, and a few seconds later she was cruising along again. In this way, she passed four more downspouts before she reached the end of the storm drain where it emptied into the bog that had once been a river.

Just as Jillybean said, she could see the remains of the bridge: broken chunks of concrete and rusting steel in a vast river of mud. What Jillybean had neglected to mention were the dozens and dozens of zombies, many very close to the bridge.

She had also forgotten to add that there was a barred gate sitting right across the front of the tunnel.

They weren't thick bars, only a half-inch or so in diameter. "*Only*," Emily whispered as she pulled off the hacksaw and began to run it back and forth along the metal.

Hours went by and back and forth went the single blade. Blisters formed on her hands and once more she used the Corsair jacket to protect her soft skin. Nothing could help the pain in her shoulders or the muscle spasm in her back, or the cement digging into her rear.

When the bar finally snapped off, she fell back and let the cold water wash over her thinking that if she ever got home, she would never go on another adventure as long as she lived. No, she would go to school every day, mind her manners, and marry the most boring boy on the island, which happened to be a ninth-grader named Joseph DiPaolo. She had always turned up her nose at him since he wasn't athletic at all and only talked about raising sheep.

Right up until she began to shiver, she laid there, staring up at the curved cement, thinking that being a sheepherder's wife would be perfect.

"W-wool and m-mutton and weird milk, what could be better?" she muttered as she crawled out of the drain and hopped to a large mossy flagstone, where she wrapped her arms around herself and shook from head to toe, picturing herself in a grey wool shift with woolen stockings. The picture in her mind's eye was not as unappealing as one might expect. Like her mother, she had the rare gift of making any outfit look good.

There was nothing she could do about the cold until she got to the other side of the river.

"If I g-get to the other side of the r-river." There were just so many zombies, all standing around. She counted twenty-three along this small curve of the river alone. It would only take one. There's no way I can cross here, no matter what Jill…"

An explosion to the north made her drop down low. There was a flash of light followed by a long, rolling, growl of thunder. It wasn't a close explosion, and yet the zombies all turned toward the sound. None moved. They shook and they strained and they clawed at the mud, but none so much as took a step.

"Ha-ha! They're stuck!" she cried, a grin stretching her mouth

That changed everything.

She saw the broken bridge in an entirely new light, and with the grin plastered on her face, she worked her way along the slick embankment. At times, she could hear men talking. Some were very close, or so it seemed in the dark. At one point, she crawled up the edge and snuck under an encroaching bush that should have been trimmed back years ago. Through its prickly branches she saw the city's defenses: a tangled row of barbed wire, a small forest of short spears, and about thirty yards of open dirt between her and a deep trench that had been recently dug. beyond that was a low berm where men faced out.

The grin became a smirk as she realized that by damming the river, the Black Captain had inadvertently given her a perfect escape route along its bank. Sure, things would get dicey once she got out on the bridge. Someone in the trench *might* be able to see a small dark figure scrambling among the rocks, *if* they were looking. She had to wonder if they would be. The few men in sight were chatting like the women at her mother's bridge games.

There should have been more of them. "I bet most of the Corsairs are gone after Gunner and all those dirty Santas and what not. And who knows if the ones that are left even know I'm missing?" She really doubted it. Jillybean had killed the three men who had escorted her to the police station and there had only been about a dozen altogether who had seen her when she had been captured.

"And they were on boat guard duty or whatever they call it. I bet no one knows I'm even gone. Besides, if anyone does see me it'll be in the dark with rain coming down. They might think I'm a zombie." She looked down at her ill-fitting clothes; even these she had "cute-ed" up a bit. The pants were cuffed slightly high at the ankle and the shirt had been tied at the midriff; nothing could be done about the smell of them, however.

She quickly ruffled them out and slung her soaking wet jacket back over her shoulders. Jillybean had taught her how to act like a zombie ages ago when she had been just a little girl, and now she adopted the same drooping posture and slanted walk.

As she was below the line of sight of any of the remaining guards, she didn't fear being challenged until she was out on the rocks.

It was difficult to stay in character while leaping from slab to slippery slab, and to make matters worse, the rain became a soft, sifting drizzle. Still, she might have gotten clean away if she hadn't been surprised by one of the dead.

The muck-covered beast was sucked down into the sludge up to its waist and had been sleeping flopped over when her foot skidded out from beneath her and she dropped with a loud slap. Instantly, the creature was awake and screaming in fury, one long arm snaking out surprisingly far, catching her foot before she could react.

As she was being dragged to its gaping mouth, her first reaction was to let out a shriek. Her second reaction was equally as useless. Instead of making a grab for the pistol she carried, she foolishly clung to the slab of cement as if she had a chance in hell of matching the strength of this bull of a zombie. The shriek built, tearing her throat as she was pulled into the mud.

Her right foot caught on a rock and she thrust against it pitting her entire hundred pounds against the seven-hundred of the creature. Futile as the idea was, it worked. Her sneaker popped right off and the monster stuck it in its mouth and began to chew. Like a rabid animal, she mindlessly attacked the slab, scratching and clawing her way higher to safety.

"Did you hear that?" someone asked in a whisper that carried across the mud.

Emily froze as someone answered, "What? A zed? Sure?"

"No. It sounded like a girl. Didn't it?"

With a gasp, she collapsed and very nearly slid back down the rough slab into the arms of the still flailing zombie. She kicked frantically back up as the second Corsair said, "Eh, I don't know. Maybe a little. Should we go check it out?"

Emily didn't wait to hear the answer. She leapt to the next jumble of slick rocks and then to the next, feeling that at any moment a gunshot would ring out or that she would fall and crack her skull open, or that she would stumble across another half-hidden zombie. This last fear was unlikely since every creature within a hundred yards was roaring already and doing their best to get at her.

Rage powered many of them through the sucking mud and as Emily fled, going from rock to rock, she saw them drawing in on her. And still she didn't remember the pistol she carried even as it banged against her hip.

She ran and leapt, and tight-roped her way across the broken bridge, losing her other shoe to the bog in one of her many falls. By the time she got across, she was a stinking muddy mess. The foul ooze coated her head to toe. It was disgusting and itchy and horrible—and it saved her life as she ran into another beast. Nine feet of ugly came stumbling out of a once pretty little ranch house, stomped through a white picket fence, and had her dead to rights.

Her heart froze in her chest and her muscles seized. She was a mud statue standing next to a leafless, leering tree that leaned over her like a threat. The zombie didn't even give her a glance as it moaned away.

When it was gone, she let out a long breath and looked down at herself, deciding that the muck wasn't so bad after all.

"I need shoes, though."

A pair that were only two sizes too big were quickly found in the ranch house, as were three pairs of socks which kept her feet warm and the shoes from slipping. Better prepared now, she set off heading through a hilly forest.

For the first hundred yards she kept herself on a perfect northeastern line, one that would take her across the land bridge, between the reaching fingers of Puget Sound, and then all the way to the shore opposite Bainbridge. "It's just three days away," she told herself without realizing that she was already gradually turning slightly north. Without a compass or stars or really any sort of landmark to help guide her, she continued edging north.

It wasn't until she heard the *SSSSSWUUSHHH* of a rocket firing that she had any inkling that maybe she had taken a wrong turn. Of course, she didn't know what the sound was and had she listened to her inner voice, begging her to run away, she might have remained clueless, as well as free.

Each hurdle of her implausible escape had buoyed her confidence to a dangerous degree, and even as the few undead that were left in the area began to shuffle towards the noise, Emily slunk after them, her curiosity getting the better of her.

Set down in a dale was something of a cheap knockoff of what Jillybean had fashioned outside the walled town of Highton. It was a small and lightly armored RV, sitting on stubby wheels. Not far from its only door was a bonfire which was keeping the attention of the zombies that wandered up.

They stared with blank eyes at the flames as a man on top of the RV snuck shots at them with a crossbow. A few had feathered bolts decorating their faces.

Emily hid behind a tree with slowly dawning comprehension as the next rocket shot into the sky and bloomed into light a mile away.

"They're herding them," she whispered as one of the zombies abandoned the bonfire and began lumbering toward the light hanging in the sky. "The Corsairs are using them to fight." Without realizing that the idea had been stolen from Jillybean, she thought it was despicable and utterly without honor.

She burned with anger and finally remembered she was carrying a weapon. She started to pull the pistol, thinking that if she could kill the Corsair on top of the RV, she might be able to do something, though what exactly, she didn't know.

But she never got to find out.

A shadow enveloped her as a steel hand clamped down on her wrist. "Look what we have here," a man whispered harshly into her ear. "A lost little lamb."

Chapter 12

Deanna Grey stepped out of the police station and looked up into the rain, letting the falling water wash into her gritty eyes.

They burned from a lack of sleep. After three days, she was running on fumes. They'd been three wasted, aggravating days for her. It had taken just a little under a week for the islanders to get over the assassination attempt on Neil Martin and now they were already moving on with their lives after only three damned days!

This sort of apathy stung Deanna more than she had expected. She thought her people had kept voting her into power because they trusted her ability to deal with difficult decisions during difficult times. Now, she knew they had only voted for her because she had helped build the wall. She represented the shield behind which they cowered.

Right and wrong seemed to mean nothing to them as long as the lights never went out. Unpleasant subjects, such as murder and kidnapping were best ignored until the sting of them went away and it could all be forgotten.

"She say anything new?" Norris Barnes asked. He was unexpected and unwanted, standing beneath a jutting awning in the midst of a tremendous puddle. Over his usual *I'm just a working man like you* plaid shirt, he wore a yellow slicker with its hood drawn up. He deliberately avoided using an umbrella, thinking that they made him look less than manly. Deanna didn't have the heart to tell him that whenever he wore the slicker, people made school bus jokes behind his back.

"Nope. She's still sticking to her story. It was all Eddie."

The hem of the slicker bobbed up, suggesting the big man had shrugged. "Maybe it was. She would have talked by now, Dee."

"No. She was in on it. You didn't see her eyes, Norris. When I went in, I saw it all right there. I read the *confession* in them." Three nights before, only hours after the kidnapping, Gina had been practically begging to confess. All it had taken was for Deanna to threaten her with that huge knife—no, not threaten; Deanna had been all set to slice Gina Sanders into little pieces, only Norris had barged in, spouting nonsense about rules and rights, pretty much the same crap he'd been yapping about ever since.

The shrug again, lifting the acre of yellow rubber. "But you didn't hear the confession and no one else did either. That's the only thing that counts. Listen, Deanna, you're in real trouble here. If she doesn't talk soon, you're going to have to let her go. People are beginning to, you know, whisper things."

Because of you! she wanted to scream; however, she had been a politician too long to let her mouth get away from her that badly. And yet, the mother in her wouldn't let it go. "Let them. People always talk. And Gina will talk, too. Oh yes, trust me, she'll talk. You just have to let me do things my way."

"Your way?" He gave her a sad look, his face turning down and creasing deeply like a sadly carved jack O' lantern. Other than the look, he said nothing, but only leaned forward, expectantly. He wanted her to say the word torture. He needed her to.

This was his big play for the governorship. If Deanna used torture, he would claim that they were a just community and shouldn't follow a leader who resorted to such barbarism. And of course, if Deanna didn't use extreme methods, and Gina simply remained silent, then Norris would call Deanna ineffective. He would be able to make the case that Deanna had not only been unaware of the coming attack, but had also done nothing constructive afterwards.

He was tying her hands, while at the same time playing the role of white knight, protecting the freedoms of his people. What good were rights if the Corsairs were able to kill them at will and kidnap little girls?

And what good is being governor if I allow it?

This thought struck her hard. She'd been trying to save her daughter and her people, while trying to keep her position as governor, thinking that she couldn't do one without being the other. And she was probably right. If Norris were governor he would jail her at the drop of a hat, simply to hold onto his position.

And then what good would she be to anyone? She seemed to be stuck in some sort of political middle ground where she was both powerful and useless. The situation had to change.

Deanna needed answers. She needed to know if there were other spies on the island. She needed to know how they communicated with the Black Captain. She needed to know if they had any more assassinations planned. And she needed to know when the Corsairs were going to attack—and here she was being babysat by a long string of people sent by either Norris or Andrea Clary, another of the council members who made no bones about her desire to be the next governor.

They all want to be governor, Deanna thought. *They all want the big house, the good food, and the applause when everything is going hunky-dory.*

The only person who really hadn't been around much was Norris himself. She guessed that he didn't want to be seen with her, thus the midnight visit. "You know this isn't a one-time deal," she said to him. "There are other spies."

"Maybe not. I get the feeling Joslyn was the last of them. She got spooked and took Emily and that other girl as an insurance policy. Nothing else makes sense. And, if there are others, what can they do? We have the island locked down tight. No one's getting on or off. We're perfectly safe."

Perfectly safe with your head buried in the sand, she thought. He was putting all his trust in the huge wall Jillybean had built, even though the Black Captain had just demonstrated that he could reach right through it and kill Deanna's most trusted advisor, infiltrate her people, and kidnap her daughter.

How did one argue with such a person? The obvious answer was that you didn't.

"You think so?" Deanna asked, giving Norris a weary smile that was both guileless and full of guile; it was a soft veneer over sharp angry teeth. She could get away with the look because she had a magnetic quality that was only rivaled by Jillybean's own queenly nature. Deanna's was based on an inborn charisma, and beauty that was almost a physical force, a force that she'd had nine years as governor to hone.

When he nodded paternalistically, she let her shoulders slump as if the weight of the world had fallen from them simply because of his manly presence and comforting nod. "Maybe you're right and maybe I need a break from her." She let the smile fade. "If you want to take over..."

"You know I can't condone sleep deprivation." The smile he gave her was just as much of a lie as hers had been, though far more obvious. *I would if I could,* it tried to suggest.

She didn't believe it for a second. "I guess. Hey, if this isn't the way to get her to talk, then what do you suggest? No. Tell me in the morning. It feels like I hit a brick wall. Were you going to stay? I can get you some tea, if you want."

"That sounds nice. I'll just stay for a spell."

To make sure I'm really leaving, of course.

Deanna walked him in and stayed in the lobby as he went to check on Gina. Since Talica Sears had been present all night, Gina was perfectly fine and perfectly mute. When Norris came back out of the holding area, he brought the yawning guard with him. Her usual perfectly teased hair was now a pure black bird's nest. "I think I better finish poor Talica's watch. She can barely keep her eyes open."

"I'll get that tea," Deanna said and left, wondering how she was going to get Norris out of the prison.

"A fire? It's what Jillybean would use. But it would be too suspicious. No, not suspicious. It would be too obvious. A chemical leak? Too unbelievable. An outbreak of pinkeye?"

She groaned. Nothing was going to get Norris out of there. The last thing he wanted was for Deanna to actually discover something nefarious about Gina. It would undermine his efforts to undermine Deanna.

Her mind strayed once more to Jillybean. Somehow the girl never let anything stand in the way of what she wanted, even if it seemed impossible. "She wouldn't use fire, at least not at the prison itself. She would set it well away and then use the distraction to swoop in and..." Deanna paused on the front step of her porch, realizing that she might have been looking at the problem from the wrong direction. Jillybean wouldn't try to torture someone *in* the prison. No. She would do it out of the sight of prying eyes.

"She would be trying to get Gina out, not Norris. Out to where? Oh! Her school!" It was the perfect place to torture someone. The zombies were always roaring and making a fuss. "It would drown out Gina's screams." Her moment of excitement faded as she imagined Gina screaming.

"She's brought this on herself," Deanna whispered, looking for an excuse.

As true as that was, it didn't make the idea of actually torturing her any more palatable. If she had been allowed to do it that first night, there wouldn't have been a problem. Deanna had been ready to flay Gina alive. Now that her anger had turned to frustration and exhaustion, she knew she wouldn't be half as terrorizing to Gina.

"Let's get her out of the prison first and then we'll worry about the interrogation. So, how do I do that?" All her old ideas: fire, pinkeye, etc. were still insufficient. As was an idea from a movie she had seen as a child in which laxatives were used to move the bad guy out of the way.

She needed something that would be more lasting than a bout of diarrhea. Norris had to be gone for the rest of the night, or at least a good chunk of it.

"Ha-ha! Sleeping pills." The idea was a good one. "Some decaffeinated tea mixed with some sleeping pills and he'll be out like a light." With her plan coming together, she barged into her own home. "Shelley! Are you awake?"

Shelley Deuso was Deanna's infrequent assistant, who had insisted on staying in the mansion ever since Emily had been taken. She was thirty-four, petite with close-cropped reddish hair. Her pale flesh had the appearance of being perpetually scrubbed as if she had never known dirt, perhaps not even on the bottom of her shoes, which Deanna guessed were, more than likely, laminated. She had once been a slave of the Corsairs and had gone through a womanly hell that few people could understand and fewer could have survived.

Although it was after midnight, Shelley came hurrying down from the guest bedroom in pajamas and a pink robe that was cinched severely across her narrow waist.

"Can you make some tea for...no, never mind I'll make the tea. Instead, could you..." Deanna leaned a little closer, "could you run over to Veronica's place and tell her I need her. I'm having a little trouble sleeping."

Shelley's eyes narrowed slightly; Deanna never had trouble sleeping. People could set their watches by her sleeping schedule. Still, Shelley only nodded.

"And if you could leave by the garage door, that would be great," Deanna added, then thought better of it since it made the simple errand sound dreadfully suspicious. It was too late to take it back, however.

Now Shelley's eyes widened but to her credit she only said, "Of course."

Twenty minutes later, Veronica Hennesy came up the backstairs quietly on stockinged feet. She and Deanna had been best friends for eleven years and she also knew Deanna's sleep pattern; in fact, she was envious of it.

"So," she said to Deanna, an eyebrow arched high onto her forehead. "Someone's having a little trouble getting to bed? Anyone I know?" She knew she wasn't in the governor's mansion to help her with something so simple as a sleep aide; nonetheless she had brought a bottle of valium and another of trazodone. At thirty-two, she was still young and pretty. For a woman, she was middling tall and fairly stout, though she carried her surplus poundage sensuously in that fortunate way few women could.

"Yes. It's terrible. I just can't seem to…"

"Knock it off, Dee. This is about Gina, isn't it? You still have a babysitter and you want him out of the way. Who is it?"

"Norris."

This took the edge off of Veronica's enthusiasm. "Him," she said with a sneer. "At least he deserves getting roofied."

"No, he actually doesn't. I've worked with him for years and he's a good guy. He's just also an overly ambitious guy."

"He's a turd."

Cursing had been out of style for so long that even this relatively childish word was enough to take Deanna back. "Maybe he's a little bit turdish. So, uh how much do you think I should use?"

Veronica's smile was full of mischief. "Two pills will have him out like a light, so I think we should do five!" She grabbed Deanna's hand and together they tiptoed down to the kitchen where they began experimenting with the pills, trying to decide what was the highest dosage they could get away with before the tea tasted funny.

Adding honey allowed them to cover the taste of four valium in the pot. "I should take it to him," Veronica stated. "I'll say I was heading home and was doing you a favor. It'll throw any suspicion off you if something happens. Besides," she added, purring and speaking so soft and warm, that her throat seemed lined with fur, "Norris has been after me for years. I just have to make sure my top two buttons are undone."

She wouldn't take no for an answer and with the steaming teapot wrapped in a towel, her shirt brazenly open, and Deanna following at a safe distance, she marched to the police station. Striding boldly in, she flirted without commitment, yawned so that her breasts strained the next button of her shirt almost to the point that it shot across the room and left a stunned Norris Barnes in her wake.

Deanna was in a bush just down the block where she had a fairly good view of the lobby and Norris sitting back with his feet up. As big as he was, he wasn't much of a sipper when it came to tea; he could down a cup in a single draw. In ten minutes, he had drained the pot.

The two women could see the valium take its effect by degrees. He yawned continuously, got up to walk around, sat down again, began to nod off, jerked awake and nodded off again. Finally, he locked the door and went into the sheriff's office, where the sound of his snoring could be heard through the walls of the station.

"Tell me you have an extra key," Veronica said.

She had an extra key for almost every building on the island. With a jingle, Deanna held up the key to the front door, as well as to all of the cells. "Let's go."

It felt wrong to walk into the police station on a clandestine mission while wearing tan slacks and an ivory puffy coat. A ski mask seemed to be needed at a minimum, not that it would have mattered a hill of beans. Deanna wanted Gina to know it was her doing the asking, and the threatening and the beating.

If she could do any beating, that is. The question was still up in the air as she strode past the empty front desk and into the holding area. She stared grimly at Gina Sanders as she unlocked the cell.

"What do you want?" Gina didn't bother to sit up and only reclined on her bunk. She'd grown insolent over the last few days as she realized just how impotent the island leaders really were. It was obvious that if they could have done something to her, they would have already. She figured they would sweat her for another day or so, and then she'd be able to walk free and live her life as best as she was able. She would blame Eddie if the kidnapping was brought up in conversation, play the victim card whenever necessary, and hope to God that she never saw the smoke rising across the Sound ever again.

What she wasn't going to do was admit to a goddamned thing, no matter what Deanna did to her.

Seeing Gina lie there as if she didn't have a care in the world drove Deanna into a sudden fury. The moment the door swung open, she leapt on the woman, pinning her beneath her blanket.

Gina's dark eyes showed a surprising amount of white. "I'll scream."

"Not yet, you won't." Deanna had prepared herself properly; her knife *snicked* open and glittered in the dim light. She held it beneath one of Gina's wide eyes. Deanna liked the fear in them.

"When my Emily was taken, they told me not to chase after her. They told me I'd never make it. That I'd get eaten by zombies, or I'd get lost and starve, or that if I did make it, the Corsairs would take me and do terrible things to me. And I believed them. They said I'd get her back eventually, if I just kept cool. So, I did, and today I headed a meeting concerning the Christmas play. Did you hear that? A Christmas play. My daughter's been kidnapped and people are worried about a Christmas play."

"It's understandable," Gina breathed, not daring to nod her head. "They were probably just trying to get your mind off things. You'll get Emily back. I'm sure…"

The deadly tip of the knife slid into her smooth dark skin bringing up a drop of blood. "No. Shut up. You don't get to talk about that. The only thing you're going to talk about is what happened to Emily."

"No. I'm not talking at all, no matter what you do to me. I didn't do anything and I have rights."

Deanna was feeling crazy. She hadn't expected to jump on Gina or to pull her knife so quickly, and she had to fight the desire to pop Gina's eye out. "Rights? You don't have any rights, not after what you did." Gina opened her mouth to answer, and when she did, Deanna shoved a balled-up sock into it. Gina tried to fight it; she bucked like an animal and Veronica had to add her hundred and fifty pounds to Gina's belly, crushing the thin woman until she took the gag.

Together, Deanna and Veronica tied the gag in place with strips of cloth. They flipped her over and cuffed her hands. Then Deanna took a paperclip from her pocket, bent it into an odd shape and snapped a piece off. She stuck the smaller piece into the door's lock and let the other end fall on the floor of the cell.

"Do you see how this is going to go down?" Deanna hissed into Gina's ear. "If I don't get what I want, you're going to disappear. You'll make a miraculous escape, only to turn up floating in the Sound, half eaten by who knows what."

Gina started shaking her head and began to make muffled mumbly noises behind the gag. "Save it," Deanna whispered before she thrust Gina toward the rear door of the prison.

The two women were rushing Gina along so quickly that she didn't have time to think. Her mind was taken up by a single image: her lifeless body floating around out on the dark water as sharks and other things ate her.

A scream built up in her throat and when they stepped out into the wet night, she let it go, thinking that even with the gag she'd wake up half the island. At the first sound, Veronica sent her heavy fist into Gina's belly, causing her to choke on the sock. Her knees buckled, but she didn't fall. She was carried painfully along by her trussed arms until her feet started treading the cement once again.

They're going to kill me, she thought as she was trundled along. At first, she was afraid for herself, but then she thought of little Bobby and her heart began to ache in fear for her son. What would happen to him? What would people say? That he was the son of traitors? That he wasn't worthy of living on the island? Would they kick him off?

She soon forgot the mental picture of her body floating in the Sound. She knew she could deal with that. People always said that drowning was an easy death once they took that first lungful of water. But they didn't take her to the Sound and they had no intention of drowning her. They were taking her to Jillybean's dark school. At the sight of it, Gina's legs failed a second time. The rumors about that place were far more terrifying than being drowned.

"That's right," Deanna said, seeing the stark terror in Gina's eyes. "Do you know what's in there? Something horrible. Something beyond any nightmare you've ever had."

Gina began to flail and Veronica lost her grip. The big bosomy woman was dead white; she too had heard the rumors about what sort of creatures were in the school.

Deanna knew the terrifying truth about what Jillybean had been growing inside the building. She unlocked the door and had to drag Gina in by her cuffed hands with Veronica trailing behind. The first roar from the zombies stopped the big blonde.

"It's okay," Deanna said. "I got this." Although she kicked and squirmed more than ever, Gina felt suddenly light to Deanna and she dragged the black woman across the linoleum floors until they came to the boy's locker room, where Jillybean kept her monsters. The largest one was ten feet tall. Its massive head brushed the ceiling. Like almost all zombies, it was completely naked and covered in a slime of feces. The chains around its neck and wrists were taut as guitar strings and looked like they were on the verge of snapping as it roared and gnashed jagged, diseased teeth.

"Tell me the truth, Gina. Are there more of you?"

Gina was so stricken by terror that her bladder let go and her body folded in on itself. Her muscles were like rubber and her mind was numb; she couldn't picture her beautiful son anymore. The only thing she could see was the one death that had terrified her beyond reason. The one death she had been doing everything in her power to avoid for the last dozen years.

"Are there more of you?" Deanna screamed into her ear.

Gina began nodding.

Chapter 13

With the fire burning in the north, Grey jogged back along his same path, hoping that Steinmeyer was already hurrying the little army through the gap in the Black Captain's trap. Minutes counted. The fire wouldn't last forever especially as the freezing rain had picked up again and was lashing him like a thousand tiny whips.

Grey could only grit his few remaining teeth and go on as fast as his tired body would allow. He knew that the moment Mark Leney realized that Grey's force had doubled back, he would start in with the flares again, drawing the zombies back.

In all likelihood, the Captain would also move his men out of their positions around Hoquiam and send them east, blocking off Grey's last escape route.

Their only chance was to hightail it northeast before the jaws of the trap could close again. Even then they wouldn't be safe. The Captain was a chess-master and was certainly moving his mountain bandits towards them as fast as he could.

Speed was Grey's only hope and yet, Steinmeyer hadn't moved out. Grey found his little army still standing around in the rain, chain-smoking tar and weed hand-rolled cigarettes. They weren't even keeping watch and Grey was able to come right up to where Steinmeyer and Captain Ryley McCartt were standing chest-to-chest, bitching at each other.

"They want to leave!" Steinmeyer cried as soon as Grey came huffing up.

McCartt was about to respond, when he saw Grey's face. Grey had forgotten to put his mask back on and even in the dark, he was hideous. Just then, Grey didn't care what he looked like. He stepped closer to the taller man and stared him back a few feet.

"You'll get your entire crew killed if you leave. Is that what you want?"

"Like you care, *demon*," McCartt answered, his hand resting on a .44 magnum with an eight-inch barrel, that was tucked into the waist of his pants.

It seemed stupidly big to Grey. "You're right, I don't care. I'm just telling you that splitting our forces before an enemy with superior numbers is a classic blunder. It endangers us all, unnecessarily."

"That's what I told him," Steinmeyer said, throwing his arms in the air. "Damn it, Ryley, what the hell? If you had a lick of sense, you'd know that leaving will only weaken us all."

McCartt pitched his voice low, saying, "Yeah, well I don't have much choice in the matter. My men are becoming sorta headstrong, you might say. They aren't really in a listening mood. They're in a taking-off sorta mood. They think that when you guys blunder into a fight, they'll use it as a distraction and escape."

"And if a fight finds you first?" Grey asked.

"Then things will be what things will be. One way or another, we're leaving. First, I want my bullets. One-third of the stockpile. It's only fair." Now he had a grip on his pistol and had it half-drawn.

Grey laughed at the threat; it sounded like he had chunks of coal lodged in his throat. "Not just no, but hell no. And don't even think that drawing your compensation piece will change my mind. First off, you'd be dead in a blink." He lifted his ruined chin to McCartt's right where little Lexi May was standing, her M4 pointed at the ex-Corsair. "If everyone starts firing their guns then we all die."

Lexi's knuckles stood out like little white nubs, and her mouth was clamped tight enough to crack walnuts, but the gun did not waiver.

"My boys aren't going to like it," McCartt mumbled.

Grey stepped closer. "I don't care what they like. If you're leaving, then you're leaving with what you got."

The Magnum Killers were slow to leave. There was a good deal of hissing back and forth, quite a number of glares and some generally expected curses and taunts. It was a waste of Grey's time. He tried to get the remains of his force moving, only they wouldn't "turn their backs" on the cowards.

Probably for a good reason.

Ten minutes went by before the two groups finally separated. The moment they were gone, Grey began pushing the remaining men to gather their packs and move. Although the fire on the far away hilltop was petering out and the zombies were losing interest, they still had time to cut along that incredibly narrow northeast line; only if they hurried and only if they could get lucky.

Five minutes later, a flare shooting high in the sky was the first indication that their run of bad luck hadn't left them. Grey, once more wearing his black fur and feather cape, and carrying his battle axe, began to curse under his breath. Whoever was shooting the flares had amazing luck. It had gone off directly overhead and drifted perfectly northeast.

The zombies would be coming right for them.

In response, he flattened his angle and went due east. The next flare that went up five minutes later, popped into flame three hundred yards directly in front of Grey.

"Keep going," he said to the next man in line. "Don't slow for any reason."

"Why? Where are you going?"

The temptation to smack the man with his axe was very great. "I gotta take a dump. I'll be right back." He disappeared, heading straight south on a run, orienting on the flares that were shooting upwards. The idea of going after whoever was shooting the flares, Mark Leney, he assumed, had occurred to him more than once during the frantic night.

It was a mission that seemed beyond either the surly, ex-Corsairs or the lazy Santas. The attempt would be fraught with peril. Had he been in charge of the flares, he would've made sure to have at least a company of soldiers guarding the launch site. Too many for one man to take on and he could only hope that whoever was in charge wasn't that smart.

If he'd had the time, he would've slowed and made a creeping approach from the east or the south. There was no time for playing it anything but straight forward. He slung the blade and pulled his battered Glock, thinking that he had faced worse than hundred to one odds before—more than once, in fact.

"Hit 'em hard and fast. Slip through the outer shell of guards and go straight for the rockets." It was a simple plan, which didn't make it any less effective. With the dark and the rain, and the element of surprise, it could work.

The one drawback was the "fast" part of the plan. It felt as though he'd been running all night and now he was burdened by his cloak and armor, and the axe which was more than likely useless. Regardless, he plowed on through the forest, looking more like some sort of deranged black buffalo than a man.

He came closer to the launch site but did not run into the line of dug-in soldiers that he knew had to be around there somewhere. A hundred yards away, a bright light lit up the forest and he went immediately still, watching for movement, listening for the chatter of bored men, looking intently for the ember of a cigarette.

Nothing.

It made him nervous and as he moved on, he went slower and slower until he saw the metal-covered RV, the bonfire, and the zombies. There were four of them now, staring at the flames. Another two were stretched out on the ground, black blood puddled around their heads. Clearly the fire was there to keep any stray zombie mesmerized.

But who was feeding the fire?

There had to be guards hiding somewhere close. Grey began slinking to his left, melding with the shadows, using the rain to cover the sound of his steps. He was nothing. He was a shadow. He was a nightmare for at least one of the guards. The man stood, leaning against a tree, draped in a poncho, his hands hidden.

Where were the others? There had to be more. Moving with soft, almost delicate steps for such a grotesque figure, he eased behind the sentry, and as he did, he slid the Glock back into its holster and reached for his hunting knife. Seconds later, he stuck it through the throat of the guard. It went in like it was going through cream cheese.

These sorts of things were never pretty and couldn't be scripted. The guard's rifle had not been on *safe* and in his death convulsion, he fired off seven rounds that went straight into the wet earth. The noise was outrageous.

With the thunder of the explosions rolling outward, Grey let him fall with a soft thud and pulled his pistol.

He was too slow and the gun was barely out of its holster when a dark figure seemed to materialize from the deep shadow of a tree thirty yards away. Flame and booming explosions ripped up the night as this new guard rattled off half a magazine, cutting a line of bullets from Grey's left to his right.

The first two missed all of creation, the next two thudded into the tree Grey was standing next to, the next two struck Grey flush in the chest and the rest hissed out into the dark. The bullets, two tiny pieces of metal, struck him like hammer blows and half spun him about. His good arm was suddenly not quite so good and instead of sliding up smoothly and locking in on his target. He strained to raise the weapon.

By the time he did, the other man had ducked behind his own tree. Grey didn't have bullets to waste. He leaned back as

117

well and with a groan worked his arm in a circle, trying to tell himself that the wetness he was feeling beneath his Kevlar chest plates was only rainwater.

There was no time to check. The zombies that had been on the other side of the RV were now fully enraged and came tearing through the forest. Grey tugged his ugly fur and feather coat around himself and dropped into a crouch low to the ground. His enemy was just as cool. He froze next to the tree and in the dark, it was hard to tell what was shadow, what was tree, and what was man.

The undead certainly couldn't tell. One went charging off into the forest, one stomped right past the guard and two lumbered within inches of Grey, who remained completely still, his chest aching, a snarl on what was left of his lip. The smell of the creatures was even worse than usual. It almost seemed as though the rain had spawned some sort of hell fungus to bloom in the feces that covered them.

Even Grey, who could barely smell a thing, grimaced at the stench, and had to hold in a cough. It was so bad that he closed his eyes to will them away, and thus didn't see the guard throw a stick right at him.

The man's aim was spot on and the chunk of wood dinked off his head. The unexpected blow made Grey jerk and wince, while the sound had the zombies turning. A massive hand with filthy ten-inch long fingers came reaching out of the dark for him.

The time for hiding was over. Grey's arm reacted the way he had trained it to, and up came the Glock. He fired twice at a range of four feet and couldn't miss. Both rounds blasted through the inch-thick frontal bone of the creature's head and it started to fall—right on top of Grey.

Desperately, he threw himself behind the tree; however, the giant body, twitching and flailing in its death-throes, landed on his legs, pinning him in place just as the next zombie roared at him in mindless fury. It swung one of its fists in a wild haymaker, looking to turn Grey's head to pulp with the blow, only it struck the trunk of the tree.

Bones broke as bark and ivory-colored hunks of wood sprayed across Grey's face. The zombie didn't even notice that it had crushed its own hand. It was so oblivious that it still tried to grab Grey with the dangling appendage.

It was like being mashed with a bag of sticks. Grey used his metal-capped left arm to bat the hand aside so he could have a clear shot, just as the creature opened its cavernous mouth to take a shark-sized bite from his head. It was extremely rare for Grey to close his eyes when he fired a gun, then again it was also rare that he let a zombie get this close.

Hot, black blood rained down on him as the monster fell, draping its six-hundred pounds across his chest. Air shot from his lungs in a single painful blast. He tried to suck in another breath that felt as thin as pancakes. Nothing went in, and still Grey kept his cool.

Death held no fear for him, though he wasn't keen on the idea of having his life snuffed out of him by being smothered under a twice-dead giant. It seemed distasteful.

The ugly hump on his back saved him as he was able to get an edge from its misshapen mass, giving himself a few inches in which to draw a breath. It was a long harsh gasp that he was thankful to take. The moment passed quickly as bullets started thumping into the zombie or passing just inches over the top of it.

Grey freed his hand and fired twice, missing badly. All he wanted was to distract the guard, who, unbeknownst to Grey, was already distracted. The third zombie had been heading Grey's way but as the guard ripped off shots in Grey's direction, the beast turned and charged.

With cool precision, the guard adjusted his aim and sent four bullets crashing into the beast. Even before it fell, the fourth zombie appeared. Its face looked like a twice-baked plate of macaroni. Where it should've had features, there was only a mass of squiggling scars. It only had part of one eye left and was clearly mostly blind and completely confused as to where the man was exactly. It came stomping along at an angle and might have passed him completely if the guard hadn't fired.

Two hunks of lead added to the horror of the thing's face, then the guard's gun went dry. Still cool, he shifted behind the tree as he reloaded, or rather, he tried to. The first magazine dropped as he fumbled it out of his tactical vest. The second was rain-slicked and he nearly dropped that one as well. He had to duck around the tree a second time to avoid the zombie's long arms.

Things might have gone bad for him if someone on the roof of the RV hadn't opened fire. Even for a nearly blind zombie, this one was stupid. As if the bullets smacking into it were a tap on the shoulder, the rambling beast turned and looked back. Now the rounds ripped into its upturned face; and still, it didn't fall. It was not until the guard on the ground got his magazine situated and shot it at point blank range did it die properly.

By then Grey had managed to pull the upper half of his body out from beneath the two carcasses. He didn't need much more than that. He aimed for the man on the roof first, since he was further away and could hide with a great deal more ease. Two shots went home, center mass. His arms crooked inwards and his hands crimped into claws as he fell on his side and began to drown in his own blood. It wasn't a quick death.

The other guard beat him to the grave. He turned quick as lightning and rattled off a string of bullets none of which came close to Grey. The guard then threw his back to the tree; he just didn't put it between him and Grey. The guard was side on and Grey could see his profile perfectly. One shot through the temple was all it took.

Other than the crackle of the bonfire on the other side of the RV and the patter of the rain, the night was quiet. Nothing moved. Grey didn't trust it. Tucking the Glock beneath his left arm, he changed out the magazine and then slowly stood, his battered, blood-splattered body a warped spring, ready to draw a bead on the first person or monster he saw.

Ten long minutes went by in which he did nothing except watch and listen.

Finally, a thump from the RV and a hiss of anger. It told Grey there were two people inside. Slowly, step by step, he began to edge toward the armored hulk, still moving as if he expected every step to come down on a tripwire.

"Look out!" The muffled cry came from the RV and just in time, Grey saw the black barrel of a gun poking out of a narrow firing port. He dodged to the left followed by bullets which tracked right at him, coming closer and closer—until the edge of the firing slot stopped the gun's motion.

Before the shooter could rush to another of these ports, Grey darted in toward the RV, stooped, found a rock, and skimmed it across the ground where it thumped and tumbled. The gun in the narrow port tracked the sound, aiming as low as it could, and hitting nothing but dirt.

While it did, Grey sped for the door.

The Black Captain's spies had relayed Jillybean's simple design but had not suggested the most basic of improvements—the metal slab covering the door was bulletproof; however, the cheap lock was not. Grey shot it, blowing out the low-grade components. The door shivered open a few inches and so he punched it with his metaled stump, and then ducked as it bounced all the way open.

A bullet winged overhead as Mark Leney fired reflexively.

He was adjusting his aim when Emily knocked his arm upwards. Furious, he grabbed her and crushed her to his chest. "If I die, you die," he growled, shoving the hot barrel against her wet hair, and feeling a touch of dark joy as the barrel hissed. "Whoever that is, you better not shoot."

"And why not?" Grey asked, stepping halfway into the trailer. He had his sights lined up perfectly; he could kill Leney as easily as taking his next breath.

"You shoot me and the girl dies."

Grey didn't even know the small figure was a girl. In the dark and with the baggy black clothes, he had thought it was a boy. Now that his eyes were adjusting, he saw the long, wet, blonde hair and the narrow face. "So what? What do I care if one of your whores die?"

"You can't fool me. I know you. You're that thing the Queen put in charge of the army."

"And I know you, Leney. You're a backstabbing traitor and you're going to die."

Leney thrust Emily forward as he took a step closer to Grey. "Are you sure? This is the daughter of the Governor of Bainbridge. She's worth something even to an animal like you." Goosebumps flared over every inch of Grey's body. This wasn't just Deanna's daughter, she was his daughter as well.

"Yeah?" he choked out. He could barely breathe. The air in his lungs had become confused and didn't know which way it was supposed to flow. Unbelievably, he was getting lightheaded.

"Don't play coy. I know what she's worth to Jillybean, and to that disgusting little zombie-man, and to you."

Grey cleared his throat and twitched his uneven shoulders, getting himself under control. "Right now, she's worth one dead Corsair." It was a bluff and he thought it was a good one. There was no way Leney could piece together that horrid, disgusting Gunner could ever father such a beautiful creature like Emily.

"Oh, I doubt it," Leney answered. "If you wanted to kill me, you could've done it by now. There's only one little thing holding you back." He gave Emily a jerk. "I think we both know how this is going to go."

"If you think I'm dropping my gun, you're an idiot."

Leney's eyes narrowed. "Well, I'm not dropping mine. So, what we're going to do is change places. You back your ass into the corner and I'll leave. Alone." The three of them slowly edged around in a very small circle until Leney had his back to the open door. "Now, back on up. All the way to the wall."

Once Grey had his back to the wall, Leney, still with his pistol cocked and aimed at Emily's spine, slowly backed out of the trailer before he went racing away into the night.

Grey considered giving chase. He had no doubt that he could catch the soft Corsair. *But what would happen to Emily?* he thought. She'd be all alone in a world filled with giant zombies, bandits and Corsairs. And she was cold and wet. And she was probably hungry.

"Are you okay?" he asked. She was still standing by the door, holding herself. It almost looked as though she was about to run as well. And she was. Leney had called the man a "thing" and in the dark, he looked it. He was hunched and warped, and there was something not quite human about him. Hate and fury seemed to radiate out of him worse than any of the Corsairs she had met so far.

She was so frightened that her teeth felt practically sealed together; she could only nod and even that was nothing more than a quick series of jerks.

"You don't look okay," he said, sounding angry that she wasn't leaping into his arms and beaming in gratitude. "They probably have a towel or some clothes around here. You don't want to go around soaking wet. People die from pneumonia, you know. It's not a joke." He started knocking about until he found a lantern, sitting next to a radio charger with a single radio set down into it.

A tiny green led light told him that it was ready to go and, thinking it was a match to the one he already carried, he pocketed it before hitting the spark button on the lantern.

When he thumbed it the first time, a flash of red light washed over the ruins of his face and Emily stepped back, not sure what she had seen. It looked as though he didn't have a face…but that couldn't be, and yet, when he flicked a second time, she saw that her eyes hadn't been playing tricks on her.

Leney had been right. This was no man, this was a thing, a horrible, evil thing.

Grey thumbed the sparker a third time and the flame finally caught and in the weak light, no zombie had ever looked as horrible. Emily screamed and ran.

Chapter 14

Too late, Grey realized he had lost his mask. Emily had seen his real face and she hadn't been able to take it. Had it been anyone else, he would have laughed at their fear and made sure to give them an extra big dose of his reality.

Because it was his daughter, he was stricken by a wave of self-pity and shame. "I have a mask," he called out, digging with his one hand for the scrap of stained black cloth. He hurried to the door, thinking that she wouldn't go far. She was nowhere in sight.

"Wait! Don't run! It's not safe." The deformed, melted little stubs that he called ears picked out her wild flight through the forest. She was already fifty yards away and picking up speed. She was fast and athletic. *A sprinter*, he thought, with a touch of pride, that cut through his shame like a ray of light.

Sprinting wasn't his thing anymore. His body was too warped to blaze away as he once had. He made up for it with an iron constitution and although he had either been running or fighting nonstop for hours, he took off after his daughter, worried that she was going to run into a tree and lose an eye, or blunder into a zombie and lose more than that.

Her panicked sprint took a chaotic route as she bounced from tree to tree. After thirty seconds she was gassed out and after another thirty, when she stumbled into a bog, Grey caught up to her.

"I have a mask," was all he could think to say.

"O-okay."

"I won't hurt you."

"O-okay." She didn't move. She stood with mud up to her shins, looking bedraggled and frightened; too frightened, in his opinion. After all, he had just rescued her.

Some of his old anger returned. "Look, if I wanted to hurt you, I could have. Come on. Get out of the mud you look…" She looked small and miserable and lost. And he was making it all worse. "Hey, I'm sorry. I…"

An explosion ripped the guts out of the dark, turning it inside out, creating a noon day out of the night. A tremendous fireball roared out into the forest.

Emily stared, her loose mouth hanging open. Ever the animal, Grey dropped to a knee and forgot all about the mask. In his hand was the old Glock, which he trained at the suddenly leaping shadows. As the fireball mushroomed up, the shadows grew huge and monstrous. Then in a long blink they were all gone and the night returned in full force.

"Was that the RV?" Emily asked, her voice quivering but not nearly as much as her chest was.

"Leney must have blown it up," Grey answered. "It's a good thing you ran." He stood, holstered his pistol, and began arranging the cloth across what was left of his face. When he was covered, he stuck out a hand.

The hand was almost normal, but it led to an ugly over-sized arm and then on to the rest of the warped, man-like creature. She couldn't bring herself to touch him.

"I told you I won't hurt you. I could. I could tear off your head if I wanted to, but I won't. I wouldn't do that. I'm really kind of a nice guy. Deep down, I mean. If your mom were here, she could tell you. I knew her, once." He had thrown this out like a life-preserver, hoping to salvage the situation, only now he saw the beginning of the obvious question forming in her eyes: *How did he know her?*

He stuck a finger to his mask, shushing her before she had a chance to say anything. "I thought I heard something. Come on, let's get you out of there." He stuck out his good hand and it was then she saw that his other arm ended in a metal stump.

"What happened to you?" It just came blurting out of her mouth and, as rude as that may have sounded, it was a far better question than the one that wanted to follow right behind it: *How are you still alive?* Thankfully, she wrestled her lips closed before she could let that one out.

"I never ate my veggies as a kid." This was his standard *Don't ask stupid questions* answer, though in this case it came with an interesting follow-up question, "Do you eat your veggies? You look big. How old are you now? Nine?"

She could feel him looking sidelong at her and it sent a shiver up her spine. "Almost twelve."

"Twelve. Wow."

As the two walked, in something of a daze, he couldn't seem to stop staring at her. It was creeping her out; he saw that and yet, he couldn't help it. This was the little girl he had brought into the world so long ago.

"I still remember when…" His mouth clicked shut just before he could mention how small her hands used to be. The last time he had seen her, she couldn't wrap her tiny hand around the tip of his pinky. "I, uh, remember when this used to be a nice area to live. Back before, I mean. Maybe it still is."

It was a lame attempt at a recovery, especially as a scream of rage filtered through the trees and a distant rifle went off with a long, high sound. She gave him a nervous grin. "I guess nothing's the same for you guys." *You old guys* was the unspoken implication.

At forty-six, Grey was a living hunk of gristle. He was too tough to simply fade into some sort of shuffleboard, checker-playing retirement, and no one yet had figured out a way to kill him. He feared he might live forever; an idea he found terrifying.

He grunted in answer, not trusting his mouth to just start jabbering away. If he'd had lips, he would've had them pressed tight. There were so many questions he had for his daughter—was she happy? Was her mother happy? Did she have a lot of friends? Did she have a boyfriend? Was twelve too young to have a boyfriend?

"Way too young," he said, under his breath, falling back into his habit of muttering to himself.

"Too young for what?" Emily asked, nervously.

He jerked and stared at her some more. They were both silently happy when they got back to where the RV burned. There wasn't much of it left. Only two walls were left standing and these were canted well over as the wheels on one side had already smoldered down to nothing.

Grey insisted on creeping around it in a full circle before getting closer to check things out. There were weapons to secure. There had been three guards; the first two were found easily enough; however, the third, the one that had been on top of the RV, had been thrown thirty yards away and hung from a tree. His skin was the golden brown of a Thanksgiving turkey and was dripping off of him. He had been flash-fried and not even Grey wanted to touch him.

All told, he found two rifles and five magazines filled with the crappy Corsair bullets which had a maximum effective range of about forty yards. Anything further than that would be a waste since the defects in their making would spin the rounds too far off course.

"Do you know how to work one of these?" he asked Emily, handing her one of the rifles.

She fumbled a magazine into the receiver, pulled back on the charging handle and then checked the fire selector to make sure it was on safe. "But I've never shot one. Jillybean showed me how to, you know, make it go, but my mom would never allow me to shoot one. She always said that I could when I got older."

"Hmmm," Grey rumbled, disapprovingly. "That's not how I woulda raised you. I woulda had you shooting from the moment you got out of diapers. But I guess that's neither here nor there, now. Go on and put that up to your shoulder. Good. Tuck your left arm more. Lean in. Yep. Bend your knees. Let the stock touch your cheek. Just like that."

He had her relax and then barked at her to get back into the proper firing position. He did this three times before he was satisfied. "When it's time to shoot, being relaxed and confident is key. You have to know you're going to hit the target."

"Thanks," she said, feeling a little better with a gun in her hand. No matter how many reassurances he gave her about how nice he was, Emily didn't think she would ever trust him. He looked like some sort of human/shark/skeleton/mutant hybrid, and she shuddered whenever he got too close.

Grey saw the shudders. He disgusted her. Sure, he disgusted most people and up until that moment, he had never cared. Now, he cared too much. He was being rejected, and the pain of it was startlingly sharp. With the pain came anger and deep humiliation.

Casting his hood over his repulsive face, he mumbled, "Let's go. We can't sit around here all night."

He took them on a course that he hoped would intersect the line of march of his little army. Seven-hundred men—minus those who were quietly running away—tromping along would almost certainly leave a wide, obvious trail, and although he walked bent double, he failed to find anything. Gradually, he changed his search to the north, thinking that they might have had to detour.

Three miles later he was still searching for any sign of his army when he came across a little cabin that he knew well. For years, it had been a snug, comfortable place; exposed just enough to be well lit by the sun in the day, while at the same time close enough to a backing hill to keep the wind from getting at it and chilling it at night. Like everything else made by man, it was fading and dying.

Moss had begun creeping up the walls on the north face like leprosy. Its gutters were filled with years' worth of acorns and leaves, and now rain poured down the sides and went right to the foundation. Inside, long jagged seams, like lightning, ran up the walls from floor to ceiling.

Still, it would be another decade before the small house became unlivable and just then they were desperately in need of dry clothes and warmth. Emily's teeth had been chattering for some time and she had gone stiff and white; when Grey stopped and looked back at her, she looked pale as an upright corpse.

He worried over his little girl so much that he missed certain small signs that he would've never had missed on his own: the windows darkened by blankets, the boot prints in the mud, the shadow that didn't belong next to the ancient Ford pickup that had been parked with its rusting nose jutting into the forest.

The first indication he had that he had blundered into a recon team of mountain bandits was the scrape of wet sludge on the first step of the porch. The next clue was a glob of snot that someone had hawked onto the handrail. The sight of it froze him in his tracks.

Emily bumped into him. Although the cloak he wore looked horrid, it smelled only of rain water. She began to rub her nose when he gently reached out with his stumpy, metal-covered left arm. Emily retreated from it with two small steps; enough room for Grey to slowly turn.

Once more, the night had gone *too* quiet. Even the light wind had gone still, as if the darkness was holding its breath. Emily was slow to realize the danger. Her mind was as lethargic as the half-frozen blood sluggishly pushing its way through her veins. She didn't see the man standing by the pickup truck, his zipper hanging wide open, his right hand caught between his still dribbling penis and the Ruger set in its holster at his hip.

The too quiet moment seemed to go on endlessly and was only broken when someone inside the cabin called out in a low whisper: "Wes, is that you?"

Years of practice had made Wes deadly fast. His hand moved with the speed of a whip as he snatched the pistol up in a blur and fired twice before Grey could drop his axe and pull his Glock. The first bullet grazed his hump, while the second smashed high into his ballistic plate armor and came so close to blasting through that the slug bent the material into a bird's beak that drove into his flesh.

The pain was negligible and easily ignored in the heat of battle. Grey's body was knocked back and to the left. He didn't fight it but turned to make himself less of a target as the axe fell and the Glock came to bear. He and the bandit traded shots, the bullets blazing past each other. Grey's round passed through the man's face, entering below his eye, tumbling like a pinball, and coming out through the side of his neck.

The thug's third shot went wide and, as he fell back in agony, choking on blood and a chunk of his tongue. He fired convulsively, the two bullets whipping shockingly close to Emily. Her reaction was less than desired. She went stiff, the rifle clasped in her grip as effective as a teddy bear.

Grey was on her like a lion. He spun her around; looming over her, his hard eyes running up and down her body, making her wonder if he could look straight through the bummy rags she had on. "Are you okay? Were you…" A growl of voices from the cabin. He knocked her behind him with that stunted arm of his and aimed the Glock at the door.

Someone inside knocked over an end table; there was a crash of glass and a cry of, "Wes! What's goin' on?"

"Don't go out there, damn it," someone else shouted a second later, the fear making his voice as high as a third grader's. Grey fired seven times; three into the door at chest height, and two into the walls on either side. There was a gurgled moan followed by another crash and another frightened cry. Grey began to shift to his right when an automatic rifle began ripping rounds, first through the door, then through the wall, and finally through the little rectangle of a front window.

Emily cringed down into a squat, still holding the rifle uselessly against her chest. If she could have found the courage to move, she would have run out of there at full speed. The beastly man had the opposite idea. He was as mad as he was hideous, and he rushed towards the cabin, ignoring the bullets that were flying everywhere.

For five wild seconds, the night was alive with ear-splitting gunshots and a strobe effect coming from the cabin, then the brigand's gun went dry and in the odd, echoing silence that followed, Grey could hear the man's frightened, labored breathing. Grey oriented on it, fixing the man's position just before he kicked in the front door and fired his pistol at the cowering shadow. The man died with his face contorted and his eyes wide. If it wasn't for the holes in his chest and the gallons of blood puddling on the floor, one might think he had been frightened to death.

Slowly, Grey swept the room with his nearly empty handgun. Nothing moved and nothing breathed. Satisfied, he leapt down from the porch and, as he switched out his magazine, he gazed searchingly at Emily. "What's wrong? Are you sure you're not shot?"

She was shaking uncontrollably and was shocked to realize that she was on the verge of crying. Everything had happened so quickly that the smell of gunpowder was still in the air and her ears were still ringing, and the man by the truck wasn't quite dead. The blood had almost filled his lungs and the wet, gurgling sound he was making was awful. On top all of that, she was embarrassed that she hadn't done anything to help the stranger.

"Were you hit?" he asked, again, reaching out a bloody hand to her wrist as if to draw her closer.

The thought of that hand and that monster touching her turned the quivering into something close to convulsions. She yanked her arm back. "I'm f-f-fine."

An uncertain growl escaped him. "That's good. I guess. Come on." He glanced once at the man lying in the shadow of the truck and knew he'd have to take the axe to him or he'd linger all night. That wasn't something he wanted Emily to see. He hustled her inside, stepping over the body stretched across the threshold.

"See if you can find some dry clothes and don't touch anything. And don't..." He bit back any more of the useless fatherly advice, thinking it wasn't his place. "I'll be right back."

Putting the bandit out of his misery and rummaging through his quickly cooling corpse took seconds. After, he walked a slow circle around the cabin to make sure they were alone. Satisfied for now that they were, he crept back and then almost went barging straight inside, only stopping when a thought struck him: *What if she's changing?*

Hesitantly, he tapped on the front door. "Uh, are you decent? You know, dressed?"

She had found a duffel stuffed with clothes that were somehow dry and yet smelled as if they had just been fished from a clogged toilet. She had picked through them to find two overly large outfits, which she held clutched nervously to her damp chest. "Yes, sir," she answered, hoping he wouldn't be angry to discover she hadn't changed. She had wanted to, but the idea of getting naked with him lurking outside had proven impossible.

He scowled when he saw she was still in the old wet rags. "What are you waiting for? I got you a poncho. It's only a little bloody. I can wipe that off. Go on into the other room and change. Go on."

Without taking her eyes off of him, she backed down a short, dark hall and entered a room that was windowless and nearly perfectly black. Emily couldn't have asked for a better place to change. The darkness hid her skinny body, her weakness. Next to the stranger, she felt small, like a child.

Being dressed again was marginally better. She came out warmer and dry, and just as haggard looking. Grey, who had been bashing his armored chest plate smooth again with a rock, gazed at her and the part of his face she could see seemed disappointed. And in a way, he was. He didn't like how she was cloaked in filthy black rags, how covered in mud and blood she was, or how there was a spark of anger hidden deep in her eyes.

She was too much like him and that wasn't right. She needed to be in a dress, one that was yellow or perfectly snow-white. Her hair needed to be washed and styled. A red ribbon... no, a blue one in it. No girl had any business looking like him, even if she had been fighting for her life for half the night. *She should look like Deanna,* he thought.

He was about to suggest that she run a brush through her hair and perhaps wipe the mud off her face but then thought better of it. The cabin was no point of refuge. The sharp battle— in his mind it was nothing more than a scuffle—had been heard for miles. More thugs were probably heading their way even then. And zombies, of course. The brigade of undead that he had tried to draw off were certainly heading straight for them.

This was no world for a little girl.

"Don't take that poncho off unless I tell you to," he ordered. "And keep the hood up at all times. I don't want to see your hair."

"Yes, sir."

"Hmmm. And don't say 'yes sir' like that. Your voice is all high and squeaky. Try to make it sound deeper. And from now on, your name is Emmet. Pick your own last name as long as it's not Grey."

Emily felt like she was being unraveled. She had gone from kidnap victim, to tradable pawn, to escapee, and now with him bossing her around, she was afraid she had become some sort of combination servant, prisoner and child-bride. The way he looked at her, as if he had some sort of perverted feelings for her, made her stomach twist into knots.

Yes, he was definitely a pedophile and the idea that she might someday become Mrs…wait, she didn't even know his name.

"What should I call you?"

Grey hadn't expected the question. It had come out of left field and knocked him for a loop.

"Gunner. My name's Gunner," he whispered, thinking about how she had shuddered every time he came close to her. He was a monster to her. He would always be a monster to her. Captain James Grey had died ten years ago and he had to stay dead.

Chapter 15

"Gunner?" Emily asked, more than a hint of suspicion in her eyes. "I know who you are. When did you ever meet my mom?"

"Before," Gunner answered, gruffly as he started marching off, heading due west to where he had last left his small army. He wasn't in the mood for answering questions. "Keep up. I'll leave you behind if you don't."

She didn't know if she believed that, and she didn't believe he had ever met her mom. She knew all the old tales from during the apocalypse. Jillybean, Neil, Veronica and Kay had told her the wild and terrifying stories from those earlier days, and one thing Emily knew, her mom had been a bad ass. She wasn't someone who would hang around with a piece of filth like Gunner.

On the boat ride from Bainbridge, Mike and Jenn had told her about how they had met the hideous troll in the wild and how he had forced them to act like spies. They thought he was working with the Corsairs, and Emily guessed he'd still be with them if Jillybean hadn't upset the applecart.

Emily scurried to catch up, the M16 already weighing her arms down. "You didn't know her. Neil Martin told me that he and Jillybean and my dad kicked your butt way before they met my mom."

"Don't believe everything you hear."

"If it's coming from you, I won't. How do I know you didn't save me just so *you* could turn me over to the Black Captain?"

Gunner grunted out a laugh. "Because I don't work for that chump. Now quiet down, please. The dead are near." He gestured with his stump of an arm to what Emily had thought was just a boulder. It was a massive zombie. Its huge misshapen head seemed to sit directly on its broad shoulders as if it didn't have a neck at all, though it must have since its face swiveled in their direction.

Emily stopped suddenly, her eyes wide and blinking in terror. She didn't think she would ever get used to being this close to the monsters that had haunted her nightmares for years. The great wall had always been there to protect her; now there wasn't anything but thirty feet of muddy ground and a few skinny pines between her and the massive ogre.

There was also Gunner, of course, though she was sure he would gladly feed her to the giant zombie to save his own horrible hide. In fact, to her, he seemed more closely related to the dead than to the living. He knew them well enough. Slowly, he went to one knee, found a rock, that he tossed far to their left where the woods thinned out even more.

Like a giant dog chasing a stick, the zombie tottered after the sound of the rock bounding away. As Emily watched in sick fascination, the creature tripped over a downed tree trunk, falling onto a spear of a branch which drove deep into its putrid gaping mouth.

It got up without noticing two-feet of wood sticking straight out of its face. Gunner found this funny and snorted laughter as he moved off to the right.

Reluctantly, Emily followed after him. She didn't want to go anywhere with him and had it been daytime and there were fewer zombies about, she might have considered striking out on her own. Her imagination suggested the hike back home would be over in a quick montage of sneaking around, seeing amazing natural scenery, running across a few deer or cougars, then standing on a bluff and gazing thoughtfully down on Bainbridge, looking serene as the sun rose over the eastern mountains.

Her reality was much different. She was tired and hungry, and the only water she'd had since climbing out of the harbor hours before was the rain that trickled down out of her hair.

But she didn't dare complain. Gunner didn't look like the kind of man who put up with complaints. He had been shot and yet he hadn't said a word. Emily decided that she would just have to toughen up and march on.

Ten minutes later, "My feet hurt. I think I'm getting blisters." She felt stupid the moment the words were out of her mouth, thinking that the only thing she could expect from him was a snide remark. Instead, he dropped down and inspected her feet. He even lifted one of them up, causing her to almost fall. To keep upright, she had to grab hold of him and found herself clutching his hump.

Her throat went suddenly tight and when she swallowed it was very loud.

He ignored it. "We'll get you some dry socks when we catch up to my men. I'm sure someone has a pair they'll let you borrow. It shouldn't be long now."

They should've run into the army ages before and Gunner was in silent fury. He had already begun bending back west and south and pretty soon he would find himself right back where he had left his men over an hour before. If he did, someone would have to answer to him and he wasn't in the best of moods. He too was tired and hungry.

Plus he had his own pain to deal with. To go along with his usual throbbing pains, the wound from the bullet that had grazed his hump burned when his cloak rubbed it, and his chest ached where he'd been shot. For him, though there was no use complaining.

"I could carry you," he offered.

Emily had been raised to be courteous and supposed that manners should even extend to monsters. "No, thank you. If it's not much further, I should be fine." *And if you touch me for even a second longer, I'm going to scream!*

It wasn't much further. Half a mile later, Grey saw the orange glow of a cigarette. Moving closer, he caught the first whiff of the ugly scent of the smoke. The homemade cigarettes could have anything in them, but for some reason, whatever combination of grasses, herbs and old tobacco was used, always yielded a noxious stench.

Gunner followed the scent until he came upon a ragged line of men, plopped lazily down in the middle of the forest. Unbelievably, his little army had moved less than two-hundred yards.

"Where the hell are Steinmeyer and May?" he demanded the moment that he emerged from the brush.

Everyone jumped, and a few even jumped to their feet and acted as if they hadn't been caught lounging around. In response to the question, hands pointed up the line of men to the east. Gunner went stomping off in his scuttling crab-like walk. Emily was, at least temporarily, forgotten and if she had wanted to she could've slipped away. Only, she was more turned around than ever and didn't think she could even find the cabin again, much less home.

She ended up trailing after Gunner, limping and somewhat hunched, looking like a small imitation of him. They passed a hundred surly men, their curse-laden gripes freezing on their lips. Most huddled at the base of trees to keep the softly sifting rain off of them, but one group had a small pit-fire going. It wasn't for warmth, but to cook the confused hedgehog that had scurried out of the brush and into their midst twenty minutes before. It had been killed, skinned and butchered in seconds and was now popping and sizzling.

It didn't smell half-bad to Emily.

With her stomach rumbling, they kept going to the head of the column where a small crowd stood about in stony, angry silence. There seemed to be two separate groups, each eyeing the other with complete mistrust.

Once more, the people jumped when Gunner swept into their midst. "What the ever-lovin' hell is going on? I gave explicit instructions to keep going."

"And I wanted to," Steinmeyer said, pointing an accusing finger across at Lexi May. "She wouldn't budge. She said that we should wait because no one knew where the hell you had gone."

"It's not my fault Captain Gr..."

His heart leapt into his throat. "Gunner! My name is Gunner," he snarled, his eyes flicking to Emily who was standing just to his left, holding her rifle at the ready. She hadn't noticed the near mistake.

Lexi May looked confused for a moment before shrugging. "Sure, Gunner is fine. Either way, how was I to know what happened to you? For all I knew Steinmeyer had stuck a dagger in your back and was leading us into a trap."

"So, you have us camp out right in the middle of a real trap? That doesn't make any sense!"

"That's what I told her," Steinmeyer cried. "Ask anyone." He jabbed a thumb over his shoulder at his men, who were all nodding in unison like a silent chorus of bearded puppets.

Gunner glared until the bearded puppets ceased their moronic nodding. "And how long were you going to sit here and wait? No. Don't answer that. We need to get moving. Steinmeyer, form the men up, properly this time. I don't want us stretched out over a God-damned mile. I want them in a real damn formation in ten minutes. Emmet...Emmet!"

Emily jerked, remembering who she was supposed to be. "What?" she asked in her lowest register. The word came out croaky in her ears.

"Stick with Lexi May. Keep her from doing anything stupid."

He disappeared then, rushing out into the night and as he did, Steinmeyer began giving out instructions, sounding like a

7th-grade gym teacher on a power trip. Emily went with Lexi May. With her camouflage coat and her hood thrown over her face, Emily could only guess that Lexi May was, in fact, a she by her name and because she was smaller than everyone around her including Emily.

"Does the Captain like little boys now?" Lexi May asked.

The question was confusing. "The Black Captain? I don't know. I've never met him."

"No. I meant Captain...or Gunner, or whatever he's calling himself now. I meant him." She gestured over her shoulder and mimed a hump on her back as she tortured her face into an ugly snarl.

"Oh, him? I don't think so. I doubt he knows any. He also doesn't seem like the kind of person who likes anyone. He can be very rude."

Lexi May stopped and came closer, peering into Emily's hooded face. "You're a girl! Where on earth did he find you? Were you out for a walk or what?"

"Yes, I was out for a walk." Emily tried to smile and nod through the lie; however Lexi May's raised eyebrow, arched into a perfect hook, made it clear she wasn't buying it. "Okay, no, I wasn't out for a walk. I escaped from the Black Captain's place, and then was sort of captured again, and then Gunner came and killed everyone. I don't really know what's going on. Are all you guys ex-Corsairs?"

"No. Most of us are Santas and I tell you, we don't even know what's going on. One day we were minding our own business and the next," she snapped her fingers in front of Emily's face, "we're royal subjects of the Queen. It's been messed up ever since, going here and there, fighting and digging and marching about. Still, I never thought we'd end up here."

Emily felt lucky to have run into this girl, who didn't seem that much older than herself. "I feel the same way. Three days ago, I was at home, and now I'm out here. Hey, do you have any extra socks?"

"Yeah, I guess. Hold on for a sec." Lexi May clapped her hands and began yelling for her men to get up. Most of them jawed back at her. Although she was both young and small, she didn't back down. "Take it up with the boss. I'll go get him, if you don't get up." No one wanted to deal with Gunner's anger, which everyone assumed went beyond simply "volcanic." He looked like a man who would resort to killing as a first option if the mood was on him.

The Santas grumbled to their feet and pressed forward into what looked more like a mob than a formation.

"Now what?" someone drawled.

"Now we wait for orders," Lexi May shot back. "And no one sits. You all know how he is." She turned to Emily. "He likes to sneak up on people and just start yelling. It's a pretty good motivational tool when you look like he does. Let me get you those socks."

Emily felt self-conscious as everyone stood around staring at her as she put on the socks and re-tied her shoes. She was about to get up when Lexi May told her to relax. "Won't they get mad?" she said, eyeing the Santas nervously.

"Yeah, but what are they going to do? Nothing. They don't dare. The Queen's locked up and they're still scared of her."

"But you're not?"

Lexi May shrugged. "Not really. The Queen likes me. She picked me out of the crowd. She said I had spunk." She laughed and said, "At first, I thought that meant something dirty, but it means she thinks I'm tough. Either way, boom, just like that, I'm the leader of the Santas. You know what I think? I think the Queen made me leader just to shame all these men. You know, to put them in their place."

"I like the way you call her 'Queen' it sounds so dignified. I just call her Aunt Jillybean."

"She's your aunt?" Lexi May leaned in closer, looking for the family resemblance, but not seeing it. Whereas Jillybean had fine elfin features that accentuated her already abnormally large eyes, Emily had a girl-next-door prettiness that was maybe only months away from developing into prom-queen looks. In contrast, Lexi May had a chipped front tooth and a bit of a pug nose that had rain dripping from it.

"Not for reals," Emily told her. "She's just very close to my family. She kidnapped me once when I was a baby. Everyone says…"

She stopped as she realized Lexi May wasn't listening. The young leader had a faraway dawning look. "You're from Bainbridge! You're that girl the Queen traded herself for. How the hell did you get way out here? You were supposed to be on the *Queen's Revenge*. Did it sink?"

Before Emily could answer, Gunner returned, silent even though his chest heaved. Because he did not trust anyone in his army, he had to do his own reconnaissance and had been running again. "Lexi! Turn your men around. We're going west."

"West?" the nearest Santa cried. "We can't escape to the west."

Gunner thumped him in the sternum with his metal-capped left arm and sent the man sprawling into the mud and gasping for air. "The next person who questions an order will get this shoved down his throat up to my elbow." He held up the stump for all to see; no one said a word. "Good. The zombies are spread out a quarter of a mile north of us, the bandits are ranging to the east and I would bet my ass the Black Captain has some of his morons heading north to trap us. Our only option is west. So get turned around, now!"

As the Santas turned, Gunner pulled Lexi May aside. Emily followed, listening as Gunner gave his orders. "Book it three miles west to that river we crossed earlier. Re-cross it and then get north as fast as possible. I want you jogging at a minimum. Just keep following that river even when it bends back east."

"What are you going to be doing?"

"Causing a distraction. That's all you need to know. Emil... Emmet, I mean, go with her. Do not leave her side and don't talk to anyone. I'll catch up in an hour."

Lexi May had her pug of a nose turned up to look at him, which she did with the shrewd eyes of someone much older. Growing up among gamblers and thieves had made her shrewd, indeed. "And if you don't show up?"

Gunner's eyes flicked to Emily before he said, "I'll show up. Even if I'm carrying my innards in a bag, I'll show up."

Chapter 16

Emily was still a little gimpy because of her blister, yet she resolved not to say anything. If Gunner could run around half the night as twisted and lame as he was, then she could at least keep her whining to herself. Not that she had anyone to whine to.

The Santas were surly and gruff, and the Coos Bay Clansmen were even worse. She had made the mistake of slowing too much because of the stupid blister and had found herself near their formation. Without having done a thing to them, she found herself the target of abuse, ridicule and at least one rock.

After that, she made sure to keep up with Lexi May, who followed Gunner's commands to the letter—for the first mile. After that, the energy of the men waned and they began to drag and complain. Lexi tried to instill the fear of Gunner into them, which only led to derision.

"He's left us high and dry," one man said.

Another added, "Yeah, I bet we're the distraction. I bet he's using us to get away."

"You know what I think?" asked another. No one got to find out what he thought because just then there was an explosion of gunfire from far behind them. It went on for a minute and then there was a long silence during which the formation ground to a halt and everyone stared eastward.

The firing recommenced with such suddenness that everyone took a step back.

"We gotta get outta here!" someone cried. This set off a stampede that carried the mob west to the Humptulips River. It was wide and up to hip-height on most of the men. They stampeded right across.

Emily didn't join them. She had enough of being cold and wet and was willing to risk death to keep her feet dry. Truly, it didn't seem like much of a risk to her. Gunner was drawing every zombie in the area to him, and it wasn't like she could get lost as long as she followed the river.

She figured there had to be a bridge sooner or later. After a mile there was no sign of one, but she did stumble across a house of sorts. Once it had been a hunting lodge, now it was three walls and a lot of broken glass. Everything about the place was wet, musty and green. Luckily, one of the intact rooms had been a bedroom and in its single dresser, beneath a layer of fungus-covered pajamas, she found more socks, and in a hamper, another set of clothes and in a closet that had a tree branch transfixing it, a backpack.

Once she had on another set of socks, she made good time and crossed the river just south of the town of Humptulips. There was no sign of Gunner's army and no sign of Gunner. She found it inconceivable that she could have beaten Lexi May to the town. Still she waited, somewhat warm and completely dry, beneath a massive pine tree that sat in the middle of a park that sat in the middle of a square that sat smack dab in the middle of the town—there really wasn't much to the town besides the usual sort of buildings: church, grocery store, gas station, bus depot, all of which were in a miserable state of disrepair.

Emily heard the group before she saw them. It wasn't as if they were being purposely loud, it was just that there were so many of them, that their shuffling feet made a rumbling sound that wasn't natural.

Not wanting to get shot, she hid behind the pine and called out, "Lexi May! Over here, it's me." Too late, she remembered she was supposed to be passing herself off as a boy. "It's me, Emmet," she tried again, deeper this time.

"What? What are you doing here?" Lexi May's face was twisted with anger, one pug-nostril flared wide and the other only a slit. "I thought you had run off."

It hadn't crossed her mind and now that it had, she was a little embarrassed. She didn't trust or even like Gunner, and although Lexi May was nice enough, the Clansmen and the Santas disgusted her. Not only that, they looked like very poor fighters, not that she was an expert on the subject of fighting, but none of them had that barely contained fury that Gunner possessed, and none had that uneven bit of discipline that was the best that could be said of Bainbridge soldiers.

To Emily, they were more or less jerks with guns. She should have run away. "It never crossed my mind," she answered truthfully.

"From now on, you stick with me. Have you seen Gunner, yet?" They both turned to look through the boughs to the east where there seemed to be a good-sized battle brewing. It seemed like a moot question and Lexi May's shoulders slumped. "So, I guess we wait here."

"That's not what he said. He said to book it, which I think means to hurry. Which we haven't done. And he said to keep following the river even when it turns east.".

"And we did," Lexi May replied. "We went east and here we are. But there's no way we're going to keep going into all that. If you want to try to talk the men into it, then by all means, go ahead."

Even if she could pass herself off as a boy, they wouldn't listen. "So what are we going to do? Just sit here? That doesn't seem right to me."

"Thank goodness it's not up to you. Gunner left me in charge and I say we stay put."

"Look, Lexi, I don't know you and I don't know Gunner, and I don't know if I want to know you guys. Don't be mad. I just want to go home and it's that direction." She didn't add, *I think*, although she was only sort of sure. "So that's the direction I'm going to go."

She turned to leave only to have Lexi grab her arm. "No one's going off by themselves. You either stay put or I'll have Little John sit on you, and Little John weighs two-hundred and fifty pounds, so be smart. Chances are that Gunner will come rolling into town bitchin' and moanin' that we stopped. Until then, take a break from worrying."

Emily would have threatened Lexi with her rifle except she thought it would seem childish.

Lexi May made her sit beneath the pine and then had her men spread out in the buildings all around it. Emily sulked, wondering what was going to happen to her. Nothing good she was sure. In the morning her disguise of mud and a hood would be useless; then she would have to worry about the evil men who were close, as opposed to the evil men who were a few miles away.

She got the feeling that Lexi May would help protect her a little, but if push came to shove, she would step out of the way. If Gunner were there, he would make sure nothing happened to her, but probably not for a good reason. Whenever he was around, he would stare at her, making her skin crawl. He wanted her. On some primal base level, she could sense that he wanted her for his own.

It was sick.

Running away seemed like her best option. She had a gun, some extra clothes, and there was clean water everywhere she looked. The only thing she lacked was some food and she figured she would find something on her way; an orchard or a lone deer she could kill.

She was just thinking that maybe it was for the best that they had stopped. She would slip away when Lexi May wasn't looking and who would come after her? Not these bums, sitting around picking their teeth, that's for certain.

Of course, it was then that Gunner returned, his wrath double what it had been. He cornered Lexi May right outside the confines of Emily's tree and reamed her out. "Whose side are you on?" he demanded. "I'm out there risking my life and this is as far as you've come? This is ridiculous. Jillybean screwed up when she chose you. Where's Steinmeyer?"

He reamed Steinmeyer as well, and that too occurred with Emily sitting too close to escape. When he was done, and had ordered the men to form up again, he pushed through the boughs and glared at her. In the dark his features morphed into something hideous; it was as if she were seeing him again for the first time.

"Jillybean trained you, right? You can throw a bandage on a wound and not lose your lunch, right?"

"I haven't had lunch and I don't know about the rest of it. Jillybean was teaching me some things but I never tried it on anyone."

He shrugged off his heavy cloak and then began to undo his ballistic body armor, one-handed. "This would go a lot faster if you gave me a hand," he grunted. Emily took a step back; he wanted her to touch him? "Come on! We don't have time for shyness."

Although she could do nothing about the way her face was twisted in disgust, Emily screwed up her courage and stepped up to him and began to release the odd wooden toggles that held the front of the armor together. When the last one was undone, she cringed, expecting to find him naked beneath.

Thankfully, he had on what looked like two layers of bloody long johns. "Splash a little alcohol on the wound and then wrap it tight."

He was scraped and cut in so many places, she was about to ask *Which wound?* when he thrust his left arm at her. It was something of a relief that the metal cap was still on it. Unlike his right arm, which had a bowling ball for a bicep, this arm was

143

something closer to normal. The bicep was *only* the size of a softball, though it was rock hard like the rest of him.

Just above it was a three-inch long gash. It was half an inch deep and bled freely.

"One of them got off a lucky shot," he explained. "An inch higher or lower and the plates would have stopped it. Be quick now. The alcohol is in my pack."

She hadn't noticed that he had a pack. It had been hidden by his hump and had fallen with his cloak. Inside the pack, among a variety of necessary items, was a first-aid kit of his own making.

"Make sure you get the alcohol deep."

The alcohol was home brewed and so pungent it made Emily's eyes water. "Doesn't that sting?"

"I guess a little. Give it a second to air dry." While they waited, they watched the men forming up. It was a slow process. "Their lives are on the line and this is how fast they move?"

"Maybe they're tired."

He gave her a sharp look over the cloth he wore strapped to his face. "Wrap it," he grunted. There was a white bandage which she wound around his injury. As always, he stared at her as she worked. "Tighter. Yeah, like that. Are you tired?" She shrugged. "Hungry? I have almonds and beef jerky."

Hadn't she always been taught never to take candy from strangers? "No, I'm good. How is that? Tight enough?"

Gunner flexed the arm and for a moment she thought the bandage would tear in half. "Yeah, it's fine. I want you to eat." It wasn't a request. As he struggled back into his heavy armor and thick cloak, she nibbled on the almonds. They had a light sheen of oil to them and were heavily salted. They were also better than she expected.

"Good," he grunted. Before slinging his pack onto his back, he pulled out the radio he had taken from the trailer. It was on channel 12 he noted with a skeletal grin. He changed it to channel 18 and handed it to Emily. "Keep this on when I'm not around but use it sparingly. It can be tracked."

"Are you going somewhere?" She hoped she didn't sound too eager.

The hope in her voice didn't escape him. "Likely. I can't trust anyone here to scout ahead. And I can't trust anyone to lead them. Steinmeyer is only a yes-man and the girl, no offense, is just a girl. She can't control her men, which makes her useless to me."

"I like her," Emily said. "I think she's doing a fine job. It's not her fault the Santas are the way they are. Nobody is going to get them moving east."

Gunner gave a short chuckle. "You like her because you're just like your mother. She always looks for the best in people."

She folded her arms across her chest. "That's a compliment if you ask me."

"Take it as one if you want, but sometimes there isn't any good in some people. Remember that and you might live to see her again."

Picking up her M16, she glared and said, "I'll remember. With you around I don't think I'll have a chance to forget."

He grunted laughter, saying, "Good. At least you'll learn some sense." He strode out from beneath the pine tree and marched along the brooding, shadowed men. "Those of you who wish to live will have to keep up with me. We have a small window of opportunity. All that shooting you hear is the bandits fighting the zombies. They've moved a few miles south which gives us a clear path across the north of them. But only if we hurry. Now's the time to suck it up and drive on."

Without looking back, he began to stride off into the dark. Emily started after him; at first, she was the only one. Then Steinmeyer sighed and began hurrying to catch up.

Gunner set a torrid pace that had Emily gasping. Still, she fought on, the "just a girl" comment had really burned and it motivated her to show that a girl could be just as strong as a man. All the motivation in the world could not overcome nature, however. It wasn't long before she tossed aside the backpack. This helped and for another few miles she kept the pace.

Then the M16 started to feel like it was a hundred pounds. Gunner took it from her and gave up his Glock. "Keep going on this road and don't slow down."

"You want me to lead? Where are you going?"

"Someone's got to make sure the way is still open." He jogged off, disappearing into the dark.

With Steinmeyer grumbling on her left, she didn't think she could slip away as she had planned. Without any other option, she went on, picking them up and laying them down endlessly. She found a groove and plowed on and, although the pace still slowed, it wasn't by much. She had an advantage over the men. Most of them were smokers and very few of them ever exercised. They were also burdened by guns, ammo, food and extra clothes.

Gunner was gone for an hour and when he returned, he was quiet, which was better than the way he usually showed up: ranting and furious.

"We need to turn north."

"I thought the way was clear."

He sucked down half a canteen of water and then handed it to her. Her mouth had been parched and she completely forgot about not taking candy from a stranger as she finished it off. "It was clear, but now there's at least a company-sized element about four klicks east, just waiting on us."

Klicks? Element? These were not words that made sense, yet she understood the gist: there was a trap ahead. Gunner immediately left the road and shot across country with his army trailing after, some "accidentally" getting lost in the forest.

Emily was terrified of the forest. Anything or anyone could be hiding among the black sentinel trees, and she was sure that if Gunner left her again, she would get lost in minutes. Luckily for all of them, Gunner didn't leave. He led them unerringly north, crossed the same Humptulips River where it was so wide it was more of a slowly running marsh, and then kept pounding north for another two miles before coming out on a narrow strip of dirt that had once been a fire break.

Ignoring Steinmeyer, he had Emily lead the way east as he went ahead to scout. In spite of her disgust for Gunner, Emily felt a touch of pride that he trusted her to lead. She redoubled her efforts which had Steinmeyer chuffing along next to her, glaring.

"Who the hell are you?" he demanded, trying to see past her hood.

"My name's Emmet," she answered, tucking her chin, and trying to sound tough. "I'm with the Santas."

Steinmeyer edged closer. There was something odd about the kid, though he couldn't put his finger on what it was. "Did you know Gunner from before? He acts like he knows you."

"Nope." She made a further effort at speed and, to get his mind off of her, she asked, "Did you know him?"

"I knew of him. We all did. He was something of a myth, you know, like Bigfoot or something. Few of us ever saw him up close, but sometimes someone would get a glimpse of that funky cloak of his, or they'd come across a still smoldering fire. Every once in a while, someone would go missing. You know someone who would never run. And," he lowered his voice, giving a quick glance around at the fading night, "sometimes we'd find a body, strung up in a tree or with their throat cut. Everyone thought it was that guy."

So, Emily thought, *he's every bit as awful as she had imagined.* "If he's so bad, why do you follow him?"

Steinmeyer shrugged and muttered bits of words and the beginnings of syllables. Despite not being an actual language, she had sudden insight that was unlikely for an eleven-year-old. They all followed him because they were used to following strong leaders, even if they were evil men. Following was so much easier than taking the risk of standing out, of confronting, or of blazing one's own way.

Emily decided right then that she would leave and of course it was right then that Gunner came racing back, his mask askew, sweat gleaming off the revealed bones of his face.

"Another trap!" he said in between gasps. "We have to turn back. Steinmeyer, get the men turned around."

Steinmeyer looked as though he wanted to say something, but his courage wasn't up to it and with a theatrically weary sigh, and his heavy slumped shoulders sagging, he turned to obey. Emily also turned and that was when Gunner grabbed her from behind, his one hand gripping the back of her neck in a vice.

"There's a spy among us," he told her, his breath washing over her like a hot wind. Her back muscles wriggled uncontrollably at his proximity. "Stop that! You have to figure out very quickly whose side you're on. Jillybean gave me this command for a reason. It's because she trusts me. She's known me for a long time. These others can't say the same thing and one of them is feeding our enemies information about where we're going. It's the only thing that makes sense."

With his muscular hand holding her, she couldn't even nod. She stammered out, "I-I g-guess."

Gunner leaned in even closer so that what passed for a mouth was only an inch from her ear. "I'm going to need your help to flush him out."

"Me? What about Lexi or Steinmeyer? And, and, and there's like six hundred of them. How are we supposed to figure out which one it is?"

"You're the only one I trust, Emily." His grip suddenly tightened, becoming painful. "You're the only one who's really

147

good. I know it." For just a terrible, fleeting moment, she thought he was going to try to kiss her. If he had, she would have screamed. The moment passed and he hurriedly began to explain, "We'll use the radios. You'll set yours to channel 12. When I give the command to move south, listen and watch. Someone will probably step out of formation or maybe duck beneath a poncho to use a radio. It'll take seconds, so make sure you stay focused."

She didn't like that he was relying on her so much. In the pit of her stomach, she knew she was going to screw up. "But what if I don't see who it is? There's a lot of them and it's dark."

He released his grip and looked down into her soft face and the creepy, adoring look in his eyes had only gotten worse. "I'll make another course change. We'll get the bastard, don't worry."

And what will you do with him? String him up in a tree? Hack his head off with your axe? She didn't dare ask, afraid that he just might tell her. Not that it mattered because first, *she* had to catch the spy. It seemed impossible.

"I can't do this," she whispered as she hurried to the front of the formation once again. It was too much responsibility. It was one thing to be tough and march down a road as if leading a parade, but catching a spy was another altogether. What if the spy had help? What if there were a dozen of them? What if...

Lexi May darted out of the formation to walk with her; she seemed just as frightened as Emily. "Another trap? Damn it, Emily, I don't like how this is going. We can't run forever; doesn't he know this? What are we going to do when the sun comes up?"

For one thing, Emily's weak disguise would be useless in the light of day, and the idea of being surrounded by six-hundred or so villainous men made her stomach curdle. At least she had Lexi with her; being with another girl helped, but only a little.

Emily leaned in close to her until their wet shoulders were rubbing together. "I'm thinking about taking off." The idea, the same one she had been kicking around all night, was once again front and center in her mind. Jillybean might have given this command to Gunner and she had put Lexi May in charge of the Santas, but she had also told Emily to escape and to stay away from the fighting. It was past time she left.

Lexi May rolled her dark eyes and tried to pull away. "No! We've already gone through this. You'll be a sitting duck out there alone."

"You can come with me." Emily pulled her to the side and whispered, "Gunner thinks there's a spy with us and he's got a cockamamie scheme to find him. He wants me to, to, never mind. It doesn't matter because it's not going to work. The only thing that will work is running away. He's going to turn the formation south and when he does, I'm going north. That sounds like a good plan, right?"

"No, it doesn't. We don't stand a chance out there alone and I'm not going and neither are you. Promise me right now that you won't or I'll tell Gunner." Emily was so furious she began to sputter parts of curses she had never been allowed to say. She even squared up on Lexi May, who scoffed, "Back down. You're just embarrassing yourself."

"Fine," Emily snarled, though what she meant by that, she didn't know. Furious, she stormed away, heading to the front of the formation. She had only taken a few steps before the radio in her pocket crackled.

"They're moving south," a soft voice rasped in a whisper.

Emily spun. She knew the voice. Yanking the radio from her pocket, she tried to turn up the volume while at the same time running back along the formation of tired men. They were all the same: bearded blurs who walked with an old man's shuffle. She didn't pay them any attention. The person she was after wouldn't be among them. *She* would be in the woods.

Emily caught up with Lexi May just as both their radios crackled, "Say again. Was that south? On what road?"

They both ignored their radios; their eyes were locked across fifteen feet of shadow. Lexi May's left hand caressed the strap of her M16A2 that hung loosely on her shoulder. "Aren't you the biggest pain in the ass?" Emily said nothing. All she could think was that the Glock was stuffed too deep in her pocket for her to get at quickly.

Lexi May lifted the radio. "I have a situation. The girl caught me. Do I continue with my mission, or bring in the girl? I can't do both."

It seemed like ages before the radio came to life again. "Get rid of the girl. Destroying that army is what matters now."

"You heard the Boss," Lexi May said with a little shrug. "Sorry. And don't bother running. It'll only make things worse."

Now Emily felt perfectly idiotic. Running hadn't crossed her mind. She could've been darting through the trees by then. Instead she had gone for the Glock with numb fumbling hands and terrified eyes as she saw Lexi May spin the M16 A2 off her shoulder like she was twirling a baton.

Chapter 17

"I'm sorry. Please, I'm sorry," Gina Sanders whispered over and over again, her tear-streaked face held just an inch over Deanna's fur-lined boots. She had already kissed them, much to Deanna's annoyance.

She didn't want kisses, or promises to be good, or any of that. Deanna wanted her baby back home, safe and sound, and the information Gina had given her hadn't helped a bit.

Veronica Hennesy stood half in the doorway, looking ready to run. The shimmer had gone out of her blonde hair and the thin lines on her face had deepened as if she had gained ten years in the last half hour. She thought it was no wonder that Gina had wet herself. Deanna had held her within inches of a zombie that was bigger and stronger than a draft horse. Its teeth were the size of Veronica's fingers and each was broken and sharp, and dripping with disease.

And it had all been for nothing. Gina knew very little about the spy network on the island. She knew the signal for Eddie to cross the Sound, and she knew where he dropped off his reports and picked up his bullets. That was about it. In fact, she only guessed that there were others, and hadn't known for sure until she had heard about Emily's kidnapping.

"What are we going to do with her?" Veronica asked.

Deanna Grey stared down at Gina's trembling body. She wanted to stick her hunting knife between Gina's ribs. That would've been justice. But it would have spawned a great deal of injustice. She would be removed as Governor and probably banished. Veronica as well.

"First, she'll write out her confession," Deanna stated. There was no question that she would. It was fact to her. There would be a confession or Gina would get the knife...slowly. "Go find a pen and paper." When she was gone, Deanna dragged Gina back from the screaming beast.

"What are you going to do to me after I write, you know, the confession?" The whites of her eyes were the size of cue balls in her dark face.

Deanna had not given it any thought. "Put you back in your cell and, as long as you keep all this between us, that's all that'll happen to you. Other than your trial, that is. If the people of Bainbridge want to hang you, that'll be up to them. I won't stop them. And if you even think about making a peep about any of this, I want you to know I have access to all the zombie blood anyone could ever want. It won't end well for you, Gina."

Gina dropped her head and refused to look up after that. Even when she wrote her confession, she kept her head down. It stayed down all the way back to the police station and only came snapping up when they found Norris Barnes, red-eyed and puffy-cheeked, standing in the doorway of Gina's cell.

"Norris," Deanna said, in greeting with a little nod. She brushed past him, unlocked Gina, set her on the cot and handed the confession to Norris. "It turns out she knew all about what Eddie was up to. Including the kidnapping."

"What did you do?" Norris demanded.

A shrug. "I put a scare into her. Or as Jillybean would say, I offered her an inducement to give us an honest confession. Which I got."

His reaction was a bit of a surprise to Deanna. The anger twisting his face was replaced by a mixture of hope and fear. "What did she say? Are there really others?" For just a moment, he was willing to put aside partisan politics, knowing that if Deanna had gotten answers, it could mean real, actual trouble for the island.

"Yes, probably." He groaned at the word "probably" and threw his hands in the air. "Hold on, Norris. Remember that picture of Bobby that Eddie had? The one demanding that he grab Emily *Tonight?* Gina certainly didn't take it and Joslyn was with me for most of that day."

"But not all of it. There was plenty of time for her to have done all sorts of things. How long does it take for someone to snap a picture? Ten seconds?"

Deanna planted her hands on her hips. "And what about the killing of Danny McGuinness, Todd Karraker and Steve Gordon? Did Joslyn Reynolds really kill three grown men all by herself? Because that's not the Joslyn I knew."

"No one knew Joslyn, apparently," Norris answered before running a large, soft hand over his face. "You screwed up, Deanna. What you did was beyond the pale. You can't go around torturing people for information. As far as we know, Gina is innocent."

"I have her confession right here!" Deanna waved the piece of paper in his face. "If you had been there you would have…"

Norris snatched the paper from her hands. "I would have stopped you, for your own sake. This confession isn't admissible in a court of law. Everyone knows that."

"Everyone who's not governor, perhaps. You forget that according to our by-laws, I am the highest ranking member of any court that's convened. I am the judge in this case."

"And the lead investigator, as well? No. That's not how this works. Next, you'll be making yourself the prosecutor. And then what? Defense council?"

None of these were bad ideas. Crime was so rare on the island that there wasn't a permanent prosecutor or public defender. These were usually short-term appointments, assigned for single cases. The only investigator on the island was Deberha Perkins and she really was much more of an awe-shucks, deputy dog type who had kept her job for so long because she played favorites with everyone. If she could look the other way and let something slide, she would.

Her skills as an investigator had never been put to a real test, until now, and it was a test she was failing. Neither Eddie Sanders, nor Joslyn Reynolds were first-rate minds and yet Deberha hadn't uncovered any evidence of their guilt. No incriminating letters or diaries, or pictures, or anything.

"I don't know about defending a piece of crap like this," Deanna said, "but someone's got to look into it. Deberha is clearly not up to it." She had a sudden inspiration. "I should put you on the case. Sort of like a special prosecutor." This would put him on her side and finally make him publicly accountable for something of real importance.

"Perhaps if you had thought of that three days ago we wouldn't be where we are right now." He looked up at the ceiling of the cell and heaved a big sigh as if the sigh itself could be construed as exercise.

She could tell that he was screwing up his courage. "Alright, I'll bite. Where are we?"

He cleared his throat and thrust out his keg of a chest. "We're at the point where I take over as interim governor pending a full investigation. As of now, you are only a citizen with all of a citizen's rights and responsibilities, and no more."

Deanna actually laughed. It came tumbling out of her, beyond her control, not that she tried to hold it back. She needed to let *something* out of her. She thought it would be rage or a shriek of misery, but it was a belly laugh that came from down deep. During the long gales of laughter, Norris and Gina shared a look. Even Veronica, who had wisely kept out of sight and was now tiptoeing out of the building, stopped and glanced back.

"Sorry, sorry," Deanna finally said, brushing tears from her eyes with the back of her hand. "It's just the way you said that, so importantly, so *manly*, it was just funny." She sighed, giggled again and then forced her face back into a neutral setting so that she could deal with Norris, soberly. "I'm afraid that if you think you have the power to arbitrarily become acting governor, just like that, just by saying it, you couldn't be more wrong. Sorry, Norris, it takes the vote of two-thirds of the council to make that change."

"I know this," he replied stiffly, much more angry that she had laughed at him than over the fact she had snuck Gina out of her cell and had tortured her.

"Interesting. You know the law and yet you make that statement. This suggests that you've been plotting against me. Have you convened the council without my knowledge or have you been going around behind my back? Interesting question with interesting ramifications, wouldn't you say?"

They both knew that Deanna's only genius lay in the political arts; she could spin situations and people better than anyone. She was especially dangerous when someone opened themselves up as Norris just had. His first reaction was to retreat before she could play the grieving mother card.

"Look, no one's gone behind anyone's back. Let's get that straight right off the bat. But you and I both know that the council will never stand for these sorts of shenanigans. Throwing fear into a suspect is the same thing as mental cruelty, which is a form of torture!"

"Which is something the entire council must decide, not one man. And where exactly does it state that the first accuser gets to take over? Don't you think that is something for the entire council to consider, as well? Really, Norris for someone worried about the sanctity of law, you seem to have no problem arbitrarily disregarding those that get in your way."

Norris' face became the color of brick. "Don't turn this around on me! This is about you and the way you bend the law for your own purposes."

"MY PURPOSE!" Deanna screamed in sudden savage fury. "Three people, including my daughter, were kidnapped and three others were murdered and you dare to say I'm acting to suit my purpose! The only purpose I serve is justice. REAL justice! Not some milk-toast version of it. Go play your political games somewhere else."

She stormed out and made it nearly halfway back to the Governor's Mansion before tears burst out of her. Although it was late and no one was out, she was still embarrassed by the tears, and she went and hid behind the hoary old trunk of a sycamore.

The tears were hot on her cheeks and soon her chest began to hitch uncontrollably the way Emily's used to when she was a tiny. It was moments like this that Deanna hated being a woman. She guessed that Norris had never cried like this in his whole life, probably not even in the middle of the apocalypse when everyone he knew was dying.

No, men didn't cry like this, and if they did it was in private because they were ashamed of their emotions. She had always thought it was a weakness on their part, not a strength. Yet, here she was hiding.

"Why am I embarrassed?" she asked herself. "I shouldn't be. They took my Emily and they infected Neil, and killed Steve and Flash...Why am I hiding behind a damned tree?"

She knew. It was because she was governor, and as governor she couldn't be a real person. She couldn't cry womanly tears. A governor had a part to play. She had to be on stage all day, every day.

Deanna wanted to give it all up and if it was someone else's kid who had been taken she would have. It was only as governor that she could help her daughter and she was going to stay governor.

Angrily, she ripped a sleeve across her face and stomped away from the tree. She stood in the street practically daring someone to come along and mock her tears. The night was cold, dark, and empty, which was fine, she didn't need a confrontation when she was angry. "No. I need to calm down. No, I need sleep." Sleep had not come easily in the last few days and she doubted that it would come easily, not with Gina's screams and the monster's roar echoing in her head.

Happily, she was wrong. The rest of the night passed in a blink and she was woken up by Shelley Deuso who came in practically hermetically sealed in spotless blue denim. Even her gloves were made of denim. This was her gardening outfit. Along with an acre of her own, she tended Deanna's plot.

In her gloved hands was a cup of steaming tea. The morning cup was the only thing that she allowed Shelley to "serve" her. She was an assistant, not a waitress. Deanna made her own meals and cleaned up her own messes.

"What are you up to today?" Deanna asked, taking the tea.

"Pulling some cabbage and plucking the second season figs," she answered, trying not to stare. Deanna was one of those extremely rare women who woke with the same radiance they fell asleep with. Shelley woke like a mole, squinting, wrinkly and wishing she could burrow back under the blankets. "You've already had two visitors. Sheriff Perkins wants to ask you a few questions about last night. I pretended not to know what she was talking about. It wasn't difficult since as far as I know you were in all night."

Her raised eyebrow told Deanna that she didn't want to know. "And the second person?" It wasn't a surprise when she told her it had been Norris.

"He says that he's called an emergency meeting of the council and that they've scheduled it for nine." It was already eight. Sighing and setting aside the tea, Deanna heaved herself out of bed and made herself presentable in record time and walked into the meeting with one minute to spare.

She expected judging looks from the council. Instead, no one would look her in the eye. It meant they had already made up their minds, which meant that they had, at least unofficially, met without her.

"It's your show, Norris," she said, taking her customary seat at the head of the table. "Let's have it."

He stood and thrust his chest out, showing off a bolt of his best plaid. "We're here to vote you out of office. I've explained the situation to everyone *without* asking for their opinion. I don't want anyone to think I went behind your back. You are being dismissed for willfully disregarding the rights of a person in our custody. A person who has not yet been found guilty of anything, mind you. A person who you forcibly kidnapped…"

"Let me just stop you right there, Norris. If you're going to do this, at least *pretend* to adhere to our laws." He gaped at her, his jaw working up and down. "As much as I enjoy your impersonation of a carp, I have things to do. Where you've gone wrong is that according to our bylaws the full council has to meet in order to vote a member out. There are only six of you."

"That's because Joslyn's not here," Andrea Clary said, looking at the other members of the council as if she had missed something. "She was the one who kidnapped your daughter."

Deanna drummed her fingernails on the table once. "Allegedly."

Norris threw his head back so that his double chin became one long tube of pale flesh. "Allegedly? How can you possibly say, allegedly?"

"By the same standard that you have for Gina. Joslyn has not yet been found guilty of anything. She hasn't been tried and found guilty. The only proof we have that she kidnapped Emily is the word of a man who disappeared hours later. For all we know, his two friends kidnapped Emily and Joslyn."

Now it was Norris' turn to drum his fingers. "Really? You're going to play it this way? Come on, Dee. It's embarrassing."

"I agree, it is. A war is being fought fifty miles from us. We have three dead...no, four dead citizens if we count Neil, and the island's biggest worry is about a damned Christmas play? This is a failure of leadership on my part and last night I decided to do something about it."

"So you admit to torturing Gina?" Norris demanded.

Her eyes turned flinty and just then she wished she had her dead husband's strength; she would have knocked Norris' head off his shoulders if she had been that strong. "I admit I tried and will continue to try to protect this community. And unless you plan on circumventing our laws you will back down."

"I won't," he stated fiercely.

"Then what is the point of having laws at all?"

"That's what I was asking you last night. What's good for the goose and all that."

Deanna stood. "What I do, I do for the betterment of the Island and her people. What you do is for the betterment of Norris Barnes. Don't pretend otherwise. Expect repercussions if you try to drive me out this way."

Meek Jonathan Dunnam, the Island's Chief of Engineering and Maintenance raised a soft hand. "This was going to be the easy way. Sheriff Perkins is investigating what happened last night. You're facing a count of kidnapping, a count of malicious cruelty and a count of witness tampering. If you're found guilty, the minimum sentence is banishment."

"But we can make that all go away," Norris added. "No one wants to see you go down like that. It'll be a blow to the entire island."

"Sheriff Perkins?" Deanna scoffed. "I'll take my chances with her. In the meantime you will do your jobs. Norris, make sure there are two backups for every one of the searchlights. Dunnam, give me an up to date, no, up to the minute inventory on our food stocks. If the Corsairs have any hope to take us, it'll be by starving us out. Wayne, I think you should start running drills on a daily basis."

She started walking to the door, saying over her shoulder, "If anyone needs me, I'll be at the Sanders' doing the Sheriff's real job."

The island wasn't very large and she found herself on the front stoop of the Sanders' home five minutes later. This would be her third time inside. Afraid that the third time wouldn't be the charm, she decided to snoop around outside first.

Right off the bat, she saw Eddie's cigarette butts. It was here that he stood every morning, rain or shine, waiting for the signal. The view wasn't great. Between two houses across the street, she could see a strip of the Sound and beyond that was a tiny spec that she knew was Alki Point Lighthouse.

Other than the view and the butts, there was nothing else of interest in front. In the backyard she found Bobby's toys, all of which were hard, brightly colored hunks of formed plastic. He also had a swing-set that Eddie and five of his friends had hauled all the way from the north side of the island the year Bobby was born. Everyone said he was a great dad.

"Everyone was wrong," Deanna mumbled, kicking over a plastic bucket. "A good father wouldn't spy on his people, or commit murder, or kidnap innocent little girls."

There was nothing outside; no clues at least. Only a lot of sadness. She went into what seemed like the home of a happy little family. Supposedly it was a home where, according to Gina, fear had dominated, where fear had driven Eddie to do terrible things.

Deanna didn't see it. Deanna saw a cozy little place made all the more comfortable by the blood money Eddie had been paid every month. "Lucky Eddie," she whispered. It's what everyone called him. Deanna wished she had been the one to kill him.

That was still on her mind two hours later as she was going through each of Bobby's *Dr. Seuss* books one after another, looking for stashed notes or incriminating pictures, or any sort of clue, when someone began thumping on the front door.

"It's open!" she yelled from the second floor. She more than half-expected it to be Norris and she wasn't disappointed. Sheriff Perkins, looking tired and glum, came into the room after him. "What now? I'm busy. If it's about Gina, forget it. I'm not talking. And whatever she's saying is probably all a lie. After all, she's been lying to us for years. Nothing much has probably changed."

"I'm afraid something has, Governor," Deberha said. "Someone killed her this morning and a lot of people are pointing the finger at you." Norris cleared his throat and Deberha sighed. "Okay, everyone's looking at you. I'm afraid I'm going to have to arrest you, Dee."

Deanna's beautiful features turned sharp and she gave Norris a hard look. "I was here the entire time and you know it."

He shook his head in such a sad manner that even his swinging jowls looked glum. "I'm afraid I don't know it. I was at home working. I have no idea what you've been up to."

Deberha sighed again, this time as she fetched a pair of handcuffs from her belt. "Do you have anyone who can vouch for you?" When Deanna shook her head, Deberha sighed a third time in such a drawn-out manner that it seemed she had a medical condition. "Then you're under arrest for the murder of Gina Sanders."

Chapter 18

Jillybean was given a new set of handcuffs and was subject to another inept search of her body that, as before, centered on the man's carnal desires more than on actual attempts at discovery. It was understandable. The mind was programmed from birth: containers, such as garbage cans and pockets *held* things, the seams of clothing did not. Neither did hair for that matter.

She accepted the Corsair's slowly groping hands on her body with only one question. "What's your name?"

The Corsair, a wicked man with a stench of decay about him, leered down at her, unafraid. He was a vastly stupid man who thought his size and strength made him superior in all ways to anyone smaller than him. "Roy J Bost, why? You think you can play me? You think you can work your wiles on me? Like you did them?"

He gave the stiffening bodies laid out in the station lobby a sneer, thinking they had died because this woman had seduced them—they had dropped their guard for a pretty face and she had killed them.

The fact that she had escaped from a pit in the earth, a feat that was possibly beyond even Houdini, before taking on and killing five armed men in a desperate fight in order to allow a young girl the chance to escape, was utterly dismissed by the man. He could not look past his own prejudices. In his mind, she could only have used her sexy parts to be where she was.

"My wiles?" Jillybean smirked. "You're obviously too sophisticated for the wiles I possess. No, I only asked so I know who to kill. I have a list, you see, and I want to add your name to it."

He laughed, spilling the unpleasant stench of rotting teeth across her face. "Ooh, a list. You hear that, boys? I'm on the naughty list and I ain't even done nothing, yet. Maybe I should earn it." He spun her around, shoved her against the wall, and began thrusting his hardening member against her rump, uncaring that he was standing in a pool of blood.

Some of the men around him laughed, though not all of them. Most, in fact, did not. They were still trying to understand what had happened. For twenty harrowing minutes they had been involved in a desperate street fight, thinking they were taking on the Queen's entire army.

The chaos had been unimaginable. In the dark, no one knew who was who, and at first, the fight was centered around the police station, but then it spilled over into the surrounding streets as more men flocked to the sound of battle. Most fired at anything that moved.

Then, as suddenly as the battle had exploded into life, it had ended as the Black Captain sent his personal guard to find out what was going on. Leading these hardened soldiers was a softly spoken man named Chuck Snawder. Behind his back, people called him Chuck The Cadaver because of his slack, pale, expressionless face. He not only looked three days dead, his hands were perpetually cold. On top of this no one had ever seen him break a sweat even on the hottest day in summer.

He was in a towering rage, though it wasn't exactly obvious as he walked into station. His unemotional face seemed incapable of forming itself into a simple frown, let alone the glare that the situation called for.

"Roy, if you wish to keep your penis attached to your body, I would advise that you move it away from her this instant." He spoke without menace as if it really was just advice he was giving and not an actual threat he would have carried out in the next second if Roy hadn't leapt back.

The Corsair pulled his pawing hands in to his chest. "I didn't know she was yours, Snawder. Really. I barely touched…" The Cadaver silenced him with a small shake of his head. He then turned his steady gaze on Jillybean, who matched his calm as she readjusted her long leather coat.

"The famous Queen Jillian," The Cadaver said. "Even from prison, you manage all of this." He gestured with a soft hand at the dead bodies laid out in a row. There were five, and one was still smoldering. "How?" he asked. She said nothing; she only stared.

If he was perturbed by this, it didn't show. "I understood that I could expect courtly manners from Her Highness. That appears not to be the case." More silence from Jillybean brought about his first human reaction: he lifted his eyebrows momentarily.

Jillybean had no intention of speaking to this man. If anyone could break her it would be him and she was starting their "relationship" off the way she planned on ending it: without a word.

"Which ones were the jailers?" he asked Roy, waving a few fingers at the dead.

"I dunno, 'cept I know that guy there was Lou McCulloch. He was the third officer of the *Midnight Raven*. Wait, I think this guy here was Mailbox, but I don't know the others."

Snawder gazed down at the bodies, one of which was mostly charred down to the bone. Five dead inside, twenty-two dead outside, and yet she hadn't run. "Why? Why did you stay? Did you get unlucky? Did these three happen to come by for some fun and you were able to snatch a gun?"

Her answer was to mock him with her steady gaze.

"It's okay. You'll tell me, eventually. Everyone talks. Everyone." He folded his lips into a bent little smile that lasted barely a second. "Roy, find five more just like you and escort the Queen up to headquarters. And do I need to remind you?"

"She's not to be touched."

"And?"

Roy swallowed loudly before answering, "And if she gets away, you'll kill me."

Snawder nodded. "If she doesn't kill you first, which I would wager she would. I don't think she likes you very much."

He didn't care what the little bitch liked. All he cared about was getting far away from The Cadaver. That guy gave Roy the creeps something bad. The stench of the roasted Corsair didn't help either. Roy couldn't remember being in a less sexy mood.

After rounding up another two men, he held Jillybean by the arm and marched her to the largest, nicest home in Hoquiam. It sat on what had once been known as Bennet Hill, but was now called *The* hill since it was the only hill in Hoquiam.

Surrounding the home were two fences made from rolls of concertina wire reinforced with a hedge of spears. Between the two fences was a run in which a pack of trained dogs roamed; these were all quite a bit more ferocious than the cocker spaniel. Even Roy and the five Corsairs were nervous passing through the barriers.

Behind the second fence and slightly higher up the hill was a seven-foot high wall with four concrete towers, each twenty-feet tall with slits to shoot from.

After all this, the home was something of a letdown. It was big enough and yet it was a dark brooding place with bars on the windows and heavy curtains thrown over them. Lanterns lit the main room, where they were met by the same brutish thug who had accompanied Jillybean up from the harbor hours before.

Without a word, he took off Jillybean's cuffs and began frisking her. "I already did that, Eustace," Roy volunteered. "The Cadaver seems to think that some of the guys tried to have some fun and she snatched a gun."

"That's nice, but if she escapes from here, it's my ass."

Jillybean assisted with the search by sliding off her black leather coat just as Eustace's hand swept along her shoulders, heading toward her hair. Everything was back in its place, though what good escaping her handcuffs or a cell would do she didn't know. She had already counted eight guards and guessed there were another five or six hanging around somewhere.

There were also the Captain's slaves to deal with. Lounging like cats on the sofas near the fireplace were three of them, each wearing next to nothing except a silver collar and a bit of silk. What they were doing awake at this time of night, Jillybean didn't want to know.

The women stared, though they did so out of the corner of their eyes, afraid to show too much interest in anything except the fire. Currently they were no more than decorations; however, Jillybean was sure they were also there to fulfill other *positions*.

"Somewhat medieval," she said, glancing around. The foyer opened onto a great room, where, lined up along one wall, leaned another group of slaves. Just in front of her was a wide curving staircase, and to the right was an office and a hall that went directly to a dining room which held an immense and shining table. Everything, from the floor, to the stairs, to the table was gleaming dark wood. "But at least it's clean," she muttered. Nothing else about the town was clean.

"Shut up," Eustace grunted. He dropped a heavy hand onto her shoulder and took hold of her black silk shirt. "Don't think you'll get away with anything here. The Captain doesn't put up with any funny business."

Jillybean believed it. There was nothing funny whatsoever about the house. In fact, it was decidedly gloomy and sad despite all the gleaming wood.

Eustace propelled her through the dining room and into a gourmet kitchen that boasted spotless matching appliances; none of which worked. Hoquiam had no running water, electricity or flowing natural gas, and again Jillybean thought: *medieval*.

163

Off the kitchen was a back stairway that could only be accessed through a heavy oaken door. On a hasp was a weighty Yale padlock. The key hung nearby, Jillybean noted.

Eustace unlocked the door and then had Jillybean go down first. When he came after, the door was both shut and locked behind them. *That's going to make an escape tougher than expected*, she thought. It was about to get worse. There were three cells in the basement, each looking as if they had been lifted straight from a zoo. The walls were bars and the cell's ceiling was capped by metal.

All three were empty, but only the furthest had a chair and table set in front of it. On the table was a lantern turned down low.

"Your Highness," Eustace said, holding the last cage door open for her. It clanged shut behind her. "By the way, I don't have the key to the cage. And yes, you will be watched twenty-four hours a day."

This was going to make escape next to impossible. "Will I be allowed any privacy?"

"No," he answered with a chuckle, settling himself down in the chair. He surprised her by pulling a paperback out from an inner pocket of his jacket and cracking the spine.

"You can read? How unexpected." He said nothing and she guessed he had spoken just about all that he would. She tested the bars of the door, giving them a firm shake—they didn't so much as rattle. None of the bars budged, although the welds holding them in place were crudely done.

Other than the bars, there was only a single mattress laying on the floor, a pillow that looked used and a pale blue blanket. Setting aside her boots and her coat, she laid back fully clothed and wondered if she would be able to fall asleep.

Her mind was still racing from everything that had happened that night. Where were Jenn, Mike and Stu? Had they been able to escape? How the hell had Neil managed to fall off a boat? And was he dead or undead? Had Emily gotten away? What was going on with Captain Grey? And finally, where were the voices?

Other than the soft, and excruciatingly spaced, turning of Eustace's pages, there was only silence in the basement...and in her head. It felt unnatural. Like she had been deserted in her time of need.

She wanted to believe that it was a good thing and tried to tell herself that now, she could make her plans and think her way out of the basement, uninterrupted. After all, she still had all of her tricks about her: the razor blade, the acid, the handcuff key, all of it.

And all of it useless with Eustace sitting ten feet away, doing the opposite of speed reading. It was horrible. Two minutes to read a single page of a dime-store paperback? Who had ever heard of such a thing?

Somewhere between pages seventeen and eighteen, she fell asleep. It was a deep, satisfying sleep that lasted five and a half hours.

Eustace woke her, saying, "Hey! Queen! The Captain wants to see you." There was a second man in the basement, a grizzled, veteran Corsair with twenty-four slashing blue-green tick-marks working their way up his neck like the rungs of a ladder. He was missing his right ear. There was just an ugly squiggly hole in the side of his head where it should have been and for some reason he wore his hair very short on that side.

He had the key to her cell and she guessed that she would have two Corsairs accompanying her whenever she left her cell —escape was beginning to feel like a dream.

Behind the men was a slave. She was probably only twenty-five or so, but she had a used look about her, as if they had been twenty-five very hard years. Still, she was pretty, with long blonde hair and kind blue eyes which she kept demurely pointed at the floor.

The two men stepped back to let her into the cell. "Your Highness," she whispered, dipping into a curtsey. She managed this despite carrying a basin of water. "The Captain wants you presentable." Her eyes flicked to Jillybean's wild mane, which was something of a fiasco, even by her own lack of standards. "I have a mirror and a brush."

She carried a purse that was so large Jillybean considered it more of a satchel. The woman set the basin down and pulled out the mirror from the purse and held it nervously in front of Jillybean as if she were presenting it to a vampire.

Jillybean gave a glance at her hair. It was atrocious and she didn't care. She ignored the brush and ran her fingers through it once. The woman looked pained. "It'll be okay..." Jillybean began.

"Tanya," she whispered. "My name's Tanya Read." She stared over the mirror, looking like she wanted to say more.

"It'll be okay, Tanya. It won't matter what I look like, the Captain is going to do bad things to me, regardless. Come on, Eustace let's get this over with."

Jillybean threw on her boots and her black leather, and followed after the one-eared man, who led the way up to the basement door. He gave a quick knock. "We're good," he said, and the door was unlocked with a rattle of metal on wood. Another barrier to overcome. They were being over-the-top careful, wasting valuable resources. And for what? So the Black Captain could break her?

She pictured him showing her off, perhaps chained to the wall of his living room, clad only in a straitjacket, and drooling, perhaps with a mock crown on her head.

The door opened and a growly, filthy Corsair said, "She ain't cleaned up. What the hell, Say What?"

Jillybean couldn't tell if the one-eared man had just been called *Say What*, or if it had been some sort of bizarre passcode or some strange inside joke.

"She, you know, declined. It's not my fault." The way he answered and because of the missing ear, she guessed it might just be his name. She followed Say What into the kitchen where the light beaming in through the open curtain was both gray and dazzling. She made a show of reacting to it; she threw a hand across her face and leaned back into Eustace, acting like she had just emerged from three weeks trapped in a cave.

Her real purpose was to give herself a few extra seconds to inspect the kitchen. Two pretty slaves wearing ridiculous French maid costumes that left little to the imagination, were bustling in from the three-car garage, carrying trays of food. Through the open door she saw two older women cooking over a wood fire. Both wore dirty aprons over dirty rags that covered their dirty bodies. Behind them was a watchful Corsair.

So no one gets 'accidentally' poisoned, Jillybean thought. From what little she could see, the garage had bars over its windows and a heavy lock on the back door. If a fire got out of control, the women would be the first to die.

Eustace gave the Queen a shove and she strolled casually after Say What through the kitchen and along the hall to the dining room. Lined up on one side of the hall were twenty-two slaves, some in lingerie, some in bikinis, some in jean shorts that had been so scandalously cut that they left little to the imagination. All twenty-two stared silently at Jillybean.

She gave them a nod of greeting before entering the dining room which was dominated by a long polished table with eighteen equally gleaming chairs around it; only four were filled. Along with the Captain was Chuck "The Cadaver" Snawder, a man tied to one of the chairs and a Corsair with a shocking growth of black hair that seemed to be slowly encapsulating his entire head—his eyes were like blue buttons, his nose, a pink island in all that hair and if he had a mouth it was hidden somewhere deep.

The Black Captain stood when she came in, prompting all of the men to stand as well, all except the man tied to the chair, of course. "Your Highness? Your hair?" the Captain asked with feigned confusion. "Weren't you told to come to breakfast in a presentable condition?"

"Actually, no. Neither of these two morons mentioned anything of the sort."

"The slave should have said something. Hmmm, sad. She'll have to be beaten. Say What, give her thirty lashes. Try not to mess up her face."

Although it wasn't Jillybean being beaten, she took a deep breath and readied herself, nonetheless. Tanya was going to be beaten, but it would be Jillybean who was being tortured by it. They would start small; a beating for Tanya, a cigarette stamped out on the arm of one of the serving girls, perhaps a few lacerations to the face of the uglier of the two cooks—that's what she could expect from breakfast.

Between lunch and dinner, she would get her own beatings. Perhaps nothing obvious at first, maybe the soles of her feet would be smacked with a bat, or her toes would be hammered one at a time. After dinner, if she was to be given one, she would be subject to sleep deprivation or perhaps they would strip her and douse her with ice cold water every ten minutes.

She could only assume it would be horrible. And where were her friends when she needed them? Where were Ipes and Sadie? Where was Eve? Eve could take torture and only scream for more. But she wasn't anywhere to be found.

Chapter 19

Say What took a great fistful of Tanya Read's blonde hair and pulled straight up until the woman was on her tip-toes. She whimpered as he started to walk her out of the room.

"Hold on," Jillybean said. "Where's he going? I was hoping for a show. You are beating her in an attempt to affect me in some manner. Won't this be more visceral in person? Don't you want me to shed tears and beg for you to stop? I can't very well do that if he takes her out behind the barn, now can I?"

The Black Captain showed white teeth in his grinning face. "By all means." He gestured for Say What to begin right there.

Tanya, looking pale and stricken, but resigned, dropped to her knees. It wasn't her first beating and it wouldn't be her last. She didn't look at Jillybean which made it that much easier for the Queen to keep the bland expression on her face. She had to pretend to be bored by the entire thing. She had to force herself not to respond, and not to care. It was obvious the slave was being beaten simply to get at her and she had to keep reminding herself that Tanya would have been beaten one way or another, no matter what.

Jillybean sat without asking, her elbow planted on the table, her cheek propped on one hand. She waited until after the first blow had fallen to cry, "Stop!"

Say What had his arm raised with the belt back, poised to strike again. He looked toward the Captain, who was looking at Jillybean with a wry smile. Jillybean pointed at the steaming plates of food. "I don't mean to interrupt but can I get some of those eggs, please. A Queen has to keep up her strength, you know."

"Of course," he said, smoothly. He spooned out the fluffy eggs himself and added venison sausage and toast to her plate. One of the serving girls placed it in front of Jillybean and retreated as fast as she could before the Black Captain found some reason for her to be beaten as well.

The eggs were perfectly seasoned and the venison sausage was amazingly juicy, and yet they tasted like sawdust to Jillybean. Tanya's muffled screams drilled straight down into Jillybean's soul. Regardless, she smiled and ate with relish, noticing the uncertain darkness on the wall behind Say What for the first time.

It seemed like a shadow; however, it was larger and deeper that any of the other shadows and, with a strange sense of nostalgia, she began to think it was her old mental problems returning at long last. It was something of a relief. She knew she was mental for a reason—she couldn't handle the terror and pain of this new undead world. She *needed* to be crazy.

Noooooooo, the word came from the dark spot in one long, cold whisper; it didn't just send a shiver up her spine, it physically shook her. When she looked up, she saw the Black Captain smiling at her.

"Something wrong? Is this bothering you? The screams, I mean."

"Hmm? What? Oh, no, don't be silly. Why would they bother me? She's *your* slave. I think it's silly that you are beating your own slave and to what purpose? Are you trying to make me feel bad? That's like you punching yourself in the face and expecting me to say ouch. You can beat them all to death for all I care."

He took a small bite of toast. Just a nibble. "I doubt that. I really do. My spies tell me otherwise. They tell me that you wear black and make threats but that deep down you are peaches and cream."

Jillybean's eyes flicked to the dark patch on the wall. It whispered in a voice like a wintery hiss. The words didn't sound English. She turned her cool gaze back to the Captain. "Peaches and cream? Sorry, but you're getting bad intel this time. Deep down…well, deep down I'm worse than you."

"Deep down? And how do we get deep down?"

"You of all people don't want to get too deep down." The beating ended a few seconds later. Tanya lay on the hardwood floors shaking and crying. Jillybean couldn't look at her and so she pointed at the man tied to the chair. "So, who's this unfortunate soul? Another person you plan on torturing so I can learn my lesson?"

"Him? This is Trevor Waldron, former captain of *The Hammer.* Somehow, he allowed little Emily Grey to stow away on board his ship. Then he went and left his ship unattended and while he was gone, she tried to steal it, the little scamp. She managed to sink one of my boats and was in the process of blowing up *The Hammer* when she was caught." He watched her closely, looking for the telltale "lack" of reaction when he mentioned Emily's name. He wasn't disappointed with her poker face. "That Emily was a clever girl. It's too bad that she was also such an unlucky girl."

Jillybean did not fail to note his use of the word: was. The chilling whisper from the dark spot grew louder.

She wanted to play it cool and act like she was unconcerned, but she could feel the flush of fear constrict the bones in her chest. They began crushing inwards. "Was?"

"Yes. She was shot to death. Sad, sad, sad. The poor girl careened wildly from one dangerous situation to another and it was only a matter of time before her luck ran out. It's too bad since she would have been safest right here. What a great bargaining chip she would've been. Yes, she would have been treated like an honored guest but because of you she's dead."

Jillybean could barely breathe now. "No," she said, in a voice that had no strength.

He gave her a sympathetic head tilt. "I'm afraid it's the truth. It's been a tough night for team Jillybean. First, Leney stabs you in the back, then your entire navy deserts you, then your niece is killed, and now we hear that poor, pathetic Neil Martin drowned in the harbor."

Nooooo. The darkness on the far wall was creeping up to the ceiling and it was deep now and so very black; it was endlessly black. And the whispers coming from it were both alluring and terribly dreadful.

She wanted to run from it, only she couldn't feel her hands or feet. The only thing she could really feel were her ribs crushing inwards. The bones inside her had come alive and were like a giant's long fingers squeezing her insides. Squeezing and squeezing. Her head was beginning to spin…they had killed her Emily, and now Neil was gone, too?

She couldn't breathe.

"And your little army has fallen apart," the Captain was going on in his mockingly sad voice. "McCartt took half of them and ran off, and now the other half is surrounded. To top it all off, your Governor back on Bainbridge is being arrested for murder as we speak. Everything you care about is crumbling away into ruin and decay, and here you are, playing games. Here you are in your black leather pretending to be cool, when everyone knows this is all your fault. You know that, right? That all of this is your fault?"

Jillybean's eyes strayed to the darkness. It beckoned. No, it didn't just beckon, there was a pull. It felt as though if she let herself go it would suck her in. Inside the darkness, she'd be able to breathe again. She'd be free of the pain. There was no sorrow in the darkness.

It took a colossal force of will to drag her eyes from the deep, dark stain and when she did, she found herself looking directly into Ernest Smith's bland, peasant face. He was sitting at the table as if he had every right to be there.

Don't, he said. Just the one word.

He had been the one who had started her down the path to crazyville. He had cracked her skull open and, like Athena bursting from the head of Zeus, Eve had been born and Jillybean's life had never been the same. She hated Ernest Smith with a passion. And she hated Eve with a terrible familiarity. Eve's brand of evil had once been like that darkness, deep and rich, and limitless. But Eve had gradually changed over the years. She had lost that boundless hatred.

Now, Jillybean had found it. It was in the darkness and somehow, impossibly she discovered that pure hatred was good and necessary.

Don't, Ernest said, again, almost pleading now.

"Why not?" Jillybean snapped. Why not give in to the temptation that the darkness offered?

Because there's no coming back, he answered and then dredged up a memory that Jillybean had hidden away deep inside herself. She suddenly saw her tiny, eight-year-old self, holding a dark knife. There was blood, but not on the blade, it was leaking down her inner thighs, leaving long streaks that reached her ankles. There was semen in the blood. She had been raped by a true monster deep in the bowels of a slaver's truck and now the deep, unlimiting darkness was on her. It was a cloud covering her brilliant mind. She could've run away; she should've run away, but the darkness was on her and so was the irresistible need to kill.

She couldn't remember how many times she had driven that knife into the raper-man, she just knew the next day she had blisters on her palm and there had been dried blood everywhere, even in her ears. She might have slathered herself with it. She might have rolled in the raper-man's mutilated corpse.

It was the darkness that had made her do it. The darkness was mindless. It was also easy. It was a siren's call to leave everything behind and just destroy and kill and rage.

"That was simple enough," The Cadaver was saying. "She's already falling apart."

Jillybean realized she had been talking to herself and that she had been staring at an empty chair. She pulled her eyes away from it and watched Snawder choose a hardboiled egg from a wicker nest filled with them. He gave it a sharp crack on the edge of the table and then rolled it beneath his palm. The one crack in the shell became thousands.

They're lying to you, it was Sadie now, sitting where Ernest had been. As always, she was dressed in black and as always Jillybean saw past the faux-goth exterior. There had always been too much happiness waiting to bubble out of Sadie for her to have ever been truly goth. Sadie was shaking her head. *How could they know all this stuff? How could they know about Emily and Deanna and McCartt? Don't listen to their lies, Jillybean.*

"Yeah, that's right. How do you know about all of this?" Jillybean was flailing around looking for help, even if that help came from the Black Captain.

He had been sitting back, nibbling on his toast, enjoying the show as the Mad Queen unraveled. "If you were more yourself, you would remember that I have spies everywhere. I personally gave the order to have Emily killed. I had to choose between letting her live or letting your army get away. For the greater good she had to die."

"The greater good?" Jillybean hated the saying. She hated the concept. Her hate fed the darkness which suddenly opened like a mouth, sucking the dining room wall down its forever throat. She had to hold onto the gleaming table to keep from being sucked in as well. "What about Neil?" she asked, clutching at a last straw. "How do you know he died? Did you find his body?"

"I can answer that," The Cadaver replied, as he peeled away the shell from the egg in the same way he would flay a person. "I heard it first hand from one of our captains. He thought Neil was a kid at first and so I asked him about the scars and that messed-up face of his, and the missing fingers. It was him alright and...Your Highness? You seem a little out of sorts." He was mocking her, but she was beyond caring.

At the news of Neil's death Jillybean turned just in time to see Sadie sucked into the darkness. She didn't scream and the look on her face was one of infinite sadness. Neil had been her father, too and she couldn't live even this semi-life without him.

Now Jillybean was utterly alone.

A deep rumbling explosion suddenly echoed in her head, or at least she thought it had been in her head, but the others reacted as well. The Black Captain smiled at the sound. "And now McCartt is dead." He sat back and thumped his black boots on the table, his hands clasped behind his head in perfect satisfaction.

"How do you know?" Her voice sounded far away, as if it wasn't coming from her mouth, but from deep in the darkness.

The Captain chuckled, which set off hearty laughter from everyone, including the tied-up Trevor Waldron, who was trying to get back into his good graces. "How do I know that was him? Because we have a spy in with him, who just happened to have a bomb and instructions to use it. I knew McCarrt would cut and run the moment things got tough and now his men are leaderless and isolated, and what's worse, they know for a fact that I can reach out and kill whoever I want, whenever I want. I wanted them to know that they will never be safe."

He drew a long, thin knife from his boot. "You keep looking over there," he said, pointing the knife at the great black hole. "What do you see?"

"A door into hell," she lied. It was actually a gory wound on reality and in the darkness, she could see a figure. Although it was shadow on shadow, she knew the fly-away hair.

The Captain wasn't fooled by the lie. "Who's going to take your place when you flee? Do you have any choice? No? Jillybean, look at me."

She could barely see him. He was dark-skinned and now the world was veiled in darkness as if the lid of her coffin was only an inch from closing.

"Make it be Eve," he ordered, holding the knife between them. "Everyone says she's the tough side of you...the evil side. I want to destroy her, because once she's gone, what are you? A frightened child with a large vocabulary? A girl who can memorize a few math problems? A broken girl? Just a fragment of something that could have been great?"

The knife glittered in the darkness, the tip disappearing under her chin. Jillybean couldn't feel it because she wasn't there. She was standing in the dark watching this and knowing she had made a huge mistake in not fighting harder.

There was something else driving the car. It wasn't Eve and it wasn't Ernest, it was just that, an *it*.

173

"What? No snappy come backs?" the Captain asked, still with the knife out. Still in complete control.

"You should have killed her," the *It* said in a rough imitation of Jillybean's voice.

The Black Captain threw his head back and whooped laughter. "This...this is what scared half the Pacific coast? I can't believe it. She must be playing. No one breaks this easy."

But she had, and not because of fear. She had broken because of sorrow. Jillybean knew it had been a mistake to give in to the dreadful sadness. It had been so easy to let go and now, no matter how hard she fought, she couldn't seem to get back to the surface, and it was important that she did.

It was plotting, not to escape to help Captain Grey, or to free the slaves, or even to race back down to San Francisco to arrange some sort of defense. No, the *It* was plotting to kill the Black Captain, something that was completely impossible, even for Jillybean.

Chapter 20

Neil Martin's body floated in the harbor for eight hours before it washed ashore. Falling in should have been expected by everyone, especially Neil himself, but he had been taken completely by surprise and could picture the moment with laughable clarity. It felt like he had been wearing roller-skates. The deck pitched and he had slid back, standing perfectly straight, as if he was standing in line for a movie instead of on the see-sawing deck of a sailboat in a storm. The rail struck him in the back of the legs, just beneath the buttocks, and folded him in two at the waist.

His arms stuck out in front of him, stiff from the disease that was killing him, and as he splashed into the water, he felt like a plastic Ken doll—Neil knew he couldn't pull off any comparison to a G.I. Joe, even in this.

The dark black water must have been very cold, though he couldn't feel it. It didn't even feel wet to him. The water was just there, all around him in what seemed like giant, white-capped waves. *I could drown*, he thought as he began flailing around spasmodically, his arms and legs making herky-jerky movements. Drowning was a very real possibility and he knew he should make some sort of an effort to get back to the *Queen's Revenge*, except it just seemed like so much work. Even treading water struck him as a great burden and his attempt was half-hearted.

A strange lassitude overcame not just his conscious mind, it also killed off his survival instinct. He simply didn't care if he drowned, and he stopped fighting to live.

He floated in a pre-death, dream-like state, looking much like the other corpses in the harbor. At some point a Corsair ship sailed up and someone gave him a poke with a boathook. His reactions were so amazingly slow that by the time he shifted his sky-blue eyes over, the ship was already moving on.

Then, sometime later, he felt sand beneath his back and the rolling breakers were throwing him on shore. Eight hours had passed in one tremendously slow blink. Another half-hour passed with him being tugged up and down the beach by small, relaxing waves. The rushing sound and the gentle back and forth movement was comforting; it was like being rocked to sleep by nature. He would have slept, if sleeping was possible for him now. Zombies didn't sleep like real people; they just sort of shutdown for a time to recharge their rage.

His mind was still in shutdown mode when a seagull decided to have a bit of him for breakfast. "Do you mind?" he groused in a croaky voice. "I'm not completely dead just yet."

The gull, usually an expert on such things, didn't believe him and gave him another peck, going for his right eye. With a most zombie-like groan, Neil sat up, causing the gull to scream at him as if to say: *I wasn't done eating you!*

"Yeah, you were." He gazed blearily around, wondering where the Corsair boat had gone. Hadn't it just been there? "Did I dream that?"

The bird cocked its head in answer. It still wasn't sure whether Neil was alive or dead. Neil had to agree. "I should be dead. That's the only thing I know for certain. I should have frozen to death. Or hypothermied to death. Is that a word? It doesn't sound like one." But the idea was right. His core body temperature had to be dangerously low. Of course, just then, he didn't know what his core body temperature was supposed to be.

Ninety-eight degrees was the first number that "popped" into his sluggish mind. "No. That's the temperature of my tongue. I think. Either way, I should be cold." He decided to do something about the cold he didn't feel.

Not far up the beach—an unknown beach to Neil—was a house. It looked to be waving at him. When he got closer, he saw that the front windows had been smashed and that dingy, threadbare curtains were flapping through the opening. He took it as a good sign, which it wasn't.

Every window was broken and the place stank of mildew and stagnant water. The basement had been flooded for so long the knee-deep water was thick with green slime. Algae and black mold competed for space on the walls and everywhere else, for that matter.

Even a zombie like Neil couldn't stomach the idea of wearing anything he would find inside.

"I'm too much of a bourgeois zombie. Hmm, that sounds French." He didn't like the idea of sounding French, though he couldn't explain why to himself and the seagull would never understand. It had been keeping pace with him, waddling along in the hope that he would keel over.

"Sorry to disappoint you, buddy." And he was, a little. He was hungry, too. "If something falls off, you can keep it." The bird didn't think that was funny. "Sophisticated zombie humor wasted once again. Let's hope there's something in there."

He and the bird were almost to the next house on the row. This was much nicer but it had its own resident zombie. Neil could see it standing in the living room, with its head practically scraping the ceiling. That it didn't come rushing out to eat Neil was a little unsettling. "I am still a person, after all. I must look a mess." He patted his rain-slicked hair as he gazed down at himself.

"Oh." His clothes were in tatters and he was missing a sock. It took him a moment to realize that he was also missing his shoes. "My Crocs! Well, that's just the worst. No wonder he doesn't want me. I look like a vagabond. You're lucky you're a bird. Look at you with your perfect feathers, all white and..." His stomach rumbled. He was hungry enough to eat the seagull. "But I won't. You have the solemn promise of a zombie." This had him cracking up and he giggled all the way to the next house, which was a big three-story affair with a dramatically pitched and gabled roof.

Neil sauntered, zombie-style, through the open front door as if he owned the place; the bird waited outside. He made his way to the master bedroom on the second floor, where he discovered that the real owners were an unmatched set.

The man of house had once played football for the Washington Huskies and was both wide and tall. His wife had been comparatively petite, which made for a difficult choice for Neil. He could either go about looking like a little boy wearing his daddy's clothes or an adult man wearing his wife's.

The deciding factor came down to the shoes. Neil could never fit into the man's size thirteens, while the wife had feet only a smidge larger than Neil's. She also owned Crocs! They were powder blue and didn't at all go with the rest of his outfit: a green *Lacoste* sweater, a peach *Michael Kors* jacket, and *Lucky* blue jeans, but that was okay since he planned on changing out the entire outfit just as soon as he reached the next suitable place.

"It'll be just for a little bit," he told himself as he laid out the clothes. "And it's not like I'm wearing a bra or anything." Assured that his masculinity would remain undiminished, he stripped off his rags.

Looking down at his leg, he noticed a strange, jagged black hole just above his knee. He thought nothing of it at first, and it was only when he was pulling on the *Lucky* jeans that it struck him: "I was shot!" But by who? And when? It took him a few moments to work it out. "That guy did it. Uh, uhhhh, Eddie. Eddie Sanders. What a jerk." Wearing a look of profound disgust, he tested the limits of the hole with the tip of his finger. Thankfully he could barely get his finger into it up to the second knuckle.

"At least it doesn't hurt. That's something." But was it? He couldn't decide whether the hole in his leg didn't hurt because it was healing, or because the bullet had hit a nerve, or because his zombie brain just didn't care about such things anymore. "It's good that it's fast healing," he told himself, working the jeans past the hole in his leg.

The jeans were so awkward fitting that he soon forgot all about the bullet wound. They were way too tight in front and strangely roomy in the rear. And worse, they had little blingy designs on the back pockets, made of shiny metal. It made his butt feel somewhat armored. "That's weird," he said, trying to see behind himself and almost spinning into the carpet.

His rumbling stomach drove all thought of fashion or bullet wounds out of his mind. He even forgot about the seagull as he stepped out into the early morning light. It was a sharp, brittle light that made his eyes ache, but at least it was warm. He stood, facing the east, letting the sunlight fall on his gray face. It didn't just feel good, it also got his black blood flowing more quickly in his veins and soon he was on the march again, heading north which just happened to be the only direction left to him unless he wanted to wade back into either the harbor or the Pacific.

After a quarter of a mile or so, he came upon a body, lying face down in the shallows. There were flies buzzing around it in clouds. They were cold, winter flies that moved slow, and like Neil, didn't realize that their lives were on a timer that would soon run down.

Neil's stomach growled again and then crimped as he realized what it had been growling for. "Disgusting," he tried to tell himself. "But you could have some if you…" He had been talking to the seagull, only he just realized that it wasn't around anymore. "His loss."

It also felt like Neil's loss and he felt not just hungry but also lonely as he walked on. Not far from the corpse, he came upon the remains of a Corsair ship, its back broken on some rocks, and a gaping hole in its bow. At the risk of soaking his ridiculous outfit, he braved the slippery rocks.

The rubber grip of the crocs kept him dry and he made it to the boat safely. "Hello?" he whispered, suddenly feeling cold again. There was something decidedly spooky about the boat. It should have been quiet except for the light surf splashing around its edges. Instead, he heard little scritching and scratching sounds coming from within the dark galley.

Moving closer to the stairs, he said again, "Hello? Anyone there?" More of the scratching. It sounded like the bony hands of a skeleton scraping at the deck. Hunger drove him down into the dark where he did find a skeletal hand. It wasn't what was making the noise, however.

The corpse of a Corsair was sprawled on the floor, almost completely hidden by a wriggling mass of voracious little crabs. Neil's stomach twisted into a knot and he was sure that if he hadn't been a zombie, he would have puked up a rush of green stomach juices.

"That's it. Crab is forever off the menu." He turned his chin away as he eased around the body, moving to the tiny kitchenette where he found bags of dried fruit, nuts, salted beef, smoked fish, and gallons of water. He stuffed himself silly, right there next to the pile of crabs; he even talked to them, though he found them far less attentive than the seagull.

He also found an M16 type gun—he had no idea what its subtype was, and frankly didn't care. There were also buckets of bullets, more than he could carry. Feeling very satisfied with himself, he dumped out one of the half-dozen packs that he had found and filled it with food and bullets.

"Now what?" he asked the world, once he was back on shore. As far as he understood things, he had two choices: he could go to Hoquiam and try to rescue Jillybean or he could head north and flounder around in the hills looking for Grey to help him.

Both choices were silly. Captain Grey was the most able commander left on the planet and if he needed Neil's help then his cause was already lost. And he had to wonder if Jillybean was still even a prisoner. She had gotten out of more prisons than Neil could count. Chances were that Neil would only make things worse by showing up in Hoquiam and getting captured himself.

"Then she would have to rescue me as well." Without a good choice, he wandered north along the beach, thinking that he would find Grey and fight alongside of him once more. "Like old times," he said.

Tightening the peach Michael Kors jacket around his waist, he set off into the hills at a plodding speed. It wasn't long before the clouds gathered again overhead and once, he was out of sight of both the bay and the ocean, he became lost, though he didn't know it.

As far as he was concerned, north lay in front of him and east was to the right, while behind him was south—no matter how many twists there were to the road that zig-zagged all over the place.

He was going northwest when he ran into a pair of Corsairs, snooping in the remains of a Lincoln Navigator. They saw him ten wasted seconds later. During those moments, he might have ducked out of sight or he might have checked to see if his gun was even loaded, or at least pointed it at them. Instead he only stared and now he could think of nothing except to wave at them.

"Hi there," he said, before remembering that these could be bad Corsairs. A grey, washed-out memory informed him that Grey had landed his army west of Hoquiam and although Neil was wrong about which way north was, he knew he was somewhere west of the Corsairs' lair.

The two jerked their guns around when they saw Neil. "What the hay-ell?" one asked, his face screwed into a look that was a perfect mix of revulsion and confusion.

"Hail?" His accent was so thick that it threw Neil off. "No, I said 'Hi there.' Is hail like your word for hello."

"Whut? Who are y'all? And whut the hay-ell are you doin' out here?"

"I'm Neil Martin," Neil blurted out, forgetting that there was a time when his name was associated with rather large bounties. It also slipped his mind that he was supposed to be dead. The assassination attempt felt like a long time ago.

The second Corsair was a mangy creature with a bald spot the size of a saucer on the very top of his head; long straggly hair, like a curtain, hung all around it. His hair was so foolishly long that he had to give his head an exaggerated waggle so he could see Neil properly. He did not know what to think.

"I don't care who he is. What I want to know is what is he? What's with your face?"

Neil touched his cheek, thinking that maybe he had some food still on it from breakfast, which would have been embarrassing. It seemed fine, however. "My face? What's wrong with my face?" The Corsair with the long hair gave his head another waggle and then pointed at Neil, his revulsion far outweighing his confusion now.

"Oh this," Neil said, letting out a quick, nervous and high fake laugh. "This is nothing. Uhhhh, it was an industrial accident, you know from before." Another fake laugh erupted out of him, though what it was supposed to be attached to even Neil didn't know. "They always said not to mix ammonia and bleach, and I went and did it. Talk about dumb, right?"

"Y'all look like one-na the day-id."

Neil blinked at this, a warped smile on his face. "I look like what? One-na what?"

"The day-id," the man repeated with great solemnity.

It was like a light blinked on in Neil's mind. "Oh, the dead. Well, that's just silly. The dead can't speak." *And they certainly don't use words like silly,* he reminded himself, *and neither do Corsairs. I better toughen up before they suspect I'm not one of them.*

It was far too late for that. The southerner's long-haired friend was nodding and waggling his head about in agreement. "And what's with the outfit? Those are girl clothes. Do you like dressing up in girl clothes? That's freaky. Hell, everything about you is kind of freaky."

Too late, Neil realized he hadn't changed into something more mainstream. *Thank God, I didn't put on the bra*, he thought as he pulled the collar of the peach-colored coat tighter around his neck, as if trying to gather the remains of his ruined dignity around him. After all, even he knew that, *Lacoste* or not, the green sweater didn't go with the coat, while the sky-blue crocs just made the outfit something of a train wreck.

"It's just temporary," he answered. "I couldn't find anything that fit…in black, I mean. I only dress in black, you know. So, what are you guys up to?" He was desperate for a change in the subject and commenting on the weather didn't seem like a good play.

"Whut are *you* up to?" the southerner challenged, cocking an eyebrow. "You spyin' or whut?"

181

Neil offered his most innocent smile—it came across looking like a curdled rendition of a grimace. "Spying? On you two? I'd never do that. That's just sil...I mean stu...I mean I would never do such a thing."

"He didn't mean spying on us, he meant spying *us*, the Magnum Killers. Were you?"

"No. I would never do that either. I'm with you guys. I know McCartt. I met him last night at the Captain's meeting on board the *Queen's Revenge*." McCartt had stared at Neil all through the meeting with undisguised perplexity. Steinmeyer had been far more circumspect, glancing at Neil out of the corner of his eye, but McCartt had stared openly and quite rudely. He stared as if looking at a magician's trick.

The southerner's eyes were now suspicious slits. "Y'all know McCartt? Really?"

"Really."

"Really?"

"Really," Neil assured, wondering how long they'd be in this loop.

To Neil's relief, long-hair gave his head yet another flick and grabbed his friend's arm. "Hey. McCartt did say the Queen had some sort of creature with her. Is that you? Are you the creature?"

"This is getting silly. Why don't you take me to McCartt and he can settle things?" The two thought this was a splendid idea and it wasn't long before Neil was escorted down the road and through the front doors of a church, where he was stared at by an entire congregation of murderers.

"Yeah, I know him," McCartt said. He was reclining on a pew and digging at his nose. "So what? What do you want? Did Gunner send you? If so, then tell him that we're quit of you guys for good. You go your way and we'll go ours."

Neil knew there would be no way for him to change McCartt's mind, since his anti-zombie bias was on full display. "Uh, which way is your way, so I know not to go in that direction." He was starting to get the feeling that north wasn't in front of him anymore and he didn't want to look stupid.

"South."

"Okay well I won't go in that...wait there's nothing south of us. The land runs out and then it's only water. I just came from that direction."

McCartt stood and stretched, saying, "No freaking duh, the land runs out. We're crossing the mouth of the harbor."

All around Neil, men were standing and gathering their belongings. None of them seemed confused by what McCartt had just said, which was very confusing to Neil. "It's at least half a mile across. Do you have a boat?"

"We have these." He and another man began rocking a wooden pew back and forth until it broke free of the bolts holding it to the floor. All over the church men were pulling up the pews.

"That's the stupidest thing I ever heard," Neil blurted out.

"Maybe," McCartt said, "and maybe it's just so stupid it might work." He and three others began hauling the pew out into the early morning light.

Neil hurried after them. "No, it's just stupid. You'll be sitting ducks out there. And it'll take forever. And what happens if the pews sink? They look pretty heavy to me and…"

McCartt stopped in the doorway of the church and pointed an angry finger at Neil. "No one asked you, dead-boy. These are wood and wood floats. Everyone knows that and you would know it too if you weren't a freakin zombie. Now go sit your ass back down and don't even think about following us."

"Why would I want to follow you out there?" Neil muttered, turning, and walking into the back of a pew that was being carried by five men.

"Watch it!" one snapped.

"Sorry," Neil said, a split-second before McCartt evaporated in a blinding flash of light and heat.

Chapter 21

The *Queen's Revenge* shot away into the night, outdistancing every one of the Corsair ships as if they were being piloted by stray dogs instead of experienced seamen. The people on board were too wilted from the stress of the chase, the near misses from so many torpedoes, and the crazy explosions, to let out a cheer.

They all found something to sag against.

All except for Mike Gunter, who was completely in his element. He was in command of the finest sailing ship he had ever laid eyes on. He had *his* queen by his side and he was going home, hopefully for good. Mike was tired of battles and wars and evil Corsairs. He was tired of adventures and tired of constantly getting shot at.

He didn't think he would ever get tired of the beautiful white ship, though. The wind came off his starboard beam just perfectly and the boat barely heeled. She was a stiff one and so gorgeous that he could barely stand the idea of someone putting a single bullet hole in her. No, that sort of thing had to be at an end. The great ship was going to take them home and that was that.

"Turn around," Stu Currans ordered.

They were not twenty minutes from the mouth of the harbor and were just coming to grips with the fact that both Neil and Emily had gone overboard during the crazy, dangerous flight from Grays Harbor and the vast Corsair fleet.

"You want to go back there?" Mike asked, his voice cracking in the highest octave it could reach. "Back there? It'll be a hundred ships against one."

"It's the right thing to do," Knight's Sergeant Troy Holt declared as if he were the final arbiter of right and wrong. This set off an argument that gradually split the little crew into three factions: those that wanted to run away, those that wanted to go back, and those that were stuck in the middle, afraid to go back, despite knowing it was the right thing to do.

Mike was in the latter group.

The two Santas had voted to go back home, as had Deaf Mick—the ex-Corsair, and current saboteur. He had been shocked to his core seeing the torpedoes racing at the *Queen's Revenge,* and the hissing rain of bullets screaming by had almost caused him to drop a load in his week-old underpants. Didn't they know that *he* was on board? Didn't they know *he* was on their side? Clearly not. Going back to certain death was not an option. "You say the girl jumped in or dove in?" he asked, resorting to his version of logic.

"Dove," Jenn answered, her heart-shaped face pointed back the way they had come.

"Then she can swim," he said, scratching the underside of his chin, and finding something crusty in the midst of his scraggly beard. He casually flicked it into the heaving seas. "And we really don't have to worry about that zombie guy. Zombies float. Everyone knows that. He'll be fine."

Troy gave the man—the pirate, in his mind—a curdled look; not exactly rejecting his argument but rather dismissing him altogether. "I'm with Stu. We're turning around. It is the only thing that makes any sense. I understand morality can be somewhat pragmatic with some of you, but I can't believe you'd let a girl drown."

Jenn's eyes had been unfocused, her mind drifting through too many emotions. Her gaze sharpened as she took in the handsome knight. "Emily is strong. She may not drown, probably won't, and Neil..." She pictured the near-zombie's horribly gray face. "Well, it might be better if he did drown. As for being pragmatic; I'm not sure what that means, but if you think we have wishy-washy morals then maybe you're right. I know I'm still young, but not everything is cut and dried."

"And it's three to two," Deaf Mick stated, giving Jenn a nod and a wink. "The ayes have it. It looks like we go on."

It was three to two because neither Mike nor Gerry the Greek had said anything at all and both wore matching guilty looks because of it. Mike finally mustered up the courage to say, "Voting doesn't mean anything on a ship. I'm captain and what I say goes. And I say we let Jenn decide."

"So, you've decided to let someone else decide?" Deaf Mick sneered. "Some captain you are. Who the hell made you captain, anyways? The old queen? She's done for now. The Black Captain will break her into little pieces and there..."

"Shut your hole," Stu barked, advancing on the ex-Corsair, a violent gleam in his eye. "Jenn is the new queen. We listen to her and that's that."

No one moved. Mike glanced at Jenn who drew in a long, deep breath of wet salt air. Yes, she was queen. Queen of what exactly, she wasn't sure. At the moment, she was only Queen of the Boat. She held authority over those onboard, and *that* felt like too much responsibility. In her heart she knew that she wasn't up to even this.

But if she didn't lead, who would? Mike had already kneeled to her, Stu could think of nothing but Jillybean, and Troy Holt was still something of a stranger. He was from another city and seemingly from another world; none of the others would follow him, willingly. The two Santas were weak, morally and mentally; Gerry the Greek's will had been crushed during the First Battle of the Bay, and that left Deaf Mick, whom Jenn didn't trust in the least.

It would be on her. "We can't go back," she said. "It would mean the death or capture of all of us. I can't be taken. It's not because I'm special or anything, it's because our people need to rally around something or someone and right now, I'm it."

"We should rally around our firm belief that God will save us from our enemies," Troy affirmed.

Jenn wished the world was that simple. She had a strained belief in a vague sort of deity that had never done much to help her no matter how much she prayed. "Not everyone believes in God," she told him.

Troy was ready with a stock answer, "You may not believe in God, but He believes in you. We should pray on this." Without asking, he took hold of Stu's hand and then reached for Deaf Mick's, who snorted and backed away as if Troy's clean hand could dirty up his own filthy one by imparting some kind of God germ.

Undeterred by the rebuff, Troy took Mike's hand. The teen looked shocked to be holding hands with another man. It was weird; still, he didn't want to offend Troy and didn't fight it. Troy waited until Mike took Jenn's hand and Stu held out a hand to one of the Santas.

"Heavenly Father," Troy began. He bowed his head as he said his prayer. The others did as well, all except Jenn, who looked up at the night, hoping that God would send her a sign— and he did, in a way. The storm had churned up the sky, whipping up mountains of black clouds and, at the same time, tearing holes in them. Just then there were two: one to the south and one east. They were so clear that little stars winked at her from within them.

At first, Jenn thought God was just pointing out the dilemma she was facing and telling her to make a choice. Then she realized that east wasn't the exact direction that Troy and Stu wanted to go; they wanted to go northeast. Then what was east?

"A compromise. I get it now," she said when Troy had finished with an "Amen" and a traced *Sign of the Cross*.

"Get what?" Mike asked, nervously. He knew her well enough to know what the complacent look on her face meant. She had seen a sign and now the pressure was off of her. "You saw something, didn't you?"

Troy looked askance at the idea. Put out that her mind had been on the occult during his prayer, he sniffed, "Praying is a form of communicating with God, of opening up to him. It's not about signs or zodiacs or any of that tarot business."

"*He* communicated with me," she answered with a shrug. She pointed up at the eastern hole in the clouds that was rapidly being crushed by the storm. "That way, Mike. We're going to put in. Anyone who wants to go ashore will be allowed to."

"I want to," Stu said, immediately.

"As do I," Troy responded quickly, as if in some sort of competition. "The life of that young lady may hang in the balance."

They both turned to look at Mike, who subconsciously gripped the wheel, holding on tightly just in case he accidentally agreed to go. His mouth came open, apparently without purpose, because he said nothing. Before he could complete the act of saying nothing, Jenn interrupted, "I don't want you to go, Mike. It may be selfish, but I'm going to need you with me."

When the different southern groups hear about the loss of not just Jillybean, but also of the entire fleet and most of the army, Jenn figured that the coalition the Queen had put together would fall apart. She couldn't allow that to happen. With each group acting alone they had no chance against the Corsairs, but if they could band together, there was a possibility that they could hold out.

Without the Guardians, it was a tragically slim chance. She didn't want to let Troy go on what seemed like a suicide mission; however, her gut told her that if she tried to forbid him from going, it would backfire on her. He would stay but with such reluctance that it would erode her chances of getting the Guardians to commit to her as queen. And she would need them to commit.

From what she had heard about Bishop Wojdan he seemed like a gentle man of the cloth, which was a wonderful thing in its way. Jenn wished she had grown up in Highton with a gentle leader like him. Gentleness was not a trait that desperate people would rally around when battle was imminent.

"Stu, can you write a letter for me?" she asked. "I need something that will make the Hill People see me in a different light. You know, so they accept me more readily as queen."

He leaned back, disliking the idea of writing anything. He had a childish scrawl at the best of times. On a heaving boat, his words might not be decipherable. "You want something like a letter of recommendation? But you were already queen and everyone followed you just fine."

What she was really after was a similar letter from Troy and this was her way of hinting at one without coming right out and asking him, something she felt was a little degrading. "Yes, but I won't have you there backing me up. I assume Gerry will speak on my behalf to the Islanders."

"Yeah, sure," he said, glad that she was asking him to speak instead of writing. It had been so long since he had written anything that he wondered whether he still could. "You were good. You know, as a queen. It's a tough gig and you pulled it off."

"Thanks," she said, blushing at the unexpected praise. Gerry had always been somewhat rough around the edges with her and, as far as she could remember, this was the first compliment he had ever paid her. Still with the pink in her cheeks, she turned to Phillip Carter the slightly more outgoing of the two Santas. "I will need you to represent the Santas for me. Can you do that?"

Carter blinked in surprise, looking like a malnourished owl. "Yeah, yeah, I can no problem. I always thought Lexi May was a weird choice, you know. Everyone thought so, too."

Jenn smiled at him, imitating the way Jillybean would smile in her "queenly" way. "Jillybean likes to put her trust in women, especially young women. Maybe she thinks they're more innocent or good or something."

"Yeah, I guess some of 'em are. I won't let you down. I promise."

"I know you won't," Jenn answered, distinctly hearing the lie with Troy watching her closely. She didn't know anything about the Santa other than the fact that Jillybean had allowed him on board, which she supposed meant something.

There was a lull in which the mast creaked and the wind tried to fight itself, first going this way and then that. One at a time everyone looked at Troy, who had never taken his strangely youthful gaze off of Jenn.

Finally, he spoke, "I'll write a letter for you. I think I was wrong about the Queen. The other Queen, I mean. She was far more selfless than I gave her credit for. I also realize now that it was a mistake for the Guardians not to join her in her war against the Corsairs. For her it's a crusade against true evil. If we had looked at it like that and had come along, maybe Leney wouldn't have defected."

"Not in a million years," Deaf Mick remarked, wearing a greasy smile that showed the many gaps in his teeth. "He would never have taken the chance with you guys tagging along. So, in a way, this is all your fault."

"As I just admitted," Troy answered, without any resentment. He turned back to Jenn, took a deep breath, thought about giving her a full bow, but only bent mid-torso. She accepted this gratefully.

Stu and Troy went below where Stu agonized over his penmanship and the spelling of the simplest words. The concept of commas was lost on him and so he added them here and there almost as decoration. He knew that periods ended sentences just as he knew that capital letters began them. What he forgot until he was halfway through the ordeal was that a capital "I" was far different than a lower case one.

With a curse, he balled up the paper and started again. The shore loomed and the sound of the crashing waves had magnified by the time Stu finished and came up on deck.

As if looking on a boy who had just been paddled, Mike gave him a sympathetic smile. "I had some food wrapped for you and some extra ammo. We're putting in at a place called Willapa Bay. Deaf Mick says there's a dock that's still workable there."

Stu snuck a look at the ex-Corsair and whispered, "Don't trust that guy. Keep a weapon hidden on or near you at all times."

"I'm not worried about him. I'm worried about you. You're going to do something stupid; I can feel it." Stu began to interrupt, but Mike continued, "Don't. Jenn needs you and so does everyone else. Even Jillybean needs you not to throw your life away, uselessly. Promise me, Stu!"

The Hillman dropped his eyes. "I'm not going to throw my life away uselessly. I promise. I'm not going to just run out and let someone shoot me. She isn't worth it."

Mike laughed. "You're going to have to work on your lies if you're going to be hanging around Saint Troy. He'll see right through them and then he'll *judge* you. You can see it in his eyes."

"It's a good thing I don't plan on lying to him. Is that your dock?" Something long, thin and low was jutting out into the bay.

It was indeed the dock and despite Mike's misgivings, it was a sturdy thing with cement pilings. The hundred slimed-over hardwood boards were warped and as slick as oil. Troy went first, did a crazy dance to keep his feet and had to grab hold of the offered boathook to keep from falling into the cold, black water.

Deaf Mick laughed and nearly lost the rest of his teeth when Mike balled a fist. Jenn restrained him, glossing over the situation by looping his arm over her shoulder before moving in to hug Stu in a three-person embrace. It had been a joke of a move, but in a flash, it became serious as each of them felt the weight of the moment.

The three of them had started their journey together, coming together on a dock in San Francisco. It seemed a year ago and half a world away.

"*The Puffer*," Mike said, fondly, remembering the little sailboat. "You couldn't even pilot that little boat, Stu."

"And you couldn't ask a girl out properly, Mike," Jenn said, remembering the botched attempts he had made at courting her.

It was Stu's turn to say something about Jenn. He was suddenly too flooded with emotion to say anything at all. In fact, he had to fight not to cry. He was about to say goodbye, and this time he knew in his heart that it was going to be permanent. Troy might be on a wild goose chase to find a girl in the middle of a storm, but Stu knew he was going into hell.

Stu had given up Jillybean when she had traded herself for Jenn because, in his heart, he knew it was going to be a temporary situation: Gunner would destroy what was left of the Captain's armies, while Mike bottled the last of the Corsair fleet in that man-made reservoir. With Jillybean's smoke bombs, her drones, and her bombs, the war would be over in two days.

Now, it would never end. With Mark Leney's defection, the Black Captain would crush the weak allied army in no time. Once that little chore was over, the only thing stopping him from taking over the San Francisco bay area was Jenn Lockhart and a handful of men. Even if the guardians mustered their entire strength they would be of little help; they lacked ammunition, coordination and the killer instinct found in the hearts of less civilized men like the Corsairs.

Someone had to kill the Black Captain and Stu armed himself for just that purpose. Along with an M4, he had a knife hidden in each boot; a neat little .25 caliber pistol tucked in the back of his belt and a stubby .40 Taurus in his coat pocket.

It wouldn't be enough, but he had to try. Somebody had to try, even if it meant suffering inhuman torture.

Stu pulled back from the triple embrace, kissed Jenn on the cheek, shook Mike's hand without looking him in the eye and then vaulted over the side of the heaving boat, landing perfectly on the dock without the tiniest slip.

"I'll take that as a good sign," Jenn said, with a choking laugh.

"Yeah," he agreed, thinking that it didn't matter that his first step was perfect. What worried him was what his last step would be like.

Chapter 22

After the explosion, Neil never lost consciousness; instead he experienced the passage of time much as he had the night before while floating in the harbor. He saw smoke and shouts and people going every which way. Someone tripped over him and shrieked in a high voice.

There were also threats and fights and more than one gun was pointed.

He sat up almost in the middle of it all, with his head feeling like it had grown to twice its original size.

"That's the spy!" someone bawled and now guns were pointed at Neil. "That's the guy who blew-up McCartt."

"Huh?" He touched his head and found that not only was he bleeding, he had a hunk of wood stuck in his skull. That was far more alarming than being accused of something he didn't do. "It wasn't me. Say, how big is this?" Gingerly, he touched the end of the wood. His hands were numb as if he'd been sitting on them. This would've been indicative of traumatic brain injury; however, they'd been numb for days now.

One of the Magnum Killers peered down at him. "Kinda big." Although this ranked low on the helpfulness scale, at least he wasn't waving a gun in Neil's face.

"Don't talk to him," his accuser cried, wild-eyed, and pointing a revolver. To Neil the gun looked like a gleaming smile; his eyes weren't focusing that well. The man behind the gun was somewhat russet in color; his beard and hair that is. His clothes were a mismatch of blue jeans, camo shirt and black jacket. "Tell me, freak, who sent you? Was it Gunner? Was it the Queen? Was it the Captain?" His name was Emanuel Powers, but he hadn't had the guts to ever use his first name around the Corsairs. Everyone knew him as Powers. He liked that.

"No one sent me. I fell off the boat last night is all. Really, if I was going to explode a bomb, would I do it while I was standing fifteen feet away? It wasn't me. It was one of you, and it had to be the Captain behind it. He has spies everywhere."

They all knew this and yet hearing it aloud, caused eyes to shift back and forth, and now more guns were being raised.

"Does anyone have a mirror?" Neil asked. It was almost as if the hunk of wood was messing with his reception. Everything seemed foggy. "Or a bathroom? Anyone know where the bathroom is?"

"You're not going anywhere." The gun was closer now but was still only a blur of iron. "No one is, not until we figure out who did this. I think we should tie this guy up and beat a confession out of him. Who's with me?"

Half the hands in the room went up which was something of a math problem for Neil. Did that mean half of everyone wanted to torture him, or did everyone want to torture him but only raised one hand apiece? It was an equation that was beyond him. "Hold on. Do I look like a spy to anyone? Aren't spies supposed to be sneaky?"

"Maybe," Powers agreed, reluctantly.

"I know that I don't look at all sneaky, and you guys know that I don't look at all sneaky because every one of you has been staring at me from the moment I walked through the doors. And did anyone see me trigger a bomb?"

One man raised his hand and for a moment panic seized Neil's heart. Was he going to say that *Yes I did see him blow up McCartt?* There'd be no coming back from that. Displaying manners not usually found in a thug, he held the hand up until Neil acknowledged him.

"I was looking right at you when the bomb went off and your hands were empty."

"I know because I didn't blow anyone up. With everyone looking at me, the real assassin was free to wait in the back until McCartt stepped out of the building and then bammo, he set off his bomb." He didn't mean that the man was literally in the back of the church and yet everyone turned to look at the few people standing near the altar.

"It wasn't me," one said right off. The others all began denying knowing anything about bombs, detonators, or anything on the subject.

A long, loud argument ensued and Neil made the mistake of rubbing his aching head. He touched the hunk of wood which he had momentarily forgotten. "Alright, listen up!" He clapped his hands like a football coach until everyone was staring at him. "The only way to figure this out is for everyone to be searched. But we can't do it one at a time; it'll take too long. So, I want you guys to form into two lines. Come on. Get in two lines and face each other. Pair off right here in front of everyone so we know there aren't any tricks."

There were so many of them that the double line went up the main aisle and then branched off in two directions before the altar. It looked like one of those gimmicky mass weddings from back before the apocalypse, only it was the dirtiest, ugliest, and gayest mass wedding imaginable.

Two-hundred men stared angrily into each other's eyes. Neil, who was standing on the raised dais so he could watch the search, couldn't help himself and intoned, "Dearly beloved, we are gathered here today to join these filthy Corsairs in holy matr…"

He was shouted down and pelted with anything available, mostly bibles and hymnals, which flapped at him like dusty birds. "Sorry! It was just a joke. Quiet down! Before we start the search, I want everyone on the right side to shift down three people, just in case we have more than one spy. I don't want them trying to pair up."

The men grumbled, and Neil suspected they would grumble over everything, but they still shifted. "Alright, let's start. The men on the right will empty their pockets and get searched first. We're looking for something that looks like a remote control for a TV. Or maybe even smaller, but it will have batteries."

Trouble set in right off the bat. Two men began pointing fingers at each other. "He's got something!" one cried.

Immediately, the second shouted, "No! He tried to plant that thing on me. I swear it wasn't me."

"Stay in your lines," Neil shouted. "It could be a false alarm." It wasn't. Sitting on the carpet between the two men was a detonator. Neil sighed, knowing that one of them was going to die horribly very soon. "The spy will have a radio, as well."

The shorter of the two began to swallow repeatedly and his deep brown eyes were showing whites like a frightened horse. Just as Neil found the radio in his pack, the man said in a strangled voice, "I didn't mean it."

"You didn't mean to blow up McCartt?" Neil asked, with another sigh. "I doubt that."

"I doubt it, too," someone shouted practically into Neil's ear. There was a rush of feet and some screams from the spy as he was beaten down. Neil backed off, retreating to the altar where he sat in the great chair that was set behind it; it looked and felt like something of a throne. The chair, with its dusty, red velvet cushion and its intricate beveled woodwork, was covered in gossamer strands of wispy grey silk as if uncountable spiders had made it their home for a thousand generations.

Neil felt as though he was sitting in the middle of an archeological dig and that he was part of it; he felt old and tired. Closing his eyes to the torture, he slipped into his dozy zombie sleep.

Later, when the spy had been tortured to death and his remains had been hacked into little chunks and flung about, the remaining Magnum Killers all turned to Neil. With his grey and scarred face, and his stunted size, he looked like some sort of goblin.

But a dead goblin.

"Hey," Powers said, through his russet beard. "Hey you."

"His name was Neil," one of the others pointed out. "I think he's dead." They all thought so. There was no telling how deep the shard of wood in his head went.

Powers stepped up and poked Neil with his M16. Neil's eyes were as freaky as the rest of him. His baby blues swam in a sea of blood red, and when they popped open, Powers jumped back with an unmanly cry.

"We finished," Powers said, jerking his thumb back at the bloody mess. "Do you want to come with us across the harbor?"

The question was surprising. He figured that they wouldn't want anything to do with him because of his minor zombie issue. What he didn't understand was that the Black Captain had purposely and aggressively culled anyone who might become a threat. Beyond a chosen few, if a person showed the least bit of leadership or ability beyond running a ship they would be "disappeared." The Captain wanted his Corsairs brutish, wicked, and servile.

Out of the two-hundred men in the church, no one had thought to change McCartt's original plan.

Neil had to keep from snorting at the idea. "I don't think so, but I wish you well." At least half the men did not want to chance a trip across the harbor in the bright light of day, but they were used to following orders. As if this was their only option, they hefted their heavy pews and trudged out into the morning which was already back to grey and cold.

Morbid curiosity had Neil trudging along with the group, holding the peach-colored coat closed against the cold. When they got to the farthest edge of land, the Magnum Killers, a notoriously blood-thirsty gang, paused, testing the water with dainty toes, like children on their first trip to the beach.

They all agreed with vibrantly vulgar profanity that the water was indeed cold. "We don't have a choice," Powers said, in clear contradiction to reality. Neil would agree that they didn't have good choices, but this seemed like the least good choice of them all.

With words of encouragement, and a good deal more cursing, the Magnum Killers picked up their pews and waded into the water. The pews turned out to be a menace. Without the weight of the men, they seemed ambivalent about the idea of floating. At best it could be said that they wallowed. With six men clinging to them, they couldn't even do that; they hung suspended in the water a few feet below the surface.

The men weren't going to drown, but with the pews partially submerged it became a terrible struggle to propel them along. What made it worse was that the pews spun like paddle-wheels unless someone with long arms was holding onto them.

Still, the Killers struggled on, valiantly but foolishly. The attempt finally ended after half an hour when a black sail was spotted moving away from the mass of Corsair boats lingering near what had once been the mouth of the Hoquiam River.

Neil spotted the ship first and began waving his arms and pointing. A near-panic ensued as the Killers tried to turn back around, a task that was so difficult that it would've made more sense to press on to the far shore. Pews crashed into other pews and men jostled and fought as if they were drowning. Leaderless, the men were sitting ducks as the ship came flying up. They couldn't simultaneously tread water and fight, and the Corsair ship seemed to know this.

They would've died if Neil hadn't been there. He settled himself in among the larger rocks and began jerking off shots at the boat. His aim, never all that good before becoming a zombie, was terrible. The ship, with its acres of canvas was equivalent in size to the broad side of a barn, and to prove the adage only partially correct, barely half his bullets hit anything at all.

The Corsairs were much better shots and the rocks all around Neil were chipped and marked-up. They were better, but when it came to death, he was lucky and remained untouched by the flying lead. As the bullets didn't scare him in the least, he kept up such a steady fire that eventually one of his rounds came close enough to the captain of the ship to cause him to lose heart.

Much to Neil's amazement, the ship turned about and fled back the way it had come.

The Magnum Killers cheered Neil and, when they finally came back on shore, exhausted and freezing, a few of them considered shaking his hand, but thought better of it. Neil had forgotten the big hunk of wood sticking out of his head and he looked too gruesome to touch.

Gruesome or not, they needed a leader and so far, he was the top contender. The only one who was strongly against the idea was Neil himself. "I'm a zombie, in case you haven't noticed," he told them.

"Maybe Powers can do it," someone suggested. Powers shrank at the idea. It would be a thankless, and likely a quick job, as well. They were all the way out on a mostly barren little peninsula and with the Black Captain's command of the sea, they could easily be bottled up with suicidal frontal charges their only option to break free.

Neil went to rub his head and felt the shard of wood, again. "Son of a bitch!" he snarled, yanking the hunk out and tossing it aside. This impressed the Killers even more and they clamored for him to lead them. "Let's hope you all live long enough to regret this," he said, thinking that this deft bit of word-play would inspire his men, when at best, it was only confusing.

"Huh?" someone replied.

"Exactly," he shot back, with a dreadful rendition of a wink.

Some of them were already regretting the choice in leadership. It was no matter to Neil. He had zero faith in his abilities as a military leader, but he had plenty of faith in his natural wimpiness. As far as he understood the tactical situation, he saw that their only chance was to run away and run away quickly.

After their fright in the harbor, the Killers took to their heels and followed Neil northward. Despite their exhaustion, they covered two miles in twenty-three minutes, which got them out of immediate danger; their longterm danger was still just as great, however. Climbing a hill, they saw an even dozen black boats, crammed with men, slipping along the northern edge of the long peninsula that stretched out ahead of them for another four miles.

"We can't stop!" Neil cried, before charging down the hill and angling to the west, hoping that they'd be able to slip out of the trap by scooting up the Pacific side.

It wasn't long before he saw that wasn't going to work. A further twenty-three boats had just come out of the harbor and were working their way north, with a light breeze on their beam. Although the boats were merely plodding along, they were still going faster than Neil's men who were slowing with each step.

Neil felt barely winded, or if he was winded, he didn't care. His lungs pushed and pulled air in and out, and it seemed like someone else's business altogether.

"Where will they put in?" he asked Powers, whose lips were tinged purple; he was soaking wet, cold, and as miserable as a man could get.

"If they got dinghies, they could unload anywhere with how calm this sea is. If not, they'll have to moor up at Copalis Beach. It's about five miles further on."

They all secretly wished for the Corsairs to go on. Five miles was a long way and the hope was they'd be able to cut between the two companies of Corsairs. It was not to be. After only a mile and a half, the boats dropped sail and began nosing their way slowly towards the coast.

The Killers stopped running; there was no point, now. "We're going to have to attack," Neil told the men. They were all bigger than he was, and stronger and meaner, as well, yet they were afraid while he wasn't in the least. "What could go wrong?"

They'd be attacking over open ground in broad daylight and without the least bit of reconnaissance, so the obvious answer was: everything, of course.

Chapter 23

I should have run, was the last thought that went through Emily Grey's mind as she fumbled for the Glock that she had foolishly tucked way, deep down in her coat pocket.

The wet night took on the slow-motion quality that Emily had always thought was reserved strictly for nightmares. As if she was some sort of drum major, Lexi May spun her M16A2 from a slung position on her left shoulder. Even with time slowed, the gun was a blur and it seemed to Emily that it had to have gone around at least twice before it stopped with a precise slap, its deep, black bore pointing directly at Emily's throat.

There was a pause in which Emily took a single high breath that got caught in her larynx precisely where the bullet would hit her. Before she could swallow the breath, there came a tiny *click* sound as Lexi May thumbed the weapon from Safe to Fire.

To Emily, it was deafening. Her mind centered on it, knowing she was in terrible trouble. She was about to be murdered in cold blood. Lexi May would blast out her throat and the only thing Emily could hope for was that the bullet would take out her spine as well. If not, she would lie in the mud, choking on her blood as the rain pooled in her eyes.

She would die slowly and her mom would never know what had happened to her. Would Gunner bury her? Or would she be left out to rot? Emily pictured her face covered in green mold as worms burrowed sickly tunnels throughout her body.

"Please don't," Emily said, her throat now so tight that she could hardly choke out a whisper.

Lexi May shrugged without letting the bore budge an inch. "Sorry. Captain's orders." She was more than pitiless; there was a small, evil grin on Lexi May's lips.

She wants to kill me, Emily realized, shocked at the idea. "But I didn't do anything."

"Since when does that matter?"

It mattered a lot to Emily. If she hadn't done anything, then maybe the Captain had made a mistake. Maybe he would change his mind if Lexi May would just call him back—but she wasn't calling anyone back. She lowered her face to the stock of the rifle, and for a moment Emily thought she was going to kiss it. Of course, she didn't; she was only lining her eye up to the rear sight.

In the next second, she would pull the trigger and kill Emily in a flash of light and, in all the tumult that followed, Lexi May would zip through the forest to the head of the formation and emerge from the woods just as shocked as everyone else that someone could kill such a sweet child as Emily Grey.

And there was nothing Emily could do to stop it. The Glock was good and stuck in her pocket and the only person who *might* want to stop her murder from happening was a hundred yards away, bawling at the men in that horrid, inhuman voice of his.

Lexi May should have fired her rifle right then, but for some reason she raised the barrel until it was pointing at Emily's face, and now her smile was beyond cruel.

Instinctively, Emily threw herself back as her hand closed around the grip of the gun in her pocket. She pulled the trigger in the same instant that Lexi May did.

In a strangely zero-gravitational instant, her body drifted nearly horizontally to the wet black earth, and the golden mass of her hair floated just above her head as if she were underwater and looking up at a dark surface.

In that fraction of a second, she felt beautifully serene— then something blazing-hot scorched a path through her hair only an inch from her scalp. It sent a terrifying jolt through her body, causing every muscle to constrict. It also caused the order in which the world spun to jerk out of whack. Somehow, she heard the explosion of Lexi May's M16 come *after* the bullet passed and this was followed by a brilliant flame, like dragon's breath, belching from the bore.

The one thing both she and Lexi May missed was the sound of the Glock firing a nano-second after the M16. Its bullet punched a hole through Emily's coat pocket and shot away the very front lip of her right shoe before spinning out into the forest. Even before it thudded into an oak tree a hundred yards away, Emily landed on her back, knocking the wind out of her with an advantageous: "Oof!"

The sound and Emily's weird contortion confused Lexi May, who hesitated for just a second, thinking that she just might have missed. It was hard to imagine since she had been so close, and yet, it was dark and the girl had flailed oddly at the last moment. To be on the safe side, Lexi May decided to administer a quick coup de grâce, and, thinking she was safe as kittens, took two steps forward, once more aiming the M16.

With the Glock still in her pocket, Emily fired from the hip. The slug winged Lexi May, blasting off the top two inches of her jutting hip bone. The pain was immediate and so frightfully fantastic that it took over her entire being. From head to toe, her body spasmed, and just before she crumpled, a loud, long shriek tore from her throat.

The agony eclipsed her mind. The M16 was forgotten, as were Emily and Gunner, and everything else. She writhed in the mud, her face now warped into a Halloween mask.

Emily didn't know what to do. She scrambled up and fought the Glock from her pocket and held it pointed at Lexi May. As she watched, guilt and sadness built up until they came out in hot tears. "It's your fault, Lexi. You shouldn't have tried to kill me. I didn't do anything to you or anyone."

Lexi May was now panting and holding herself, as if she were about to give birth to a half-grown steer. Emily could feel her pain and it was agonizing. It blotted out what little medical training she had been given.

She dropped down to her knees. "What can I do? Do you need a-a-a tourniquet or a bandage or a…"

A huge, bat-like shadow suddenly emerged from the dark and she nearly screamed. It was Gunner, looking simultaneously deeply concerned and viscerally enraged.

"Explain," he commanded.

"She's the spy. And…and…and she tried to k-kill me." Emily's chest was beginning to hitch as if she was five-years-old and a boy had pulled her pigtails on the playground. She had never wanted to hurt anyone like this in her entire life. She was sick to her stomach with grief. Gunner managed to cure her of it by putting his terrible arms around her.

He was hugging her!

With a shriek she pulled herself out of his arms. "Emily, look, I didn't mean…" She brought the gun up. He gave it an embarrassed laugh. "I guess that's about right. Sorry about that, I guess I forgot my place."

"Don't ever touch me again, freak." Her voice was shrill, too much like a kid's voice in her ears. She tried again, forcing the shrillness out of her words. "Don't touch me again, you got it?" This time she came across as cold as steel. It was a proud moment for her.

"I said I was sorry," Gunner answered. Although most of his hideous face was covered, he had expressive eyes. Even in the

201

dark, she could tell he wanted to say more. He hesitated, drawing in a deep breath. It came out with a tired sigh. "What happened here?"

They both regarded Lexi May, who had gritted her teeth against the pain and was just reaching for her rifle.

"She's the spy," Emily accused, raising her voice as if volume lent credibility. "She has a radio. The Captain told her to k-kill me. I heard it and she was all, 'Sorry. Orders are orders.' And I said, like, 'Don't. I didn't do anything wrong.' And she shot at me for no reason."

Emily remembered the burning sensation and she touched her head. Her hand came away with a few long filaments of golden hair. She choked at the sight of them. "She shot me!" The words were filled with disbelief.

Gunner forgot himself as he grabbed her. "Where?"

"In my hair."

He pushed her away. "Your hair?" He was annoyed.

"Yes. An inch from the top of my head." She held up finger and thumb. "I was this close to getting my head blown off. God! There's a hole in my hood!"

"And I got a hole in my hip," Lexi May said, gasping. "I say we're even." Her hands were slick and wet; the bleeding hadn't stopped and she was beginning to think it wouldn't—not that she would live long enough to worry about that. She might have been able to talk the girl into letting her go, but him, never.

Unless she could parlay his secret into some sort of freedom. The fact that he had gone by Captain Grey right up until little Emily Grey had shown up was not lost on her. It seemed impossible that this inhuman creature was her father, but Lexi May had no other cards to play.

"I had to spy for the Captain to save my daughter," she lied. She had no daughter; only a fool would allow a child to be born into this world. "You understand about saving daughters don't you, Captain…" She left the end of the sentence dangling.

"It's just Gunner." His dark eyes flicked nervously towards Emily. "Once I was a captain, but that was a long time ago."

"Eleven years isn't that long. Still you understand the need to protect one's daughter. You should let me go and everyone will be safe and sound."

Emily had been just putting the Glock back in her pocket. "No way. She's the spy, Gunner. I don't care about her daughter.

No one cared about me and no one cared about my uncle. No. We can't let her go."

Lexi May opened her mouth, poised to spill her secret. Gunner shook his head. "Maybe we can. I'm not going to carry her. She'll only slow us down. Our only other option is to kill her. Are you willing to do that?"

The air in the little clearing became sharply tense and the rain that passed through did it with such purpose that each drop was amplified and instead of a gentle patter, it felt to Gunner as if he were being riddled by soft hail.

"No," Emily finally answered.

"Good," Lexi May said, grinning despite the pain radiating throughout her body. "You're a good girl. Now you two go your way, and I'll go mine and that'll be that."

Emily was frowning, two little lines between her brows marring her otherwise perfect skin. The situation was going in a direction she couldn't have imagined. Gunner seemed cowed by the girl, all because she had a daughter. A lot of people had daughters; it didn't make them good people. And this was a bad person who could still do a lot of bad things, even with her wound.

"What about the radio?" she asked. "We should at least take that. I don't trust her with it."

"Take it. I don't care. It's in my coat pocket."

Emily was just about to kneel down to search her coat, but she pulled back. What if the spy had a knife and planned on finishing the job the Captain had given her? She even said, "How do I know you won't try to do something?"

"She's harmless," Gunner growled. He knelt, looming over her, looking wide and menacing. "Let's have it, and no funny business."

"I'll say the same for you," she whispered. "It'll just take one word." They locked eyes as she held out a blood-smeared two-way radio. Too late, she saw that he had his metal-capped left arm out to receive it. His right hand held the axe beneath his cloak and as her eyes and mouth opened wide, he brought it around in a fast, vicious arc and split her head in two.

His wide, muscular body and great black cape blocked the sickening view of Lexi's death. Still, he ordered Emily to, "Look away."

Emily was glad to. She was shaking again and was worried that if she saw Lexi May's brains splattered everywhere, she'd puke, and she didn't want to hurl in front of Gunner. He already thought she was weak and useless.

"I thought you were going to let her go."

"Nope." He wiped the edge of his axe on Lexi May's coat and then rifled her pockets, taking food and ammo. "She deserved to die. I just didn't want her to play some sort of trick." He held out the radio. Along with the blood there was a spat of ick on it that had Emily's stomach rolling over. "I need you to check in with the Black Captain. Tell him the job's done and that we're turning south."

Her hand shook as she held it out. He seemed to sneer at it from behind his mask. "Maybe you should practice first. Just say: The job's done and we're turning south. That's it."

"I don't sound like her." It was terrible excuse.

"He'll hear what he wants to hear. He's expecting a girl's voice. Put your hood up and say the words low and slow."

She had to practice the simple lines five times before Gunner allowed her to do it for real.

"The job's done and we're turning south." Even with the practice, she rushed the sentence and ran the words together.

"Who is this?" a coarse voice answered, seconds later.

She looked to Gunner, who pointed down at the dead body. "I'm, uh, Lexi May of the Santas."

"Oh, great code name, Lexi May. Jeeze. What road are they on?"

"Uhhh."

Gunner rolled his eyes as she covered the radio, and begged him, "What is it? What's the road?" As far as she could remember, with all their twists and turnings and back and forths, they had passed only one very faded street sign, which had been impossible to read because of the dark—and because she was tired and hadn't paid it any attention.

"It's the Wynooche Valley Road," he hissed in that harsh, gravelly voice of his. As he was without lips and missing part of his tongue, whispering really wasn't his thing.

Emily couldn't understand him in the least. When he whispered, he sounded like a snake with a mouthful of gravel, but he had such a quick temper and was so frightening that she didn't dare ask him to repeat himself. "It's the In-nooty Valley Road."

The radio crackled. "The what? In-nooty? I don't see anything like that on the map. Is it a dirt road, or what?"

"Win-new-che," Gunner repeated, attempting to hold back his anger. To Emily, he looked as if he were about to explode and hack her head off with that axe of his. She still had the sickening *ca-chunk!* sound of him splitting Lexi May's skull open echoing in her ears.

She repeated, "Win-new-che," into the radio and received a simple: "Got it," in return.

"Good job, kid," Gunner told her.

She felt a little stab of pride at this, which was offset by the way Gunner was looking at her; like he wanted to touch her or maybe even hug her. She would scream if he tried to.

He only pointed at her hair. "Remember, you're supposed to be a boy, though you sure are pretty. You remind me so much of your mother. You have her…" She was looking at him with such disgust that he couldn't go on. It was a mistake anyway.

"Just keep your hood up and get some more mud on your face," he growled over the hump on his back as he stormed away. "And keep up. You don't want to get left behind."

"Maybe I do," she muttered. Running away still seemed like her best option, if only she wouldn't get lost so easily. She followed after Gunner as he made his way to the front of the formation, kicking the men to their feet. After a long night of marching, they were so tired that many fell asleep with their backs to trees and rain pattering off their hoods.

It took Gunner some time to get his army up and moving again. They slogged northward with a dismal gray dawn gradually revealing itself on their right. Even the slackening rain and the first rays of sunshine breaking through couldn't invigorate the men, who evacuated the area so slowly that they were nearly caught as hundreds of mountain bandits rushed by just a few hundred yards south of the last man.

The Black Captain had fallen for the simple ruse and Neil Martin was about to pay for it. He had no idea that his Magnum Killers were now completely surrounded and facing seven-to-one odds.

The sudden, intense barrage of gunfire behind Gunner's army was the only thing that could have got them moving faster. Afraid that it wouldn't last, they scampered north, disappearing into Olympic National Forest and leaving Neil to his fate.

Chapter 24

Deanna Grey balked at the handcuffs. "Put those damned things away! Search me if you wish, but I'm not leaving in handcuffs."

"It's standard procedure, Deanna," Norris said, puffing up importantly, his chest like a plaid barrel.

"That's bull! We don't have a standard procedure for this because it's never happened before. Now step aside before I lose my patience with you."

Norris was no fool. He knew that he would gain nothing by arguing with Deanna on the subject and, that if he tried to force the cuffs onto her, he would likely come out of the scrape clawed up and perhaps missing an eye.

He stood aside as Deanna fast-marched past him and out the door. Sheriff Perkins had to jog to catch up, one hand holding her campaign hat in place on top of her head, the other on the butt of her revolver to keep it from falling out of her holster.

"How'd she die?" Deanna asked.

"I don't know if I should answer that," Deberha replied. "It being an open investigation and all. And you the chief suspect. I should at least wait until you give an official statement."

Deanna grunted out a laugh. "Here's my statement: I didn't do it. I'm innocent. I went directly from the staff meeting to Gina's house and have been there ever since. No one is going to be able to say otherwise. You see all these people?"

She waved at a pair of kids cycling by. Other than Gina's murder, it was a normal Bainbridge morning. People were busy doing their thing, going through their morning rituals; heading to and from the market, or to church, or to school. Quite a number of people were just sitting on their front porches, smiling at their neighbors, and waving to the same people they waved at every morning.

"Not one of them will say that they saw me come from the police station, or even in the direction of the police station."

Norris had been keeping up, though he was already slightly winded and a little dizzy. He was more of a stroller than a marcher. "You might have swung out the long way to make it look like you came from a different direction."

"Then I want you to gather thirty people and start canvasing any neighborhood you want to, Norris. Go find your eyewitnesses."

He only stared at her as he walked, his jowls no longer glum; they were perky and swayed to the beat of his long stride. She stopped and stared back. "I mean it, Norris. Call up the Fast Response Team. I want this done right now."

"You don't get to make demands anymore, Dee. This is murder we're talking about. You've overstepped the bounds big time. You won't be able to play political games with this one. If the council doesn't step in then the government is over. It'll be anarchy."

"That's why you need to find your witnesses as soon as possible!" Deanna cried, hammering a fist into her palm. "Find someone who saw me leave the meeting and then find someone who saw me heading towards the station and so on and so forth. Because right now, you don't have any evidence to convict me. Go get some before I go free!" She actually snapped her fingers and pointed for him to go.

"Fine," he snapped, before stomping away.

Immediately, Deanna turned and began marching again. Deberha hurried to catch up. "What was that about? You act like you want to get caught."

Deanna shot her a look out of the corner of her eye. "Do you think I actually did this?"

"No, not really. I think if you wanted to kill her you would have done it last night. You had the perfect opportunity."

"Exactly. And that means if I didn't do it..."

Deberha was slow to finish the sentence and when she did, she did so incorrectly. "Then someone else did?"

"Not exactly. It means there's at least one more spy on the island." Deberha stopped, her mouth coming open. "Don't do that. You look like a carp," Deanna said and began striding on again. "The only people with motive to kill her are me, Norris and the spy."

The sheriff pitched her head back to stare up at Deanna, nearly losing her hat in the process. "Norris? Why would he kill Gina Sanders?"

"To be governor. It's a weak motive, I'll grant you that, but people have been killed for less. And, by his own admission, he doesn't have an alibi either. But he didn't do it. I've known Norris for too long. There's another spy on the island. There is one thing that Gina, Eddie and Joslyn all had in common: none of them were exactly geniuses. The way I see it there has to be someone else with some sense running things on the island or they would have been caught a long time ago."

"Maybe," Deberha sniffed.

Deanna was forced to reactivate her politician's smile. "Come on, Deb. Don't take offense. It's not like they've been obvious, right? No one even knew there were spies on the island until three days ago." No one except Jillybean, that is. Five years before she had warned the council about the possibility that the Black Captain had been setting up "sleeper agents." Everyone had laughed at her.

Not Deanna, of course, but then again, neither did she implement the counter measures Jillybean had suggested.

The two women walked in an uncomfortable silence until they came to the police station, where Deberha found herself in a bit of a pickle since she needed to lock Deanna up without her touching or even viewing the crime scene.

Deberha asked Deanna to look away as she led her past Gina's bloody corpse. Deanna wished she had. Gina's throat had been slit and not in a dainty girlish manner, either. The cut was so deep and wide that her head was flopped far further back than it had any right to be.

"My God," Deanna whispered as she turned away. "How could anyone think I could do that?"

"It took a lot of anger," Deberha answered. "And you're the only one who has reason to be that angry."

As Deberha opened her cell door, Deanna had her lips pressed together, afraid that if she opened her mouth too wide, she'd vomit up her breakfast. Whenever she blinked, she saw an image of the corpse; she didn't dare close her eyes.

"I'm going to have to take your clothes and photograph you," Deberha explained, holding out a pair of green hospital scrubs. The sheriff's investigation was done quickly enough and soon, Deanna was left to sit in her cell. It was walled on three sides and thus she couldn't see what was being done to or for Gina.

Not much it seemed as a few minutes later, a grim-faced Deberha Perkins came to see her. "We're going to have to check out your house. We won't be gone long. If you need anything, um, well, we'll be back."

Deanna didn't think to ask if they had moved Gina's body until after they had gone.

The cell felt suddenly cold and the quiet sank deep into the grey cement walls. She couldn't help herself as she listened for the slightest sound; the scrape of a shoe, the drip of blood, the soft squeak of a cell door easing open. All she heard was her own heartbeat—her own guilty heartbeat.

"But I have nothing to feel guilty over. I didn't do anything." Except kidnap her and threaten to feed her to the scariest zombie on the planet. "Other than that, I mean."

Her words were swallowed up by the silence as if what she had said had been rejected in some way. For reasons she didn't want to think about, she held her breath, straining for any sort of response. There was nothing from the second cell over and she had to bite back on the urge to repeat herself more loudly.

It almost seemed as though Gina was listening.

"If she's even here. They might have moved her for all I know." This was a whisper spoken so low it might have only been a thought. Deanna crept up to the bars and pushed a soft cheek into them.

She could just make out Gina's bare ankle and foot, lying in a drying pool of deep red blood—she was still there all right.

Her killer had opened her cage and slit her throat from behind just as she was about to walk out. Blood had sprayed out of her like it had come out of a hose. Deanna pulled away from the bars, whispering, "I didn't do that." Those moments in Jillybean's school, when she had Gina by the hair and was thrusting her at the terrifying zombie, had been Deanna's test.

The rage and grief over what had happened to Emily had reached a peak inside her, causing her desire for justice to turn into a hunger for revenge. She had wanted Gina to die and she had wanted to do it with her own hands. And she had wanted it to be bloody and terrible. And she wanted Gina to finally feel the pain and fear that Emily must have been feeling when she was taken.

In the end, Deanna hadn't been able to finish the job. Yes, Gina deserved to die, and to die horribly, but Deanna couldn't do it. Her lust for revenge could not overcome the inertia of her civilized upbringing or the unseen pressure of society, and she had pulled Gina away.

The moment she had, she knew she had failed her test.

209

Gina deserved to die. Banishment wasn't good enough. Deanna understood this on a visceral level. On a cerebral level she had her excuses lined up: she was governor, not an executioner; she had an obligation to uphold the highest moral standards; they had laws and policies in place to deal with these situations; killing without the authorization and consent of the governed was the very definition of murder.

She could tell herself that these reasons were all very nice and proper, just as they were also so very pathetic.

In that moment when she lost her nerve and pulled Gina back, she knew an instant of pure weakness. She knew she had failed in some way. Bainbridge was wonderful; her people were honorable; her laws were just; and her walls were grand, but in the end, it was only a temporary refuge.

One day, maybe even sooner than she could have ever guessed, it would all end and she would once again be fighting for the merest survival. In that fight, there was no room for such weakness.

It was a lesson she thought she had learned already once before. Had not life *Before* been just like this? Compared to the great expanse of time, when human life had less value than dirt, the end of the "American Century" had been idyllic. Yes, there was crime and evil, and people were mean to each other, but starvation had been all but ended across 95% of the planet, diseases were being eradicated one by one, and people argued over the most minor of differences.

It was time taken for granted, and if it hadn't been the undead that had destroyed that world, something else would have, and everyone would have stood around crying: "If only…"

Deanna felt as though she were in that same place. If only she had let the monster eat Gina, she wouldn't be locked up, and Norris wouldn't be on the verge of taking charge. What would he do when the Corsairs came? What sort of concessions would he give? Would he, God forbid, pay the Black Captain a monthly tribute?

"What would I do?" That was actually a much tougher question. As far as she knew, the Captain held her daughter hostage—it meant he had a great deal of leverage over her. "Perhaps too much leverage. Maybe it's for the best that I'm stuck in here." With her daughter's life held against her, the weakness she had already shown would be exploited fully. It was no surprise; she had known from the beginning that she would gladly pay any price, any *tribute* to keep her Emily safe.

Deanna sat down on her cot and tried to figure out the best way to get Emily back without endangering her people. It was a puzzle without a solution and, after an hour, she was no closer to figuring it out than when she started.

Norris Barnes' blaring voice ended the mental stalemate. "You are done, Deanna!"

Her first thought was: *He's found a witness of some sort.* It would have to be a confused witness or a paid one since she knew she hadn't killed anyone. She waited patiently in the cell until he came down the hall, the sound of his labored breathing preceding him.

"I never thought you would stoop so low," he said, with sincere, if over-the-top theatrics. He held a shoebox in front of the mound of plaid he called a belly. The box was closed.

"You've accused me of murder. Some would think you can't get lower than that, but I'm game. What did I do now? Did I kill a pet hamster?"

He opened the box, again with such theatrics that she felt a chill, expecting to find a severed hand or maybe a still beating heart. It was almost as bad. Inside was a heavy knife with dark blood dried along its edge.

"I found this in my garbage can!" he cried.

"I told him not to touch it," Sheriff Perkins squeaked from behind him. "It's part of a criminal investigation, and no one should be handling it but me."

Norris turned his large, reddening head at her. "If you were doing your job correctly, I wouldn't have had to. Explain this, Dee! Explain how this just happened to show up in my garbage can an hour after you hinted to your little friend here that I have a motive in this killing, too."

Deanna's head had begun to spin. "I-I don't know. Unless someone planted it to make me look guilty."

"Ha! You actually think that someone is setting you up by setting me up? That doesn't make any sense. None at all. What does make sense is that you stuck the knife there after you killed Gina." Deanna started shaking her head in something of a wobble—Norris was right, it was the only thing that made sense. If someone had wanted to set Deanna up, the knife would have been stashed in her own garbage can.

"Hold on," Deberha Perkins cried. "Right now, we don't know enough to go pointing fingers. All I know is that you both had motive and opportunity. Whatever you *guess*, Norris doesn't mean much in a court of law. Personally, it doesn't look good that the knife ended up in your possession."

"You think I did this?" he cried.

The sheriff held up her small hands. "I'm just going with what the evidence suggests."

"Then what do you think about that!" He jabbed a finger at the knife and shoved the box in Deberha's face. She squinted and then went pale. Norris then held it close to the bars for Deanna to see. Perfectly positioned on the stainless-steel blade was a fingerprint. It hadn't been obvious before; now it was all Deanna could see.

It was a whole print, but a small one. Norris had big, thick hands. The print was too small even for his pinky. "A woman did that and there's only one woman who would stand to gain anything at all by framing me."

Again, he was completely right. Feeling light-headed, Deanna stepped away from the bars. The knife, the print, the murder, none of it made sense. *Unless you're crazy*, she heard a soft voice in her head say. She shook the thought away with difficulty.

"It wasn't me," she whispered, not under her breath and not to herself, but to that damned voice. From the corner of her eye, she saw Norris' eyebrow shoot up. "I said it was not me. Sheriff, I want you to take my fingerprints and compare them to the one on the knife."

"Hold on!" Norris bellowed. "She's not trained to examine fingerprints. No one on the island is."

Deanna agreed. "Then we'll get two other random people and have them all make their separate assessments. This sort of thing was done before computers, it can be done again." This was agreed to. While Norris left to find the other two people who would inspect the prints, Sheriff Perkins struggled through what seemed like a simple process of smushing Deanna's inky fingers onto a blank piece of paper.

"You know you're putting your fate in the hands of three people who don't know what they're doing, right?" Deberha asked. "They're more likely than not to get a false positive, you know what I mean? Loops and swirls, they all start to look alike after a while."

"Yeah," Deanna whispered, her stomach starting to ache. A false positive didn't worry her as much as an actual positive match. She wanted to think she wasn't crazy and yet, the only thing that made any sense at all was that she had killed Gina and had stashed the knife—and then had blanked the memory.

She knew such things were possible; Jillybean had been doing it for almost her entire life. Sometimes Deanna wished she could forget the hateful moments that had happened to her; there had been times when she was envious of Jillybean's craziness.

Just at that moment, she wasn't envious at all. She was sick with the idea that she had taken a life and that she had been walking around with a bloody knife. What if someone had seen her? If she had been crazy enough to kill Gina and frame Norris for it, maybe she had been crazy enough to get rid of any witnesses.

"Just make sure you get it right, Deberha. I want the truth." She had to know if she had killed Gina, even if it meant being banished...or worse.

Chapter 25

Neil Martin's first battlefield experience ended in a complete disaster. It didn't begin that way. The beginning of the battle was something of a middling disaster, but by the end, he had generaled his men with such exact ineptitude that the disaster was whole and complete.

In fairness, it wasn't entirely his fault.

To begin with, Neil faced a strategic situation that was utter crap. He was surrounded without even the most remote possibility of retreat. It made sense that he ordered an attack. What didn't make sense was the direction: east, directly toward the fortified town of Hoquiam, four miles away. Even if he managed to break through the first line of Corsairs that had spilled from the dozen ships minutes before, he still had a swollen river to cross before he was confronted by two wire fences and newly dug entrenchments that were studded with machine gun nests.

His soldiers were not up to the task. They were of a low order, ill-trained and ill-equipped. They were a surly lot, used to grumbling and questioning any order that they didn't understand. The few officers among them had almost no experience in land warfare. They knew very little beyond commanding sailors on relatively tiny boats, where any order could be heard by everyone on board and very few of these orders were ever really unexpected.

Raise the main; lower the jib; clean the head. Life on board a forty-four footer was the very definition of routine. On the other hand, battle was orchestrated chaos, and that was if it was done right.

Neil hadn't done much right, starting the moment the first bullet careened past his face after clipping the edge of a birch. He blinked as he was dusted by the white bark and for a moment, he thought the light rain had turned into a strange pelting warm snow.

More bullets smacked into the trees around him, sending up a blizzard of bark and chips of wood. Confused, he put his palm out while all around him the Magnum Killers were diving for cover. It took a moment for him to connect the sharp, snapping explosions with the actions of his men.

Someone was shooting at them...but what was with the weird snow? That part didn't make any sense.

"Are you seeing this?" he asked Powers, holding his hand out to show the flakes of white.

"Get your ass down!"

That seemed like a lot of work. They were supposed to be attacking, why would he want to get down? "You guys should get up. Come on, now. Up an at 'em. I thought you guys were supposed to be tough."

"We are, but this is stupid!" someone down the line cried. "This is never going to work. We gotta get outta here!" He sounded hysterical.

"It might work if we all hop up and get going. It doesn't sound like there's all that many of them."

Neil had led his company of Magnum Killers through a little subdivision, foolishly marching right up the middle of a road. By happenstance, the route he had chosen was lightly guarded and split the defense exactly in two. It was a fantastic opportunity to drive a wedge in the defense and roll up the Captain's fighters in an unstoppable flank attack.

An initial victory that could have led to his company escaping the trap they were in was in his grasp, if he only knew what he was facing. Unfortunately, having forgotten the basic concept of reconnaissance, he was tactically blind.

Relying on luck, he had blundered forward at the head of his column; which had ground to a halt, his men huddling in fear, strung-out along the road. Even a novice like Neil knew this was a recipe for disaster. His solution was even worse.

"If you're all too afraid to attack, then we'll go this way!" Without waiting for anyone, he took off across the street, heading north, moving straight in front of the Captain's defensive line. He made it safely to the other side of the street, pushed through the remains of a fence and dashed through someone's backyard before heading into a little copse of trees which were being riddled by rifle fire.

Because the trees sat in a slight depression, the lead flew too high to do anything but scare the Killers, who stood in a hunch, breathing heavily as if they had run half a mile. "So far so good," Neil yelled to the men over the barrage. "Let's keep going."

Everyone waited on him to go first.

Without a real plan in mind, Neil aimed himself at a hill a few blocks away. He wasn't sure about the importance of hills, but in every war movie he had ever seen, some rough, partially bearded sergeant would invariably go on about needing to "take" this or that hill, usually at all costs. He didn't think he needed to go to that much of an extreme, but he felt a hill should be taken.

"Perhaps it has psychological value," he wondered aloud, his words accompanied by the hiss of bullets. There were grunts of pain and agonizing cries, but these went unnoticed by Neil. Since becoming a zombie, he sometimes had terrible tunnel vision. His mind was centered completely on the hill.

For him the few blocks went by in something of a quick dream. People died around him, and people shot at him, and the rain came down in a drizzle. The only concession to safety he made was to advance up the back side of the hill. He was hit twice, losing little chunks of himself. The wounds hurt if he thought about them, which he didn't.

At the top of the hill were five houses crowded onto each other as if the owners had fought their own battle to put down stakes. In each house were a handful of men who didn't care about holding the hill at all. Their only goal in the battle was survival and to that end, none of them dared to expose themselves even to shoot.

Hundreds of wasted bullets punched holes in the Washington sky and fell harmlessly to the ground a mile away. Their own fear of death caused the deaths of many of them. They were too afraid to fight and many were too afraid to run when they had a chance.

Only when the hill was swarming with Neil's Killers did they attempt to flee, most being shot in the back as they took to their heels. The hill was won at modest cost. Neil had lost seventeen men to bullet wounds, and a further thirty who had found a good place to hide and didn't plan on coming out of their little holes for another day or two.

During this "battle," the Black Captain could have held the hill if he wished to, or he could have made the advance up it a bloody affair for Neil's men by sending in reinforcements, but he hesitated giving the orders.

The attack, perhaps because of its very foolish nature, caused the Black Captain a moment of doubt. He sat on his roof, high up on "The Hill" in Hoquiam, and watched through a telescope as Neil's Magnum Killers came on in a ragged wave, running from house to house.

He couldn't help but shake his head in wonder. "Have Raul hold his position," he directed his battlefield commander, whose only job was to relay the Captain's orders as quickly as possible. The Captain did not believe...no, he *could not* believe that this initial attack was for real. He was sure it was only a feint to draw his forces east so that his enemy could then bust through his not yet solidified lines either north or west.

It's what any competent commander would have done. And so he waited and watched, wondering where the real attack would occur.

Neil was not competent. He wasn't stupid, he just didn't know the first thing about battles, at least not from a leadership point of view. Like everyone else, he knew attack and defend, but that was about it. Since he had attacked his hill and won it, he really didn't know what else to do besides defend it, especially as the attack had been so laughably pathetic.

When he had come to the realization that they were trapped and that their only real hope had been attacking against odds, he had envisioned something much greater than the weak demonstration he had just witnessed. He had pictured his men crying *Huzzah!* and charging in one great gambit for freedom. Instead they had hung back, waiting for him to do everything. It wasn't a winning strategy.

"I think we should dig in," he told Powers.

"I guess," was Powers's mumbled reply. A piece of shrapnel had cut a groove through his mustache, slicing a small furrow through the flesh just above his lip. His beard was no longer the russet color it had been.

Neil didn't like this sort of wishy-washy answer and gave Powers a glare, which went unnoticed; Powers didn't like looking Neil in the face. Neil sighed. "Have the men set up one of them circle things around the hill."

"A perimeter?"

"Yes, a perimeter."

This would be his third mistake. Having accidentally fooled the Captain into thinking an attack was going to land somewhere else, he squandered two full hours in which he could have sent out sorties and probed for weaknesses, of which there were a surprising number.

Not a quarter of a mile away there was a hole in the Captain's lines as wide as a football field. Two miles northwest was a huge gap where the Mountain Bandits were busy hunting about for Gunner's forces and hadn't yet linked up with the Corsairs.

Neil missed his chance to escape when the Captain finally realized that Gunner had slipped away. The Captain's only consolation was that Neil had done nothing after he had trapped himself.

The Corsairs and the bandits closed in and could now attack whenever and from whatever direction they wished. Always miserly with his ammunition more than his men, the Captain decided to extend an olive branch, accept Neil's surrender, and torture the Magnum Killer to death in a very public and leisurely manner. He sent out his field commander to make the offer, certain that the ridiculously named "Killers" would agree.

Captain Dave Reedy had been promoted to his current position after the death of Phillip Gaida and Tony Tibbs. He had a lot to prove.

His chief claim as a military leader had been his time spent in Iraq during the rebuilding effort years after the second Gulf War. He told everyone who would listen that he had been Special Forces, but in truth he had been a cook, and had been receiving disability checks when the Apocalypse broke out. He had been claiming PTSD for an incident that had happened to a friend of his.

But since there was no one around anymore to set the record straight, he had used his self-proclaimed reputation to secure a position as Chief Training Officer for the Corsairs. He had trained them to bully, overpower and overawe their opponents; something that came naturally to them even without the training.

Although he was going to demand their surrender, it was the one thing that he did not want. With a proper battlefield victory, he could overshadow both Gaida and Tibbs, and that jumped-up Mark Leney. He wasn't heading up the hill to offer surrender; he was going to pick a fight.

He chose two of his most brutish thugs to accompany him. One carried a white flag insolently on one shoulder. He looked like he was ready to smack someone with it. The other walked with a gorilla-like attitude, hunched with his muscular arms crooked to show off their tremendous biceps. The two were without weapons but were completely unafraid, as if their very size and fearsome scowls would keep anyone from trying anything.

They marched up to the thrown-together defensive lines that Neil had built. Reedy laughed at what he saw. "Oh no! A bed frame! How are we going to get past a bed frame? And is that a refrigerator? I can't tell if they're having a garage sale or they've built the *Great Wall of Crap* to keep us out." The two brutes laughed at this wit as if jokes had just been invented.

"It looks like a wall of crap," the gorilla-like one echoed and then laughed again, spoiling the fun with his feeble attempt to add to the humor of the moment.

Reedy tried again. "It's a *Great Wall of Crap*, Larry. Like the one in China, right?" He gave the bed frame a quick shake. "Ooh, scary. Maybe we should be the ones surrendering."

Neil watched them from atop a minivan with something of a sneer on his face; of course, his face had a permanent sneer, so it was hard to tell if he was angry or constipated. The Magnum Killers around him looked nervous, all except Powers, who had eased back behind the van, hoping not to be seen with Neil.

"Excuse me," Neil called. Larry the gorilla looked up at him and thought he was a propped-up corpse and looked away again just as quickly, forcing Neil to try a second time, "You-hoo, up here."

"What the hell is that thing?" Reedy asked. He had planned on being disrespectful to the *n*th degree, something that he figured would be difficult because of his servile and sycophantic nature, but this was going to be a breeze—the similarity between Neil and a goblin had increased. "No, really. What am I looking at?"

The sneer on Neil's face deepened, the remains of his top lip curled back to show surprisingly white teeth. "I'm the leader here, so show some damned respect."

"*You* are the leader? Ha-ha! You've practically turned. How much time do you have left before you go full zombie? An hour? Jeeze! You know they're using you, right? They know what the Captain does to the leaders and so they made you *King Turd of Crap Mountain*. What a bunch of chickens!" He yelled this as he gazed about in contempt. No one would meet his gaze and Powers slid deeper into the shadow of the minivan.

"*King Turd of Crap Mountain,*" Neil repeated, judiciously. "That seems about right."

Reedy bent at the waist in a mock bow. "It does, your High Turdness." His two brutes also bowed, elbowing each other and chortling as they did.

"What do you want?" Neil snapped. "Did you come here to make fun of me or to talk?"

"Maybe both, King Turd."

Neil stared at Reedy as he reached into his pack and found a bag of beef jerky. He tore a chunk off with his teeth, chewed and swallowed. Without hurry, he took another bite. And another. It seemed to be making Reedy mad, and that was just fine with Neil. He hadn't needed to be reminded what would happen if they surrendered. The Captain would do terrible things to him, unconscionable things. And he would probably do similar things to the Magnum Killers as well.

But there was a chance that he would use the Killers as cannon-fodder against Grey. Even Neil knew a few hundred more soldiers could make all the difference in a battle.

And if Grey failed, the Captain could turn his full attention on Bainbridge with no one to stop him except for whatever inept force Deanna could scrape up. Neil couldn't do much to hurt the Corsairs, but he would try. He took another deliberate bite; he had to pick his own fight.

"You're just going to sit there and eat?" Reedy asked, incredulously. "Diplomats come to parley and you're just going to eat? This is a waste of my time. And it's insulting. We should leave right now."

Another bite; Neil relished the smoky flavor more than ever. "What's stopping you?" Neil knew, of course. No one went against the Black Captain's wishes.

Reedy cleared his throat and stepped closer. He spoke quietly so that only Neil and a few others could hear. "Listen up, freak. Out of the goodness of his heart, the Captain is going to allow you to surrender. It will be unconditional surrender. Your men will be protected and given the chance to return to his good graces."

"I don't believe you," Neil answered.

"A zombie doesn't believe me? That's rich. I give you my word that your men will be safe. Scouts honor." Instead of holding up his first two fingers as a real boy scout would, he only held up his middle finger.

Once more, Neil said, "I don't believe you."

"That's your choice, freak," Reedy replied with a shrug and a grin. He had done his duty and now he was going to get his battle; the idea gave him a warm feeling. "You know that when you insult me you insult the Black Captain?"

"I don't believe that either. Then again, I don't really care. There are no words in the English language to encompass the correct insult I would have for the Black Captain. But..." Now it was Neil's turn to grin. "There are some actions that might convey my hatred." He set aside the beef jerky and picked up the M16 that had been resting by his bloody thigh. There was a hole in the blingy jeans that he hadn't noticed before.

Musta got shot, he thought as he looked down the iron sights. "Any last words?" The misting rain had slicked Reedy's hair. It also made it look as though he was crying.

"Y-You can't do this!"

Neil pulled the trigger. He had been aiming center mass, but because of the wonky spin on the Corsair bullets and his own bad aim, he hit the man in the side. It was a fatal wound nonetheless since it blew out his left kidney. Gasping in pain, Reedy plopped down in the mud as his two brutes began backing away.

One wore a panicked look until Neil's next bullet smashed into his chin; he died, screaming and choking on blood. His friend was shot in the back by four different men as he tried to run away. It just seemed like the right thing to do.

"Well, that's that," Powers said, in a hollow breathless manner when the last gunshot echoed into nothing. There wasn't much else to say.

"Yep," Neil answered, taking another bite of his jerky.

The battle began an hour later. Taking a page from Jillybean's playbook, the Black Captain's Corsairs lit off the big smoke-bombs they had taken from the fleet. These did not have the effect they had hoped for since the smoke only swirled around the base of the hill without actually mounting it.

The actual bombs catapulted over the makeshift fence had a much greater impact on the battle. They destroyed parts of the wall of crap, and had men running back and forth like frightened children. There was nowhere to run.

On of the Corsairs had the idea of using a catapult to heave smoke-bombs up the hill which really only added to the confusion to what was already the most confusing battle of the war. Because there was smoke on and around the hill, the Corsair attacks seemed to occur randomly, and sometimes even accidentally. One attacking company got lost in the smoke, crested a shoulder of the hill, and went down the other side and right into another company. A fierce firefight broke out in which both sides killed each other with utter abandon.

When the will of both sides broke simultaneously, the remaining men fled only to run into more Corsairs who blasted away. The din of the battle raged in what appeared to be a black and white world where men appeared like formless wraiths, rushing out of the smoke, guns blazing.

Very little made sense.

A well-placed bomb started one of the five hilltop houses on fire. This inferno spread to another house and then a third. Not to be outdone, one of the smoke-bombs shot from a catapult did not make it to the top of the hill but landed on a slope and went rolling back down where it stopped, nestled in a thick growth of underbrush. In minutes a new fire began to spread.

Neil's battle ended after only twenty minutes or so. One of the bombs went off too close to him and tore the top of his head right off. He fell back and still couldn't manage to die like a real person. An astounding amount of blood gushed down him as if he were standing in an iron-smelling shower. Along with this came a feeling of intense exhaustion and slowly, very slowly he faded into nothing.

But he still wasn't dead. He felt like a ghost in his own body, unable to move and unable to bring himself to care.

This twilight feeling lasted well past the end of the battle which dragged on for a surprisingly long time. Blearily, Neil watched as men walked about, stripping the dead. With them were others with pitchforks or large mallets. When they came on people who were still half-alive, a sharp poke or a proper thump would end their misery.

Neil didn't even get that luxury. He looked so dead that no one poked or knocked him until nightfall and then the man doing the stabbing had a spear. He raised it up without ceremony and drove it home.

Chapter 26

As the long day faded, Deann's cell had grown smaller, grayer, colder. What hope she had diminished right along with it. What replaced it was the feeling of encroaching doom. She had made mistakes and now they were coming back to bite her in the ass.

The print analysis had proven to be inconclusive.

"That's impossible," Deanna said through gritted teeth. "Fingerprints are foolproof. No two are alike. Everyone knows that."

Sheriff Deberha Perkins sighed. "Yeah, but the one on the knife was never really good to begin with…"

"What did you do?" Deanna's eyes were at slits, the grey showing through was sharp as daggers.

"I was trying to help you and, and, I might have smudged it a little. It wasn't my fault. Look." She held up a book on processing forensic evidence. "In here it shows you all the steps there are to 'lift' a print and enhance it. My hand kinda shook and, well…" She ended with a shrug.

Deanna was glad she couldn't reach Deberha through the bars or she'd be in trouble for a second murder. "And what's going to happen to me?"

"I don't know. Norris is pushing for a preliminary trial to happen as fast as possible. He wants something like a grand jury trial, which is a trial to see if there should be a trial. I think that maybe you should consider getting a lawyer."

"No. Just getting a lawyer will cement my guilt in people's minds. Only guilty people need lawyers. Besides, who could I get?" The only people she really trusted to save her were Neil and Jillybean, both of whom were far, far away. "I'll be my own lawyer."

The idea didn't sit well with Deberha, but Deanna was adamant. "I'll need a copy of all the evidence. I mean everything."

Deberha seemed to be ready for just that request and in less than an hour, Deanna had a box of photographs on one side of her bunk and a box of statements and investigative notes on the other. There wasn't a whole lot of evidence, one way or another. The case against her was largely circumstantial, which didn't make it any less compelling. Only she had any real motive to kill

Gina. No matter what parts of the case she could attack, it would always come back to that.

Norris Barnes had meant it when he said he wanted to rush the preliminary trial—he had scheduled it for that evening, stating, "That the island's government was paralyzed in a time of crisis while the case was hanging over their heads."

The minutes before the preliminary trial crammed together, each pushing past the next in a great hurry. An hour went by in a blink and the next went by even faster. Deanna began to sweat and check the clock with every other breath, or so it seemed.

She tried to tell herself that it would be good to get the trial over with. After all, it wasn't like she was going to find some surprise witness. The island was too small for that. Everyone who had seen anything that morning had already come forward. And there wasn't going to be any new evidence discovered that would change anyone's mind. There'd be no DNA, no carpet fibers, no blurry video footage; all of that was a thing of the past.

Her only hope lay in creating doubt. That was their law: she had to be found guilty beyond reasonable doubt.

"But how?" When she looked at the few bits of evidence, it all pointed, in a very reasonable manner, to herself. "There's got to be something here." She dug again through the written evidence. The photographs were no help whatsoever and she would have to downplay them as much as possible.

Seeing Gina splayed out in a pool of her own blood would increase not only the anger in the jurists, but also the desire to enact some sort of vengeance.

"It's time." Deberha Perkins had appeared out of nowhere and now stood at the bars, looking glum. "I'm supposed to cuff you, but I'm not going to. You'll be cool, right?" Deanna only glared. "Alright. I had to ask. It's my job on the line."

"I would also like to change my clothes. There's no law saying I have to stand trial in prison clothes. That's not how they used to do it."

Deberha reluctantly agreed. Standing in the twilight outside the jail was a crowd. They had been murmuring to each other in a soft rumble; when she came out, they went silent, craning their necks to see the first person ever accused of murder on Bainbridge.

"Hello John," Deanna said with a small wave to John Houghton, a man she had known since Estes Park. "Linda. Kay, it's good to see you."

"I know you didn't do it," Kay said, her voice sounding far less confident than her words.

Deanna nodded. "I know it, too. Thanks, Kay."

She walked through the crowd with her head held high. It wasn't easy, especially as the whispers followed her all the way home and then, when she was changed, to the council chambers. The entire crowd started heading in after her; however they were stopped by Deberha and a number of newly sworn-in deputies, who pushed people back, saying things like, "Sorry about that," or, "Jimmy, you know I can't let you in."

There were two council chambers, both set in what had once been a Chinese restaurant. The fake bamboo plants and the golden dragons had been removed, but nothing seemed to get the smell of old burnt sesame oil out of the walls. The main room had always been a dark, low-ceilinged place which discouraged participation in council proceedings by the islanders. It was empty save for the slightly sticky chairs and the long banquet table which had a single, ominous candle burning on it.

"They're in the private room," Deberha told her.

Deanna gave her a thin smile; she hadn't expected them to be meeting in the alley in back. With the silk prints on the walls and the black lacquered wood, the private chamber still looked very much like it belonged in a restaurant. It was at least brightly lit.

Gathered at the far end of the long table were Norris Barnes and the other five members of the council. At Norris' right hand was soft, meek Jonathan Dunnam, the Island's Chief of Engineering and Maintenance; he had been in the long process of going bald for years and his combover had been getting more and more egregious.

Next to him was Rosanna Landeros in her usual severe grey dress and as always, her brown hair was perfectly straight. Her linear bangs cut as if a T-square had been used along with the shears. Exactly three inches under those precise bangs was a single eyebrow that crossed her forehead from end to end.

Practically rubbing elbows with Rosanna was politically hungry Andrea Clary. She had been a cheerleader some thirty years before and had used her natural charisma and unfailing smile to gain the position of Chief of Logistics, a job she had been ill-prepared for and had yet to master even after five years. She always smiled or so it seemed to Deanna. Even then she

225

wore a crooked, ill-at-ease smile that made her look like she was going to vomit, but was going to be a trooper about it.

On Norris' left was stern Wayne French, Chief of Island Security, which had been mostly ceremonial until the last few days. On Wayne's left was Karen Hentz, the newest member of the council. She fidgeted with a pen and wouldn't look up as Deanna sat down at the far end of the table. None of the council members would look at Deanna.

"Weh-ellll," Norris sighed. "What a day, right?" Deanna said nothing to this. "Okay. I guess we should have a reading of the charges against you. Sheriff?"

Deberha reached into a pocket and fetched a piece of paper, squinted at it so that her nose wrinkled, making it look as if she found the charges foul-smelling. "The defendant is facing a count of kidnapping, a count of malicious cruelty, a count of witness tampering and, lastly, murder in the first degree. It carries a sentence of death by hanging."

"How do you plead?" Norris asked.

"Not…" Deanna began, only to choke a little on the word. She tried again, "Not guilty."

"Of course," Norris said, as if put out that Deanna would want to defend herself. "Alrighty then, let's start with the first counts since they're pretty much open and shut. Sheriff Perkins can you go through the evidence on the kidnapping charge?"

Deberha had been carrying a legal yellow pad tucked up under her arm. Now she flipped the pages up and over after giving each a quick scan. "There's not much of a case," she said, giving her eyebrow a lengthy scratching, as if afraid to see the shocked look on Norris' face. "According to the old way of doing things, statements from dead witnesses are inadmissible as evidence since the defense has no way to challenge the statements or the, you know, the veracity of the person making the statement. You know what I mean?"

"You're kidding me, right?" Norris asked.

"I don't think so. Everyone agreed that we would use the old ways."

Norris leaned back in what was usually Deanna's chair; it squeaked in protest at his great weight. "It should be evidence. Why would Gina lie?"

Deberha flipped a few more pages without looking at what was written on the pages. "Revenge, maybe. Or to get sympathy.

Or maybe she was still trying to do the Captain's bidding. We don't know and there's no way to find out."

Norris started to turn red and made a few attempts to form words before he wrangled his tongue under control. "And what about Veronica? Gina said she was with them when they went to the school. What did she have to say?"

The sheriff flipped a few more pages before squinting again and saying, "Veronica said you guys went to talk to Gina, but when she wouldn't talk, you guys went out back for a smoke and to talk about the importance of getting everything out on the table. And when you guys came back in, that's when you saw Norris. Is that what happened?"

She was asking Deanna. It was a clear invitation to lie. And it would be a lie that couldn't be proven false. Still, she was governor. "I'm under no obligation to testify. Currently you have the word of an upstanding citizen of Bainbridge against that of someone who had every reason to lie. At best they cancel themselves out. If there's no other evidence, then I think we can safely dismiss the first three charges."

"Hold on," cried Norris. "What about my testimony? What about what I saw? Gina had not just come from having a smoke. She was miserable and disheveled, and she burst into tears the second you left. She wasn't acting, trust me."

"I don't trust you," Deanna stated, baldly. "Not when it comes to the acting skills of these people. According to her own written statement, she and Eddie had been fooling us for years. I don't know how many times Gina looked me right in the eyes and lied with a straight face. And Joslyn..." Deanna couldn't finish. Anger welled up inside her so fiercely that she thought her chest would burst.

Four of the six council members began nodding and glancing at one another. Norris shrugged at the unspoken agreement. "I think we can lay those charges aside, at least for now. The murder charge is not something you're going to be able to explain away." He gestured to Deberha.

"Yeah, well, on that, I don't know what to say. She had motive, that's true, but so did a lot of people. Everyone loved Emily so much. And they loved Steve and Flash, too. From a motive perspective, a lot of people had one."

"Come on, Deberha!" Norris cried. "Who loved Todd enough to kill Gina? Or Flash Gordon? Please. They were great guys, but they didn't have loved ones or family. And Neil was something of a ghost. No, this was over Emily." Deberha gave the smallest of shrugs and went back to hiding behind her notes. "Okay, Deberha tell us about opportunity."

"Yeah, that's where things get a bit tricky. There's only two sets of keys to the cell. I have one and the other is kept up at the Governor's mansion."

Jonathan Dunnam patted his combover before asking, "And is that where you found the keys during your investigation?"

Deanna answered before the sheriff could. "They were in my coat pocket, but I had them on me only because I had forgotten to put them back from the night before."

A long silence greeted this. Finally, Andrea Clary, a pitying smile replacing the queered-up one, said, "So are you suggesting that Deberha might have killed Gina? If you didn't do it and she had the only other key, what else are we supposed to take away from your statement?"

"I had the keys at the station," Deberha put in, quickly. "Anyone could have snuck in and snagged them."

"Anyone in a twenty-minute span?" Norris asked. "You said you were only gone for twenty minutes and when you came back you said you found the body. *And* that it was cold."

Deberha flipped her pages until she found one that she wanted. "I said it was *getting* cold."

Norris softly thumped both of his meaty fists on the table in frustration. "I know you want to protect your friend, Deberha but we need the truth. Give us the last bits of evidence and then I'm going to need you to step out of the room."

She dropped her head and told everyone that the knife which had killed Gina had been used by a woman or possibly a teenaged boy. "And lastly, someone…a woman, wearing a tan jacket and black slacks, was seen leaving the station around the time of the murders."

"And we all know what Deanna was wearing earlier," Norris said. "A tan jacket and black slacks. That'll be all Deberha." Norris barely waited for the door to close before he raised his hand. "I've seen enough. All in favor of sending this to trial?"

Every hand went up, but only for a second, then they were hidden away beneath the table, as if the council members were ashamed of their vote.

"The ayes have it, six to zero," Norris intoned, sounding both relieved and saddened. "Now that we've got that settled, I think the question should be, do we even need a trial, Deanna? Your only defense is to pretend that someone set you up. You know that even with all the evidence against you, some people will believe it. They'll start looking at us as the bad guys and in the end, it could tear this community apart. I think you should try to see your way clear to do the right thing."

"And what is the right thing?" Right and wrong were very muddled in her mind just then.

"The right thing would be for you to plead guilty and throw yourself on the mercy of the court. I, for one, don't want to see you hang. I think I can promise banishment in your case."

But I didn't do anything! Deanna wanted to scream. She knew screaming it wouldn't do any good. Someone had set her up perfectly. "I-I'm going to need some time."

"It'll be time spent in jail," Norris told her. "I hope you understand. And you will have to be in cuffs from here on out. For Deberha's sake I think you shouldn't fight that. I've let it slide, but now, after this, we can't."

Deanna didn't remember agreeing to the cuffs; she didn't fight them either. Her wrists were held out for her, and the moment they were locked on, she was pushed out into the waiting crowd. It had grown from forty to four hundred, and the raw emotion of it had grown as well. Questions were thrown at her like rocks.

Did you do it?
Are you guilty?
Why did you try to set Norris up?

There were more. The questions hit her from all sides until she found herself wobbling, her head turning this way and that. She was pasty, her hands jittering in their cuffs, and she was no longer nodding or smiling to her friends.

The walk back seemed to take forever and the whole way Deberha kept up a constant whisper in her ear, "It'll be okay. Don't listen to them. Let's just get you back to the prison. You'll be safe there and everything will be fine."

Of course, it wouldn't be fine. She was looking at a death sentence, and a quick one at that. As she and Deberha were walking out the door, they had heard Norris talking about setting up the trial in two days' time if Deanna didn't "do the right thing."

"What should I do?" she asked Deberha when the cell door was finally closed. Inside the cage she felt safe for the first time since she had left it.

Deberha took off her hat and began spinning it in nervous circles in front of her chest. "I don't know. The case against you is pretty tight. I tried to help. You saw that, right? I did what I could, but the evidence just sort of fell into place. I mean, finding the knife right after you accuse Norris? That was like bad luck or something."

"Yeah, but what should I do? Do I take the plea bargain? What happens if Emily comes back? She'll be welcome, right?"

"I'll take her in," Deberha assured Deanna. "That's a promise. And I'll make sure no one says anything to her." That was an impossible promise, which Deanna ate up and believed. She clutched at the lie and hung on to it. It was, perhaps, the only thing that allowed her to sleep that night.

After a dreary meal of lukewarm lentil soup brought by her assistant Shelley Deuso, who made sure not to touch anything at all, going so far as to walk with her arms scrunched in to avoid scraping against the clearly germ-covered walls, Deanna drifted off to sleep.

She had chaotic, half-realized dreams and woke in a sweat, a chill dissipating on the air. Groggily, she gazed around, trying to get her bearings in the gloom of the holding area. Something was out of place, but she didn't know what until she heard the lightest *click* coming from the rear of the facility—someone had just left and they had left stealthily.

Deanna sat up, quickly, thinking that she was being set up again. Her heart shuddered, afraid that when she sat up there would be a dead body in the cage with her. There wasn't and she whispered a quick, "Thank God!" Her relief did not last. There wasn't a body, but there was a note lying on the floor of her cell; it seemed to gleam with a light of its own.

At first, she was afraid to touch it and she approached it warily like a mouse sensing a trap. And like the mouse, she was unable to stop herself. She picked it up by the very edge and, glancing at it, was momentarily transported back to before the apocalypse. The words on the paper had been clipped from an old newspaper.

If you want Emily to come back in one piece, do not plead guilty! You will follow my instructions to the letter. You now serve the black captain.

"Yes," she whispered. She would do anything for Emily. She would even betray her people for her. Her only consolation was that from jail, she couldn't do much of anything, and if she could be "sprung" it wouldn't make much of a difference. She'd be just one woman, hunted as a murderer.

Or so she thought.

She was just in the process of flushing the note down the toilet when someone slit Norris Barnes' throat wide open.

The knife, with a single bloody print, would be found the next day by Jonathan Dunnam as he went to take out his garbage. He shrieked like a girl and two hours later Deanna Grey walked out of her cage, not just as a free woman, but also as Governor.

Chapter 27

High up on the roof of the Black Captain's house in Hoquiam was a widow's walk. He stood at the end of it, as if it were the end of a diving board, a glass of cabernet in his hand and a satisfied smile on his face.

Yes, he was very satisfied. Not perfectly satisfied; no, he was old enough to know that perfection was impossible and that attempting to get it would only end in frustration.

It had been a good day. The Magnum Killers had been annihilated, the Governor of Bainbridge was now his puppet, and the disparate groups of mountain bandits had put aside their differences to join him. Better yet, they had turned out to be better fighters than his own Corsairs.

There had been minor setbacks: Emily Grey had been killed, uselessly as it turned out; the little army, led by an inhuman creature named Gunner, had somehow managed to disappear into the Olympic National Forest; the *Queen's Revenge* had made an impressive getaway, somehow sinking over a dozen ships in the process; and Mark Leney was still upright and breathing, something the Captain found hard to stomach.

He hated the idea that he was being forced to reward Leney with command of the army instead of flaying him alive.

"He'll be dead soon enough," the Captain told himself, patting one of the twin .44 caliber Colt Anaconda revolvers that he carried strapped to his narrow hips. They all would be: Leney, Gunner, the ridiculous kid queen racing back down to San Francisco. She was cute, but not cute enough to keep around.

Besides, he already had a queen.

A few feet to his left stood Jillybean gazing at him in dark silence. She was also something of a disappointment. He had wanted to break her good and proper, but so far, The Cadaver had nothing to show for his efforts. She had slipped into this glaring, sneering state and nothing he had done to her had made the slightest difference.

"I've tried some minor electrocution, strangulation, waterboarding, beatings," he paused, sighing. "I've even threatened to have her gang raped...I wouldn't have actually done it without your permission, of course. I got the biggest, meanest men I could find and had them strip in front of her. All she did was bare her teeth as if she was looking forward to biting their wangs clean off. I believe I'm going to have to up the ante a bit."

"Just don't mark up her face," the Captain had answered. "I want her to look the same so that her adoring subjects will think that she caved easily."

The Cadaver had almost smiled. "Always the tactician. I'll begin in the morning. Don't keep her up too late. I want her fresh."

The Captain was going to keep her out as late as he pleased. He turned from her and gazed out into the night. A few miles away on a lonely, corpse-strewn hilltop, a few fires were still burning. "That's where your Magnum Killers died to a man. Nothing more than the traitors deserved. And that way," he pointed north, "is where the last bit of your army is running away. We both know how that's going to turn out."

It was going to be *another* victory for the Black Captain. Although the Olympic Peninsula was large, hiding five-hundred men would be impossible, especially since they were lucky to have a day's worth of food. They would have to hunt, scrounge and forage, all of which would slow them down and make it easier for the Captain's men to track them.

"We'll pick up their trail in the morning," he told her. "And once they've been dealt with, it'll be Bainbridge's turn next. And, thanks to poor little Emily, it'll finally fall. You see, Mommy doesn't realize she's dead and, by the time she does, it'll be too late. She'll have opened the gates to us. I look forward to wintering there before heading south to finish off the last bit of resistance in San Francisco and Highton. What do you think?"

She only glared all the more fiercely and he was sure that if her hands weren't cuffed and big Eustace wasn't there guarding her, she would've tried to push him off the roof.

He laughed at her. "Make your mean faces while you can. Pretty soon you'll be like all the rest of the skanks walking around here. You won't dare look me in the eye." She was looking now, and the hatred practically smoldered out of her. "I know you're in there, Jillybean. I know you're hiding, but I'll drag you out, trust me on that."

Jillybean was inside and she was hiding. She knew it was wrong to hide. She had responsibilities. People needed her. Grey was in a bad way and it sounded like Deanna was in even worse trouble. Thousands of lives depended on her and yet she was beyond terrified. The Cadaver was infamous. He had never failed to break someone and once you were broken, you remained broken forever.

The truth was she had not been overcome by the horrifying black force inside her—the *It*—in a way, she had welcomed it.

She was no longer the Queen; that woman was gone. In her place was a small, scared little girl. She was so very weak and so easily hurt. Her body was fragile and if she got hurt, who could help her?

The *It* would make everything alright in a way that the others inside her couldn't. Eve was pure selfishness. She was Jillybean's uncontrolled desires. Sometimes it seemed like she was pure evil, but these moments were like temper-tantrums compared to the terror that the *It* could harness. Ernest Smith was something of a controlled version of Eve. He was as selfish as she, but used Jillybean's mind to get what he wanted. He appeared to be the ultimate evil because he was so calculating and cold.

Neither could hold a candle to the thing that she had once hidden deep inside her. The fire of *Its* hatred was something beyond measure. It scared Jillybean worse than anything, and at the same time, it was comforting. The vile, monstrous heat it generated had blotted out the electricity The Cadaver had sent through her body, and it made the water torture seem like a day at the beach. The sharp whacks with the baton to her elbows, knees and the bottom of her feet had felt like only taps, and the bag over her head had been meaningless.

Breathing was nothing compared to the hunger to kill the Black Captain.

It wanted that more than anything, perhaps because *It* thought that all of their problems would end with the death of the Captain.

Despite the madness, *It* wasn't entirely stupid. *It* endured and waited, looking for the right moment to strike.

The roof seemed like a perfect chance and there was a second where the Black Captain was looking out at the fires and the brute had glanced back at a sound. *It* was just about to lunge forward and throw herself at the Captain. They would have both gone over the side, where a thirty-foot drop awaited them.

No! Jillybean cried, afraid that the fall would only break their body and that they would be left in misery until The Cadaver came back. She could imagine him grinding her broken bones together, or taking a hammer to the remains until she was nothing but a fleshy bag of fragments.

Her mental scream had been a jolt and the moment passed before *It* could recover; they didn't get another chance.

"Have a good night," the Black Captain said, a few minutes later, his smile very white in his ebony face.

It spat at him.

He glared. "That's unbecoming of a queen. If you're not careful I won't treat you as a fallen queen, and you really don't want that. Your life would be *more* unpleasant. I could have The Cadaver sew your mouth shut. Would you like that?"

Before *It* could spit again, David Eustace crushed his large hands over her mouth, bruising her lips. He manhandled her back down to her cell. She fought him every step of the way. Even with her hands cuffed, she was a wildcat and it took two of them to get her into her cell.

"Freaking psycho," Eustace muttered as he went back to his chair and his little book. "I'll be glad when my shift is over." He checked his watch; a gold-trimmed stainless-steel Rolex that would have cost a fortune, fifteen years before.

It glared at him, the hatred reaching a peak that turned their shared mind to a hurricane of static. This wasn't something that *It* could manage forever. After a minute, her shoulders slumped. She turned and went to squat in the corner, like a child being punished.

Eustace snorted and repeated, "Freaking psycho," as he started to thumb to where he had dog-eared a page. *It* squatted in silence for a few minutes before she slowly cranked her head around so that her chin was on her shoulder. She could see Eustace's lips moving; he was back into the thread of his book.

"You'll get us out of here," *It* said to Jillybean, speaking in a gravelly, alien whisper. "You know what to do."

"I have a few ideas, but he's right there. You can't expect me to…"

It cut her off. "You'll get us out of here." It was an unquestionable demand. "You know what to do." It was a statement of complete belief—and strangely, Jillybean did know what to do. She just didn't want to do it. The danger involved in an escape like this was fantastic. Too many things could go wrong; there were too many unaccountable variables. There was too much un-assessed risk. There were too many hurdles.

She was handcuffed—locked in a cage—closely guarded—locked in a basement with the lock on the wrong side of the door—the house was filled with armed men—and lastly, she had no idea where the Captain's room was, and what sort of protective measures he might have in place.

"You will do this."

Jillybean could not fight against this demand anymore than she could fight against her own heart beating. Her hands started to move without her compelling them to; it felt like there were huge spiders attached to her wrists. She struggled to catch up.

Her hands were cuffed in front while her key was sewn into her belt at the back; this was no problem, all she had to do was undo the belt and slide it off. In no time, she had the cuffs off and had the tiny, inch-long razor blade out. The *It* began to grow excited and her hands started to move too quickly.

"No!" Jillybean snapped, pulling her hands back. "Gently, or we'll be dead in seconds."

Along the hem of her long leather coat was sewn a double-wrapped ounce of Fluorosulfuric acid in powder form, and in the left sleeve was another double bag of powder, this one a formula of her own making. Although the Fluorosulfuric acid was powerful enough to dissolve metal, it was nowhere near as lethal as the extremely toxic mixture of *Thiophosphonate*—the base chemical for VX gas, and *Atrazine*—a powerful pesticide.

Ingesting or breathing in the tiniest amount would lead to blindness and temporary full-body paralysis. There was no room for error when dealing with the substance; an ill-timed sneeze could find her on the floor twitching like a dying bug.

She sat down and stripped off one of her thigh-high boots...

"What are you doing?" Eustace demanded, looking up from his book. Without answering, she pulled off a black sock and laid it on the floor. "Hey! I asked you a ques...What is that?" She yanked her shirt up around her nose before taking the double-bagged nerve agent out and laying it next to the sock. "Is that drugs?" He sounded nervous, as if he was hoping that it was drugs.

Taking a deep breath and holding it, she took the smaller bag from the larger one, shook out a teaspoon of powder onto the sock and then resealed the bag. The second bag went into the first, her movements very careful and precise.

"Your cuffs?" Eustace was suddenly nervous. He knew she had already escaped from one prison. Everyone had assumed that the jailers had tried to rape her and that she had managed to get a gun from one of them; too late, Eustace was starting to have his doubts. Jillybean folded the sock twice, stood and walked directly toward Eustace, who had retreated, scared now, but unsure why.

Just as his back hit the wall behind him, she threw the sock. Her timing was perfect. He was just looking over her shoulder when he saw the sock sailing at him. His only chance was to duck and run, but it was just a sock. Instead, he flinched and turned, quick enough to avoid the sock, but finding himself half-facing the wall when the sock hit it. The deadly powder plumed like dust, which he sucked into his lungs with his next breath.

His lungs were paralyzed first, then, a split second later, his eyes froze open. He grabbed his throat just as the muscles of his face spasmed, turning him into some sort of sideshow freak. His jaws clenched, and teeth cracked and broke. Now his hands turned to claws and his arms contorted with a snapping sound.

Expressionless, still halfway between worlds, Jillybean watched from the corner of her cell. She wanted to feel sympathy, but it wouldn't come. The It was all around her like a black cloud, dampening her feelings and turning her cold and mechanical. She barely felt the desperate need to breathe. Backing as far away as she could, she took a tentative breath and didn't die—it was something of a disappointment.

Death might not have been a bad thing just then.

Glancing over, she spied the pitcher of water next to her mattress. The water was a blessing. She washed her hands; her right hand was already burning and beginning to crimp. In spite of the pain, she worked her hand, her fingers, and her wrist, forcing it back into full compliance.

And all the while, Eustace died a slow, horrible death. It took forty-two minutes before the last hitch left his chest. It was horrible and agreeably quiet. By the time he was finally dead, she had her boot back on, a part of her pillowcase wrapped around her face, and the cell door open.

With the last of the nerve toxin and a wire pulled from an old extension cord, she set a trap on the stairs. It was only a simple wire snare that ran to the plastic bag that she had hooked to a nail in the rafter. Anyone who tripped it would be enveloped in a light dusting, which was enough to kill two-dozen men.

Escape up the stairs was impossible and so she assessed the squat little windows that were set high-up on the basement walls; each had inch-thick bars over them. Trying to saw through these would take hours. She hoped that the Fluorosulfuric acid would act more quickly.

With her face still covered, she stepped past Eustace, grabbed his chair and carried it to the window furthest from his body. After propping up the window, she brought out the acid. It was so fantastically corrosive that she didn't dare let the smallest bit of powder touch any part of her as she sprinkled it around the base of the middle bar. The ledge was damp from the rain and it immediately started to hiss and smolder.

She leaned back away from the fumes, guessing that they were deadly as well. The wisps of smoke didn't last, so she added more acid and a sprinkle of water. This did the trick and she had to back away again as the fumes made her eyes water and her throat constrict.

"That's what we needed," Jillybean said a few minutes later when the smoke cleared. There was a little crater burned into the cement and the bottom of the bar had been melted clear away. The bar took a little convincing to come all the way out and when it did, she had a gap of just about a foot wide and fifteen inches high, which was good enough for a slim young lady like her.

Once free of the house, she took one step toward the wire fence, but only one step. *It* would not allow her to go any further. Freedom wasn't what *It* was after. Jillybean tried to fight against the darkness, only to be swallowed up in a blink.

"There's no escape," *It* told her. "You of all people should know that."

Jillybean didn't know whether *It* was talking about escaping the town or from within the darkness.

It didn't matter one way or the other. The *It* was too strong, too enormous, too horrible. It was in control and was still hot for blood. Jillybean watched herself as she bent and found a brick that had once sat perfectly aligned with dozens of its brothers to form a walkway along the side of the house. Now the formation was buckled and ruined, no one giving a single thought to the bricks for ten years. No one but her.

She liked the feel of it in her hand. She hefted it, letting it bob as she made her way to the edge of the front porch where she heard the long, tired breath of a bored guard. As well she heard scraping that didn't make sense to her.

He's carving something, Jillybean told the *It*. Jillybean hadn't gone deep within her own subconscious; *It* wanted her nearby for just such observations. *He's got a knife in his hand, we should get out of here.*

Observations were welcome, recommendations were not. As if the brick was a much more powerful weapon than it was, the girl went fearlessly over the railing, as quiet as a breeze. The guard was bent over, gathering his shavings into a pile when the old boards of the porch gave her away. He sat straight up, while she charged the six feet between them, the brick raised high. Uselessly, he held the knife up as if to threaten her.

It ignored the knife and dashed the brick full in the guard's face. The brick destroyed the man's right eye-socket and turned the orb into a mismatched glob of snot. The man was concussed by the blow and was already falling over when the brick caved in his temple. *It* used the knife to finish the job, driving it into his crushed skull up to the hilt.

It then sat hunched over her kill, watching, listening, waiting to see if anyone had heard the muffled thuds.

No one had. His M4 was sitting against his chair. It was locked and loaded and, with a flick of her thumb, it was ready to fire. And so was she. Her heart was racing. Her pulse was a perfect thrum in her mind. Her feet were light, and her steps were soundless.

The front door was locked. *It* considered resurrecting Jillybean, but she didn't like the limiting effect the old Queen had on her. Jillybean had morals and rules and ideas that went far beyond killing the Black Captain. All *It* really wanted was to kill and then perhaps to wallow in the kill. Yes, coating herself in his blood, perhaps even drinking it while it was still hot was the way *It* wanted to cap off the night.

She tapped on the door.

"Whaaaat?" a voice answered, dragging the word out in irritation.

"Gotta take a crap," *It* answered in a low growl.

"And you can't wait an hour for shift change? Son of a bitch." The lock thunked back and the door started to open.

It charged in, moving low and fast, driving the knife into the man's diaphragm, a much surer strike than trying to slip the big blade between the third and fourth intercostal spaces. Sliding the blade up paralyzed what was left of the diaphragm, keeping the man from making a peep. His mouth went so wide, the *It* figured she could drive her fist down into it and if she could drive her fist in, she certainly could drive the knife as well.

The knife came free of the man's thorax and went through the back of his throat a second later. When he died, the only sound he made was his teeth biting down on the blade as his muscles spasmed. *It* sat over the man, a smile on her face. "You deserved that, you son of a bitch," *It* whispered. A new sound to her right caused the *It* to leap up. *It* left the knife and swung the M4 around.

To the slave standing with her back to the wall and her hands by her sides in the designated subservient posture, *It* looked like a small, black demon, squatting over a fresh kill. The slave wasn't wrong.

"Where is he?" *It* asked in a soft, hungry voice. The slave was too frightened to say a word. Her eyes bugged out of her bruised face and all she could do was swallow reflexively, over and over.

It shut and locked the door behind her, before going to the girl and shoving the M4 into her soft stomach, pressing it deep. "Where is the Black Captain? What room?"

The slave's head began to go back and forth in tiny arcs. "He'll kill me if I tell you that."

Its huge blue eyes turned to huge blue chunks of ice and she was about to smash the girl in the face with the butt of the gun.

"Then don't," whispered Jillybean to the slave. It was her own voice that she heard, and it made her hesitate in confusion, not quite understanding how she could suddenly speak. Her hands were not her own, and when she tried to turn away it felt as though she were falling into darkness.

She fought her way back, searching for the slave from out of the shadows. "Who are you?" Jillybean asked, in something of a ghostly whisper.

"Glenda Jensen," the woman answered. Glenda looked and acted like an abused animal. She bore too many scars to count. Her lank hair grew in patches and where there was no hair, there was only the ugliness left behind from where parts of her scalp had been torn away by the roots. If it was possible, her teeth were worse. They had no general direction or standard color, some being black and dead, others grey and loose in her gums.

Jillybean suddenly understood why she was at least partially there. Pity had stayed *Its* hand. The fire of her hate had been doused ever so slightly by the sight of the woman cowering before her.

"Okay, Glenda, don't tell me where he is. Tell me where he isn't. Like this: he's not on the first floor or the second floor…do you understand?"

Glenda was so very nearly paralyzed with fear that she could barely nod. "H-He's n-not on this floor and h-he's n-not on the third floor."

"Good. When I get to the second floor, is his door not on the right or the left?"

"He's not on the left and his door is not the first or second one."

Before Jillybean could thank the girl, she was falling back into the darkness of her mind. *It* fought to the surface where everything was annoying and hateful. Her feet on the carpeted stairs were scritchy and loud, and the stupid light hurt her eyes so that she wanted to crush them shut, and the feel of the gun in her hands was maddening. All she wanted was to start shooting. She knew for certain that once she started blasting away all of it would all go away.

Because they will kill you! Jillybean tried to scream but her voice was muffled by the darkness that tried to thrust down into her open mouth and choke what little life she had left right out of her. Jillybean managed to spit the stuff out just as *It* got to the Black Captain's door.

The handle turned under her grip. In spite of the overwhelming demand to simply start shooting, *It* moved slowly. Slow enough to stop when she saw the glint of a chain pulling across the other side of the door. Jillybean hoped that she would be needed so she could try to talk some sense into the dark thing that dwelled inside of her.

But she wasn't needed. This sort of lock was so easily picked that anyone with a bit of stiff wire could use it to slide the chain out of its groove. In no time, the door was open, and she was looking down on the Black Captain. Although his dark features blended with the shadows, she thought he looked different. Weaker. Vulnerable. He breathed loudly, just like a bulldog.

It hated the sound and *It* hated him with every part of her being. She wanted to kill him and yet she wanted to drag the moment out, to make it last. The hunger for killing won out and

241

she raised the rifle and fired every bullet in the gun into him. His blood was soft and warm and utterly delicious.

Chapter 28

Even with the dark and unfamiliar land, the two men moved soundlessly. In spite of their youth, they were both veteran hunters, practiced at stalking game even while they were being stalked in turn.

Troy Holt trusted his spear and carried it easily, while Stu Currans crept forward with his M4 at his shoulder. They were halfway into a twelve-mile trip that would lead them to the southern shore of Grays Harbor. Supposedly, it was the "safe" shore.

Nothing had been safe so far. The land was scrub combined with ancient hardened dunes. There was little in the way of cover, which shouldn't have been an issue except there had been a surprising amount of activity for being the middle of the night. The explosions and gunfire out on the harbor had riled the dead and now they were stomping around everywhere, their inhuman moans echoing back and forth.

Along with the moans were the growly, unexpected voices of Corsairs. During the wild chase that sent the *Queen's Revenge* flying south, quite a number of Corsair boats were sunk or driven onto the rocks, and now those crew members who had been fortunate enough to make it to shore were being hunted by the dead.

It had been a long hunt that had drained the energy out of the humans, while leaving the zombies fresh. When the dead found one of the Corsairs, there would be a brief flurry of gunfire followed by shockingly high screams that seemed to bring the storm above them to a standstill while they lasted.

"No one deserves that," Troy said in a whisper. He was saddened by the pain that his enemies were in, something Stu couldn't understand.

"An eye for an eye, if you ask me," he mumbled, quoting one of the few bits of scripture that he knew. He was a Christian, just not a very knowledgeable one, and demonstrated that by adding, "What goes around comes around."

Troy sighed and leaned on his spear as if it were a shepherd's crook. "Remember, it is not for us to pass judgment. The Lord God has the final say in all things. We're supposed to love our enemies. It's one of the things, one of the concepts, that I've always struggled with."

Stu tried not to roll his eyes. "Maybe we can love some enemies, just not the Corsairs. The things they've done, man, I don't even know if you can call them human. And if they're not human I don't have to love them. I probably shouldn't. I bet that's in the Bible. Thou shalt not love demons."

"It's not."

A new scream; this one so filled with terror that Stu shuddered. "It should be. And it's probably implied." Stu was done with the ridiculous conversation. Love his enemies? Bah! It was the dumbest thing he had ever heard. No one could love a Corsair. He crept from behind a downed tree and started to angle away from the sound of the zombie. It was eating the Corsair now and amid the screams, there was a sickening crunching noise as its teeth cracked through bones. This was nothing compared to the dizzying slurping sound that came next.

Troy took Stu's arm as he wobbled. "You know the Queen tried to love her enemies." Stu gave him a shocked, angry look as if he wasn't just completely appalled by the idea, but also insulted that it could be said aloud. "It's true," Troy insisted, "and until earlier tonight I resisted...no, I hated the thought of it. I thought that deep down, she had to be as evil as they were. You know, birds of a feather flock together."

"She's not evil," Stu said, forcefully. Softer, with less assurance, he added, "She's only kinda, you know, mental."

"Mental or not, she is forgiving of her enemies. From what everyone says, if you kneel before her, she allows you into her kingdom. That's exactly what God does." Troy paused right out in the open as he followed this unexpected tangent to a startling conclusion: Jillybean was a better Christian than he was!

It was such a shocking idea that he was still standing there when Stu saw two shadows moving their way. Stu pulled the young Guardian down and tried to hide in the hip-height brown grass that seemed to grow everywhere. Hip-height or not, the grass was thin, and they were easily visible from a few feet away. They were fortunate that the two Corsairs coming their way were not actually looking for anyone. They were hiding from the zombies as well.

The two got down into the grass and began crawling, passing within a few feet of Stu and Troy.

"South is that way," one of them said, pointing.

"Thanks," was all Stu could think to say.

"There's all sorts of grey meat back that way," the other Corsair added, nodding back the way they had come.

"Okay, thanks," Stu said, and then pulled Troy along in the same direction they had been traveling. They hurried to the tree-line, where they heard branches snapping and the growls of the dead. Without words passing between them, they slunk down and moved to their left, skirting the zombies. There were more of them further on, groaning and stumbling in a wide band.

Again, the two acted without relying on a discussion. They were both experienced woodsman who had grown up with the zombie threat hanging over their heads. Troy found a rock and hurled it away, causing the groaning, slow-moving zombies to roar and burst into action. They thrashed through the forest, passing within yards of the two young men.

Then they were in the clear, save for a few hobbled, partial zombies that were missing huge chunks or limbs, and in one case, a large amount of its head.

They left the groans and the screams behind them as they trekked north while a soft, cold rain fell. It was slow going since they could never tell if there were Corsairs hidden in the smattering of homes or slunk down in the woods. The few zombies left behind were easier to locate and circle around. Eventually, with dawn breaking behind a bank of grey murk off to their right, they came to the harbor they had fled from only hours before.

Across the water from them was the fortified town of Hoquiam; a dark haze from a hundred cooking fires rising over it made it seem like a dirty place even from far away. In a wide arc in front of the town, their masts jutting up like so many spikes, was most of what had once been the Queen's fleet. They were Corsair ships once again, and they proudly floated in a sea of garbage.

In the harbor were a handful of black boats, zigzagging back and forth. "They're looking for survivors," Troy said, sounding tired, knowing that if Emily hadn't been found yet, she would in the next few minutes, and there was nothing he could do about it.

Except try to rescue her. "I guess we go with plan B." He tried to give Stu a nonchalant little smile, only it came out crooked as a dog's leg. Even with his vast faith in God, he had more than just a tingle of fear running down his back at the idea of walking into the lair of the Corsairs. It was a place of boundless misery. It was a place of evil. It was the earthly equivalent of hell, and Troy felt that if he went there without an army of angels accompanying him, he would not come out again.

Stu was feeling the same, except he didn't have Troy's faith. Angels weren't going to save him. Across the water was where he would die. He swallowed with a clicking noise loud in his ears. Embarrassed, he asked, "Plan B? How did we get to plan B so fast? And what is Plan B?"

"We break into the town, free both Emily and the Queen, and then escape. Any ideas how we go about accomplishing this?"

"None whatsoever," Stu answered, feeling the sharp edge of his fear dull slightly, knowing that he wasn't going into that terrible place alone. "I guess we take things one step at a time. The first thing to do is to get across the water." It seemed like a simple thing, except the northern shore was four miles away as the crow flies.

Stu looked to his right where part of a black boat was crumpled nose first in the rocks; it looked like an old cigarette that had been stubbed out. Beyond it was a fourteen-mile hike along the southern shore which was littered with bodies, torn streamers of sails and who knew how many zombies. It was a hike that would take them most of the day.

Going the other direction meant almost as long of a hike, interspersed with a mile swim across the mouth of the harbor. A mile was a long way to swim on a nice day; this was hardly a nice day and the thought of battling the current and the cold, choppy water while burdened with gear and weapons was too much and they both decided to go east.

Troy was all set to get moving; however, Stu needed a rest. He had been on the go for days on end and, after another night without sleep, he felt sort of hollow and jittery. "I need just an hour or two of sleep, and maybe something to eat. Then I'll be good to go."

They set off to find somewhere to bed down for a brief spell and it wasn't long before they came across a snug little home in a snug little community with a fine view of the harbor.

Snug or not, everything about the house smelled of the ocean and everything was damp to the touch, though not nearly as damp as Stu, who had been walking in the rain for most of the night. Still in his coat, he collapsed on the first bed he found and fell into a deep sleep. He was so out of it that he slept through the explosion that killed Ryley McCartt. Troy had been dozing next to a small fire he had made, and he came awake with a start at the rumbling sound, which he took for thunder at first. He sat there for a few seconds with his head cocked and his ears pricked. When nothing immediately followed, he slipped back into his semi-state of sleep.

Two hours later, gunfire woke them both. It was a more urgent sound and they staggered out onto the front lawn of the snug little house and watched as a Corsair ship exchanged fire with someone on shore. They were shooting at Neil Martin, which Stu and Troy had no way of knowing, just like they didn't know it was the Magnum Killers trying to cross the mouth of the bay using a bunch of half-submerged pews as rafts. They were so far away that the heads looked like just more trash in the water.

The pair were trying to puzzle out what was going on when they were unexpectedly hailed. "Hey guys," a smiling Corsair said, giving them a friendly wave. He was standing in front of the next home over, giving his backside a good scratching with his non-waving hand. "What do you think the deal is?"

At the sight of him, Stu started reaching for the .40 caliber Taurus he carried in his coat pocket; then he saw two more Corsairs standing behind the first. They were all properly armed, while Troy only had his spear.

"Don't know," Stu answered, trying to match the friendly tone, as if it was no big deal that he was standing there talking to a mortal enemy.

Next to him, Troy wore the oddest look. It was almost as if his natural hatred for the murdering Corsairs was being canceled out by some sort of need to show forgiveness. Stu shot him a look, which he missed.

"I think our guys might have come upon a stray turncoat," another put in, squinting with such determination that his eyes looked like they had folded into their deep sockets. "Maybe it's one of them clansmen. I hope it is. I hated those guys." Everyone agreed that the Coos Bay Clan was the worst.

When Neil managed to finally drive away the boat, there was a general cursing by the Corsairs which was followed by an argument as to which boat had turned tail, embarrassing them all in the process. It was a long argument since they couldn't even agree as to what size the boat was. The only thing they could agree on was that the boat was crewed by either a bunch of pansies or by a troop of girl scouts.

During the back and forth, two more Corsairs showed up. One turned his dirty head from the fight and gazed a long time at clean-shaven Troy Holt. "What was your ship?" he asked.

Troy's head seemed to move in slow motion as it cranked around to face Stu, who felt a moment of panic as he blurted out: "The *Sea King*."

"The *Sea King*? Hold on, she blew up down in San Francisco. I meant what ship were you on last night?"

Stu floundered for the name of a ship. All the ones he could remember had been sunk, burned to cinders or blown to smithereens. The *Captain Jack* had gone down beneath Stu on an empty shore far to the south; The *Rapier* had been dashed to pieces against the rock that was Alcatraz; *The Saber,* with Mike captaining it, had gone up in flames taking two larger Corsair ships with her. Even the *Puffer* was no more.

Before Stu could come up with a viable lie, Troy told the truth. "We were on the *Queen's Revenge* last night." He stated this with such forceful calm assurance that there was a challenging edge to his words. Stu's mouth fell open.

"The *Revenge*?" the Corsair asked, half his face cocked upward in a look of shocked surprise. "The Queen's ship? How on earth did you get on it? You chummy with Leney?"

"The Queen thought I was cute," Troy answered, setting off howls of derisive laughter.

"Cute? Like a baby duck?"

"Aw, look at the widdle cutie pie! Did she make you shave off your beard?" one asked, falling down from his wit.

Another, practically in tears, asked, "Did she make you shave your downstairs as well? How's the bikini zone this morning? Chilly, I bet!"

Amid the gales of laughter, Stu found himself staring at Troy with a stunned look. He did not know Troy very well at all; they had only met the night before, after all, but already he got the feeling that he was one of those extra devout Guardians who wouldn't lie under any circumstance. The Queen must have called him cute.

Troy caught the look and suddenly remembered the stories and rumors that had swirled aboard the *Queen's Revenge* concerning the Queen. One in particular had shocked him; she had poisoned the new queen, Jenn Lockhart, as well as Mike

Gunter and Stu Currans, supposedly the only man she had ever loved.

Because the previous night had been filled with explosions, chases, death and double-crossings, *and* because Troy was not one to put faith in gossip, he did not know the truth, at least, not until that very moment. The pain in Stu's eyes went deep.

"It wasn't actually the Queen who said it," Troy added, quickly, hoping to soften the blow. "It was one of the people in her head. Eve."

Although this set off another round of unfunny jokes, Stu was able to breathe easier. Eve was bound to say anything at all, especially if she knew it might cause someone pain. The Corsairs were all still cracking jokes when two more of them showed up.

One was a burly man with lice crawling in his black beard. He looked at each of them as if he wanted to take a bite out of them. "Why are you just standing around yucking it up? Why isn't there a fire lit for crap's sake. We could have one of them boats over here in a damn snap."

For the moment, Troy and his beardless cheeks were forgotten as a fire was lit and watches set. The burly man was Jared Hayashi, one-time captain of the *Black Dream*, only now the *Black Dream* was nothing but bits of trash floating with the current. Hayashi eyed every piece of crap that washed ashore, wondering if it had once been part of his beloved boat.

He was not in a joking mood. He quizzed each of the sailors, demanding to know what ship they had been on and where were their captains. The Corsairs in the little group represented four ships; two of their captains were dead and two others had run off.

"Son of a bitch!" Hayashi snapped, before beginning to pace up and down the beach. "Those chicken bastards!" He had thought about running as well. The Black Captain was going to be furious over the loss of so many ships. "And he's going to want an explanation." Hayashi had no idea what had happened. One moment he and Conrad were neck and neck in the chase for *Queen's Revenge*, then out of nowhere the damned *Blood Belle* exploded.

Hayashi had been thrown overboard by the blast and, unlike so many others in the water, he was perfectly conscious when the *Buzzsaw* evaporated in a shocking flash of orange light a few minutes later. It reminded him of when the *Sea King* had gone up.

Then the *Dark Gull* and another ship had begun attacking each other, firing yardarm to yardarm like it was 1776. The slaughter was fantastic but neither side gave an inch. After that, there was a good deal more shooting from every direction and then came unexplained fires that sprouted like magic on board half-a dozen ships.

Nothing about the night had made sense to Jared Hayashi and while others talked about saboteurs and spies, he knew there was only one culprit: The Mad Queen. She could call herself queen all she wanted, he knew better. She was some sort of sorceress. That was the truth and it's what he planned to tell the Black Captain, no matter what the consequences were. The Captain could call him a fool or an idiot, but there was one thing that he had learned on his three trips south to San Francisco: that Queen had to be killed and the sooner the better.

He was in a snarling mood when he saw Troy Holt pick up his spear. "Where did you get that?"

Chapter 29

Jared Hayashi had heard about spears like the one Troy had in his hand. As far as he knew, the only people fool enough to carry a weapon like that were the God-groveling Guardians. And this slick-cheeked kid had an altogether overly pious look about him. If he didn't know better, he would have sworn the kid was *judging* him.

Hayashi found one of the little maggoty creatures crawling in his shaggy beard, gave it a quick, satisfying pinch and flicked the remains at the kid. "Did you just happen to *find* the spear?" he asked, baiting Troy.

Stu had been worried someone would ask about the spear and was ready with an answer, one that was at least partly true. "He took it off the *Queen's Revenge*. No one else seemed to want it and so he took it with him when we jumped ship…which we did as soon as we could." For a moment, Troy looked as if he were going to contradict him, then he nodded and shrugged.

Hayashi didn't like the answer and he didn't like the look of the boy. There was something about him that made his skin crawl. He was on the verge of grilling him when a boat came zipping across the harbor, drawn to the smoke. With a sick taste in his mouth, Hayashi saw that it was Chuck Boschee riding to his "rescue" in the fifty-five-foot catamaran, *The Courageous*.

"Great," Hayashi muttered, forgetting the boy and his spear, at least for the moment. He held a strong dislike for Boschee, who was a mean son of a bitch with a holier than thou attitude, which he backed up with huge, hammer-like fists when he needed to. About the only person Boschee didn't intimidate was the Black Captain.

The catamaran had a shallow draft but Boschee purposefully kept his boat in deeper water, forcing the stranded Corsairs to swim. They were all shivering when they came aboard. He glared down at them. "What do we call Corsairs who have lost their boats?"

"Losers," one of his sailors answered.

"Crossing guards," another suggested.

"Piss boys!"

Boschee had the last say. "They're pathetic is what they are." He was enjoying their misery and wore a self-satisfied grin until he came to Hayashi; at that point, the grin became a wide, toothy smile. "Damn, if it isn't Hayashi, the Oriental Mad Dog.

You look a little like a kitten to me. What happened to you? Where's that raft you were in charge of? Did you misplace her? Maybe at the bottom of the ocean? Oh, no! Don't tell me that you fell overboard, again?"

His first mate, looking down the length of his snide nose, remarked, "Or he might've been pushed. We all know how much his men just love him."

Hayashi fumed at the "Oriental" dig, but he held his anger in place and started to explain only to have Boschee laugh at him. "So, against all reason, you were so damned close to another boat that when it blew up, you managed to get your own boat blown up, too. Well, isn't that just about the dumbest thing I ever heard? The Captain is going to have a field day with you. What were you thinking, coming back? You know what he's going to do."

Suddenly, his reason for coming back seemed terribly stupid. "I had to warn him about the Queen. She's a sorceress. She has to be killed right away."

"Or what? She'll put a spell on him?" Boschee rolled his eyes. "Damn Hayashi, that's just about the dumbest thing I ever heard. You get your ship blown up and this is your excuse? That she's a sorceress? All I can say is that it's been nice knowing you." The first mate snickered, and the crew elbowed each other as Hayashi shrank back. Boschee turned from him, his head shaking in disbelief. "Now, who are the rest of these losers?"

He went down the line and questioned each of the miserable Corsairs without really listening to their rambling, excuse-filled answers. They were riff-raff. Whatever rank or position they had held before the battle would be stripped from them, and if they were lucky enough to find a place on a new ship, they'd be low-men on the totem pole.

After the treatment Hayashi had received, they seemed to be finally understanding this. They grew sullen and wouldn't lift their eyes when they spoke. One man was viciously kicked into a bloody pile because he mumbled; he received laughter from everyone on board instead of sympathy. When Boschee got to Stu and heard which boat he had come off, his eyes narrowed.

"How many men were on board?"

In spite of Troy's presence, Stu knew he had to lie to protect Jenn. "A couple of dozen. She was a big boat. And fast, too."

"What kind of crew were there? Any other Corsairs besides you two?"

"Yes sir," Troy answered. "There was a fellow named Deaf Mick."

Boschee looked him up and down; he then glanced at the spear sitting next to Troy's thigh. Stu thought Boschee was going to try to pick it up, instead he only gave it a little tap with his foot as he asked, "Did you see the girl they traded the Queen for? What did you think? Will they listen to her?"

Stu almost said, *I hope*, but quickly changed it to a firm "Yes, they will," hoping that this would at least give the Corsairs a bit of a pause before heading south. His people would need all the time they could get to prepare, and even then, disaster and massacre were the likely result.

Boschee was surprised. "Really? That's not what Mark Leney said. He was adamant about it. And the Captain thinks she's just a kid."

"Yeah, that's true, but she was queen before," Stu said, wishing the man would go away. Every second spent talking to him was a second closer to getting caught. "She was sort of a temporary queen. It didn't matter, though, people still followed her."

"Interesting," Boschee muttered, staring away across the water at the foul city of the Corsairs. Signal flags were being run up the masts of the ready boats; something was going on. "We're going to have to get you two in front of the Captain. He'll want to question you about this new queen. And Leney is going to throw a fit. You better prepare for that."

Troy and Stu shared a look. Neither could be seen by Leney since he knew them both and would have them arrested on sight.

"We sure will," Stu said; however Boschee wasn't listening. A green "return" flag was flying from the signal tower, and most of the ships were already beginning to tack. He bawled for the decks to be cleared of the "Trash." By that, Boschee meant Stu, Troy, and the sailors he had picked up on the southern shore. They were kicked and pushed below deck, herded like cattle into a cramped area in one of the two hulls which was lit only by a tiny portal that was constantly awash in sea water.

The two hoped to find Emily down there, but there was no sign of her. "We can't be seen by Leney," Troy whispered into Stu's ear. "He knows me."

"He knows me, too. It'll be okay. We'll blend in with the group and try to slip away when we get to shore." If they could manage to pull off a semi-escape, Stu didn't know what they would do after. Neither of them knew anything about Hoquiam and since they were posing as Corsairs they couldn't go around asking obvious questions such as *Where do we keep the prisoners?* Or, *Where does the Black Captain live?*

It would have been smart to come up with a better, more in-depth plan, or perhaps even a secondary one for when the first fell to pieces; however neither had much of a flair for such things and since they were sitting knee-to-knee with actual Corsairs they decided they had no choice but to wing it.

The Courageous made slow, but steady headway against the wind, and yet, as they had been furthest from the town, they were the last to moor. The hatch was thrown open and the "trash" began to shuffle up into the misting morning only to be pushed back down seconds later. "Change of plans! Get your ugly asses back down there!" a Corsair roared, swinging a short length of thick rope and smacking the ship-less men with it. It was a cross between a whip and a billy club and when it hit there was an awful slapping thud and a cry.

The group was stuck in the semi-dark until the air grew thick and hot with the stench of the unwashed Corsairs. They farted endlessly, crabbed at each other over everything, bullied the smaller men and made tasteless jokes at each other's expense. Just when Troy didn't think he could take any more of the crude behavior, the hatch opened again. They weren't let out. Instead, twenty more men were shoved down into the narrow room with them. They could only sit with their knees tucked up to their chins.

"At least we don't have to worry about freezing anymore," Troy said, trying to find the bright side of the moment. Stu made no answer. Since the growing heat and ripening stench had put him into something of stupor anyway, so he decided to go with it and catch up on some much-needed sleep.

There was another long wait in which Stu lolled onto Troy, who had no choice but to accept the man's head on his shoulder as if they were two moony teenagers. Finally, the boat took on a bit of a tilt and the sound of water rushing along the hull suggested that they were moving.

"What's going on?" someone asked.

"We're attacking," was the answer. Attacking who or where, or even when, was not known.

They were part of the fleet that was moving around into the Pacific to cut off the escape of the Magnum Killers, who were not trying to escape at all, but were currently hunkering down on a hill miles away.

Thankfully it was a short trip of only two hours before the small fleet put in on and empty beach where there were no docks. The doors were thrown open and the crowded hull emptied with a good deal of shoving and shouting. Stu and Troy relished the fresh air for all of ten seconds before they, and everyone else, were pushed into the water fifty yards from shore. With his armor, Troy went right to the bottom and would have drowned if they were any further out. Eight feet below the surface his feet found a rocky bottom. He kicked off, came up for air and sunk again almost as quickly.

With Stu struggling under the weight of his pack and his gun, he wasn't any help and the only way Troy was able to get to shore was to sink, push off toward the surface at an angle, take a breath and sink again. It was an exhausting method to get to shore, though it slowly grew easier as the bottom curved upwards. After a while, he could hold his head above the water while touching the bottom. Stu dragged him onto the beach where they fell onto the sand and laid gasping along with hundreds of others.

It was an inauspicious beginning to an attack. Gradually, the captains were able to rally their men by beating them to their feet, and soon everyone was trooping inland, walking in a weary hunch.

The attack seemed like a major event and Stu kept a sharp eye out for the Black Captain. If he showed his face, Stu planned on killing him without hesitation. One slight impediment to the plan: Stu didn't know what he looked like. All Stu knew was that the Black Captain was a black man who tended to wear black clothes—which also happened to describe thirty of the men around them.

He wasn't there, of course. Stu was sure that the Black Captain traveled with some sort of extensive entourage that couldn't be missed. He decided against telling Troy his plan, since, from what little he knew about him, Stu could expect some sort of misplaced lecture on morality if he did, and this was definitely not the time or the place.

In the end, it didn't matter since the Captain didn't show. He remained protected in his hilltop compound and, at first, communicated with his far-flung forces via radio. The shoddy Corsair batteries proved unreliable and by afternoon, signal flags were being used. Against another opponent, they might have proven to be a detriment, but Neil Martin was not a real general and he wasted his remaining hours until the trap slowly closed around him.

The regiment that Stu and Troy were now part of came from the west, while mountain Bandits streamed out of the north, and a third force under Chuck Boschee came from the east. These groups crushed inwards. Minutes before the start of the battle that would end with the utter destruction of the Magnum Killers, Troy and Stu looked at each other in a panic.

"What do we do?" Troy whispered as they were marched toward the hill. "We can't fight for them!"

They had been unable to slip away, partially because Troy had refused to give up his spear and partially because they were some of the few not wearing black. In fact, Troy was still in his gray Guardian uniform. He stood out like a sore thumb and it was a wonder no one had commented on it yet.

"We'll fake it. We'll make a lot of noise and fire our guns like everyone else. Listen, if I get an open shot at one of these guys, I'm going to take it." Troy looked shocked at the notion and Stu pulled him close. "All's fair in love and war. You ever heard of that?" Even sheltered as he had been behind the walls of Highton, Troy had heard the saying. He had dismissed it as beneath him.

Now, as the smoke bombs began to billow, and the rudimentary catapults began to hurl their explosives, he was unsure of himself. Doing nothing at all would mean that he was contributing to the death of soldiers that he had consciously decided to ally himself with. It would be wrong not to help them. Yet it felt detestable to shoot men in the back.

Thankfully, the battle was such chaos that shooting people in the back was almost unnecessary. The smoke bombs were worse than useless; instead of filling their enemies with dread and confusion, it was the Corsairs who wandered about in a gray storm, groping blindly for the enemy.

In no time, it was every man for himself. Stu and Troy took shelter behind a downed tree and shot at anything that moved. And they weren't the only ones. It sounded like there were a hundred different battles going on. The fight was deafening and terrifying even for hard men like Troy and Stu. Because of the endless smoke that hung about them like a bank of fog, Troy could not catch his breath. He was constantly gulping down air, so it felt like he was always just on the verge of panic.

Many did panic and ran to and fro, making it seem like the Corsairs were frequently in either full retreat, or rushing to attack. Men were gunned down no matter which way they went. The battle was moments from being lost by the Corsairs, when pure ineptness saved them—almost everyone began to run out of ammunition at about the same time. This caused a lull which allowed the individual Corsairs time to coalesce back into an actual fighting force.

Troy and Stu, who had ruthlessly killed every Corsair that got within range of their guns, thought it wise to get away from the scene of their many crimes. They slid beneath the downed tree and crawled forward, stripping the dead that they came across like early-bird grave robbers. Among the dead were shuddering, weeping men with huge holes in their bodies and their life's blood pouring from them.

Stu mumbled a few words, "I'd help if I could," and "Sorry. We'll send someone, I promise." This wasn't good enough for Troy. He wouldn't leave the injured without at least tying off wounds or slapping on a field dressing, which was something that at least be justified, but with those that had no chance, he actually stopped to say prayers with the men.

"We don't have time for this," Stu hissed. Boschee had been scraping together men to make a final push up the hill and Stu could almost feel his scary eyes searching for the two of them amid the smoke.

"No," Troy answered, calmly. "These men are the ones who are out of time. This is their last chance to beg forgiveness for their sins and to accept Jesus Christ as their lord and savior. Saving a soul is more important than saving a life."

Out of sheer frustration, Stu wanted to pull his hair out; they couldn't be seen lagging behind. At best, people would start asking questions that they couldn't answer, and at worst, they could be shot for cowardice. Still, he knew that Troy would not be moved until the last prayer was said and the last tourniquet tightened down like a cinch.

"I'll bind the wounds; you do the praying." Things went faster, and they only had one more person to go before the call went up: *Charge!* Bloodcurdling screams burst out all around them and there was a renewed explosion of gunfire as the Corsairs surged at the hill.

Stu shifted to the last man: a stick-thin, forty-year-old who had drowned in blood the minute before. "Thank God," Stu whispered, thinking that luck was finally on their side and that they'd be able to join the others, but to his astonishment, Troy dropped to his knees and began praying over the corpse.

"But he's dead already," Stu cried, the harsh words nearly drowned out by the raging battle.

"I know. Our intervention may be his only chance."

Somehow, Stu was able to hold in a scream of rage. He waited in silent agony until Troy finished. The moment he said, "Amen," Stu grabbed him by the arm and started once more up the hill. They almost made it to the top. Their half-hearted effort to join the crowd of Corsairs so they could blend in was stopped as soon they came across more dying men. Knowing it would useless to try to stop him, Stu could do nothing but help with the wounded. It made the work go faster.

But not fast enough. The battle was over, and the daylight was fading when Boschee came up on them trying to fit a fractured femur back into place. Their patient, a middle-aged Corsair, was wailing like a banshee.

"What the ever-loving hell is going on?" Boschee demanded. "It sounds like you're torturing him."

"We're trying to save him," Troy replied, through gritted white teeth. The teeth were only a slight bit whiter than his face. This was his first time working as a medic and he had never seen so much blood in his life.

Boschee leaned over Troy's shoulder, snorted and said, "It's a waste of time. Sorry Tim, but you're a goner."

Troy glared. "It's not a waste. I've seen men come back from worse. We just have to..."

Stu was sure he was about to blurt, "Pray for him," which would have been inexplicable to a Corsair. Thankfully, Boschee interrupted, by pulling out a bowie knife and planting it with a meaty thud up to its hilt in Tim's chest.

"I told you he was a goner," Boschee said, clapping Troy on the shoulder. "Now, here's what I want you boys to do, take that dippy spear of yours and do the same for every man you come across from here to the other side of the hill. Do you got me?"

"Yes sir," Stu answered, quickly, grabbing Troy's arm before the younger man leapt up and attacked the captain. "We're on it." He hauled Troy away, pointing at the nearest body

—a man who was clearly dead already. "Get him," he ordered Troy, giving him a shove.

Troy's lips compressed as he hissed, "He's already de..."

"Just do it!" Stu barked. Seething, Troy lifted his spear and drove it into the midsection of the corpse. He couldn't bring himself to put his full strength behind the act of desecration. The blade of the spear went in and met resistance; he gave it a bit more of a shove until there was a horrible popping sensation and the tip went all the way through the corpse.

"Good," Boschee said. "Now everyone, clear the hill of any wounded. We don't have time for prisoners."

Although they supposedly didn't have time to take prisoners, they certainly seemed to have plenty of time to torture them. The Corsairs went about the act of killing off the wounded with gruesome slowness. Fingers were bent back until they snapped, knees were bashed with rocks, bullet wounds were subject to probing by sticks, eyes were put out using dirty knives and tongues were torn from mouths.

The slaughter was inescapable as were the screams of the Magnum Killers who begged and pleaded for death.

With Troy on the verge of fainting from the sheer barbarism, it was up to Stu to do what he could. He found a man trying to crawl away with half his left leg missing. He stared over his shoulder at Stu as if he were the devil himself. "Beg forgiveness from God," Stu whispered. "Hurry!"

The man whimpered through an abbreviated confession. "Now, say: I accept the Lord Jesus as my personal savior." Stu glanced at Troy who nodded, weakly. The man repeated the words and as his reward, Stu stabbed him through the heart. It was a terrible gift that left Stu sweating and his hands shaking.

"There's another," Troy said.

Stu staggered like a drunk to the man and went through the same dreadful ritual with the same dreadful results. A third man was found, and Stu wondered how long he could do this. He had killed two men and he could barely stand. This third man wouldn't beg forgiveness and he laughed at the idea of a personal savior.

"W-What do we do?" Stu asked. He was feeling his age in a way that he hadn't since he was ten. He wanted to run away.

In the light of the setting sun, Troy was paper-white. "We leave him. He might come to his senses and we owe him that."

There were more people who were ready to die with their tattered souls thinly sewn together by a death-bed confession. Four more died at Stu's shaking hand before they came to a man who was living his last seconds. The top of his head looked like it had been shorn almost completely off. He was absolutely covered in dark blood.

And yet his dull eyes followed Stu as he came up with the red-tipped spear raised. Stu wanted to just stab him and be done—the man was clearly beyond speech—but as he drove the blade home, Troy knocked it aside. "Hold on. Hey! Blink once if you wish for your sins to be forgiven."

"My shins?" the man said, sounding as if his tongue was loose and flopping around inside his mouth. "What shins?"

"Any of them," Stu said. "Or all of them. It doesn't matter. Just hurry." Boschee was not far away. He seemed to be inspecting Stu's handiwork.

Troy hushed him. "It does matter. The Lord knows your heart and if you are sorry, he will forgive. Now, are you sorry?"

"I'm sorry for the ones I'm sorry for, but not the others, Knight." Unbelievably, he sat up, felt the top of his head where half his scalp was hanging over his face, and flopped it back over with sickening *splat*. He then wiggled it firmer onto the bare bone of his skull as if he were re-sodding his head. Troy was so sickened by the display that he forgot to breathe.

The man smiled up at Stu and asked, "You don't happen to have a safety pin, do you, Stu? Or maybe one of them big diaper pins? I promised myself that if I ever lost my hair I would never, ever resort to a combover, but here I am, vain to the end."

The man had absolutely nothing to be vain about, except for perhaps his sky-blue eyes. "Neil? Is that you?"

"In the grey flesh."

Chapter 30

With Captain Boschee so close, Stu had to act fast. "Play dead," he hissed and then used his boot to knock Neil onto his back. Stu then feigned stabbing him just as Boschee walked up.

He sucked in his breath, on the verge of demanding answers. He had been watching the pair for some time and there was something completely un-Corsair-like about them. All the others were torturing and butchering the last of the prisoners, displaying appalling appetites. These two had been almost surgical in their killings. He didn't like it.

Only now he found them standing over a properly disgusting display of torture. "Way to go," he said, smacking Stu on the back and knocking him off his feet. Boschee laughed as he strolled away.

Stu had tripped over Neil, who was still playing dead. Out of the corner of his mouth, the near-zombie whispered, "Is he still here?"

"He's close. Just hold on; the sun is almost down. We're going to try to escape when it gets dark."

"Escape to where? And what are you two doing here? Where's Jenn and the *Queen's Revenge*? I swear that's where I saw you guys last."

After a quick and very obvious look around, Troy knelt down next to Neil. "She's flying south as fast as they can, I hope. Do you know where Emily is? Have you seen her? Was she captured?"

Neil forgot that he was supposed to be dead and sat straight up. "Emily? She's still on the boat. Isn't she? Right? Tell me she's safe."

"We don't know where she is," Troy answered, feeling like he had failed in some way. He told Neil everything they knew of the situation which was so limited that it took him seconds. Then he told him their plan.

"You're going to escape *into* Hoquiam? That doesn't sound like much of an escape...unless you've guys changed the meaning of the word. You know like: cool means hot or square means nerdy." The two young men shook their heads while trying to hold back little patronizing smiles that suggested they thought his little flesh wound went deeper than it had.

"That's what kids used to do back in my day." Neil heard his father's voice in the sentence and grimaced. "Never mind;

pretend I didn't say anything. So, we're going to the lair of the Corsairs. What's the plan?"

"That is the plan," Stu said in his quiet rumble as he squinted around in the gathering darkness. He didn't like how loud they were being. The dark that hid Neil's inhuman nature could also hide an eavesdropping Corsair. "First we have to get away from here. Boschee is way too interested in us." He helped Neil to his feet.

The small man swayed alarmingly as he looked around at the mounds of dead bodies, the fires that were still raging and the brass sprayed all over the ground, glittering like gold. It only just struck him that the battle was lost, and his Magnum Killers had been massacred to a man. "This is my fault," he said so quietly that he barely heard his own words.

Stu was surprised to see what looked like sorrow pass over the gruesome face. "You okay?"

"No. I did this. I was the leader and look what I did... I messed up, bad." He had his excuses: being a zombie was number one, not being an actual military leader was number two. There were more and none of them mattered. This was on him.

"I don't think you guys ever had much of a chance," Stu said. "Try not to think about it."

"Apparently, not thinking is what I do best," Neil muttered in reply and set off in the wrong direction. His brain seemed so scrambled that when he tried to walk, he had to "will" his different limbs into action, this made him look like a wooden puppet being controlled by hidden strings. "I'm just a little wobbly is all. Nothing to worry about. Just a conk on the, the ol' noggin. Oh, wait, I see the problem; I lost a croc." When Neil bent to get his flung powder-blue rubber shoe, his scalp flapped off his head and hung suspended over his right ear like a bloody shelf.

Troy, who was still a bloody mess and had seen many disgusting things in the last hour, thought this was the worst and leaned back from Neil. He kept his hand close to his chest as he pointed at the flap. "Your, uh, thing is sort of off to the side."

"Thanks," Neil said, slapping it back over and resettling it on his skull as if squishing it down would glue it in place. "I could use a hat. If you see anyone with one let me...Ha! Lucky Neil strikes again." Not ten feet away was the mutilated corpse of Emanuel Powers; he had been shot, partially exploded, and burned alive—he was still prettier than Neil.

"If you don't mind, Powers," he said to the corpse, taking the red baseball cap that he had put on to act as a disguise in case things went wrong. Neil shook out a congealing hunk of blood and brain and stuck it on his head. He then held out his arms as if to ask: *How do I look?*

Stu had no idea what to say. Neil had on a peach coat that was open, revealing a green sweater and blue jeans with little shiny crystals glued around the pockets and down the thighs. Splashed over all of this was what looked like two gallons of blood.

"We should get going," Stu muttered. He found Neil a discarded rifle, so he could at least blend in a little, and then started to lead him off to the left, only to almost run into Boschee.

They turned around just as the burly man bellowed, "Okay, we're moving! I want everyone formed up on me. I don't care about what ships you were on. Just form up, ten across. Let's go!"

Stu pulled Neil down behind a bullet-ridden Audi. The half-zombie would have fallen on his face if it wasn't for Troy, who grabbed his other arm. Through the filthy glass, they watched as Boschee gathered hundreds of soldiers together. In the dark, it was impossible to count them all. There were so many that it took an hour to get them all gathered and twenty minutes for them to march past the Audi.

They headed towards Hoquiam. "What do we do?" Troy asked, when the last of the wounded Corsairs lurched and hobbled after the main body.

Neil was sitting with his head cocked all the way to one shoulder, his eyes barely open, but unmoving. He looked dead to Troy; then again, he always looked dead. Troy poked him in the shoulder. "Neil, what do we do? They're heading toward Hoquiam."

"Isn't that where we want to go?"

It was and it wasn't. None of them really wanted to go anywhere near the lair. The thought was so horrible that it froze the soul even thinking about it. Stu found himself hesitating, his stomach suddenly twisting. Instead of picturing Jillybean, what played in his mind, over and over, were the screams of the men being tortured. The way they had begged so pitifully struck a fear-filled chord within him.

263

"I can go by myself," Neil suggested when he saw the fear that the two were trying so hard to hide. "They can't really hurt me, you know. It's the best part about being, whatever it is that I am."

"No," Troy said, almost reflexively. It galled him that he had let his fear show. "I should never have left in the first place. At a minimum, we must find out what happened to Emily. She's innocent in all of this."

Stu forced his fear back down into his trembling gut and agreed with Troy with his usual grunt. To keep Neil from falling or straying, he walked on one side of him and Troy on the other. They expected to be far behind the column and take forever to catch up. This wasn't exactly a military formation, however. It moved like an old accordion. Slow then fast, then slow again. Large gaps opened up as men came and went, stopping to use the bathroom or to smoke…or to run away.

The three imposters caught up with the walking wounded first. Stu had to hiss at Troy to keep him from helping them. "It's not that far," Stu muttered under his breath. "They'll be able to make it on their own and, even if they don't, I'm sure they'll send someone for the wounded."

"Will they?" Troy shot back. "These are Corsairs. Did you notice that during the battle no one even called for a medic? I don't think they have any. If you get hurt, then it's just too bad. Barbarians!" he seethed.

"Will you quiet down for God's sake?" Stu glared. Troy looked shocked and then glared right back. "Oh, the God thing," Stu said. "Sorry. Force of habit. Look, we can't help these people and Emily at the same time. Not right now. So, pick a side and stick with it."

Troy chose to stay, much to Stu's relief. They were coming up to the West Hoquiam River and it was black as oil. It was like crossing the River Styx, except instead of a boatman, there was a rope bridge strung across it. A squad of guards with lanterns and rifles that sprouted long bayonets inspected everyone trying to cross the wobbling thing.

"I'll make a scene long enough for you to get Neil down the rope a bit," Stu said, knowing that a lie would likely have to be told and Troy would rather see the three of them tortured to death than tell the smallest of fibs. Thankfully, a lie was needed, and a scene was provided for them by a man who'd been gut-shot. He couldn't hold onto the ropes and hold his stomach at the same time.

He was a miserable thing, mewling and crying, begging for a boat to be brought over. Even though the guards knew his name, they taunted him mercilessly. "Come on, Steve! Just reach out and grab the rope. Did you hear that, Steve? It sounds like some of the undead are coming this way. Over here! You can eat Steve."

Stu could see Troy working up the courage to go over and help Steve. "Don't do it," he growled, pulling Troy to the rope. "You go first, then Neil. Oh, Jeeze, Neil! Button your coat, please." The green sweater he wore was clearly a woman's sweater and the little crystal studs on his pants were winking in the lantern light. Fortunately, the coat was so covered in his blood that it looked brown.

Neil turned away and fumbled the button in place. He then mounted the wiggling, wobbling rope. There were three ropes: two at waist height and a thick one to walk on. It wasn't that thick, and he made it only twenty feet before he fell in. The river was already neck deep and he was somehow able to retain his baseball cap. The rest of him was completely soaked which wasn't the worst thing.

With the caked-on blood washed off of him, Neil looked nearly human. He didn't act it, however.

No matter how hard he tried, he couldn't pull himself up onto the bridge and had to either go back and try again or remain in the water, going hand over hand. Wisely, he chose the latter option. Steve did the same thing, only he was far weaker, and his hands shook. It wasn't long before his body went into shock, shunting blood from his limbs and to his core.

It was a sure sign that he was on the verge of dying, but did that stop Troy? No, the Guardian was in the water before Stu could get a word out. Troy tried to get Steve to hold onto his spear, but Steve was too far gone, and Stu was forced to lug the pole along for half a mile until he got to the far side.

Troy showed up ten minutes later, dragging a dead body through the water. "He repented," he said, nodding his head, as if he had gained a partial victory.

Stu didn't see it. Still, he said, "Good. Now, if you'll let the current take him, we have to get out of here." Thankfully, Troy agreed, and he slogged out of the water to stand next to a dripping Neil Martin.

"I'm officially repenting, too," the zombie said. "I don't know if you guys feel it, but this place isn't right."

They could feel it as well. The air stank of death and decay; not far away was a partially decomposed body lying in a gutter. Besides the bodies, there was more than one, there was trash everywhere lying in piles and in some places, drifts four feet high. Beside the smell and the unsightliness, there were sounds that made Stu doubt the wisdom of coming.

Screams came frequently, as did the crack of whips. A man was yelling at a slave, telling her that he would beat her until she got his toast done right. There was laughter as well, but it was either cruel or mocking. There was no joy in the Corsairs' lair.

The screams coming from a squat brick building down the street from them were particularly loud. It was windowless and dark, and as they stared, two men came out of it hauling a third by the ankles and armpits. The two, walking with short waddling steps, took the man and tried to fling him onto what looked like a small hill or a mound. The man, who was clearly dead, kept rolling to the bottom and the two kept trying to pitch him higher up.

"Wounded go that way," a Corsair drawled, pointing toward the building. "The rest of you are too late. The boats are full, so you'll be getting your exercise; Mount Olympus is a long hike." He chortled. "Come on, get marching. Follow the rest. Hut, two, three, four. Hut, two, three, four!"

Neil, who looked like a walking corpse, but who otherwise felt fine, started to march along with the slower half of the Corsair army. Stu turned him toward the hospital. "Go that way," he whispered and then fell in beside him, affecting a limp. When Troy didn't immediately follow, Stu gave him a quick look that said: *Start limping or start marching.*

Troy sighed and began to limp toward the hospital, using his spear like a staff. The limp was a form of a lie and he felt as if the ugliness of the town was infecting him already. He was a knight, not some skulking thief. "Remember the mission," he told himself, "And remember God's plan." Troy had no idea what God's plan was, and he had to be okay with that. The Lord worked in mysterious ways.

This mystery deepened as they limped along with twenty others to the low building and saw that the mound was completely unnatural. For the most part, it was made of human bodies.

Stu stumbled past it, his head turned to stare, not realizing he was walking in a bloody stream that ran from the building. With his head cranked around, he knocked into a pale-faced slave—this one was a man with a thick, rusting collar around his neck.

"Sorry, I didn't…" His words deserted him as he saw that the slave was a blood-dripping horror. He had on a useless apron which was as soaked in red gore as the rest of him. In one hand, he carried a bare arm that looked as though it was made of white rubber and in the other hand he had a foot. He threw it at the mound and Stu thought he was going to puke.

"I can't do this." These were his thoughts and yet they came from a Corsair who had dragged himself all the way from the battlefield. From the front, his injury looked like one of those "movie wounds" that the good guys would get in almost every action movie that he had ever seen growing up. He had a hole in his shoulder that leaked a convincing amount of blood. Inside of him, things were not nearly so camera ready. The bullet had destroyed his clavicle, ripped through layers of muscle and cartilage, torn bands of tendons and shattered his shoulder blade into pieces. The one wound was really closer to fifty and each one bled profusely, though the blood was almost all internal and was collecting around his heart and lungs, making it difficult to breathe. What seemed worse was that he couldn't feel his left arm. It hung from his body, swollen and strangely heavy.

It was a testament to his strength that he had made it this far. "I can't go in," he said to Stu.

"You're not supposed to leave," the slave whispered, glancing inside, nervously. "The Captain doesn't want a bunch of corpses all over the place. If you're gonna die, you're supposed to die here."

Stu glanced inside. It was no hospital, it was a butcher shop where the copper smell of blood was dizzying. As they stared, limbs were sawn off and the stumps burned. Belly wounds were uselessly bound, while sucking chest wounds frothed with pink foam. Those who begged for death were unceremoniously knocked on the head with a short-handled sledge hammer before their bodies were trundled out to be added to the pile.

The slave, thinking that Stu was hurt, tried to drag him inside. Stu grabbed the man's wrist and held it in an iron grip. "I'm not going inside." He might have broken the man's wrist if Troy hadn't touched his shoulder.

"He's not our enemy. Let him go." Troy led them back outside, where they sucked in great gulps of air, trying to rid their lungs of the terrible stench. "What do we do now?"

"If you get me back to my place, I have about ten gallons of good hootch," the Corsair with the shoulder wound said. "Drinking myself to death seems just about right."

With no other plan and no other way to get information, they decided to join the man. He only made it a block before his eyes dimmed, rolled up in his head and he fell. "Don't let me die in a ditch," he whispered. "That's not right for a man."

Troy and Stu pulled him into the shadow of a burned-out husk of a house and rested his head on a tree stump. There were no trees left in Hoquiam, only stumps, all cut as close to the ground as possible. "I need you to do me a favor," Troy said. Stu groaned because he knew that the Knight was about to go into his "repent" sermon. Troy pushed him away from the Corsair. "This is the last one, I promise. Sir? Look at me. You have to repent now before it's too late. God loves you despite your sins."

"Repent?" He began laughing and wheezing and coughing all at once. "Are you crazy?"

"No. I have a duty to…"

The man lifted his bloody right hand and grabbed Troy. "I know you. You're that Guardian. It's me, Garret. I saw you in Highton."

Troy gave him an uncertain smile. "Yeah, sure. I was in Highton, but right now, let's concentrate on finding a path to heaven. Can you do that?"

"You were supposed to protect the Queen," Garret said, softly. Troy had been about to go on; he sucked in air but nothing came out. "She's gonna die, now. They have her up at the big house. I saw that dumb Roy Bost bring her up last night and *The Cadaver* was with them."

Stu had been all set to let Troy have his Christian way with Garret until he heard him mention the Queen. "Where's the big house? Where did they take her?"

Garret had a sleepy look about him as his blood pooled and his blood pressure dropped. "Up the hill. You'll never get that far. There's fences. And…and…guards."

Neil crowded in close and shook Garret until his eyes opened wide. "Was there a girl with them? She's slim and blonde and just a kid. Her name's Emily. Did you see her?"

The corsair stared at Neil, his eyes beginning to bug out of his head. Things were becoming increasingly unclear. First there had been talk of heaven and now he was looking into the face of a demon and to make matters worse, bent over as he was, Neil's bloody scalp outweighed the baseball cap. The one fell off and the other swung out, and to a suddenly terrified Garret, Neil's head looked like a horrible jack-in-the-box, from which something terrible was about to spring.

"I repent!" he gasped.

"What about the girl!" Neil growled.

"Yes, there was a girl," Garret cried, desperately. "They say she disappeared or escaped. That's all I know. Please! I said I would repent, okay?"

Troy pushed Neil back. "Do something about his…his, you know, his head," he whispered to Stu.

"Yeah," Stu agreed, handing Neil his hat. "Come on." He took Neil by the arm and went to the nearest intact house, uncertain what he would do if anyone was home. It was empty, as were ninety percent of the homes in Hoquiam. The Corsairs had won one battle, but they still had Gunner and the Coos Bay Clan to deal with, which left the town mostly deserted.

He called softly, disturbing the rank-smelling air. When no one answered, he went in, stumbled about until he found the fireplace. For kindling, the Corsair who had lived there had been using Bible pages. Stu didn't know until he had a little fire going.

"Don't let Troy see you doing that," Neil said, either blinking blood out of his eyes or perhaps winking at Stu.

Quickly, Stu pushed the Bibles behind an old leather couch that was being held together by duct tape and crusted blood. He fed the little fire with pieces of a chair until there was enough light to give the room a proper search. A lantern was found and with it he discovered a little bit of ammo, a very questionable store of unidentifiable dried meat and a sewing kit that must have belonged to the previous owner.

An hour later, Troy entered to find Neil happily eating his way through the meat and Stu pinning the top of his head back on. Although Stu's face was queered up as if he had eaten some of the rancid meat, he hadn't touched a bite.

"Can we switch patients?" Stu asked, not expecting a serious answer.

"My guy died," Troy said, keeping close to the door.

Stu shrugged. "So did mine. What's your point?"

Troy tried to laugh at the joke; however, the view was too unsettling and the smell in the house was making him gag. He could only hope it wasn't Neil. "I think Garret might have been saved. I hope so at least. He told me that the Queen freed Emily and she disappeared. No one knows where. He also says that Jillybean is in the house at the top of the hill. Apparently, there's only just the one. I took a quick trip to check it out and unfortunately it has fences and guards just like he said."

"We knew it wouldn't be easy," Stu said, struggling to tie a knot without stabbing himself with the needle. "A woman lived here. Can you check to see if she had any make-up? Sorry Neil, but you've gone over to grey."

"A man wearing make-up?" Troy asked with a curl to his lip. "That's not natural." Then again, a man getting his head sewn back together wasn't either; he shrugged away the comment and went looking for make-up, grabbing everything he could find. This was as far as he was willing to go in the process and Stu was right there with him. They left it up to Neil to experiment with base, foundation, powder, lipstick and rouge.

His first attempt made him look like the scariest clown that had ever existed. "What? Too much?"

They both nodded. "And do something about your eyes." He had left them untouched and they were gray circles of crazy in an overly white face.

Neil made a few over-exaggerated blinks as if trying to feel his eyes with his cheekbones. "Like, do what? Add mascara?" Neither of the young men knew anything about women's make-up and they both shrugged. Neil came out ten minutes later looking like the scariest transvestite who ever tried on his wife's panties, and that was saying something.

"Better?" he asked.

Stu nodded, shrugged and twitched. "It's probably as good as we're going to get. We've been talking about how to get up to the big house. We'd like to use your, uh, fame."

"My fame? I'm not famous."

"You are to the Captain. He tried to kill you, remember? We figured we would bring you up there and say we found you trying to sneak into the city."

A spark of understanding came into Neil's dead eyes. "And you'll want to ask for a reward or something to get close to the Black Captain? Then we kill him or hold him hostage. Yeah, that was the beginning plot to *The Empire Strikes Back* and it didn't work for Princess Leia."

"Princess who?" Troy asked.

"Never mind," Neil sighed. He tried to rack his meager, under-worked brain for a better plan and came up empty. "I say let's do it. What do we have to lose? No one else is going to try and take him out."

They fake tied up his hands and were just about to lead him up the hill when someone else tried to take him out. The second floor of the Captain's home was suddenly lit as an M4 started rattling round after round. They stared with slack jaws as the gunshots echoed across all of Hoquiam.

"Someone beat us to him," Stu said, feeling a sudden need to laugh and dance.

Chapter 31

The darkness inside Jillybean drew back, retreating like a hell fog before the warmth of a beautiful sunrise. What lay in front of her was not beauty. It was a symptom of man's inhumanity. The blood was very dark and glistened against torn and riven flesh. She had killed the Black Captain.

Red bubbles ballooned up from his chest. Each popped in turn only to be replaced by the next, surging up from below. Jillybean should not have been able to hear those delicate, tiny pops and yet somehow, even with her aching ears ringing from the thirty explosions she could.

The tiny sounds were magnified, both in sound and importance. To her, they meant so much more than the thunder of feet racing up the stairs. There was nothing she could do about the men coming for her. The *It* that had festered in her mind, had made no plans beyond the killing of the Black Captain. His death was its soul desire and now it was up to Jillybean to deal with the consequences.

And that was okay with her. She would gladly accept her fate. The greater good had finally been served in a proper guiltless manner. She could now die, knowing that with the Captain dead, the war would not be able to go on. Only he had the charisma and force of will to hold together so many lawless evil men. Without him, they would fall to bickering, and the greatest threat to the civilized world would dissipate just like the evil thing inside of her had.

The empty gun clattered to the floor just as the first man burst into the room. He had a pistol aimed at Jillybean's face. She coolly appraised both the gun and the man, neither of which frightened her in the least. His hands were perfectly steady and she assumed that his aim would be perfect as well; if he fired, she would die instantly. What was there to fear from that? As far as deaths went, there was nothing better.

He edged to his right as another man came in, eyes flicking back and forth. A third man carried a lantern as well as a pistol. The light revealed the assassination, fully—she hadn't missed with any of her thirty shots. The amount of blood was amazing and shocking. The man with the lantern glanced once at Jillybean, once at the body, swallowed loud enough to drown out the popping of the last bubble, and then went around the room checking to make sure no one else was lurking in the shadows or under the bed.

A fourth man slipped in on cat's feet. He was small and wiry, his face puckering after a quick peek at the body. He frisked Jillybean with shaking hands.

"Clear!" he called.

The one word sent a chill down her back. Something was wrong. Steps in the hallway. These were measured, easy and sure. They shouldn't have been. There should have been panic in them. There should have been urgency. There should have been a sense that the world was unraveling. There wasn't.

Jillybean knew who would walk through the door even before the Black Captain appeared, wearing a cocky smile. At the sight of him living and breathing, she felt something lurch inside of her. Something like panic. Something urgent and frightened.

"You are amazing," he said, bringing her back from the edge of darkness. It was a different kind of darkness than what she was used to. It was an empty darkness. No Eve, no Sadie, not even *It* was there. It was almost like there was nothing to the darkness, like it was only a shadow. That should have been reassuring, but it was one more unexpected thing.

Pull it together! she ordered herself. She took a breath, fixed a quizzical smile onto her pale face and asked, "I amaze you? How did I manage that?"

"By escaping…again. The first time we all told ourselves it was a fluke, but now I don't believe it. I feel like a kid watching a magician and all I can think is How did you do it? You picked the locks, that's pretty much a given, but how did you get past Eustace? Of all my men he's one of the best." He read her eyes correctly. "Oh, he *was* one of the best. Interesting. Tim, go check on Eustace. And take Hester with you. Find out how she got out."

This time Jillybean made sure to guard her look. Tim and Hester had been professionals—it would be a good thing for them to die in agony with their bodies twisting like pretzels. She felt that would be very, very good.

The men left and while they waited, the Captain had another of his guards strip her naked and cuff her hands behind her back. He then grinned down at her. "Just a skinny little piece of ass without your fancy clothes." She said nothing, which didn't seem to faze him. He glanced down at the dead man in the bed.

"Ray here said there was no way you'd get out a second time. No way at all. I told him to put his money where his mouth is."

"And if he had been right?" Jillybean asked, raising her voice slightly. She had heard a thump and rattle from somewhere deep in the house. Tim or Hester had probably just walked through a small cloud of VX dust. "What would Ray have won?"

The Captain had heard the sound, too and his eyes shot to hers. He cocked an eyebrow. "You still playing games?"

"Just talking. My guess is that Ray wouldn't have won anything." Someone was stumbling up the stairs; Tim or Hester more than likely. Whoever it was didn't make it, and there was a shout. "Not even bragging rights. You don't like to lose. You throw tantrums."

The accusation rolled off his back and his smile returned. "The thing is, I don't lose. I have set-backs like everyone else; for instance those little victories you won down south. What did I really lose? Anything? A few men and a few ships? From where I stand, I am stronger than ever. I've rid myself of dubious allies and gained much better fighters in the different mountain gangs. And what does little Jenn have left to fight with? A handful of women and children, and a few spear-chucking Guardians."

He laughed without humor. The laughter was pure self-satisfaction. "And does it look like I lost here tonight? My stock will only rise after tonight. My reputation will grow and grow as again, I remain unkillable, impervious to death. Yes, tonight I have won!" His eyes gleamed triumphantly in his dark face.

She couldn't deny the truth in his words and, naked and chained as she was, there was nothing she could do to wipe the satisfied grin off his face. It was up to Chuck "The Cadaver" Snawder to do that for her. He paused in the doorway, surveying the bloody bed, the mutilated body, the naked woman, the Captain standing over her in victory.

"We have to leave the house immediately," he said, as usual without any inflection that might hint at emotion.

"Is it a bomb?" the Captain asked.

"We're not sure what she has done. Come with me." The Cadaver left unhurriedly with the Captain following. Like a human train, a guard went next, then Jillybean and finally another guard. Each of them paused in the hall long enough to see Hester contorted on the stairs. It wasn't his twisted limbs that made them hesitate, it was the shrieking fear stamped on his ballooned, purple face.

"You're quite the winner," Jillybean said, as the little train hurried on. "Every winner runs from their home in the middle of the night."

He said nothing and now it was her turn to wear a self-satisfied smile. It was an act, just like his had been. Neither of them had won anything.

They fled into the night along with an unbelievable number of frightened slaves and a dozen or so nervous guards. They all stared at the house as if expecting it to suddenly burst into flames. The Captain collected himself first and pushed The Cadaver aside and marched down the hill towards a large home a hundred yards to the west.

One of the guards ran ahead and by the time they arrived, lanterns were being lit and the occupants: a favored ship's captain and his twenty-two slaves were on their way to being evicted.

The moment the Captain walked in, he began barking orders, rapid fire: "Nettles, set up a new perimeter and double the number of guards. Someone wake Kountz and tell him to get his forge running asap. Where is Christi? I want the sheets changed on all the beds. Don't look at me like that, Tupperman. Everyone knows your appetites are insane. I don't want to catch anything. Snawder, I'm going to want you to begin again, tonight. I want to know what she did and how she did it."

People began to go in every direction as Jillybean was dragged back out into the night, where the cold tented her bare skin in thousands of goosebumps. With her were two guards as well as The Cadaver; no one offered her a coat. As they walked, and she stepped gingerly to avoid as much of the broken glass as she could, The Cadaver kept taking peeks at her from the corner of his eye, which at first, she caught by doing the same thing. Finally, she simply stared.

"I'm surprised you're back so soon," he said, conversationally. "I didn't think we would see you until tomorrow night at the earliest." She didn't answer, verbally or physically; she only kept staring, committing his face to memory. He would die by her hand if she ever got the chance.

"Still not talking? I thought that was just your darker side. You will, eventually. Trust me on that. You'll tell me all your deepest, dirtiest secrets. Oh, here we go," he said, changing gears, smoothly. "And look, Kountz has his forge going already." It was no forge, it was a crematorium that had been converted into a blacksmith's shop. Heavy black smoke piled out of the chimney and the glow from the dreck-covered windows was devoid of the usual nostalgic warmth one associated with a fire.

Even with the fire raging, everything was dim, seen through a haze of smoke and fumes.

"What the hell is so damned important that it couldn't wait until...Snawder!" Harper Kountz blanched, his sallow skin going a grey-white. He was a hairy man with black tufts erupting up from the collar of his shirt and from the depths of his ears. More dark hair flowed down his arms and all the way to his knuckles. "Excuse me...I didn't know...I got the forge going... it'll be ready in a minute." He seemed to be choking on his words and could only spit them out three or four at a time.

"Take your time," The Cadaver intoned. "We have all night." When he looked at Jillybean, he finally showed some emotion. It looked a little like love. A sick, sick, depraved sort of love, but love nonetheless.

Kountz looked at Jillybean as well, though he did so with a frown, which blinked into surprise. "Say, is that the Queen?"

Snawder nodded once. "She has already managed to escape twice. You will see to it that she can't do it a third time."

"Oh, yeah, sure. We'll give her a few weights and let's say two secondary chains. As long as you guys keep the locks out of reach, she won't be going anywhere. Do you know if the Captain is looking for anything nice? I can do gold for the collar. It would make her real fancy."

"Yes. Do that." One of Snawder's lips almost turned up. "She will be the Captain's most prized possession."

Kountz smiled enough for both men, his teeth looking extra yellow by the light of the fire. He scurried out of the room, yelling to back off on the fire and yelling for the "ing-gots" and yelling for the "special" mold. "No, the one on the top shelf, damn it to pieces, Jeff!"

When the fire was brought to a dreadful orange glow, the gold was lowered down into it on a thick tray. While it melted, Jillybean was seated on an uncomfortable, heavy wooden chair with her arms chained to the rests. A towel was draped over her shoulders and then two thin pine boards, each with small half-circles cut from them were joined around her neck so that her head sat a few inches above the wood. She felt like she was about to have her head chopped off.

"That is the neck of a queen," Kountz said, approvingly. "The hair, not so much. Jeff, do something about that for goodness sakes. How's the gold coming?"

"It's coming. Get the mold ready."

Jillybean had her wild mane trussed up with hairbands and string before a two-piece plaster circle was set around her neck and locked in place. A smaller towel was worked between her flesh and the plaster. "Whatever you do, don't move," Kountz warned. "It'll be hot, and it'll sound and feel like a snake is coiling around your neck, just don't move. Do you understand?"

"I do."

The gold was rushed from the fire, tested by Kountz with a small steel rod, and was then poured into a funnel that was set uncomfortably close to Jillybean's face. Heat baked into her cheek and there was indeed a snakelike hiss as a weight settled around her neck.

"Almost, almost, almost," Kountz said and then abruptly pulled the container holding the gold back. A single drop of gold struck the pine. There was a curl of smoke around the perfect edge. "Don't move a muscle. We have to let the gold sit for just a little longer. Jeff! The water. Make sure it's cold. Not icy, mind you."

The water was poured around the mold and drained through the towels and the opening of the boards. She shivered even though the water was tepid and the heat from the furnace was appalling. "Almost, almost, almost," Kountz said again, adding more cold water. After two minutes, he touched the mold with both satisfaction and sadness. "It's a one-off. Let's hope it was worth it."

Taking a monkey wrench, he gently cracked the plaster in two places and it fell away. More water was poured over it, partially to continue to cool it and partially to clean away any dust. "Almost," he said once more as he took out a cloth and whipped it around the metal, like a shoe-shine boy. He began to grin.

"Perfect," he whispered. "It's fit for a queen. Here let me show you."

Excited, he called for a mirror. One was produced and Jillybean was shown the intricate vines, the near life-like flowers and the tiny hummingbirds worked into the gold around her throat.

"It is perfect," The Cadaver said, again, almost smiling.

Jillybean didn't think so. The artistry was amazing, that couldn't be doubted, but what it was on, made it horrible. She stared at herself, naked except for the gold collar. She was now a slave.

Chapter 32

Gunner found Emily asleep leaning against a tree. Her snores were soft and wonderful, and he felt like he could listen to them all night, if the Moon Dogs weren't boiling up from the south to kill them all, that is.

He was even more exhausted than she was, having been on the go for days now, snatching brief naps whenever he could find a moment. Just then he couldn't afford to rest even though his twisted body demanded it. This was a make or break battle that stank of desperation. If they lost, or if his men ran, that would be it. If they ran, he knew they would scatter to the winds and would be hunted down and destroyed in detail.

It's why he had to be on top of every detail. The one thing he could not control were the Moon Dogs themselves. The fate of five hundred men and one girl depended on whether he had been able to lure the gang of killers far enough ahead of the rest.

For three hours now, he had fled before them in a feigned rout, taking advantage of their aggressiveness. If they weren't alone, if the Mawks had kept up, Gunner was going to lose his third fight of the day. He just didn't have the numbers to secure his flanks properly. The last two times, they had come boiling up his left flank and nearly turned his position. Hard fighting had kept the combined Santa/Coos Bay Clan army from annihilation, but they were all running on vapors now.

They had to have a win, and Gunner had done everything possible to make it happen. He had set a trap that was both psychological as well as physical. The Moon Dogs would be caught in the open at the end of a valley. Their own left flank would be turned by the picked men Gunner had already stationed behind a low rise. If the Moon Dogs did *anything* except turn and run, they would be in trouble.

Gunner didn't want them to run; it's why he left an old dry riverbed on their right unguarded. The wide sandy lane led directly to where Emily was sleeping against the tree. She and a hundred men would be in the perfect position to rain hot lead on the Dogs.

Paradoxically, he felt that she was in the safest place on the peninsula. Everything to the east of them was crawling with hundreds of monstrous zombies. To the west, companies of Corsairs were marching, and soon, if the wind ever changed, more would be landed at intervals at the north end of the peninsula by their navy. The trap was closing around them and nowhere was safe.

He sighed and gave her a gentle poke on the shoulder. "Hmmm?" she mumbled. She was bleary-eyed, slow-witted, and so incredibly beautiful that it hurt Gunner's heart.

"It's go-time in fifteen. Do you have your fields of fire set?" In answer, she pointed in a diagonal to her left and then to her right. "Good. Now listen, don't be afraid, okay? They're going to be taking fire from three sides. It won't be all you. It's one of those things all newbs have to learn. The battle is not about you. You are just a small, but important piece. Play your part well and we all win. Okay?"

She gave him a shallow smile that he read correctly: she didn't trust him in this or in anything. From her point of view, all they had done from the start was run away, and when they had stopped to fight, each battle had been a near disaster.

All his men probably thought the same way; not that he cared what they thought. They could choke on their complaints since they were the sole reason for the endless retreats. The clansmen were weak-willed and had failed each test put before them in the long-running battle.

As good as they were on the sea, they were sorry fighters. Just like the Magnum Killers, whom Neil Martin had led to their ultimate destruction two days before, they made crappy, whiny, weak soldiers, and it had taken all of Gunner's skill to keep them alive for this long. Most of the mountain bandits were far better. They were tough, hard-charging men who understood camouflage and subterfuge. They were also much better marksmen.

Their leadership had not proven equal to the quality of the soldiers. They were overly brash and foolishly confident. They made a sacrament out of frontal attacks, basing their reputation almost completely on bravery. If Gunner had a halfway decent force, he could have whipped the lot of them three times over.

If. Always if.

"Let them come in close," he told his daughter. "The closer the better. And don't be afraid. Trust me, they'll be far more afraid of you." She gave him another disbelieving smile. "It's true. When the bullets start flying, they won't picture you as an eleven-year-old girl, they'll imagine they're up against some sort of badass ranger."

"Ranger?"

A boast swelled in his throat. He quickly swallowed it. "I'll explain who the rangers were after the battle. Stay safe. Got it?" Forgetting himself, he leaned in to kiss her forehead. Thankfully, he came to his senses before he could embarrass himself.

When he left, a shudder ran through her. "He was going to kiss me," she whispered in disbelief, her eyes suddenly wet with tears. She was afraid that whichever side won, she would lose. "Pull it together," she told herself, wiping a sleeve across her eyes. "You're supposed to be a boy, remember?" She wondered if anyone still believed that lie. Earlier that day, she had caught a number of men eyeing her with odd looks on their ugly, bearded faces.

Just then, she was too tired and too afraid to care about that little problem. It didn't matter what Gunner said, she was frightened right down to her toes. She wasn't anything like her mother. "She was a Valkyrie." Emily knew that was some sort of girl warrior with wings and golden hair. Except for the wings that was Deanna Grey through and through.

Emily knew all the stories from the old days. Her mother had been as tough as any man and had singlehandedly turned the tide of the last great battle in the war with the Azael. "*She* would never let some creep kiss her," Emily seethed. She took out her jackknife and gave it a flick so that the metal gleamed. "Anyone who tries to kiss me will get this," she vowed.

For just a moment, she felt as tough as her mother, but then there was a sudden ripple of gunfire and her strength left her. Quickly, she scrabbled for her gun, dropping her knife in the process. It no longer mattered to her in the least. Her vow was all but forgotten. Still, the blade winked like a silver eye at her. What if someone saw it?

With shaking hands, she reached for the knife and nearly closed it on her thumb. "Jeeze," she whispered, sticking it back in her pocket. The need to cry began to grow stronger as the thunder of gunfire rose and fell, and then rose again louder and longer. This wasn't another skirmish, this was a full-on battle and everyone knew little girls were not meant to be in battles. She was meant to be home with her mom. It was past her bedtime and...

The sound of the battle suddenly shifted. It had shifted slightly to the south. The Moon Dogs had tried their usual flanking maneuver and had run up against the men holding the low ridge.

"It's working!" someone in the dark cried. It set off excited whispers all around the old river bed. The whispers became a growing babble, which died altogether as the firing suddenly changed direction again. Now it was coming right at them. Men began licking their lips and checking their guns for the tenth time and then the eleventh. Someone began shushing people who weren't even talking. He was shushed roundly in turn.

Seconds later, they heard the first of the Moon Dogs. They were panting like real dogs as they ran. They were frightened!

This should have filled Emily with confidence, instead, she shrank behind the M4 Gunner had given her the day before. From the outside, it looked as though she were hiding behind it. "Go. Go away," she whispered. "Please go. Please…" The shadows began to shift in front of her. They grew and surged like a black wave heading right down the river bed, heading right for her!

One thing she knew for certain: there was no chance in hell that any of them was even remotely as frightened as she was. Her fear escalated so quickly that she reached the point of petrification—a very brittle petrification. She felt as brittle and as thin as a cracker, and she guessed that if she fired her gun, she would simply crumble into dust and be blown away by the northerly wind.

Then she saw the first of the bandits, materializing with such suddenness that he seemed as if he had been formed from the shadows. He stopped right in front of her and she saw him with perfect clarity, noting his forked beard and the Dodger logo on his faded baseball cap. He was so close she couldn't miss— not that she could shoot with numb, frozen hands.

The bandit must have suspected something, because he jerked his gun up and had it aimed as he slowly traversed it from right to left. When the barrel swept across her, she let out a gasp. To her own ears the gasp was theatrically loud as if she was trying to get his attention, which she did. His gun swung back and centered its black hole directly on her forehead.

That was the very worst moment to shoot and yet, inexplicably, her gun fired on its own accord. It just went off and she was so surprised that she almost shrieked and threw it from her. But it was her only real weapon, even if it was defective. How else could she explain the weak sound it made. From her limited experience, guns made lots of noise and yet this one hadn't made any, not even a cough.

It fired with a whisper and a spark, and instead of banging hard enough against her to bruise her shoulder, it barely jumped, making her wonder if it had fired a bullet or a sweet pea. She decided that the nudge, which should have been a kick, was her gun's way of telling her to shoot for real.

She had every intention of doing so; however, the fork-bearded bandit crumpled and fell practically at the base of the tree she was hiding behind. He began gurgling and gasping, dying right in front of her. Emily didn't know what to do. Running felt like the best idea in the world, but could she just leave the man? Didn't she have some sort of responsibility to help him?

Her indecision whether to run or step forward to help, kept her rooted in place long enough for another bandit to materialize. He was huge and hulking, running in a crouch. For a moment, he reminded her of Gunner. The moment ended with her gun going off a second time. They were both surprised.

"What?" the man growled, his hands groping at his chest as if searching for something in one of his pockets.

Emily's gun had lowered slightly. Now, it came back up, ready to shoot—ready to kill. *No, it's me*, she thought as the hulking man took a step back. His right leg buckled and he fell on his face, his searching hands failing to break his fall. He didn't move, not even to turn his face from the dirt.

I killed him. Emily didn't know if she felt sad or triumphant, or what. Before she could figure it out, another man ran diagonally in front of her. He was screaming but he had a voice like rushing static. This time, she took deliberate aim with the gun and she felt the kick and heard the blast. The man spun as if he had been struck by an invisible sledgehammer and fell. He didn't die like the others and she fired again, and again until he finally stopped twitching. Sickened, she looked around and discovered she was in the middle of a tremendous battle.

In the dark, it was simply bewildering. Little lights were blinking everywhere as if both sides had deployed regiments of fireflies. The sounds generated by the intense fight were equally confusing. The explosions of the guns formed a background curtain of noise that was meaningless compared to the hissing bullets sizzling through the air inches from her head. Along with hissing, people were screaming in pain and others were bellowing orders at the tops of their lungs. There was also someone laughing which was almost as scary as the hissing bullets.

The strangest sound was that of knocking. It was like someone was hammering on her front door. At least a minute passed before she realized the knocking was bullets thudding into her tree, sending bark and chips into the air. Her first thought was insane, *Were there enough people firing at her to chop it down?* She wondered where she would hide.

"Nowhere," she realized. If the tree came down, she would die. The bullets would get her. It made no sense, but this spurred her on to a desperate defense of her tree. She fired at the sparkling lights until she ran out of bullets. In a new panic she dug in her pockets looking for more and when she couldn't find any, she scurried about in the leaves at the base of the tree like a squirrel, picking up hot shell casings, glancing at them and tossing them aside.

In the middle of this insane behavior, she was stopped by a great cheer. Popping her head up, she saw the clansmen around the riverbed jumping up from their hiding spots and advancing inward; the Moon Dogs were giving up! Bright joy lit her insides and she cheered along with the rest, jumping up and down like a maniac.

One of the clansmen was giving out hand-blistering high-fives and in her enthusiasm, Emily raised her small hand to receive her share, only the man froze in front of her, a stunned expression on his face. "You're a girl," he told her.

Someone had lit a lantern and in its soft light, everyone around her could see her golden hair and her delicate features. During the fight and the mad scramble to find a bullet, her hood had fallen back. "So what I'm a girl?"

"It's just weird is all. Does anyone else think it's weird?" A few men shrugged, a few agreed with him, and the rest leered like vultures.

"It's not weird," Emily answered, holding her M4 close to her chest. "I'm allowed to be here. *Gunner* said I could be here." Evoking his name caused some of them to draw back into the dark and it made the others waver. Emboldened, she began nodding. "Yeah, Gunner said that if anyone touched me, he'd break their you-know-what's right off."

This seemed like something he would do and every one of the clansmen quickly lost interest in her. They hurried to scrounge from the dead, the wounded, and the new prisoners. Emily went with them, desperate for some way to protect herself. Dropping Gunner's name might work in the short run, but it wouldn't shield her forever.

She searched what she considered were her kills and found four full magazines and two partials. It was something of a relief to slap one of the full ones home. She also found some dried fruit and some meat that had an old cheese smell to it; she kept both; the meat just in case things got bad.

While everyone else was rounding up the prisoners, she began nibbling on the fruit, which had been dipped in crystallized honey. It was sticky but good and she was just cleaning her hands with her tongue when the first of the wounded was shot.

"I'm just putting them out of their misery," the shooter said with a shrug. Others joined in and soon the wounded were riddled and very dead. Then there came a tense moment as that first shooter gazed at the remaining Moon Dogs, kneeling in the lantern light. "What the hell? We ain't gonna let 'em go so we might as well…" He finished his sentence with a long burst from his rifle.

The slaughter was over quickly. Too quickly for Gunner to put a stop to it, although no one really knew whether he would have bothered. He stormed into the area with that ugly, crab-like walk of his and though he frowned at the carnage, his mind was entirely on Emily.

When he saw her with her hood thrown back, he reached to pull it up again. She stepped back from his hand, feeling every eye on her. "It's too late for that," she said in a whisper.

"Are you hurt?"

Before she could answer, someone snickered, "Look, it's beauty and the beast."

Gunner rounded on the little group of men. "Who said that?" Hands pointed to a rail-skinny man, who took a step back and started to bring his rifle up. Gunner already had his Glock out. "Take it back!" he thundered.

"I-I'm sorry. I-I was just joking, and I didn't mean it, I swear."

This seemed to satisfy Gunner, at least partially. "Find five men and get a fire going. We're moving out and I want zombies all over this place."

"We're moving out?" Alec Steinmeyer asked. He threw his hands in the air. "We can't. Men are dropping like flies. We need our rest."

"And you'll get it. Five miles northeast of here is a little community. We'll be able to rest there. We'll be out of the wind and the cold. Trust me, we'll get more rest there than plopping on the ground here. I don't know about any of you but I want to sleep in an actual bed if I can, with a fire and blankets."

This won the men over and they were able to find the energy needed to drag their tired bodies to the little cluster of homes and businesses that made up Big Loop, Washington. Emily made it, but only barely. The battle had taken everything out of her and she staggered and fell so frequently along the march that Gunner carried everything of hers and then considered carrying her.

She was in a semi-conscious stupor by the time they reached the town. "This is it?" she blurted. There were maybe seven or eight little homes, a gas station, and a convenience store; clearly there weren't nearly enough beds for all the men. A disappointed groan went up at the sight of the dinky town.

"Stop your whining!" Gunner snapped. "Anyone who wants to sleep out in the woods can do so. The rest of you are going to have to get comfy cozy with one another. I want a minimum of two people per bed. If you're afraid to sleep in a bed with another man, then by all means, you can sleep on the damned floor."

There were two exceptions to the two people to a bed order. One was Emily; Not only did she have her own bed, she had her own room as well. The other exception was Gunner. No one wanted to share a bed with him; he wasn't exactly broken up by this.

After setting Emily up in her own room, he took a mattress and plunked it down in front of her door. Before bedding down, he went through the house to make sure the fires that had been lit, one in the fireplace and two on old, rusting garbage can lids, were not going to kill them all. He also went in search of dry clothes for Emily.

He had to wake her up and she was so out of it that he was afraid he was going to have to change her himself. The idea frightened him worse than having to fight a dozen men. "I'll just get her started. Emily? Emily? Wake up." He sat her up and she lolled forward like a ragdoll, her head slumped on her chest. "Okay, I'll just take off your coat."

She had on two coats, which he managed to get off without waking her. Next, he went to work on her wet boots. When he was tugging one off, she woke up.

"What are you doing?" she asked, in a frightened whisper, tugging the blankets up to her chin. In the dark, he looked like a hideous nightmare monster and her first bleary thought was that he was going to eat her. It was only when she came fully awake that she thought about the other danger a strange man in her bed could mean.

"Nothing, I swear. I have dry clothes for you. That's all. Honest."

Honest? Nope, she couldn't believe that. Her hand went for her knife, but it had been in one of her coats, and her rifle was against the wall. She was an open book that he read with sadness. Holding up the clothes, he placed them on the bed and backed away.

"I'll be right outside in case you need anything." Feeling like a creep, he left her and was just settling down when the door cracked open an inch, just enough for one blue eye to be seen.

"I have to use the bathroom," she said, barely loud enough to be heard. He scrambled up and stood away from the door, lurking in the shadows. He pointed a stubby half-finger at a door down the hall. She tip-toed past his mattress and to the bathroom only to find it occupied; one man was sleeping in the tub and another laid out on the floor.

The smell coming from the toilet was violent in its stench. She turned away, her throat seizing. "There's another one downstairs," Gunner told her. Halfway down the stairs, she stopped. Every inch of the livingroom and hallway was covered in sleeping men.

How many of them were as creepy as Gunner? she wondered. *How many were worse?* Gunner could have raped her ten times by now if he had wanted to. She turned to him and saw that he had come forward silently; in his hand was his Glock. He wanted her to take it. Even that didn't seem like enough protection. What if someone grabbed her from behind? What if they came in while she was on the toilet? Was she supposed to carry the gun even then?

"Could you come with me?"

"Yeah," he said too quickly and with too much excitement in his voice. Guarding her on the way to the bathroom was the closest thing to a daddy-daughter date he'd ever had with her and he felt a stupid sense of pride—but she had heard the excitement and looked about to rescind the invite. "I mean, I guess so. Follow me," he said, making sure his normal gruffness was back.

He led her down to the first floor to the small powder room off the hall. It had no tub and was too small for anyone to sleep in. Unfortunately, it was also too small to have a window and, if anything, the smell here was far more appalling than the bathroom upstairs. Emily didn't dare lift the lid of the toilet.

"I can't," she said, feeling her stomach flutter threateningly. Even though squatting in the woods meant she would be alone with Gunner, she couldn't hold it any longer and some things had to be risked.

They were back inside in under a minute. He had stayed discreetly back a good thirty feet and didn't once take a peek. It had been such a long grueling day that it was the highlight—she had been able to pee in peace. Although he had won a desperate battle and had saved his little army from destruction, that one minute was the highpoint of his day as well.

He was feeling almost euphoric and for just a moment before he fell asleep, he wondered if the tide was turning for them. All he needed for that to happen was for the wind to keep howling down from the north. According to the eavesdropping he'd been doing with Lexi May's radio, the fleet had been almost stalled for nearly the entire evening. If this kept up, Gunner pictured setting another trap and if he could pull it off, the entire course of the war could be changed.

He fell asleep, making his first military error since assuming control of Jillybean's army—he forgot to set his watch. He meant to sleep for four hours, instead seven went by, and during that time the wind changed, coming out of the west in a beautiful steady breeze.

Corsairs were landed in six different spots north of him and began closing steadily in, while at the same time the *Mawks* and *Meat Hooks*, spurred on by threats from the Black Captain, had marched without sleep and were only a mile away.

There was nowhere for Gunner's army to run and nowhere to hide.

Chapter 33

The torture and the pain started early, basically right off the bat as the Queen walked back up the hill wearing the golden collar around her neck and not a stitch of any other clothing. After the heat of the furnace, the night was dreadfully cold and the pavement was like walking on rough ice; her feet ached unimaginably with every step. She said nothing, knowing that complaining was useless. The Cadaver's one job was inflicting pain and he had a reputation for enjoying his work.

He proved worthy of his reputation over the next two days as he broke out every horrible trick in the torturer's manual. He even proved equal to his name.

The man was dead inside. His heart was as cold as the barren cement floor that Jillybean slept on when she wasn't being tortured. He never cracked a smile unless she screamed and then he produced a creepy leer as if hoping the scream would progress into something worse, like a chronic disease, cancer perhaps. If she could stifle a scream, he didn't get mad, he would return to that endlessly bland look of his. The look made it seem like he could wait forever for the next scream, even if he had to take the bat to her shins again. Which he did, a lot. He wanted her to beg for him to stop.

She tried to swallow her tongue instead.

Don't think about it, she thought as he picked up the bat once more. Sweat ran into her eyes, stinging them, blinding her. That was good. She couldn't bear the sight of the bat or the hammer or the jumper cables. *Do more than endure the pain,* she told herself. *Live it. Crave it. Enjoy it.*

She had read that there were people who liked pain. They enjoyed it, sexually. It seemed crazy and yet…

Snawder smacked her left shin with the bat. He didn't hit her hard because he didn't have to. Both of her tibias had hairline fractures running up and down them and were bruised and swollen. It took very little effort to send her into a convulsion of pain. Her teeth slammed together so hard they looked like they were about to crack, as her beautiful face morphed into a hideous mask. Her full lips drew back, her eyes bulged, and the tendons of her neck went taut as cables.

She had already vomited twice, and she felt a third wave building. After a few seconds, she was able to pant it back down, gulping air.

"You know you can end this," he said, stooping so that their eyes were level. "Just talk to me. That's all I want."

LIAR! she wanted to scream. This wasn't an interrogation. Sure, he had asked her many questions, most concerning Bainbridge. He had pretended that it was very important to know about the island's defenses and its military. She wasn't fooled. These were just excuses. All he cared about was breaking her. It would start with giving up secrets about Bainbridge, but once the dam was broken, she would say or do anything to stop the pain. She would beg and grovel and lick his feet, all for nothing.

The pain wouldn't stop until her spirit was well and truly broken. It wouldn't stop until she was too afraid to look up past his knees, or until she peed herself at the sound of his voice, or until she trembled uncontrollably when he walked in the room.

And even then, the pain would never stop. The Black Captain had already collared her, but when she was broken, he would lead her around on a leash, making her crawl on all fours. He would debase her. He would steal her humanity. He would make an example out of her.

The bat struck her on the left shin again. Her arms flung wide, the chains snapping tight. She was on a crude, homemade chair that was stained with blood and piss and every other fluid that could come out of a person. She added a quart of watery vomit to the mess.

"Oh, Jillybean," he said, sadly. "You know you can't go around making messes like that. Look what you did to that pretty collar of yours. I'm afraid there's going to have to be a punishment." He tapped the bat on the floor three times and all she could think was: *Not the left again, please. Hit the right.*

Snawder whistled for his assistant, a big nervous man with blank eyes and no tongue. He also had no teeth for that matter. "Put her on the stand," Snawder said the man.

"N…" The word *No* had almost slipped out of her mouth. She hated the stand with all her heart and soul. It was a simple enclosed cage-like device about the size of a telephone booth that allowed for only two positions: standing or kneeling…on sharp rocks which were glued to the floor. Those little rocks made everything worse.

She couldn't escape the pain of them for a second. She could only twist or go from foot to foot or change positions constantly. And then, when the tortures were added on top of everything, the agonies were magnified, and there was no let up, no rest, no moment to just breathe.

"I'm sorry, did you say something?" Snawder asked. She almost shook her head, stopping herself with her chin canted to the side. "Ooh, that was close. You're slipping Jillybean. It's still Jillybean isn't it?" He grabbed her chin uncaring about the vomit that covered it. With irresistible force, he turned her face to his. She closed her eyes, not willing to give away anything.

It was her. Eve wasn't even a ghost in her head. Just when Jillybean needed her, she was gone, driven away by the cocktail of drugs that Snawder was pumping into her veins. It had been a shock to know that Eve wasn't coming to her rescue.

"I want to break the Queen, not some loony half-ghost," he had said the night she had been collared. "When you first came to me you were being unresponsive to my advances, but look at you now, all bright-eyed and bushy-tailed. Do you wonder why that is?"

She hadn't known five-seconds before; she did then. "You've been spiking my food or water," she had answered, and although she sounded confident, she was terrified beyond measure. If there was one good thing about being crazy it was the ability to escape from reality. Without Eve, she had been unable to hide from the horrors of her torture.

Two days of endless pain and she would have done anything to get Eve back.

"Look at me or you'll get the stand," he said, his fingers gouging the soft flesh of her face.

Jillybean's life had been such hell that she took her pleasures where she could get them. Snawder had just made a mistake. He had already ordered his mute helper to put her on the stand. Was she supposed to be doubly frightened by this? A smirk came creeping onto her lips.

He grunted, his fingers relaxing. "The stand," he said.

There was no reason to fight the hulking mute. She went in without a struggle and the pain began immediately. The rocks bit into her delicate feet. Both her heels already had bruises that went deep into the bone and her arches were swollen from being hit repeatedly with Snawder's bastinado.

She began to go from foot to foot and it wouldn't be long before she couldn't bear her weight. Expectedly, she grabbed the bars of her cage.

"Let's start the juice," Snawder said.

Jillybean clamped her lips shut on a whimper. The generator was turned on and the electricity coursed into her hands. She had to let go and now the rocks were digging into her feet. There was nothing she could do; the pain was ghastly no matter what she did or which way she turned. Soon, she was a quivering, writhing mess, and there was nothing she could do to stop the screams.

But she didn't break.

At some point, the electricity was turned off and she was pulled from the stand. "The Captain would like to see you now," Snawder told her. "Actually, he asked for the Queen, but I told him the Queen was gone. All that's left of her is a thing coated in urine and vomit."

The nasty words went past her without registering. The only thing she cared about was that the electricity had been turned off.

Snawder demanded that she stand up, but she only laid there, dribbling vomit-tinted sweat onto the floor. The mute had to pick her up and half-drag her out into the grey cold morning. She was still naked but the cold didn't bother her so much; she welcomed it. The idea of freezing to death sounded wonderful. If she'd been allowed to, she would have curled up on the street and gladly died there.

The mute kept her hobbling along. There was only one saving grace, at least she had no one staring at her naked, bruised and vomit-covered body. Save for the many slaves that scurried by without daring to look The Cadaver in the face, a few wounded men and the minimal number of soldiers to guard against the unexpected, Hoquiam was empty.

A thousand men had marched north to act as the anvil, as an equal number were sailing around behind Gunner's trapped army to act as the tactical hammer. The Black Captain expected to smash his last real foe between the two sometime that day. In the meantime, he stood at the front window of his new home watching Jillybean struggle.

He chuckled and then yawned. It had been a long week. "I wonder if we should put down some plastic," he said to his new head of security. He had gone through so many guards lately that he was scraping the bottom of the barrel using Dean Bridge. The man had a fine reputation as a sure-shot who was cool under pressure, but the Captain didn't like how small he was or how sallow and unhealthy he looked. He had felt safer whenever Eustace had been around.

It wasn't something he cared to admit.

Not that he was worried about Jillybean. She looked like a frail, beaten old woman as she limped through the doorway. He noted how her toes curled gratefully on the soft, warm carpet. After taking a moment to collect herself, she lifted her chin.

"Captain," she said, with the tiniest of nods—one equal to another.

He burst out laughing at the display, slapping his hand on his thigh. Everyone in the room laughed along as well, including the nervous slaves, though their laughter was forced. They knew they were one spilled wine glass away from sharing Jillybean's fate.

Along with the Captain and eighteen slaves, there were four guards and The Cadaver, who managed to crack a genuine, but small smile.

"You've still got some fight in you, I see," the Captain said. "Impressive. Few people last even this long with ol' Chuck playing their frayed nerves like a Stradivarius. Still, I guess it won't be long now."

"That I can't say," The Cadaver replied. "It could be tonight, but like you said, she still has fight in her. I'd like to undermine that, with your permission, of course. The rumor is that she has a soft spot for others; especially women."

Jillybean's face froze and her eyes dropped to the floor, which elicited another laugh from the Captain. "Your poker face isn't what it used to be, your Highness. Who'd you have in mind, Chuck?"

"Glenda Jensen, the slave who told her which room was yours. I figured it would make a fitting punishment and throw a good scare into the other girls."

The Captain began slowly clapping, his wide hands coming together as loud as gunshots. "Bravo. A perfect two-for-one deal. Let's do it."

The slave was brought forward, led by a chain hooked around her collar. She had four other chains on her collar, each attached to twenty-five pound weights that she had to drag behind her.

Beneath her collar, her throat was red and blistered. More of her lank hair had been torn from her head. Every inch of exposed skin was bruised or bloody. She stared about the room with haunted eyes and when her frightened gaze fell on the Black Captain, she collapsed to her knees and hid her face.

"Definitely get some plastic," the Captain said at the sight of her. He would have preferred a public display so that everyone could learn, once again, the penalty for crossing him. It's a lesson he liked to impart four or five times a year, and he thought it was especially needed considering how quickly his captains had turned on him. The problem was that his captains were all out fighting, and it made no sense to get cold and wet for nothing. Where once the Captain had made an ally of the elements, he called for more wood for the fireplace.

Once the fire roared, and plastic sheeting was gleefully found, Glenda was dragged forward by her collar. The mute started to strip her; however the Captain called for him to use his whip to remove her clothes. She was whipped bloody before the last of her rags were torn from her limp body.

Her screams left Jillybean shaking.

"Tell him what he wants to know," Glenda begged.

Nothing had been asked during the whipping, then again, what did that matter? "He knows everything already," Jillybean whispered, without looking up at the Captain. "He just wants to break us."

"That's not altogether true," The Cadaver said. "We still don't know how you escaped or what you did to Eustace." He almost smiled, it was there behind his dead eyes. "You could explain that…if you don't want to see poor, poor Glenda in any more pain. Don't you think she suffered enough?"

Glenda turned her bloody face up to Jillybean. She was missing her right eyebrow, it was replaced by a red gash. Her mouth had been extended an extra two inches, so she looked like a cross between a clown and a frog. More of her hair had been torn from her head—and they had only just begun to torture her.

Jillybean stared into her eyes, noting how the left one sagged slightly. "It doesn't matter what I tell them, they'll keep hurting you."

Snawder replied for Glenda, "If it doesn't matter, then why don't you answer? Maybe we should send her into the house? Maybe we should send her down into the basement. What do you think will happen to her?"

She knew exactly what would happen: Glenda would die, trapped in a twisting, twitching body, suffocating slowly. It would be a horrible death, and yet, it would be a better death than the one she was facing.

"Don't listen to him," Jillybean said, without looking at Snawder. "You know this is all a lie. If I could save you, I would, but there isn't a single thing I can say or do that will help. You know that."

Deep in her heart, past all the fear and the pain, Glenda knew Jillybean was right. "I don't blame you," she said and closed her eyes, knowing what was coming. The whip struck a second later, and then three seconds later, and then three seconds after that. It came like clockwork until her flesh was hanging off her in ribbons.

Her pain hurt Jillybean so much more deeply than her own tortures. The guilt brought out a richer, more exquisite sting because Jillybean couldn't help but think that there was the tiniest chance that she was wrong. That maybe she could end Glenda's pain by begging the Black Captain to stop. But where would the begging end? It never would. Once she started, it would be all she had left, and it was exactly what he wanted from her.

"No," she said under the screams. "I won't break." There were real reasons why she was so adamant about holding it together. The first was obvious: cringing and crying and begging uselessly for mercy would not save her or Glenda. The second was that she had been broken her entire life; however, her mental fractures had been coping mechanisms to protect the real girl beneath all the mess. Breaking now would expose that girl and destroy her.

Without her, Jillybean didn't know what would be left—the dark *It* that only cared about killing? Something worse? A sad, sickening half-human like Glenda? Probably.

She closed her eyes and her mind to Glenda. This was something that the Captain wouldn't allow, and he pointed the mute's whip at Jillybean. The pain from the first lash was shocking. It seared like fire across the bare skin of her back, and yet it was something of a victory. She would take all of Glenda's pain if she could.

The whip only fell on her three times before it went back to striking Glenda with the sound of gunshots. Jillybean immediately closed her eyes again, hoping to take the woman's pain. The Captain must have guessed her intention and didn't strike her again.

Eventually, Glenda was beyond pain and the Captain became dissatisfied with her. "Chop her hands off and give them to the Queen to wear." Everyone thought this was a wonderful idea and an axe was brought forward. Glenda gazed at it dully out of her one remaining eye. She wasn't frightened. Fear was beyond her.

Her hands were hacked off and she bled out, both quickly and gratefully. The hands, still dribbling blood and interstitial fluids were pierced with a heavy needle and thread and then tied to the golden collar that hung from Jillybean's neck.

"They look nice on you, your Highness," the Captain said, laughing in his throat. "I think you need a few more." He glanced around at his slaves who were all pale and trembling.

"Can I suggest using someone she knows?" a woman said from behind Jillybean. She knew the speaker: Joslyn Reynolds. She stood in the doorway doing her best not to look at Glenda's remains. As usual, her dark hair was brushed to a luster and her smile had that, I-know-more-than-you-think quality to it. It was a quality Jillybean had dismissed for years, much to her detriment.

Jillybean, naked and kneeling in a foul mixture of blood, sweat and tears, snarled, "I'll gladly wear your hands. I'll even take them off for you."

Joslyn was about to snap back when the Captain came between them, moving with the fluid ease of a panther. "Ladies, please." Jillybean glared at him, while Joslyn backed meekly away, afraid of the man she had cast her lot with. He grinned at her fear, enjoying it. "Who'd you have in mind? Colleen?"

She had just started to answer when there was a knock on the door. It was a tattooed Corsair; his face was mottled blue-green from the ink. The designs themselves had faded or blended so as to be unrecognizable. He gave a stiff bow.

"We have them, sir. They're trapped. Gunner and the last of the rebels, I mean. You know, Steinmeyer and his stupid clansmen."

The Black Captain instantly forgot about Jillybean. Now that she was collared and chained, she was for fun. "Where? And are the Santas with them? I don't want any more surprises."

"Yes sir, they certainly are. We got 'em bottled up on the Skokomish River right in that little valley by Mt Stone. They ain't going anywhere!"

"Excellent! Sorry Snawder, this takes precedence. Jos, that was a good idea. Get Colleen ready. I'll be back tonight or tomorrow. Probably tomorrow." He stepped over Glenda as if stepping over a mud-puddle and kissed Joslyn hungrily, before giving Jillybean a quick wink and sauntering from the house.

"Do you have Colleen White?" Jillybean asked. Joslyn raised a smarmy eyebrow in answer. "I don't like her, you know," Jillybean said, quickly. "We never saw eye to eye on anything."

Joslyn added a smug smile to the smarmy eyebrow. "Then you won't mind when she gets her pretty face wrecked. Of course, she'll blame you, either way. After all, everything that's happened so far is all on you, and this," she indicated the gold collar and the dangling hands, "is exactly what you deserve."

Chapter 34

Because Troy Holt was simply too clean cut to pass as anything but the altar boy that he was, and Neil Martin looked like a zombie, acted like a zombie, and smelled like a zombie, it had been up to Stu Currans to play the part of the spy.

It was not a role he was very good at. As far as he knew, spies had to be suave, slick-talking and charismatic, and he was none of these things. The only thing Stu had going for him was a month-old beard, the gravelly growl in his voice and the steel in his eyes. These attributes were enough to allow him to travel safely among the Corsairs, passing himself off as one of the *Mawks*, though he had no idea who the *Mawks* were. Someone had said, "You must be one of them *Mawks*," to which he replied, "Yeah," and that was that.

He figured a *Mawk* had to have a reason for being in Hoquiam so he affected a limp and told anyone who asked that he had been shot in the thigh.

Not that he talked to a lot of people. The Corsairs usually kept to themselves and sneered at any outsiders. They were hateful and suspicious, and questions only made them more hateful and suspicious. Stu tried to talk to some of the many slaves running around the town; however they were so frightened of their masters that they would never give away anything that could possibly be construed as disloyal.

This made finding out information a very delicate and time-consuming process. Stu found that the only way to discover anything was to lurk outside open windows and in the shadows near bored guards. It had taken a day and a half to figure out where the Black Captain's old home was, where his new home was, and that Jillybean wasn't there. She was being tortured by the man everyone called The Cadaver.

"He's *un-making* her," one guard had said the night before. Stu's chest had tightened to the point he began to worry he was in the middle of a heart attack. The conversation went on, but no one mentioned where this Cadaver person lived. Stu went in search of screams and found himself going in circles—the Corsairs liked their women to cower at the least frown, which in their mind meant frequent beatings.

Screams rang everywhere though none were Jillybean's. She stifled her screams, denying Snawder anything full-throated.

And so, their second night in Hoquiam passed as uselessly as the first.

In the morning, Neil was almost feverish with anxiety for Jillybean. He paced and added a new wrinkle to what he called the "Empire idea" in which they fake tied him up and brought him before the Black Captain.

"We can sew a bomb into my stomach lining. Trust me, it won't hurt, unless it goes off and then it won't hurt for long." They didn't have a bomb, otherwise Stu would have agreed. Any other attempt would be a waste of time since Stu had watched every person getting frisked and questioned as they went into the Captain's residence. There was no way Troy would get past the first wire fence.

Stu knew what he had to do. "We're going to have to *question* someone," he told the others at just about same the time Glenda was being brought up from the police station to be whipped to death. They knew what he meant by "question."

"I'm all for it," Neil said, without hesitation. When it came to killing Corsairs, he was all for it. He had never been a hateful person; as a zombie he was much different. He could go from smiling to furious in no time under the right circumstances and Corsairs always made it the right circumstance.

Troy was harder to convince. He had his morals, and these did not include torture; however, they did include acting as a lookout. They also included "blending in" so he allowed his uniform to be torn and dirtied. He also left his spear behind. Neil was also left behind. In broad daylight there was no difference between him and a gargoyle, except of course, for his blingy jeans.

The two men walked out into the stench of Hoquiam and both fought to keep their noses from wrinkling.

"This is a hateful place," Troy said. "I cannot imagine Sodom or Gomorrah being any worse. Could we find fifty righteous people here? Could we find five?"

Stu guessed this was more Bible talk. Troy hadn't been able to stop himself with the Bible talk. "Righteous? Probably not. That's not really our job right now. We need to find one lone man. If he's righteous then that's great, if not…then it's not." Stu felt the sand running out of their hourglass with every breath. He had heard about Gunner being trapped and he had heard about Deanna being arrested.

Their chances of any sort of victory were growing slimmer and slimmer, and it was hard to look for God's blessing here.

Still, they found one in the form of a scream. It wasn't Jillybean's, however. This was from a girl who had perfected her scream over the last four years. She knew she couldn't be too shrill because it only made her master angrier. It couldn't be too loud because he liked to build up and if she hurt her throat and couldn't do her part, he would get mean. And the scream couldn't be too soft, or he wouldn't think he had hit her hard enough at all and she would be hit again whether it was needed or not.

The scream was just the right note. It sent Troy Holt into hero mode from which it was very difficult to get him out again. Stu was forced to race after him as he bounded over a low hedge and bashed his way through a sagging fence. Troy charged through a back yard, tripped over a tire that had been hidden in the overgrown grass, but was back up again in a flash. Stu caught up to him just as he stormed into the screamer's house; by then it was too late to do anything.

"What the hell?" Paul Lester demanded from around the remains of a hunk of salmon. He was a potbellied Corsair with sagging pecs, sagging jowls and sagging earlobes that hung below his jaw. He was wearing nothing but a pair of greying boxer shorts and a pair of athletic socks that had progressed to nearly black.

Across from him was his one and only slave. He called her Jenny, though her real name was Zophie Williams. She stood in something of a hunched cower, a fresh bruise beginning to form on her cheek. It would have to fight through the green sheen of older bruises.

"Hold your tongue," Troy said, his gun still held true. He could pierce Lester's eye with a single shot. "No one asked for your blasphemy. Why did you strike this woman? And do not lie!"

Despite his various sagging parts, Lester did his best to stand perfectly erect, trying to match the two men in height so that he could convey the proper manliness and indignation. "This is *my* house, boy. You don't come into a man's house and threaten him unless you plan on carrying out that threat, and you don't have the guts to pull the trigger."

Troy's eyes flared, and the red was high and bright in his apple cheeks. He set the gun aside. Stu had seen enough and pulled Troy back by the collar. "You say you're the man of the house?" he asked Lester. "You live here all by yourself with just the one girl?"

"Yeah and I'm the third on the *Blood Sword* so if you knew what was good for you, you'd turn your ass right around and get the hell out of here."

Stu grunted out a laugh as he also set aside his rifle and took out his hunting knife. "You aren't wrong, friend. We don't know what's good for us. No one does, not anymore. Sit down." He had the knife held low and close to his side where, even if Lester was quick, he wouldn't be able to grab it.

Lester licked cracked lips. "Why?" Stu didn't answer, he advanced threateningly. Lester did the smart thing and dropped into the closest chair.

"Good," Stu told him, moving to his side. "We're here for answers to some very easy questions. Let's start with the man people call The Cadaver. Where's his...place?" He had choked on the words *torture chamber*.

A slowly dawning realization came over Lester. These weren't Corsairs or even any of the mountain bandits. These men were with the Queen and they were going to try to free her. They were going to fail. They had no chance at all, which meant that it would get back to the Black Captain who had helped them —and that meant Lester was a dead man one way or the other.

"It's not that far," he said. "It's on the corner of screw and you." He crossed his arms over his sagging pecs and calmly waited for the bluster. Sure, they would threaten and raise a fuss, but they wouldn't be stupid enough to actually do anything. Someone would hear.

Stu was beyond caring if someone heard him or not. He couldn't stop picturing Jillybean tied up and crying; it was making him crazy. Without warning he slammed the butt of the knife down on Lester's knee. It was as hard as a bannister and cracked like an egg. Lester sucked in a breath to scream, but before he could let it out, Stu drove the butt of the knife as hard as he could into the man's solar plexus.

With his diaphragm in spasm Lester couldn't scream; he seemed to be choking on the air left in his lungs.

"Stu!" Troy cried.

"Get out of here," Stu ordered, "and take her with you. Go out back or take a walk. Just get out of here."

Troy saw the madness in Stu's eyes. "I'll pray for you and for him."

The Hillman wasn't listening. He had shoved a balled-up washcloth into Lester's mouth and was tearing strips of cloth from the curtains when Troy scooted Zophie outside. Her eyes were wide, and her fingers were like claws, scritching on his armor. "Don't let him hurt Lester, please."

Surprised, Troy took a step back. "Why? Is he your husband? If so, his actions are not those of a proper man. The bible tells us in…"

"He's not my husband! My husband died twelve years ago." The two stared at each other; their cultures clashing so badly that neither really understood the other.

"If he's not your husband then why do you want to protect him?" Troy said at last.

A muffled grunt of pain from within twisted her battered features into a grimace. "It's not allowed. He's an officer. You can't touch them or it's death. Tell your friend that. Hurry!" Troy didn't move. The lady wasn't being truthful, and he wanted to know why. Under his steady gaze, she slowly collapsed into herself. "He'll blame me for whatever happens, and he'll take it out on me."

Troy nodded in understanding. "If it's any consolation, I doubt my friend will leave him alive."

"It's not," she said as a scream rose from the house. It was cut off suddenly. She shuddered. "The next one will be twice as bad, if I even get a master. I'm getting old."

"You *want* a master? I don't understand."

She turned and stared at the house. "I want *one* master. Lester's gone a lot and when he comes back, he spends most of his time drinking and gambling. It could be a lot worse," she said, sighing, tiredly. "I could be a ship's whore or barrack's rat. I don't want that. No one wants that."

"We'll take you with us when we leave," Troy said, deciding on the spot, thinking that Stu would just have to get over himself. He would raise a stink about worsening chances and…

Zophie began laughing and crying, interrupting his thoughts. "You're not getting out of nowhere," she said. "Two guys against all the Corsairs. No. No way. Leave me out of it."

Stu was suddenly in the doorway, sliding a newly cleaned knife back into its sheath. "We can't. You'll talk and that'll ruin everything. I know where The Cadaver's shop is," he told Troy. "We need to go there right away. Neil can watch her."

Troy's shifty smile was the closest thing to a lie that he would allow himself. He figured that Zophie would freak when she saw Neil.

"What-is-that?" she asked ten minutes later from the doorway of the house.

"That is Neil," Troy said, pressing her gently forward. "Neil, this is Zophie Williams. She's our friend and we don't eat our friends, remember?"

Neil's face crumpled in what might have been a frown. "I'll eat you if you keep talking to me like that. What's she doing here?" Stu explained the plan which did not include Neil coming along. "Jillybean is my daughter and I'm going."

"No, not in the daytime," Stu said. "You'll give us away in a snap. Besides, there are only two of them, this Cadaver person, and some mute that he keeps as an assistant. We'll take them down, snatch Jillybean and come back here. When it's dark we'll make our escape. That is the plan and yes, the two of them will have to die. If you have a problem with that Troy, then I will have to chance taking Neil."

Troy took a deep breath before agreeing. Aside from what amounted to assassination, it was a good plan. Even Neil agreed. His thin shoulders slumped at his role. He then glanced at Zophie and asked, "Do you like backgammon? There's a backgammon board in the closet."

"Sorry, I hate backgammon," she replied, feeling in the mood to hate everything.

"Well, it's either that or spin the bottle."

Her eyes bugged at the thought of kissing this half-man. "Maybe we can try backgammon. I actually don't know how to play."

"Me neither. It always looked foreign, you know like French or Portuguese, or something. I mean, what's with the checker pieces? And what's a gammon?" She shrugged and settled across the table from him, making sure to keep her hands on her side of the board. Stu and Troy left them struggling over the instructions: she needed glasses and he needed not to be a zombie.

Hoquiam had that quiet before the storm feeling to it. To Troy it felt like a dam was about to burst. The slaves in the streets hurried about faster than normal, getting inside as quickly as possible. A victory celebration was being planned and that meant the city would be filled with drunk Corsairs. It was a scary time for the slaves.

The guards and the walking wounded were acting like it was Christmas Eve. They were like kids, laughing, playing catch with a football, and hurling good-natured insults at people who passed by. Beardless Troy got his share, but no one questioned the two men. It's not like the Corsairs had uniforms or an intricate rank structure that required knowledge of when and who to salute. They were tall, tough-looking men in a town that respected these attributes.

They fit in so well that Stu decided against breaking into The Cadaver's home. He knocked politely with his left hand, while in his right was the same hunting knife that he used to slit Lester's throat. No one answered and so, he thumped louder.

After five minutes of this, he tried the door, found it unlocked and the two slipped in. The first thing they noticed was the cold. It was a cold that went deep into the bones of the house. It stole into them and made them shiver. Stu called out and got no answer.

"Maybe it's the wrong place," Troy suggested.

Stu wanted to ask: *Then how do you explain the pure evil in the air?* Of course, that might have been all in his head. "We'll check the basement. That's where he does his work." It was the right place, or to be far more accurate, it was the exact wrong place. Everything wrong with the world was found in that basement. In a closet they found moldering bones. In one room they found a heap of corpses; the air was warm and wet, and so incredibly foul that Stu went instantly white and slammed the door.

They stopped looking behind doors at that point. In the main room, where the "Stand" took center stage, they found Jillybean's blood. It was almost completely dry.

"I suppose we wait, then," Troy suggested.

It was a long dreadful wait. They stood at the ready for an hour. Then they "sat" at the ready for a further hour. The final hour and a half they despaired, fearing that they had been too late. Eventually, with the sun beginning to set, they decided to go check in with Neil, each with a small but very real worry that he might have eaten Zophie.

They slipped out the back door and went around the side of the house. Once on the street they were surprised to find it crowded with people—men mostly. There was a great deal of excited talk. Stu tugged on the chain of a passing slave with black hair and filthy rags about her. Even though he hadn't tugged hard, she winced and put her fingers beneath her collar and for a moment, she looked like she was going to spit nails.

In a soft voice, he said, "Sorry about that. Do you know what's going on?"

"You didn't hear? The Captain won a great victory. The Coos Bay Clan and all those stinking Santas were wiped out."

The devastating news stunned Troy and left him feeling somewhat hollow. He did not know God's plan, but it was becoming more and more likely that his part in it could not play out much longer. His fate was closing in on him. Regardless of the evil surrounding him, he drew the Sign of the Cross on his forehead and chest.

The same news rolled over Stu, gripping his heart, and squeezing it with icy fingers, and yet it wasn't the reason he stood transfixed, looking as if someone had just whacked him with a mallet. The slave girl wasn't just any slave girl. He found himself staring Colleen White square in the face. He had known her since she was a squeaky little eight-year-old. He had known her mom. He had known her step-dad until he had died four years before. Unbelievably, it was her in the middle of Hoquiam.

Chapter 35

"Colleen," Stu's voice was tight and rasping. He sounded like he was in pain. "What are you doing here?"

For a few seconds, she wore the same bewildered look as him, then: "Stu!" she gasped when she realized why the man looked so familiar. "What the hell are you doing here? And Troy? What the…" She stared around as if expecting to see more faces she would recognize.

"Not so loud," Stu warned. "We're here to save Jillybean." Her eyes immediately went to slits and he quickly added, "And you, too. Of course, we're going to save you. We just didn't know you were here. Is there anyone else from the Hilltop here?"

The word "Hilltop" made her cringe and she looked around to see if anyone had heard. She then grabbed his hand and pulled him off the street. "I don't think so, but I haven't been everywhere yet. Stu, you can't stay. The Black Captain will be back tonight and then that'll be it. There'll be no getting in or out."

"I'm not leaving without Jillybean."

Anger washed over her pretty features. "Then you're not leaving. They'll kill you, Stu. And that's if you're lucky. If they capture you alive, they'll torture you just like in the stories we used to hear from the traders. I used to think they, you know, exaggerated to give us a scare, but it's all real. They'll do terrible things to both of you."

"I believe my path has been chosen for me," Troy said.

Stu agreed, "Mine too. Do you know where she is? Or what about a guy they call The Cadaver?"

Colleen rolled her blue eyes in exasperation. "What is with every guy when it comes to her? You all completely lose your minds. She's not that great and she's definitely not worth dying over. I can't believe…" She turned away for a moment, shaking her head. "I'm supposed to be going to the jail and they say she's there. I might be tortured you know."

"That's why we're going to get you both out," Stu told her. "Where is it? We'll go there right now."

"So, you can die a hero for her? No. There's like thirty guards on duty. They're all over the place. If you want to commit suicide, there are easier ways." She turned away, tugging at her collar as she tried to figure out what to do. "I think…I think the only good time is when the Captain comes back. There'll be a big celebration and a parade that everyone's been ordered to attend. I bet there'll be a lot fewer guards and in the middle of it, you might be able to get in. It's either that or the three of us leave right now. We could take a boat and go to Bainbridge…"

Stu shook his head. He hated the idea of waiting even a minute, knowing the pain Jillybean was going through, but he wanted a real chance at saving her.

"Fine," Colleen said, her lips drawn in an angry line. "He's supposed to get back around nine. I'll try to get here before then. Don't try anything without me. I don't want to get left behind."

"You shouldn't even go," Troy told her. "If you're going to the jail, it's not for a good reason. Stay with us. We'll protect you."

"I don't need protecting. Unlike you two, a lot of guys around here think I'm alright. They won't hurt me. They bluster and go on, but I'll be okay. The only way there'll be trouble is if I don't show up. Now, I gotta go. You guys will be here at nine, sharp?"

They both agreed, though neither felt good about letting her go. They threaded their way through the crowded streets back to the house they had left Neil and Zophie. The two had moved on from an attempt at backgammon and were now making a stew and chatting like old friends.

Colleen White was a half mile away, approaching the jail with shaking hands and shy, nervous steps. Finding Stu and Troy was something like a miracle. Getting anywhere near The Cadaver was a curse. She had never been tortured by him or seen him in action and yet he had such a reptilian, inhuman air about him that she didn't even like being in the same building as him.

"Sorry I'm late," she said as she walked into the lobby. It was the same room that Jillybean had killed three men in and there were still specs of blood on the walls. She didn't notice. The Cadaver and his hulking mute were there along with three other men. She couldn't look The Cadaver in the eye and said to the closest of the men, "I got caught up…"

The mute punched her in the stomach, sending air blasting out of her. The shock of the punch was followed up a moment later by another. His knuckles, ridged and hard as the spine of a mountain took her in the temple, the cheek, and the corner of her eyebrow sending her to the ground.

Dazed, her head ringing, she blinked away hot blood as she struggled to draw a breath. Chuck "The Cadaver" Snawder leaned down and whispered in her ear, "Know your place, bitch. You think a pretty face means anything? I can carve it off of you if you piss me off. Then where will you be?"

He waited for an answer and she was able to choke out, "Nowhere."

"Exactly. Now get up." He turned to the largest of the guards. "Put her in the cell next to the Queen. We'll let them get re-aquatinted. It'll make everything so much better."

Colleen was dragged to the second cell and was thrown inside. Through the bars she could see Jillybean sitting in a hunched ball, naked and shivering. Water dripped from her hair and lay about her cell in puddles. Colleen was about to say something when the mute came up with a green mop bucket that was filled with nearly freezing well-water. He dashed it on Jillybean.

The act was carried out in silence by both of them.

When he left, Colleen edged to the bars that separated their cells. "Hey, Jillybean, it's me, Colleen."

"Yes, I can see that."

Her nasty tone was surprising. "What did I ever do to you, besides help you? I was the one who got the Guardians on your side, remember?"

"They are not on my side and they never have been."

Colleen was very taken back by Jillybean's entire attitude. "I tried, which was more than most of your people. If I had known this was the thanks I was going to get I wouldn't have bothered."

"Listen carefully: you don't want to be my friend. Not today."

In truth, Colleen never wanted to be Jillybean's friend. The two sat in an uncomfortable silence until Colleen couldn't take it anymore. "Aren't you even going to ask how I got here?"

Jillybean finally moved, turning her creaking, aching neck to take in Colleen White, noting the collar, the new bruise, the blood, and the rags. "I figured you would tell me without me having to ask," she said, after a minute.

"Well, now I'm not going to tell you. Sheesh! You are impossible! Is it because you're jealous of me? No, don't pretend you aren't. It's okay, most women are jealous of me. It's something I've learned to live with. Though I am surprised you are having an issue with it."

"I'm sure a great many things surprise you."

Colleen was about to snap back, however the simple put down held quite a bit of truth. "I'm surprised I'm here. This is what happens when you trust the wrong people. The guys I hooked up with said they were done with the war, just like me, except that was a lie. And they said I wouldn't be treated like the other girls." She grunted out a laugh and then flicked her metal collar with a polished nail.

Jillybean said nothing to this. She only crouched in her ball as time trickled by. Colleen tried to engage her a few more times and got the same non-reply. Soon Jillybean was blue-lipped and dull-eyed. She barely responded when the mute threw more water on her.

"You're going to kill her, you know," Colleen said. "And your boss isn't going to like that."

The guards watching over the Queen conferred, casting suspicious glances at her as if she could somehow fake hypothermia. Eventually, they decided that she wasn't faking and that she really was going to die if they didn't do something. She had her arms and ankles shackled before she was towel-dried, set in front of the fire, and wrapped in a blanket.

She lost track of time and of Colleen and even of The Cadaver. At some point, when it was dark out, she found herself back in her cell with something poking her foot.

"Please, please. You have to wake up." It was Colleen with her face pressed against the bars, reaching in as far as she could. She was clearly worked up about something. When she saw Jillybean's big blue eyes crack open, she beckoned her closer. In the lightest whisper, she said, "Don't say anything and don't react. We're going to be rescued."

Jillybean's complete lack of reaction was shocking. She blinked once. "Sure, we are. By these friends of yours?"

"No, by Stu Currans." Colleen cocked a half-smile that was chock-full of smugness as she watched Jillybean's mouth come open. "He and Troy Holt should be here any moment."

"I don't believe you," Jillybean said, her eyes boring into Colleen.

The girl shook her head in disbelief. "Why would I lie? And why would I lie about this?"

For once the woman with all the answers was at a loss. It felt like a lie because it was exactly what Jillybean had been praying for. She hadn't been praying for just any white knight; she had been praying for *him* to come and rescue her, and yet she knew that he wouldn't. Her soul was too stained to expect a miracle, her luck just wasn't that good, and karma owed her ten lifetimes of disappointments.

Still, she came back to the question of why would Colleen pick this particular lie? Was this a form of psychological torture? Had it been anyone else she might have considered it; however, Colleen just wasn't that smart.

Jillybean searched the woman's eyes and saw much that was hidden, much that she wanted to remain secret, but in this one thing she was being utterly honest.

"He's really coming?" She could hear the desperation in her own voice, and so could Colleen.

"Yes, he really is," Colleen said, enjoying the moment. For the first time since she had met the Queen, she was the superior woman, and when Jillybean began to cry, she had to hide the look of triumph in her eyes.

Chapter 36

The battle began fourteen hours earlier and the small allied force was doomed from the start. In truth, they had been doomed for over a year, though only the Black Captain had known it.

He had never liked the idea of Coos Bay being its own separate town. In his mind, the entire population should have been moved off that steep-ass hill of theirs and brought back to Hoquiam, preferably in chains. But like the Magnum Killers, they had never been properly conquered and so they had negotiated a nation within a nation kind of status.

They had been a thorn in his side ever since. "Never again," he told his captains. He would not let the same thing happen with the mountain bandits. It would be easier since they wanted Bainbridge as their reward, which was perfect since he fully planned on being king of Bainbridge when all was said and done. They could bow to him like everyone else.

He was sick of Hoquiam. The place stank.

Practically the only thing that stood in his way was Gunner and his paltry force, and so far, they had managed to stay one step ahead of Mark Leney, stinging him here and there, making him doubt himself as a general. The Black Captain did more than doubt him; it's why he had shot north the night before to take charge in person.

That, and he wanted the victory to be his alone. Victory seemed like a foregone conclusion when the mountain mists drew back, revealing the smoke from the enemy fires drifting lazily up from every house in Big Loop. They hadn't moved out; it didn't even look like anyone was even stirring.

Mark Leney sensed a trap. In fact, he hoped for one. Having the Black Captain suddenly show up, out of the blue and steal his hard-fought victory wasn't just a blow to his ego, it was a slap in the face.

The Captain felt the trap as well and he moved with caution, taking his time, making sure to place his troops precisely where he wanted them before giving the signal to attack. But there was no trap, there were only a few hundred exhausted men who were low on food and even lower on ammunition. Given the opportunity, they would give up and go to their deaths, meekly. Gunner wasn't going to give them that opportunity.

He had come awake fifteen minutes before, blinking in confusion at the strange grey light beginning to fill the house. "Damn!" he cried, leaping to his feet when he realized he had overslept. There was no need to check his watch to know time had suddenly turned against him.

Without knocking he raced into Emily's room. "Get up," he ordered, going to the window, and throwing back the curtain. The mists were just beginning to lift. Even though he couldn't see his enemy, he knew the Corsairs were out there and that they had minutes to make their escape.

Just as quickly as he came in, he charged back out again, hissing, "Everyone get up. We move out in two minutes. Where's Steinmeyer?"

"Next door," someone drawled. He was moving as slowly as his words. They all were.

Gunner punched the man square on the jaw. "I said get up! Anyone not outside in two minutes will answer to me."

This got them moving as Gunner ran to the next house. This time he started with the hitting, rousing the entire house, and sending men sprinting for the other houses in the little town. Four minutes later, with half the men yawning and the other half peeing off the side of the road, Gunner had them moving. He knew there were men still hiding in the town, but there was no time to hunt them down. His hope was that they would cause a distraction for the Corsairs.

"Take the lead," he told Steinmeyer. "Double-time it up into those hills. And I mean double-time. Only slow down once the last man is safely under cover. I'll join you when I can."

Emily caught his eye and looked as though she wanted to say something. *Good luck*, maybe? *Be careful*, perhaps. *I love you*—that would never come from her mouth.

"Stick to the middle of the company until I get back. If I don't make it, slip away and head to the highest peak. That's Mount Olympus, cross over its southern shoulder and go straight east. It'll be your best bet to make it back home." It would be her only chance. The terrain there was rugged and forested, and a single girl on foot might be able to slip past any patrols.

But Gunner did not plan on dying. His plan was to draw the Corsairs' attention away from the main company for as long as he could. To that end, he jogged back the way they had come and climbed up along a gulch. Just as he slid into the shadow of a boulder, the mist lifted completely.

He had a perfect view of the little river valley. To his right were hundreds of *Mawks* and across from them were a milling group of *Northbenders*, while on a peak to the west flew the jet-black flag of the Corsairs. And unfortunately, he also saw the last of his company straggling up into the hills.

If his daughter hadn't been among them, he would have washed his hands of them right then. Instead he propped his rifle on the side of the rock, took a bead on a clump of the closest group of *Mawks* and let fly half a magazine worth of lead. It was nice to see four of them drop; however his main goal was to focus attention away from where his daughter was struggling up a steep incline three-hundred yards away.

He got all the attention he would ever want as a hundred guns opened up on his position. The boulder offered some protection and for half a minute he lay behind it, lifting his rifle occasionally to fire blindly in the general direction of the *Mawks* just to keep them interested in him.

His position, to put it mildly, was unenviable especially as a group of *Northbenders* were hurrying down from the hills to flank him. With the rain of bullets pelting the hillside, kicking up dirt and chipping away at the boulder, there wasn't much he could do. The bandits were almost through the town when suddenly gunshots rang out from one of the houses.

This changed everything. Gunner was immediately forgotten as the town became everyone's new focus. It wouldn't last. Cowardice had caused a handful of strays to remain behind and although someone had panicked and fired his gun, the rest would not put up much of a fight.

Gunner crawled up to the ridge of the hill and then scuttled like a crab along it until he saw his men moving with dreadful slowness up another hill. He longed for a radio so that he could scream at Steinmeyer to get him moving, but the cheap Corsair knockoff batteries had ceased working the night before.

"I'll just have to scream in person." Although weighed down by his armor and axe, Gunner was fully rested and was able to cut down the backside of the hill, wade through an icy stream and charge up the next one to cut off his company. In fact, he beat them to the peak and had a few minutes to see how much trouble they were in.

The next set of hills to the northwest all had black flags flying from them—they were being hemmed in. To the northeast was another stream which would eventually wind around and feed into the Skokomish River. It was an inviting path and everyone on the hills opposite him should have seen it. "And that makes it an obvious trap," Gunner whispered to himself. "And that leaves what?" The answer was nothing.

There was nowhere to go that the Corsairs couldn't cut them off. "How do I get us out of this?" His mind spun uselessly while his stomach began to ache with fear; not for himself, of course. He was afraid for his daughter. If she were captured, the Black Captain would use her against Deanna. It was the only reason she'd been kidnapped to begin with.

Deanna would do anything to save Emily, including turning over Bainbridge to the Corsairs. In the end, it would gain her nothing. The Captain would get the island as well as both mother and daughter. Gunner didn't want to think about what sort of cruelties would be levied against the two women he loved.

All of this meant that from that moment on, every action of his, every order he issued, and every single life under his command was to be given with one purpose in mind: saving Emily. He would let his men die horrible deaths to ensure that would happen. He was no exception to this. She was the only thing that mattered to him.

"But how to save her?" What could he possibly do that would give her the opening to flee? With the Corsair's numerical advantage, their fresh legs, and their fleet's ability to leapfrog men all around the peninsula, he would have to do something completely unexpected. This was difficult since he was limited to defending one of the hills, attacking up one of the hills or giving up.

He wasn't a man who usually needed much help in this area, but just then the question came to him: *What would Jillybean do in this situation?* He had listened intently to Stu Currans as he had described the battles that had been fought in and around San Francisco. Jillybean was not shy about using the dead to take the place of soldiers. "And she liked to use smoke to her advantage. Fire will bring the dead and smoke will confuse the Corsairs."

The inkling of a plan was just beginning to form when Steinmeyer huffed up to him. "We're trapped," Gunner told him, curtly, ~~pointing out~~ the surrounding hills. The clansmen went pale at the sight of the flags. "We need to make a very big fire as fast as possible."

Now his pallor was touched by green. "That'll bring the dead. That'll bring them right here."

"I know." Gunner's grinning leer was only partially hidden by his mask. "They'll have to get through the Corsairs first. We'll use the distraction to attack. If we don't falter, we'll send them running and we'll be free. It's either that or we give up and hope the Captain doesn't torture you and me to death. What do you think the chances of that are?"

Steinmeyer's only answer was to turn from green to putrid green. He began nodding chicken-like before barking orders in a high, strangled voice. Working without rest, Gunner's company gathered all the dead wood they could find and piled it at the base of the largest trees on the top of the hill and set it on fire.

With its branches still clinging to its autumnal leaves, the tree went up very quickly. It blazed like a huge torch in the early morning light. While it burned, Gunner quickly prepared the men for what he hoped wouldn't be a suicidal attack. He broke them up into two teams, with the plan to attack the hill across from them in two directions.

Whichever team made it to the top first would wrap around and help the second team. It was a bold plan without any chance to succeed. The Black Captain had already countered Gunner's fire by lighting three of his own. What dead were drawn in were captivated by these fires and didn't come anywhere near the battle. Thankfully, the smoke from Gunner's fire masked this partial disaster from his troops and he ordered them forward against a thinly spread, but fully prepared enemy.

They met their first resistance at the base of hill, where the smoke was thickest. The men faltered, confused by the smoke, not sure if they were attacking in the direction they were supposed to.

"Up! Up! Up!" Gunner cried, throwing men forward, seemingly unafraid of the bullets winging high. The men went forward bent at the waist as if heading into a stiff rain. Some fired their weapons, but most only followed after those in front, some going so far as to walk directly behind other men to use them as cover.

Emily had been told to stay as close to Gunner as possible. As much as she feared and loathed him, she did exactly that until they were the last ones at the base of the hill. Reluctantly, she started up in the direction of the sporadic, half-hearted shooting, but he grabbed her.

"No, you're coming with me," he said, pulling her back down to where the smoke was thickest. A thin breeze was pushing it down the narrow gulch between the hills.

They hadn't gone more than a hundred yards when through the haze, they heard heavy breathing, the clank of weapons, and the crunch of old leaves. The Corsairs were already on the move, moving up to attack Steinmeyer in the flank. Of course, the right thing to do would be to shout a warning. Instead, Gunner pulled Emily in next to him and covered them both with the strange fur and feather cloak of his.

Emily was shocked to find him trembling; she would have been even more shocked to find out why. Gunner knew there were too many of them to fight and he was just coming to a terrible realization. The same question as before had just popped into his head: *What would Jillybean do in this situation?* The answer—the only logical answer turned him weak.

If it was Jillybean hiding beneath that cloak and they were discovered, she would kill his only daughter. *But she loves Emily like a sister.* It wouldn't matter. Jillybean would still do it because it would be the right thing to do. For one it would be a mercy.

"But could I kill her?" he whispered, so quietly that even Emily couldn't understand the words. "No." Emily heard that and gave him a shadowed look which only made him grunt as if hurt.

If he couldn't kill her, what were his options to escape? There weren't many. If they were taken captive, he could only hope to get amazingly, miraculously lucky because once they got back to Hoquiam there'd be no escape. He had heard about the pits beneath the prison; no one could get out of them, not even Jillybean. And even if he and Emily could, they'd have to try to run away while wearing nothing but collars of welded metal that were weighted down.

No. There'd be no escape and no jail break. His only chance would be to get away before making it to the lair. And how likely was that? They would undoubtedly chain him like a wild beast and exhibit him freak-show style. He and Emily would be their prizes and watched like hawks making it impossible to even attempt to pick their locks. Not that he could. He didn't have any tools and even if he did, he had never picked a lock in his life and his one hand was only good for wielding his axe.

A sigh escaped him as the men came closer through the thin smoke. There'd be no escape, there would only be rape and torture until Deanna gave in and betrayed the people of Bainbridge. And after that? More rape and torture.

Gunner slid his battered Glock from its holster. He had made up his mind. He would kill her with a single shot to the head and then kill as many Corsairs as he could before he died.

It wasn't just logical, it was the right thing to do.

Chapter 37

Despite his better judgment, Deaf Mick found himself impressed by the young queen. He had expected her to be either haughty and so full of herself as to be unbearable, or timid, afraid to make decisions and always looking for answers from someone else.

For a sixteen-year-old—she'd had her birthday three days before during her short captivity and hadn't even noticed—Deaf Mick thought she was remarkably composed. Then again, she had to be. On the quick trip down, she'd only been able to turn to her blonde boy-toy for advice. Everyone else was practically useless. The two Santas were barely yes-men, Gerry the Greek was gun shy and dithered unless told exactly what to do, and Deaf Mick, well he was a pirate and wished he was back with the other Corsairs where he belonged.

The girl didn't trust him and that was some smart thinking on her part. And that left only Mike Gunter for her to turn to. When it came to decisions, he left everything to her and supported her wholeheartedly, unless it pertained to the boat, then he overrode everyone. In this regard, Mike was as impressive as the Queen.

He was as natural a sailor as Mick had ever seen. The *Queen's Revenge* was a big boat that took a steady, well-experienced hand to guide her. The double-masts were tricky bitches to coordinate even for a man born to the sea like Mick. When he was at the helm, he found the two tremendous snowy sails were constantly undermining each other or working at cross-purposes, making the *Revenge* gripe and want to crab sideways.

Somehow, although most of Mike's sailing career had been spent on twelve-foot dinghies, he could feel the rhythm of the sails and made piloting the boat look easy.

When they got to San Francisco, Deaf Mick was less impressed by what he saw. The Golden Gate was strung with rope and buoys, and in some places a little chain. It was a fine start to a defense, but the people guarding it were almost all women, and were they armed with machine guns or rifles? Why, no they weren't. They had crossbows, which they waved over their heads as if the return of the *Queen's Revenge* represented some sort of great victory.

A gap was opened in the ropes and Mike slid the big ship through the defense with ease. As they approached Alcatraz and the *Floating Fortress*, two thousand people lined the sea wall and stood on the roofs of the buildings. They cheered the beautiful sails and the elegant ship and the majestic white and gold flag.

Their cheering faltered and ground to a shocked halt when Mike hove to and drifted the boat side-on to the dock as easily as if he were parking a Mercedes and not a sixty-foot ship using nothing but a light breeze. The crowd choked on their cheers when they saw it was Jenn Lockhart at the top of the gangway and not Jillybean.

For starters, everyone thought Jenn was dead—many of them had seen her body, some had touched her cold, lifeless flesh, and practically all of them had seen the sinking *Captain Jack* towed out to sea as her final burial spot.

And yet, miraculously, here she was. The shocked silence soon gave way to an excited whisper that raced along the waterfront as she descended onto the dock. She was somber and did not smile, which they took to be a bad thing.

Donna Polston stood before what was left of the old coven. "Jenn? Is everything alright?" she asked. Her head was spinning at the sight of Jenn Lockhart. Dazed, she looked and sounded older than her forty-four years.

Right behind her was Miss Shay, searching desperately for her son, Aaron. "Where is he? Where's my boy?"

"And where's the Queen?" Rebecca Haigh asked. "The *real* Queen, I mean." She was supposed to have been acting governor, but there had been all sorts of inter-factional squabbling and she was very ready to give up the job altogether. She had hoped Jillybean was here to take charge again.

"I am the real Queen," Jenn said, speaking loudly. "Queen Jillian appointed me queen before she was taken captive by the Corsairs. Mark Leney and the entire fleet went over to the other side. Our army was trapped and more than likely has been wiped out by now. We barely escaped. And I'm sorry Miss Shay, but I believe Aaron was on a Corsair ship. Chances are he is a prisoner."

For as long as Jenn had known Miss Shay, she had never been exactly healthy looking. Now she was deathly pale. She raised a trembling, accusing hand and pointed at Jenn. "This is your fault! You are unlucky...no! You are cursed and I will never follow you. None of us should."

Jenn only nodded. She turned and walked back up the gangplank to the rail of the *Queen's Revenge* so that everyone could see her. "I was anointed queen by the old queen," she yelled and then paused so that what she had said could be transferred by whispers to the people furthest away. "But that means nothing if you won't follow me. Who should lead you instead of me?"

The whispers went back and forth like waves in a bathtub, clashing and throwing up angry shouts. The factions could only agree that they didn't trust each other all that much. The Santas were too pushy; the Sacromentans were too whiny; the Islanders thought they owned the place.

"What about the Guardians?" Charmel Gilbert suggested. "We could let them protect us and their bishop could be our king."

"No way, Charm," Rebecca said. "They wouldn't fight the Corsairs before, what makes you think they'll fight them now?"

This caused a new argument to break out among the people: Were they supposed to fight? Were the Corsairs coming? How could they possibly win without an army and without actual soldiers? They didn't even have a fleet except for the one boat. Would the Guardians save them and if so, at what price?

The crowd turned to Jenn for answers. "Yes, we will have to fight and yes, we can win. We've already proven that. But we can only win if we band together. I don't know this Bishop of the Guardians, but I met one of his Knights and he was a good man and a stout, courageous fighter. If the Bishop is like him, we'd be lucky to have him as our leader."

"He's not," Donna Polston said. "The Bishop is a pacifist. He won't fight unless he has to and whatever help he'd give us will come too late with too many strings attached. He's already demanding that everyone gets baptized."

There was a murmur of disgruntled agreement. Jenn sighed. "This leads us back to the question of who will lead you?" It was a page right out of Jillybean's playbook: show the people that they have no other viable option and then step in, assuming a mandate without actually having one.

"I say Jenn Lockhart should be queen!" Mike Gunter cried, almost as if the entire thing had been scripted, which it had been the day before. "*They're not going to accept me,*" she had told

Mike while standing at the bow, far from the others. "Then we'll have to convince them," he had said.

Together they had hashed out a subtle Jillybean-like plan and in the end, she had envisioned something exactly like what was happening, only on a smaller scale. There was no way she could have known that *everyone* would be on hand. Jillybean would have used the crowd to her advantage, while Jenn felt like she was just along for the ride. But now, at Mike's cry, they looked up to her—another thing they had planned out, that she would be *above* them while they looked for a leader.

"I'd go for Queen Jenn," Fi Findlater, the last living Sacramento slave, called out. "She was the queen once already."

Donna Paulson surprised them by saying, "I second the idea, but I think it should be Queen Jennifer. We have a yes vote from Sacramento, the Hilltop, and the Islanders. What do the Santas say?"

Jenn turned to Phillip Carter, the man she had asked to represent the Santas for her. She couldn't have guessed that putting her trust in him would pay dividends so early. He nodded. "The old Queen said she was the one and I gotta think that has to mean something."

Queen of what? Deaf Mick wondered. There were barely a hundred men among the crowd and not one had stepped forward to lead or even to ask to lead. They were weak-willed beta-males and the Black Captain would make short work of them. He expected more trouble from the women, who he secretly referred to as the "Bitch Brigade."

But not that much trouble. With Jenn as queen, they did not suffer from leadership; their main problems were: ammunition, experience, and the savage will to win at all costs.

It became increasingly clear that without the Guardians they had no chance of survival. The bridge was a formidable barrier; however it couldn't be held if attacked from either of the two land approaches. Once the bridge was taken, the Captain would be able to use Jillybean's own smoke tactics against the Bay Area people, taking or sinking the *Floating Fortress* before either storming Alcatraz or starving them out.

They had to have the Guardians on their side. Jenn had no sooner thought this than a dozen white sails were spotted approaching the bridge. A cheer went up and echoed throughout the bay. They all took it as a sign: they were going to be saved!

Chapter 38

Emily Grey could feel the old Glock scrape up her spine; clicking up each vertebra. It was a countdown of sorts and when it got to the top...

Gunner was going crazy. He clearly loved her in some creepy *If I can't have her, then no one can* sort of way, and he was going to kill her. She knew it. His smaller left arm had her around the chest and in his right was the gun; it loomed like a cannon. She ran out of vertebrae and now she could feel the black bore of the gun pointed at the back of her head. It was a negative space, a deadly round tube that she imagined was growing larger and larger.

The Corsairs were closer now and the gun began to tremble, the worn sight snagging in her hair, making her wonder if her head would catch fire when it went off. The thought made her shoulders hunch and she had to resist the urge to put her fingers in her ears—because the explosion from such a huge gun would deafen her. It was just about the stupidest thing to think, and yet there it was, taking up all the room in her noggin.

She didn't dare move her hands. She was too afraid to even shudder. Any movement, even a twitch, might tip Gunner over the edge.

"Is that a bear?" someone whispered.

"Holy crap! I think it is," someone else hissed.

A third person spoke excited words; however, they were drowned out by the tiny sound of the Glock's trigger spring being compressed. It was a nothing of a sound and yet it held Emily's fate. When the trigger came all the way back...

"Do not fire, you idiot!" a Corsair captain growled. "Go around the damned thing. Do you want to give away our position, for Christ's sakes?" Rocks were kicked, more leaves crunched, and pebbles slid down the walls of the gully as the squad broke and went far around the strange mound of black fur.

Gunner counted slowly to twenty before sliding back his cloak and looking behind them to where the sound of battle had just increased. Emily noted the sweat dripping out of his patchy hair. It hadn't been hot beneath the cloak, it had been deathly cold. The pent-up shudder rolled in a wave from her shoulders and down her back, leaving her shaking and weak.

"Come on," Gunner said. He went to grab her hand, but she pulled back, the fear once more clouding her eyes.

She moved to the side, skirting around him, easing up the gorge. "I think I can make it on my own from here, thanks. The Sound can't be too far off. East, right?" Without taking her hands from her M4, she jerked her head to the northeast. "If you ever come to Bainbridge, I'm sure my mom will give you a reward or something."

"You aren't safe. Not even close." He went to reach for her and she scurried back again, bringing her gun up. He rolled his eyes. "You're acting like a kid. Sure, you can get to the Sound but which part? If you knew anything you'd know it's not like a river that you can cross with ease. It's a damned maze. And how do you plan on getting past the hundred or so orcas that live there or the thousand zombies, for that matter?"

"Oh yeah," she said, struggling to find a comeback. "How do you plan on getting across? Can you even swim?" With his armor, his huge axe, his one hand, and his heavy cloak, she assumed he would sink like a rock.

"I have a boat."

That took the wind out of her sails and her eyes began to shift about as if looking for a reason he couldn't come with her. She walked sideways so she could keep an eye on him, while at the same time as putting some distance between her and the battle. He was doing the same thing on the other side.

Eventually, she said, "I-I don't need a boat. I'm sure...I'm probably sure I can find a way across. Or I can signal the island. People do that, you know."

"Not when there are Corsair ships heading to the Sound even now. I don't know why you're acting like this, but you need to stop right this..."

"Yeah, you do," she shot back, raking him with an accusing blue eye. "You know why. You have some sort of *thing* for me and it's not right." Now that it was out on the table she seemed to grow while he, on the other hand, shrank into himself, uncharacteristically uncertain.

Should I tell her? he wondered, nervously. It seemed like the perfect time. She wanted answers and they didn't have time for nonsense. It would clear the air and make him look far less creepy. The idea was sane, it was honest, and it was likely the morally correct choice—a girl deserved to know the truth about her father.

The idea was also frightening, even beyond Gunner's courage. He kept picturing the movie: *The Empire Strikes Back.*

Luke tried to commit suicide rather than face the reality of who his father was…and he was a grown man! A whiny little bitch of a man until that point, but still a man. Gunner imagined the worst of Emily's possible reactions to the news and he knew he couldn't be honest with her.

"Just forget it," he said. "Jillybean trusted me with her army and you…you got no choice. I'm going to get you back home and that's that." He started stomping off up the gorge and could only hope she was tagging along.

She was moving but slower. "Jillybean trusted you and look what you've done. You've abandoned them. You left them to die because of me."

"No! That's not what happened. They were doomed from the start, and what are you even saying? Do you want to go back and die with them? Is that it? After everything I've done for you, this is the thanks I get." Before she could formulate any sort of response he was storming off for real, saying over his hump, "You're not even a teenager yet. Your mom has done a bang-up job raising you. Bravo to…"

He heard her sneaker feet running at him. He expected to get an earful, and rightfully so. He shouldn't have brought up Deanna. Raising a child singlehandedly, in the middle of a zombie apocalypse, couldn't have been easy. He was about to apologize when Emily kicked him in the back of the left knee. She was big for an eleven-year-old and her aim was beautiful. His leg buckled just as she hauled back on his cloak. It was nearly a picture-perfect takedown and had he been almost anyone else, he would have landed square on his back.

His crabbing walk kept him low to the ground and he was able to pivot on his right leg, stab down with his strong right arm and stand again, coming up face to face with his daughter.

"You leave my mother out of this!" she spat. "She's everything you're not: kind, loving, smart, and strong. And I'm not talking physically strong. I'm talking emotionally and spiritually strong. Look at you. You hide behind a mask because you're afraid. You're afraid of what people will think. Coward!"

She stormed off and for a moment, he couldn't find the strength to follow after her. She was right. He had never tried to live without the mask and didn't know if he could. It was hard enough having people stare at his deformed body; his face was beyond hideous. Even he didn't like to look at it. His own face made him sick.

Touching the mask, a habit he had no intention of breaking, he hurried after Emily and fell in beside her. They were quiet for a minute as they walked out of the smoke. The morning seemed overly bright.

"We should get to high ground, so we know what's happening." Gunner didn't like the gorge anymore. Without the smoke, he felt trapped. She only grunted and started up the hill to her left. "No. This way. That's north. Remember, the sun rises in the east."

"No, it doesn't," she said, matter-of-factly. "The Earth rotates eastward, in prograde motion, making it appear that the sun rises and sets. Jillybean taught me that. She taught me a lot."

Gunner shot her a look and wanted to ask: *What the hell does that mean?* He held back, saying instead, "When we get to the Sound you can have my boat and I apologize for my comment about your mother."

"And I apologize for calling you a coward," she said, stiffly. "You are clearly not one."

"Alright then."

To which she replied, "Alright."

They made it to the ridge line and he scampered beneath a pine to peer back at the "battle." It was already over. "Damn!" he barked, causing his cloth to flare and giving Emily a peek of jawbone and a streak of white tendon. "That's the real reason I left them. Useless sons of…"

In the middle of what would have been a long curse laden diatribe, he glanced over and saw Emily was standing right out in the open, clutching her green coat about her. The hood was cast back and her golden hair seemed to give off its own luminescence. "Get down!" Gunner hissed, sliding out from beneath the pine and hauling her in close to the tree. "Never be conspicuous. Always assume that someone is searching for you. Oh, jeeze because they are. Look." He pointed with his stub at the line of hills across from them. Something was twinkling in the patchy woods, catching the light just so and sending out shards of crystalline white.

It was someone with a scope or maybe binoculars. Emily's heart began to race as the whole forest seemed to move. Dozens of men in camouflage started creeping down the hill, taking an angle that would cut the pair off from the Sound.

"Do you see that peak?" Gunner asked, pointing to a two-thousand foot mound of rock and snow, some miles distant. "Get to it as fast as possible. Go!"

She had a hundred questions, starting with: *Where's the boat?* but she discarded them and took off down the hill towards the gorge, while he ran down the hill a few feet and then crabbed speedily across its front, looking like some sort of hideous alien. She pulled her eyes from him; she couldn't be distracted by him or the hundred or so clansmen throwing their hands in the air and giving up their lives to a man with a notorious and well-earned reputation for inhuman cruelties.

Emily couldn't spare a moment to think about any of that just then as she ran down the rocky slope. One false step and she could break an ankle and then it would be her giving up and praying for the chance to be repeatedly gang-raped day in and day out—anything was better than being sawn in half or roasted alive or skinned by the unholy creature they called The Cadaver.

Even she had heard of him.

Was this why Gunner had threatened to kill her just when they were about to be captured? She stumbled just as she got to the gorge, her stomach flipping. It had to be. Which meant that if the Corsairs got anywhere close to her, she might expect to be shot out of hand by Gunner. As if to pound home the point, a lone rifle sounded from up on the hill, causing her to twitch.

It got her moving again and she ran with her back hunched until she was out of sight of Gunner, who was blasting away at the Corsairs at extreme range. They practically fell all over themselves as the bullets began chipping rocks and whacking into tree trunks.

Emily couldn't see any of this and imagined them cresting the hill to her right in an overwhelming black torrent any second. She would be caught in the open and if they didn't kill her, Gunner would. It was a dreadful thought and she ran with her chest constricting in fear which all gushed out of her once she went up and over the next ridge. She was swept by a wonderful wave of relief.

The relief spurred her on and she ran faster, feeling like she was running from both Gunner and the Corsairs. She wanted to leave it all behind her; the war, the pain, the evil in men. She was only a child and thought she should only have a child's worries: bedtimes and chores, and best friends and school.

That's what her life should be and that's what she ran for, so she could get it back.

The peak she was aiming to climb was much further away than she figured, but with the gunshots keeping pace, she went on and on despite her growing exhaustion. Hours went by before she made it to the top where upon she fell to her knees, her lungs burning, her legs like jelly.

For a long time, she could only huddle there, sucking in the cold air, her muscles quivering. Gradually, she forced herself to come back to the terrible reality of her situation. The view to the south was wide open and she could see lines of tiny, tiny men snaking around the base of the mountain. Further back the way she had come, she saw the black flags beginning to come together into a formation as Steinmeyer, and the remains of his men, were being led away on what was to be a cruel twenty-five mile forced march back to the Corsairs' lair. Far off to the east was the Sound, and Gunner was right. From where she stood, she saw that it was indeed a huge maze of islands and green waterways.

Shaking, she climbed to her feet and went to the eastern lip of the peak, hoping she would see the walls of Bainbridge, hoping that her journey was at an end. Her island was too far away to see; it made her sad and homesick.

"We'll get you there," Gunner said, coming up behind her. She didn't jump although she hadn't heard him. She had been expecting him; she also was expecting him to put an arm around her shoulders, but he kept a respectful distance. "One way or the other you'll get home, don't worry about that."

Too late, she thought, but would not say. He already thought she was a brat, which was an embarrassment. People back on Bainbridge were always remarking how mature she was for her age. It was a point of pride for her.

Her pride was almost gone, now. It had been replaced by gnawing fear. She was very worried. Not all of the Corsairs were coming up after them. Most were spreading out to cut them off from the Sound. They were going to be trapped. "Can I ask you a question?" she asked with a nervous smile. "Could you tell me where the boat is? You know, just in case."

"Just in case I die, right?" He grunted out a wet laugh. "No, it's okay. That's a distinct possibility. Head east to the Sound, then go north about four miles to a little place called Tarboo Bay. At the very top of the bay is a huge log jam and in the forest behind that, is a canoe. But I'll be there with you. I know this land better than anyone."

He pointed with his capped arm. "You see all those guys? They're about to run into a gorge. The walls of it are forty feet high and slick as hell. Unless they brought rope and have some sort of expert climber with them, they'll be stuck going almost all the way to the Sound. By then we'll be paddling you home."

"What about the orcas? Is the canoe big?"

He laughed. "The orcas won't bother us. I was just trying to give you a scare. Now," he clapped his one hand against the metal stump as if enthused by the idea of another five-mile run, "Let's get going."

Where he got his energy from, Emily didn't know. On their jog down from the peak, he carried everything of hers and probably would have carried her as well if she had let him. He bounded from rock to rock as surefooted as a goat while she stumbled, her legs feeling like they were filling with lead with every step.

They threaded their way among boulders and sheets of ice. They slid down sandy slopes, starting mini-avalanches. They slowed their gathering momentum by going from tree to tree until they had made it safely to the thick pine forest at the base. They stopped twice after that to let her rest and eat. The day was growing late when the green smell of the Sound grew in Emily's nostrils and she found herself eagerly pressing forward.

"If you have that much energy," he said, holding out her M4. She took it, hoping it would be for the last time. She naively thought that if she could just make it home, the war would be over and she would never have to see another Corsair or touch another gun as long as she lived.

She started to sling it, just as a crow began an angry cawing. Jenn Lockhart would have considered it a bad omen. Gunner considered it a warning. The forest could talk to a person if they had the ears to hear it, and a cawing crow could mean danger was nearby.

"Keep it at the ready," he said, as he set his rifle against a tree. Chances were the crow was yapping at an owl or fox, but it could also be one of the dead and he felt more certain with his axe than a gun. "Stay back for a few."

That made perfect sense. She was not the badass her mother was and if it was something that Gunner couldn't handle, she would be of little help. He had not gone far when he and Mark

Leney came face to face across a small clearing. Leney and ten of his closest friends had dared to climb down the cliff face. Three had fallen; one had cracked his head open so that pink and grey brains gushed out. Another had broken his femur and died three days later, his leg swollen like a sausage and his brain on fire. The third had twisted his ankle and immediately turned and set off for Hoquiam and was never seen again.

This left Gunner with eight to one odds, which were bad enough, but on top of the numerical advantage, Leney and his friends were borderline suicidal. The Black Captain held deep and enduring grudges, and it didn't matter that Leney's traitorous move against Jillybean had been the only thing that kept him in power. No, Leney knew he was a marked man and so were those around him.

With the Black Captain showing up out of the blue the night before and taking credit for crushing Gunner's army, Leney had to do something to make himself indispensable—then, like magic, he had spotted Gunner and Emily Grey escaping once again.

He wasn't going to let anything stop him from recapturing the girl, especially not Gunner. The gimp was carrying an axe for goodness sakes.

"Don't move or I'll…" Leney began.

Too late. Gunner was already moving; darting left behind a tree, the axe falling to the leaf-covered dirt as he pulled his old Glock. Leney had him dead to rights and fired three times. The first missed, the second punched a hole in his cloak with a thump like someone beating a carpet, and the third hit one of his ballistic plates at an angle, ricocheted and tore a red line through the flesh beneath his armpit.

If there was pain, Gunner didn't notice. Before Leney or any of the others could fire again, he slid behind the tree. It wasn't the biggest of trees, being all of three feet wide. Gunner didn't like how things had shaped up. Normally, he would have split out of there, run for half a mile before doubling back, becoming the hunter. Only he couldn't run; Emily was fifty feet directly behind him and he wasn't about to bring all eight men right down on top of her, unexpectedly. And he couldn't attempt to shift to a better spot as he was already behind the largest tree within sight. Even the now flat ground was against him. There was very little in the way of underbrush which made crawling away impossible.

"Damn it," he growled, picturing how the fight would go down. If Leney had any sense, he would lay down covering fire, pinning Gunner in place, while at the same time he would send out a few men to his left and right. It was the simplest of squad-level tactics and even Mark Leney couldn't fail to adopt them.

Realistically, Gunner knew that if he had a minute left, he would be very lucky. "Emily! Run! Don't look back."

With these words still echoing through the quiet forest, he flung out the left hem of his long cloak. One of the Corsairs was keyed up and the flash of black drew his eyes. He fired, and the cloak caught two bullets. As it did, Gunner darted low and to the right, aiming the Glock, using his ears more than his eyes. He had the shooter's location fixed from the sound of his gun and fired twice before ducking back.

The return fire was sharp, chewing up both edges of the tree, making it rain bark. Gunner didn't dare to poke his head out to shoot and with only fifteen bullets in his gun, he didn't have the ammo to waste firing off a couple of decoy shots. He had more ammunition; however, reloading one-handed was a seven-second process which would be an eternity in combat this close.

Beneath the cacophony of gunfire, he heard someone crashing through the forest to his right. Again, hearing was more important than eyesight. Gunner could have aimed with his eyes closed as the man went for one tree too far. The key to movement under fire was to make small gains in short bursts. The Corsair must have felt over-exposed because he began firing as he ran.

Gunner ignored the bullets zipping his way, aimed, pulled the trigger, dropping the man in a flail of arms and legs.

He turned back to his left, catching a glimpse of another man diving behind a log. Gunner held his gun up, squinting down the barrel, knowing the Corsair would show himself. Valuable seconds went by before the man finally peeked up over the log. A fraction of a second after that, he fell back with a neat little hole in his head.

Gunner was shot for his troubles. Two Corsairs had gone wide right and were shooting at him with amazingly bad marksmanship. Together, they fired twelve bullets. Nine missed, two glanced harmlessly off his armor, but one got through and tore a hole in his right latissimus muscle on his side and then ran a groove through the back end of the fifth rib.

It felt like he'd been kicked—he took it with a grunt as he spun and fired in one move. His aim was off and instead of hitting the first Corsair center mass, the bullet hit high, smashing through the man's clavicle. He screamed, his collarbone feeling like it had been transformed into a hundred shards of glass.

A snapshot of the battle would have shown that three Corsairs were down, four were shooting and one was cowering. Bullets were crisscrossing inches from Gunner's extended arm as the other Corsair to his right was firing wildly without aiming, blazing through his magazine. Leney was crabbing to his right, firing at the shadow of the black cloak, while at the same time yelling for someone to: "Move, Damn it!"

More bullets bracketed the tree, some clipping it, digging grooves, others smacking into it and making its few leaves quiver. In contrast, Gunner's strong right arm was steady as a rock as he adjusted his aim slightly and shot the second Corsair on his flank, this time hitting him dead center. The man jerked as he died and rattled off his final three bullets all winging into the tree. Two embedded themselves going deep, while the third hit a knot and ricocheted, striking Gunner in the thick meat of his good arm.

The Glock felt like it had suddenly gained fifty pounds and his hand dropped to his side.

Despite the odds stacked against him, he hadn't been the least bit nervous until that moment. Dying wasn't something he feared; however the idea of being unable to fight back—the idea of being helpless was terrifying. "Son of a bitch!" he snarled as he took his metal capped left forearm and stuck it beneath his right wrist.

Uncaring about the incoming fire, he stepped away from the tree and began aiming the best he could at Mark Leney. If he could take down that turncoat before he died, that would coat his bitter death with at least a little sugar. He hit Leney twice but was struck no less than eight times in return.

His left leg buckled as blood seemed to erupt in a river down his knee. He fell back behind the tree. "Time to…" He had to pause to spit out blood gurgling up his trachea. "Time to die, Leney!" His plan was to jump out from the tree and go down with his gun blazing, but his body rebelled. The Glock had fallen from his numb fingers and his right arm was now all but useless.

With determination, he thudded his left stump into the dirt and tried to push himself up. He could only get to all fours before Leney came around the tree, a hate-filled sneer on his scarred face and blood dripping from his dangling left arm.

"Where's the girl? Tell me or you die."

"Fuck you," Gunner spat.

"Nice final words. I'll make sure to put that on your headstone." Leney raised the gun and fired, sending Gunner face first into the dirt, hot blood running like a river from the hole that went deep into him.

Chapter 39

Colleen White did not show at nine. Stu, Troy, Neil and the
slave, Zophie Williams waited in the shadows of The Cadaver's
home with increasing nervousness as the parade began.

At the head was the Black Captain, looking grand in a cape
of deepest ebony. He rode sitting on a high-backed chair that had
been attached to something that resembled a litter. It was hoisted
on the shoulders of six prisoners who had been warned that to
drop the Captain would guarantee them the cruelest death
imaginable.

He was in no danger of falling.

Behind him came Captain Alec Steinmeyer of the Coos Bay
Clan. He was chained about the neck and forced to drag a huge
rock along behind him. If he slowed he was whipped. If he
looked up, he was whipped. If someone commented on the
weather, he was whipped. He left a long trail of blood.

After him were the rest of the prisoners, all of whom were
chained or tied in some fashion. They were whipped as well. The
gutters ran red.

Along the streets were cheering Corsairs and with them
were their slaves who cheered twice as loud in abject fear.

Stu and Troy watched the beginning of the parade, looking
as though they were about to vomit. Neil watched, looking as
though he could use a tub of popcorn. "When I was a kid we had
floats and balloons," he said, scratching his pinned scalp so that
it shifted around on his head like a bad toupee.

"Balloons?" Troy asked, appalled.

"Oh yeah. I'm talking the mega-balloons; fifty, sixty feet
high. Underdog was my favorite." The others looked at him like
he was crazy. "What? You don't remember Underdog? 'There's
no need to fear, Underdog is here!' Then there was Polly
Purebred and Snoopy."

Stu began to worry about his deteriorating state of mind.
"Are you sure this wasn't all in a dream you might have had? Or
something from a book?"

"No. Snoopy is real, or he was real. But he did come from a
book, but that was only at first. Then he was real. Oh, never
mind. All I'm saying is that this isn't much of a parade. There's
no pizazz." They clearly didn't know the word "pizazz" and he

wasn't in the mood to try to explain it. "At least they didn't get Captain Grey."

If they had he would have been front and center, perhaps riding in his own caged litter. Neil hoped he was alive but was glad he was spared what came next for the prisoners. The crowd began to stone them.

"Come on," Stu said, licking his dry lips. "Colleen's not coming. We'll have to do this on our own." He forced a reluctant Zophie to show them the way to the police station. It was only a mile or so off the parade route and Colleen was right about the timing. There were only two guards out front and none guarding the back door.

Inside the station there were three more guards; two in the lobby with Snawder, his mute and one sitting across from Jillybean's cage sharpening a knife with such dull repetition that she thought he was going to hone it down to nothing.

From the corner of her cell where she was wrapped in her threadbare blanket and where the light from the single lantern barely reached, she saw that the guard was nervous. She was as well. The parade was coming closer and that meant so was the Black Captain...and so was Stu. She closed her eyes and tried to will him away. It seemed as though turning to the supernatural was the only option she had left; she had already tried praying, but the words had felt empty and weak as soon as they left her mouth, as if prayers in this hell were useless.

She had even tried to see the "signs" as Jenn Lockhart would have. But there were no "signs" in the cobwebs or the old blood splatters. There were only facts and logic.

Stu was going to die. He was walking straight into a trap and Jillybean was sure she wouldn't be able to stop it. Materially, she had but one paperclip tied into the back of her hair, and of course, her chains and golden collar, though what she would do with them, she didn't know. Watched as closely as she was, even the paperclip was practically useless.

She sat back and forced her mind from picturing Stu's face. Once centered, she was able to come up with one very shaky plan that involved using the chains hanging from her collar. Unfortunately, it hinged on something that was highly doubtful: she needed someone to love Colleen as much as Stu loved her. As pretty as Colleen was, she was also personally repulsive, at least as far Jillybean saw her.

Jillybean eased to the side of her cage where hers and Colleen's joined, and nodded to the girl, flicking her eyes at the guard as she did. Colleen was much more obvious as she glanced his way.

"I know a way out," Jillybean whispered. Colleen's blue eyes went huge and she edged nearer, giving another undeniable glance at the guard. "Be cool," Jillybean said, under her breath. "I'll pretend to fix your hair."

Colleen glanced dubiously at the top of Jillybean's head. "I think it would be more realistic the other way." She had a point. Jillybean's hair was a wreck even by her standards, while Colleen's looked like she was going for the purposefully messy, but not *too* messy, look.

"Just turn around and do what you're told for once," Jillybean snapped. She pulled Colleen's shoulders back to the bars. "Here's the plan," she whispered, taking a length of one of her chains, she snaked it through the bars and yanked it hard around Colleen's neck. The girl jerked in shock, but it was already too late as Jillybean pulled the chain tight.

Colleen began flailing and gasping, her finely manicured nails snapping on the chain. "Did you think you could fool me?" Jillybean hissed. "You're no slave. You're nothing but a dirty spy!"

Seeing the sudden commotion, the guard began pointing and stammering, "Y-You better stop. I-I told you to stop! Damn. Hey, Cadav...I mean Snawder! Something's happening in here."

Jillybean ignored him. "How long have you been working for the Captain? Put your hands down and answer the question."

When her hands were at her sides, Jillybean released some of the pressure, letting Colleen breathe again. After a few gasps, Jillybean began to tighten the chain and Colleen hissed out: "A year."

The answer was strangely reaffirming to Jillybean. She had started the war *guessing* that the Corsairs were on the verge of attacking San Francisco; this was complete validation that she had been right to step in when she had.

"Okay good. And you killed One Shot, right?" This was less of a question and more of a hope. His murder hadn't made any sense. Eve claimed to have killed him, but she was insane and could someone who was insane ever truly know anything for certain?

"Of course," Colleen answered, proudly. "You were becoming too big for your britches and I wanted to impress the Captain. I also figured I might be able to push you over the edge and I did, too. Not bad for a…"

Jillybean gave the chain another yank. "Are you really gloating about killing a man? You're pathetic." It was with difficulty that she let Colleen breathe again. "One more question: is Stu really coming?"

"Yes," Colleen said in a croaking voice. "And the Guardian, too. I'm not lying. Like I said before, what good would that do?"

Once again, Jillybean couldn't see the upside to Colleen lying, unless it was to get her to giveaway some sort of escape plan. If so, it was working. Jillybean had exposed her "grand" plan; too bad it wasn't a good one. It was all desperation and letting what little luck she had ride against terrible odds.

She was still somewhat in shock that Colleen had been the one to set up the trap to begin with. Jillybean had gleaned right away that she was no slave. She had guessed it by the way Joslyn had offered her up—she had done it as a rival looking to score points with the Captain.

Even without Joslyn's making things obvious, Jillybean had noted that although Colleen's collar had been dirtied up, it was still practically brand new. The fresh red marks on her neck could attest to the fact that she hadn't worn the collar for more than a few hours. The blows to the side of her face had also been staged. They had been aimed with precision to cause a cut without blasting out her eye socket, or bending her nose across her face, or breaking all of her front teeth.

She hadn't fooled Jillybean, but she must have been able to fool Stu, who had known her since she was a child and must have trusted her.

How Colleen managed to set up the trap really didn't matter. The only thing that did was ruining it somehow before Stu and Troy came blundering into the prison, thinking that their innate goodness and the nobleness of the act would protect them somehow.

Jillybean had to stop them but didn't like her chances. Her plan centered on one hope: that Colleen meant enough to someone that threatening her life would get her released. The hope was dashed almost right away as Chuck Snawder strolled into the holding area and almost cracked a smile—one lip twitched and then his face went completely blank; he never looked more like a cadaver than at that moment.

He came with his huge mute, as well as a cowering slave girl wearing what appeared to be a pillowcase with three new holes added for her head and arms, and two guards. The Cadaver glanced about with a mild look of contempt. "What?" he asked of the cellblock guard, who stood with his knife and whetstone held to his chest. The guard pointed the knife at where Jillybean was slowly strangling Colleen.

"A squabble among prisoners," The Cadaver commented with a shrug. "What does that concern me?"

"I'll kill her," Jillybean threatened.

"She deserves it," The Cadaver remarked with a little flip of his hand. "Traitors and spies deserve only death. You would be completely within your rights to kill her. In fact, it would be expected."

Jillybean blinked in surprise at the callousness of his answer. They really weren't going to do a thing to stop her from killing Colleen.

"Hey!" Colleen rasped, her face turning from pink to scarlet. "What would the Captain say? Huh? He's not gonna be too happy if I die and you did nothing to stop it."

The Cadaver's cold look did not falter by a single degree. "And why would that be?"

"Because I set this up! Because I found the spies and I..." Colleen's voice suddenly cracked and now her mouth hung open but not from anything Jillybean was doing. "You didn't tell him," she accused Snawder. "You didn't tell him it was me that set this up, did you?"

"It must have slipped my mind. Now, your Highness, you have a duty to carry out. This traitor deserves death. We will not interfere with the execution."

Jillybean was nearly as stunned as Colleen. Not only would The Cadaver let the girl die, he was rooting for it. He wasn't wrong about Colleen. Even without adding her other crimes, Colleen had set up Stu and Troy. In Jillybean's book, that alone should have been punishable by death. She began to tighten the chain.

"Pl...ease," Colleen whispered with the last of her breath. The scarlet color was deepening into a burgundy—and still Jillybean cranked back on the chain. To her left one of the guards said something and then laughed. In shock, Jillybean looked over and found the men were being entertained!

"No," she said, simply and released the chain. Colleen dropped onto her face and lay gagging and coughing. "An execution is not the time for laughter. I would sooner set her free than kill her for your enjoyment."

The Cadaver shrugged. "It's just another sign of your weakness. Being clever doesn't equate to being queen. Ah, look who we have, now."

Just then, Stu Currans and Knights Sergeant Troy Holt had come in through the unlocked backdoor, walking on cat's feet. They paused at the corner of the cellblock with rifles aimed. They were both furious and disgusted by what they saw. Jillybean was so covered in bruises that she barely looked like herself.

"We're here for the Queen," Stu barked. "If no one moves, then no one will get hurt. Am I clear?"

The odds against them weren't nearly as bad as they had feared they would be. There were five men, but only three were armed and all had been caught by surprise by their sudden appearance.

One of them, tall and pale, gazed calmly at the two young men, almost as if he had been expecting them, which of course he had been. "If we can't move, how are we supposed to unlock the cage?" The Cadaver asked. "You seem to be asking the impossible. Next, you'll probably tell me I can't detonate the bomb that's strapped beneath her cot."

He showed Stu a detonator, his thumb caressing the red button. Stu eyes were at slits. "You won't detonate that because you'll blow yourself up, too."

"Unless the charge isn't particularly big," The Cadaver replied. "Also I'm sure you noticed that I kept my good friend between me and the cage." He was mostly hidden by the mute, who cast a fearful eye at Jillybean's cage. The only one who didn't look afraid was Jillybean. She went to the cot and flipped it over; there was no bomb.

"Oops. Maybe I put it in the wrong cell," The Cadaver said.

"Get out of here, Stu!" Jillybean ordered. "It's a trap." She was too late. The trap was sprung as two Corsairs with guns drawn crept out of the back offices and came up behind Stu and Troy.

"Drop your weapons!" one of the Corsairs shouted, even though he was only three steps behind them.

Stu could feel death creeping up over his shoulder, calling to him. It made his shoulder blades twitch. Still, he did not move a muscle. He had the big mute in his sights and was ready to start firing.

"Is this really how you want to die?" The Cadaver asked, taking a step to the side to make sure he was completely behind his assistant. "Riddled with bullets and crapping your pants in front of the woman you love?"

"Don't listen to him," Jillybean commanded. "He's a liar. Kill him, Stu."

The Cadaver turned his dead-white face on her. "How selfish can one girl be? You don't know their fates. The Captain will almost certainly use the Guardian as a messenger to his people. He wants peace and the Guardians are not yet at war. And who knows what will become of young Stu. He can have a long and valuable life ahead of him, but if he pulls that trigger, he'll be dead in a blink and I'll still be alive and, more importantly, so will you." A ghost of a smile played on his lips. "If they don't drop their guns, kill them," he told the guards.

The two guards eased forward until their guns were poking into Stu and Troy's backs. A gun battle now would be over before it started—and Jillybean would still be a prisoner and The Cadaver, still her torturer. Nothing would change.

A second later, Troy broke. Not out of fear, but out of a commitment to his people. He knew that if there was only the most remote chance he could get back to Highton and warn them of their danger he would have to take it. He lifted his rifle into the air.

Stu spat curses at him through clenched teeth and Troy hung his head in shame.

"What are you waiting for?" The Cadaver asked. "I said kill him."

The two Corsairs glanced at each other and shrugged without care; no one was aiming guns at them. They settled in behind their rifles but before they could shoot, Jillybean ordered, "Stop!" Even without a crown or a country, she was still a Queen and her command stopped her enemies from killing the man she loved.

"Put your weapon down, Stu," she commanded, steeling herself. "You'll live. I'll make sure of it." She knew what it would cost to save his life—it would cost her everything.

Stu's weapon was taken, making The Cadaver almost giddy, which for him was a somewhat reptilian crinkling around his eyes. "That was a mistake, your Highness. You have nothing, and you know nothing that will keep him alive. There is no sweeter torture than watching a loved one under my knife. I guarantee you will feel everything he does. You will feel it all."

Chapter 40

Emily had not run. She was not built that way. She was a child of relative privilege, but she also had a pedigree that wove steel through her soul.

Within her was the blood of a warrior and she did what came naturally, sliding noiselessly to her right until she had a clear view of Gunner's fight against overwhelming odds. He was too close to his enemies to maneuver, and too out-gunned to even breathe. Had he been thirty yards further back, he would have picked them apart, but as it was, he was lucky even to have the one tree as cover.

The fight was unbelievably quick and even as she dropped down behind a log and took a bead on one of the Corsairs, she saw Gunner get hit once, then twice, his good arm dropping.

Although she had the blood of a warrior, she had the experience of an eleven-year-old. As she raised her M4 to take the Corsairs in the flank and rip through them, the strap of the rifle caught on a broken branch. Desperately, she yanked at it, her fear for Gunner making her whine high in her throat.

Too late, it came free and she brought the gun up just in time to see Mark Leney shoot Gunner at point-blank range.

Gunner tried to shift at the last moment, but he was too big of a target and Leney was too close. The bullet went into him at a downward trajectory, passing just above the clavicle and going deep. Gunner fell and Emily screamed. She didn't scream a word. She screamed hate, and fired the M4, sending Leney running.

"It's the girl!" he cried as he dove behind a tree. "She's just a kid. Don't kill her."

Just at that moment, she was no child. She had the M4 on a stable platform, one which would allow her to traverse the gun left and right without sacrificing her aim. One of the Corsairs leapt up to try and flank her, only he wasn't exactly sure where she was and ended up running almost directly at her.

Two shots dropped him. And then she went back for the rest. One man was dressed all in black and she picked him out of the brown background with ease. He was hunkered down behind one of the small pines and she had a huge, meaty target in view. She fired and the bullet caught him in the side. He screamed and tried to twist around to the other side of the tree, which gave her another shot at him. This time she hit him in the shoulder.

He began yelling about giving up. She wasn't about to let him go. They hadn't given Gunner a chance and now that she had the upper hand she wasn't going to relinquish it. At the same time, she wasn't going to waste time on a man who wasn't a threat.

She wanted Leney, but first she had to deal with one of the Corsairs thundering through the forest off on her left. She fired and he dropped, but he hadn't been killed. He was up a second later, thumping rounds into her tree. She fired in return and sent him back under cover.

"Someone get up on her right!" he yelled. No one answered. Leney had crawled off, heading back the way he had come, another had sprinted away and the man who had yelled that he wanted to give up was just realizing that he was dying; his legs were completely numb. He couldn't even feel the blood pooling beneath them.

When the Corsair realized he was on his own, he fired repeatedly, his bullets missing high. To Emily they felt far too close and she ducked down for a count of three. When she looked up again, he was in full retreat, booking through the forest. She waited only long enough to make sure he wasn't trying some sort of fake-out, then she too was running to where Gunner lay, grunting and coughing up blood.

Looking like some sort of evil turtle, he was on his back and struggling to right himself. His armor and cloak were too heavy for him now, and there was so much blood on the ground that it made a vile, slick mud. His right arm hung limp, while his left kept slipping as he tried to gain purchase.

"Can't...breathe," he said through the blood in his throat.

Emily dropped her rifle and fished out her pocket knife, *snicking* it open. She used it to cut away his cloak and then his homemade armored suit. Beneath it he wore a double layer of long-johns that were more red than white, now. She helped to roll him over and as she did, she counted his wounds and came up with nine. It was a frightening number since, as far as she knew, people didn't live after being shot once.

And he didn't look like he had that much life left in him.

"Go," he whispered, his red breath rattling in and out. "Top of the bay...behind the log jam...canoe."

She didn't have to ask: *What about you?* That was obvious; he would die. It was a wonder he wasn't dead already. She shook her head. "Not yet. I-I have time. Those guys ran the other way.

And I can help. Jillybean taught me some stuff." Her attempt at a confident smile failed. Jillybean *had* taught her some things, starting with basic anatomy and physiology, which Gunner clearly didn't possess. He was twisted in a way that didn't seem possible, and the hunch on his back wasn't like anything she had ever seen, even in a book. She had no idea what was in it.

Still, she had been taught emergency first-aid. She knew her ABCs: airway, breathing, circulation, and she knew all about hypovolemic shock.

"I'll just bandage you up and you'll be good as new in no time."

He shook his head. "No. Get to…the canoe. Leave me."

"No, no, I don't think so. That's not what the good guys do. They stay with their friends and they help them. Besides I scared those guys so bad they probably aren't going to stop running until they reach Hoquiam."

He had stopped struggling when she had called him her friend. He knew he was dying, and he knew she had to go, but he was weak, and in his weakness, he was selfish. All he could do was stare at his beautiful daughter as she took off her coat and began cutting it into strips to act as bandages.

While her clever little hands bound his wounds, she prattled on, talking because she was nervous, afraid that she might do something wrong and accidentally kill him. "Jillybean taught me and my dad taught Jillybean. He was super smart. Everyone said so. And he was really brave."

"Is that right?" Gunner whispered. She was wrapping his arm, going round and round, but too loosely. "Tighter," he told her. "Really cinch it down. Trust me, you're not going to hurt me. And then if you have enough cloth, make your knot…"

"On top of the wound. I know." She was so small compared to him that she thought about kneeling on his bicep to get the knot tight enough. *What could it hurt?* she said to herself and put a good portion of her weight on the wound. He didn't even flinch, which she took for a bad sign.

A worse sign was the dreamy, glazed-over look in his eyes. If she didn't know better, she would have thought he was happy. "Hey!" she said, snapping her fingers in front of his face. "You have to focus. Tell me how you know Jillybean."

Gunner's smile slid away. "I ran into her when she was a kid." *And I used her genius, putting her in stressful situation after stressful situation until her already cracked mind broke wide open*. That was a truth he didn't like to face. "She was smart even back then. Maybe too smart." He let a cough carry on, hoping to end the conversation.

"I don't think anyone can be too smart." She sure wished she was smarter. She knew she had to do something about the blood bubbling up out of Gunner's neck but had no idea what. It wasn't something that could be wrapped and she imagined that if she stuck a plug in it, his hump would grow larger and larger until it was like the hump of a camel.

And she didn't think that would be good.

She decided to put that wound off for last and went about binding his leg, and the laceration under his arm, and the one across his neck. Emily talked nonstop, lulling Gunner into a state that was somewhere between a coma and a deep sleep. Emily almost couldn't wake him when she was done. She had to dash water in his face when shouting and slapping him hadn't worked.

He was surprised to see how dark it was. The watery winter sun was hidden somewhere behind Mount Olympus. "Jeeze, what are you still doing here? You have to go. Go on, leave me. You've done enough."

"Not yet. You're not safe."

She put out a hand and he went to smack it away, except his right arm could only move in slow motion. "Emily, please leave. They'll be back soon and there'll be more of them. We don't stand a chance."

She knew this and at the same time she had been raised on story after story of how brave her father had been, never leaving a man behind. And her mom's heroics were equal to his; and Jillybean had been performing epic feats as a child even younger than Emily was. There were even courageous tales of timid, little Neil Martin.

Emily wasn't going to be the first person in her family to turn her back on a friend…or whatever Gunner was to her. "We'll go together. You said yourself that the Sound wasn't far."

It was every bit of two miles and he couldn't walk. He didn't even know if he could crawl and was sure he didn't want to. It just didn't seem worth it to crawl all that way just to die within sight of freedom.

"I have an idea," he told her, summoning all his energy, and putting it into a casual wave of his stump. "You go for the canoe while I head for the Sound. By the time you get it, I'll be on the beach working on my tan."

"No," she said, obstinately, sitting down and stretching her long legs out in front of her. To show that she would sit there all day, she casually remarked, "I think I have cricket legs and can't stand them, but my mom says that boys like a girl with long legs. What do you think?"

Tears sprang to his eyes and he turned away to stare at the ice-capped mountain hiding the last of the light from him. "Please leave. That's an order."

"You start crawling. That's an order, too! Don't be a baby. I'm sorry you got shot and all, but we're both going to die if you don't get moving." She had her mother's knack for being able to double down on a point by arching an eyebrow. He had never been able to argue with Deanna's eyebrow and all he could think to do with his daughter was to start whining.

He bit it back, replacing it with a long string of curses that had Emily's ears going red. He wanted to say that there were a lot more where that came from; however, his head went light and he coughed up something black the size of his tongue. Emily looked shaken but somehow held her ground, forcing Gunner to start crawling.

It was an ordeal that few other men could have faced, especially since in the end it would be a waste of time. There would be no Jillybean at the end of this trip to sew him back together again. Sure, Emily could probably handle some of his simpler wounds, but the bullet that had blasted into his thorax had hit his right lung before carrying down to somewhere near his spleen. It felt as though there was a sword of fire still in him.

Every movement brought dizzying pain and he realized that he couldn't go on in a crawl. Both lungs were filling with blood for some reason. With Emily's help, he struggled to stand and had to submit to a wave of dizziness that almost killed him right there. He could feel his heart begin to speed up. It raced in his chest and yet, when he tried to feel his pulse he found it was practically nonexistent. There wasn't enough blood left in his body and his blood pressure was bottoming out. All it would take were a few more trickles leaking from Emily's bandages and he would die.

"Good," he whispered and waited for the inevitable. But then there was Emily shoving a canteen to his mouth.

"Drink," she ordered. She gave him no choice, pouring the water down his gullet in even draughts. It hit his empty stomach and he could immediately feel it leach out into his system. Sure, it felt great, but what he needed was a blood transfusion and an operating room.

Without both, he was a dead man. He sort of felt like the dead as he stumbled along hitting tree trunks in a numb haze, staying upright only through the efforts of his daughter. His brain could think of nothing but putting one gimpy foot in front of the other. Pain no longer meant anything and with each step, he came that much closer to death; any reasonable person would have suspected that he was at least part zombie at this point.

Emily poured water into him periodically and tried to steer him eastward, but in the dark, their route meandered, something that was both a blessing and a curse. Gunner wanted nothing more than to get to the Sound, so he could lie down on its shore and die, but the route actually kept him alive longer by confusing the Corsairs who were trying to track them.

Mark Leney had made it back to his company that had been dawdling to the south. Despite his wounds, he got them moving with wild promises of women and drunken feasts on Bainbridge if they could just get the girl.

With more excitement than skill they boiled up the shore, hunting with torches and yelling back and forth if a track was discovered. They came close twice, passing within twenty yards of the father and daughter both times. She would pull Gunner down into the dark underbrush and pray until the danger passed. Then she would have to do everything in her power to get him moving again.

It was a test of endurance that she passed and he did not. When they got to the Sound, about a mile from the little bay, he was done and no force on earth would move him. They had come out onto a little spit of land that had a bottleneck to it, which meant they could hold out for at least a few minutes against an attack. The problem was that behind them was a serious forty-foot drop to the Sound. Emily tried to find some way down that had a gentle grade and maybe a little beach, but there was nothing close.

The only way down was a rickety, weather-worn set of stairs that zigzagged back forth down the cliff that led to a stubby little dock that was half-submerged.

For the moment, Gunner was too far out of it to attempt the stairs. She tried dragging him, but he was too big. Panic started setting in and all she could think to do was re-tie his bandages and give him more water, neither of which had any effect. He was still dying.

"I got a new plan," she told him. "You're gonna wait here. Okay? Gunner look at me. You gotta stay awake. I'm gonna go get the canoe and then we'll get out of here, together. Okay?"

The best he could manage was an uncertain nod, his dark eyes at slits. She turned, glanced once at the stairs and decided against them. A light wind was making them creak and sway ominously.

Going around was perhaps even more dangerous. There were Corsairs everywhere, yapping back and forth as they beat the bushes looking for them. They were a loud lot and she was able to find a gap in their line by slipping to where it was quietest. They passed around her in a ragged line and, to her horror, began to head almost directly toward where she had left Gunner. With the way he snuffled and gargled constantly on the blood choking him, even a blind man would be able to find him sleeping next to the stairs.

She needed to distract them as fast as possible. A loud shriek would do the trick, but it would also get them all right on her tail, and she didn't think a mad sprint through the forest at night would end well. An idea struck her and in seconds, she gathered a small handful of sticks and old leaves. She formed a little teepee out of them and although she could have made a larger fire easily enough, she wanted it to burn quickly and die away just as fast.

With a flick of her lighter, the fire rolled up the leaves and started the twigs burning. Just like that, she was night blind and had to stumble away with her hands thrust out in front of her. Quicker than she expected, she heard a gruff voice carry though the dark: "Hey, look over there."

She began to hurry, looking for the dirt road she had crossed earlier. It ran north and south and when she found it, she picked up her speed. Behind her, the fire faded before the Corsairs could get to it. Just as she hoped, they eventually closed on the glowing embers and stood about holding their torches over the remains and asking each other what it meant.

Her favorite answer was, "Maybe it's a trap." Just like that, nearly seventy men threw themselves to the ground and pointed their weapons outward in a circle. Tired as she was, Emily giggled as she made her way up the road in a jog. She was leaving behind a clear trail through the mud and that was okay, too; she wanted to draw them away from Gunner and by the time they got to the bay, she would be pulling away into the night in the canoe.

It was a perfect plan, just as long she could find the canoe, that is. She wasn't given exact coordinates after all—was it a hundred yards past the logjam? Or fifty? Or two-hundred?

She decided to search in a zigzag pattern and struck on the thing in the first three minutes. Although it had old branches thrown over it, there was a tell-tale silver gleam that caught her eye. It was lighter than she expected, and before long, she slid it out on the Sound—and she was free.

It was the strangest feeling she'd ever had. She wanted to laugh and cry at once. She wanted to flop over in the boat and just let it drift for a while, knowing that not even a zombie would take notice of her in the dark.

But she had Gunner to save and that took precedent over everything. Luckily, the Corsairs had found her fresh, size six prints and the entire crowd of them was jogging along following them. They were about halfway to the logjam and, by the time they figured what was what, she and Gunner would be beyond their reach.

She had just started working the unfamiliar paddle when Gunner fired his first shot.

"No!" she hissed across the water. "Stop it, you idiot!" He did not stop. He kept shooting the M4 that she had left next to his body. She had taken the Glock, thinking it was all she would need.

The Corsairs split into two groups; one group kept after her tracks, while the other group pelted back the way they had come. Frantically, Emily dug her paddle into the water, but after two strokes, she found herself spinning like the needle in a compass after a lightning strike.

She had never used a canoe before and finding the right balance between power and paddle control took time and by the time she discovered the proper balance, Gunner was fighting it out with the Corsairs. He had no armor, no cover and not nearly enough ammo.

The only thing he had going for him was a will to make his death count. Uselessly, Emily paddled on, no longer feeling the urge to laugh. All she had were tears.

Chapter 41

Neil Martin no longer had any true concept of time. As soon as Troy and Stu slunk down the alley behind the police station, he had begun to get antsy.

"We should go after them," he said after barely a minute. "Heck, we should've gone with them in the first place. What good are we doing here?"

Zophie Williams rolled her eyes. "We're guarding the back door. It's a thing, you know. We're making sure their, you know, their way out is clear. That's a thing, you know. It's important."

An entire minute went by—an eternity to Neil—before he said, "It's been too long. Here." He handed her his Walther PPK, the same one he had carried for so long that he couldn't remember when he had picked it up. For some reason Neil trusted her with the gun but did not trust her to be left alone. "If things are cool, we'll come back out. You'll see."

Things were definitely not cool. Because there was only the one lantern to light the cell block, Neil had to squint to see what was going on. Everything was so shadowy that he walked right up to the two Corsairs who had thrust Stu and Troy down to their knees and were in the process of taking their rifles.

"What's going on?" he asked. As Zophie had stopped fifteen feet back and stood almost paralyzed in the shadows, Neil seemed quite alone.

Chuck "The Cadaver" Snawder was, for once, startled into an expression. His face registered disgust. "What the hell are you?"

"What are you?" Neil shot back. "You look like my fifth-grade math teacher." Neil nodded, letting the burn sink in, before realizing that Snawder probably didn't know his fifth-grade math teacher. "He was sort of boring looking, just like you." Now, Neil smiled, silently congratulating himself: *Good one.*

"Kill him, Neil," Jillybean said, her words very precise and clipped.

Neil frowned. "It's only a passing resemblance, really. Mister Shay was much smaller and had this big belly that he'd…"

"Kill him," she repeated.

Just before Neil and Zophie had interrupted things, The Cadaver had stepped out from behind his mute and, as Neil shrugged, he tried to hide again, this time behind one of the prison guards. Seeing Neil bring his gun around to point right at him, the guard squeaked, "Don't."

It was too late. Neil was already pulling the trigger and even with his blurred vision, he really couldn't miss hitting one of them. The guard fell back, blood spurting from two holes in his chest and Snawder eagerly used him as a shield, pulling him down on top of himself.

There was a strange moment as everyone seemed surprised that a crazy-eyed half-zombie, with a safety pin holding his scalp in place, would actually shoot a gun into the small crowd. The moment drew out until the shock faded and then everyone moved at once. Troy and Stu both went at the guards who had been in the process of frisking them, and they tussled with such violence that they knocked into Neil just as he fired again.

The round entered a target-rich environment where there was one dead guard, three live ones, The Cadaver, his mute and a dark-eyed slave girl who flinched behind the mute, who then took a step back and promptly fell over her. The bullet hit one of the guards in the wrist and of the thirteen tiny bones found there, five were broken in some way and three displaced. He screamed and dropped his gun.

That left two for Neil to face. One had been standing watching what he considered to be a highly entertaining show with his thumb corked in the bore of his M16 and the butt of it resting on the toe of his right boot. He tried to yank up his rifle before Neil could fire again, but there was no chance of that. Neil killed him a second before he was shot by the last guard who carried a forty-year-old M16A1. The man had flicked it to "Auto" and sprayed his rounds like he was spraying a hose.

The bullets ran right to left, barely missing Stu and the guard he was fighting. Troy saw what was happening and twisted his opponent around as if he were giving a girl a twirl on the dance floor. Three rounds thudded across his back, one of which blasted between his ribs and hit Troy in one of his ballistic plates.

It was the ninth bullet in the magazine which hit Neil on the arm, a deep scoring laceration that he didn't even notice. He had been somewhat overwhelmed by the noise and what appeared to be flames coming from the gun, and he had only stood there as the guard blasted away.

He was surprised that he was still standing when the man, quite unexpectedly stopped firing, a round stove-piped in the chamber. The automatic rifle left all their ears ringing and so no one heard Neil's soft, insidious chuckle as he raised his rifle to kill the man.

"Ple…"

Neil's bullet tore out his throat. The half-zombie then threatened the guard with the hurt wrist.

"We can't execute prisoners," Troy said, tossing aside the body that been draped on him.

"Don't listen to him, Neil," Jillybean said. "None of these foul creatures deserve to live." She looked like she wanted to rip through the bars to get at them. Troy stared stonily across at Jillybean; she gazed back, fury and hatred stamped on her beaten face.

It took her a moment to calm herself. "Fine. We'll jail the guards; however those two," she pointed at Snawder and the mute, "must die for their crimes. They did this to me," she said, savagely, pointing a crooked finger at her face.

"What's a few scratches between friends?" The Cadaver said, holding his hands up while getting to his feet. "You won't be able to get out of that cell without me. I have the key to your cell. The only key."

Stu Currans pushed his guard toward the other prisoners and advanced on The Cadaver with his M4 raised. "Give it to me now or I'll shoot you."

"I don't have it here with…"

The bullet from Stu's gun took him in the knee and for the first time, Jillybean saw true animation on The Cadaver's face. In his agony, he looked human and she wanted Stu to do it again. Eve did as well. She fought through the drug cocktail that The Cadaver had her on and laughed, the sound echoing in Jillybean's mind.

Jillybean had to step back away from the bars. Now was not the time for Eve to show herself. She would ruin everything—if there was anything to ruin, that is. The mute was shaking his head at Stu and in a few gestures, he pantomimed: *The key is on the kitchen table*. He then jerked his thumb behind him, meaning back at their house.

"That's a mile away," Stu whispered in disbelief. Even running full out both ways, it would take him a minimum of fifteen minutes. If the Captain wasn't here in that time *someone* would be. The gun battle had not been quiet by any means. "Is there another key?"

The mute and both guards shook their heads.

"I told you there was no escape without me," The Cadaver said through gritted teeth. "I'm sure we can work out a deal."

Jillybean turned away to hide the disappointment that had hit her harder than any bullet. The rescue had failed. She was trapped and would remain trapped—*Forever*, whispered Eve. Jillybean's face fell because she knew Eve was right. After this, the Captain would double or triple his guards; she would never leave Hoquiam.

Swallowing her fear, she forced her chin up. She could still save Stu and the others. "I don't make deals with dead men," she said without looking at him. She eyed the guards who stood in a little clump with their hands raised. "Where's the key to the far cage?" she demanded.

"I have it," the one unwounded guard practically cried. "I have all the keys, except yours. Sorry. I really am sorry. I didn't know…"

"Shut up!" Stu snarled, stomping up to him, his gun pointed at his face. "Troy, frisk them and get them into the cage. Neil you watch the front and you," he snapped his fingers at the slave girl they had picked up earlier.

"Zophie," she answered meekly.

"Right, you watch the back. Let us know if anyone is heading our way. I'm going to go get the key. I'll be only a few minutes."

"You'll never make it back in time," Jillybean said, softly shaking her head. "There'll be Corsairs all over the place any minute now. Don't…don't worry about me. They can't hurt me…"

He balled a fist until his knuckles stood out sharp and white. "No! We're getting you out of here. Look what they've done to you! Look at your face. Look at your poor feet." Her feet were crimped inward as if she could barely stand, and where she wasn't bruised, she was burned, and where she wasn't burned, she had been cut. The sight of her set his mind raging. He was going to get her out, no matter what.

"I'm getting the key and that's that." He turned to leave and she called his name; he didn't look back. She was going to try to talk him into escaping without her and that was something he would never do. Not again. He had let her go once before and he had been in torment ever since. It was better to die with her than to see her in such pain. He tore out of there and sprinted for all he was worth to The Cadaver's house.

When he was gone, Jillybean's entire body slumped. The rescue was about to turn into a massacre. She tried to summon the last bit of strength she had. Taking a deep breath, she pulled the blanket closer around her bare shoulders and called Neil to her side. He was a horror to look upon and that hurt her as much as all of her wounds.

"He won't make it back in time," she whispered to him. "You'll need to lead the others to safety. I know a way out of the city." She told him about the sewers and as she did, a tear dropped from his strange, blue zombie eyes with each word.

"No," he said, shaking his head, the tears dripping from his chin, now. "I should stay. I'm your father, damn it. What kind of father leaves his..." Overcome with emotion, he began to choke on his words.

"Neil please. There's nothing you can do. The only thing that will help me is knowing that you are alive and safe. Someone has to watch over Emily and Deanna. And Stu. He's special to me, Neil. Put Troy in his way. Don't let him come back here. No matter what. Do you hear me? I can't watch him die, just like I can't watch you die."

He could only manage a short nod and even that felt like it was nearly too much for him. She squeezed his cold hand. "Good. Now, give me a gun and get of here." Her eyes settled over his shoulder at the far cell where Chuck Snawder stood with his mute and the two guards. In the cage between them, and doing her best not to be noticed, was Colleen White.

"I should do it," Neil said.

"No. They're coming." There had been a shout from the front of the building. Their time had already run out. Jillybean grabbed the Walther from his pocket and then shoved him away. "Get out of here now. Go, before it's too late."

Troy reached out and took Neil by the arm. He bowed his head to Jillybean and pulled the half-zombie out the back, shepherding the two slaves ahead of him. When Troy bent to pick up the spear he had left lying in the gutter, the dark-eyed girl ran off into the night and Zophie looked like she was an instant from joining her.

"Don't," Neil said, taking her slim wrist. "I know a way out of the city. We can be in Bainbridge in three days if you come with us." She started to nod and he added, "But first…"

Zophie's eyes turned to glaring little slits. She pulled her hand away and started marching down the alley, hissing over her shoulder, "No, but firsts. We have to get out of here right now. You can't just shoot-up a police station and hang around like it was nothing. If we're going to go, we gotta go."

"But first we have to stop Stu," Neil insisted. "He can't come back here. And you're going the wrong way. We have to go back the other way." He turned just in time to see shadows slinking towards the front of the building; the very direction he needed to go. "Oh boy."

"Oh boy is right," Zophie snapped. "I'm going to be in so much trouble because of you guys. You don't know how it is. You have no idea."

Troy took her gently by the arm and led her around the back end of the police station, out of sight of the people looking to rush the building. "You'll be fine as long as you stick with us. Where exactly are we going, Neil?"

He told them and Zophie shrunk back into Troy, wearing a look of complete disgust. "The sewers? Are you kidding me? And the river is all mud. No one can cross that, not even the zombies." She raised an eyebrow at Neil, suggesting that she had guessed what he was.

"There's a broken bridge that we can use to cross over," Neil explained. "It's not far away. You could…" A gunshot from within the prison made him jump. It was followed up by three more. They were slow, deliberate shots, all coming from Neil's Walther PPK. Jillybean had just executed The Cadaver and his mute.

Zophie immediately started to walk away, only to nearly blunder right into half a dozen Corsairs who had their backs to the wall of the next building. She squeaked and held up her hands.

"What's going on?" one of them asked in a gruff whisper.

"A jail break, I think," she answered with more honesty than Neil could have wished for. "We heard them shots and cleared out."

The man's features were hard to pinpoint in the dark and Neil could only hope his were just as difficult to see. "We're going around front just in case," he said, putting so much "growl" into his voice that he choked a little. He didn't wait for permission and started around to the front where there were already thirteen men slinking around aiming guns at the entrance.

Neil kept going, heading along the street for a block before crossing over. They ducked behind an old Buick and watched as more and more men came hurrying up.

"I think we should find a sewer entrance and get you two down into it," Troy said. "I'll go after Stu." Neil began to protest. Troy held up a hand. He pointed across the street. "You can go if you can tell me which one of those men has blonde hair?"

Even with a full-on squint, Neil couldn't tell one man from the next—or if they were men at all. At thirty yards, they were only figures in the dark. "Okay, maybe you should go," he told Troy.

"And leave me stuck down in the sewers with the freak again?" Zophie hissed. "What if he tries to eat me?"

"Slap his hand," Troy replied, tiredly. He sighed, not relishing the idea of trying to stop Stu when it seemed like he should be helping him instead. And yet it would be a suicide mission with the odds growing with every passing second. "Give us about twenty minutes. If we're not back by then you can try to cross the river, but not before."

Neil nodded, thinking he would give them a half an hour. Zophie also nodded, figuring ten minutes would be pushing it too far.

Troy gave up his spear once more and went jogging north, crossing the street after three blocks. He started down an intersecting road but stopped when he saw lights heading his way. There were hundreds of lanterns and torches—it was the Black Captain leading his parade.

"Yea, though I walk through the valley of the shadow of death, I will fear no evil, for thou art with me; thy rod and thy staff they comfort me," Troy said as he cut across the block and went down a different street. It was easily his favorite prayer and he was desperately in need of comforting. Their adventure into Hoquiam had been a complete miss and he was afraid that Stu was going to do something terribly stupid.

With a heavy heart, the knight found the one intersection that Stu would be guaranteed to pass through.

A cold minute crept by as the foul wind stole down his coat and past his armor. He had just begun to shiver when he heard the steady beat of Stu's pounding feet. Troy stepped out of the shadows and hailed his friend. "You're too late."

Stu grabbed him with desperate hands. "Too late? How? She's okay, isn't she?"

Troy shook his head. "The Captain and his whole parade of evil are at the station by now. I passed them a few minutes ago. You'll never get in and if you do…" *You'll never get out,* was left unsaid.

Stu's fear seemed to leave him. He had a hard face for one so young, but now the lines smoothed and the hard planes softened. "Maybe if you prayed for me," he said, "I could get lucky."

"No. That's not how the Lord works. If you want a sign from God, then I am it. I have told you what lies before you. If you go on, then…I don't know. You'll die. It's as simple as that."

The Hillman shrugged, a barren smile on his lips. "I've tried living without her. It's impossible. And I can't sit back and do nothing while they hurt her like that." He began nodding to himself. "If I can, I'll kill the Captain. That alone is worth going back." He knew that it wouldn't be. The only thing that would make it worth it was telling Jillybean that he loved her. He had left with his mind in such a rage that he hadn't said it, and now it was all he could think about.

She needed to know that he loved her to death.

An Epilogue in Four Parts

A— Alcatraz Island 9:13 p.m.

Queen Jennifer had waited on pins and needles for hours as the twelve white sailing ships sat just outside the entrance to the bay. She had assumed that the ships were a sign from God that the Guardians were going to join them against the Corsairs.

Then a new sign, one that was more natural than supernatural, came to her in the form of a beautiful, but utterly windless day. The ships were stranded within sight of the island. At first the crowds waved and cheered as if twelve boats were all that were needed to frighten off the hundred and forty or so black-hulled ships that the Corsairs could muster. But gradually, when the wind refused to come back, the crowds departed.

Jenn left as well, heading to the office that Jillybean had briefly used. She sat in the chair behind the desk for all of one second before she hopped up again. "Would Jillybean sit around, waiting on the wind?" she asked herself.

The idea was ludicrous. Jillybean filled every second of everyday with action of some kind—not that Jenn was going to behave like that. She just knew her time was better spent planning. "Or plotting," she murmured. "Jillybean sure seemed to do a lot of plotting."

Jenn didn't consider herself much of a plotter and thought that was a good thing. Unfortunately, compared to Jillybean, she thought she was much more of a plodder. She wasn't stupid by any measure; it was just that things came slowly to her.

To make the right decisions, she realized that she needed a lot more basic information and so she began to draw up questions that a queen should know the answers to: What did her community possess in the way of defensive weapons? Of offensive weapons? Was there even a difference between the two? What were their food stocks like? How much clean water did they have? What did they need in the way of housing? Bedding? Medical supplies? Who the hell even lived on the island? How many of them were there and what were their specialties?

And so on. When the list of questions was completed, she called for Donna Polston and assigned her the task of assigning someone to answer each question. Jenn wanted a preliminary estimate before nightfall and then a complete one within a week.

Donna took the list without comment, but then she paused at the door. "The dying wind. What do you think?"

The ex-leader of the Coven wanted Jenn's interpretation of it as a sign and Jenn was rightly flattered. After only a brief pause she said, "We're being given valuable time to prepare and we have to make the most of it."

"That seems right," Donna said, sounding relieved. She opened the door to go and then paused a second time to add, "Your Highness."

Jenn smiled at this, though there was sadness in it. She was a pale shadow of a queen compared to the young woman who had given her life for her. Determined to be the best she could be at the job, she rose and went out among her people. It's what Jillybean would have done. She would've cemented her claim by embedding the concept within them.

After making sure she was as made-up and as presentable as she had ever been, she strode out onto the small island, wearing all black, this time, not just emulating Jillybean, but stealing her clothes as well. Gerry the Greek accompanied her and, when needed, she had him growl people into bows and curtsies so that she could "remain above that sort of thing."

The pair developed a following of children who laughed and made up songs about the queen. It was a parade of innocence and happiness; the exact opposite of the horror show that the Captain was even then arranging outside Hoquiam hundreds of miles to the north.

Her little parade went to every part of the island and even visited the great ship, *The Queen's Revenge,* where Mike was overseeing repairs. The ship had many bullet holes which had to be plugged, and decks that had to be scrubbed, and hulls that had to be made snowy-white again.

He smiled down at her, his blonde hair clean and long, draped on his shoulders; she grinned back. She was very much in love and should've been ecstatically happy; however, the weight of responsibility was heavy on her. The signs pointed to a break in their troubles, not an end to them.

The very thought seemed to summon the wind—impossibly it was an eastern wind. Except for a stray gust or a fast-spinning storm, she couldn't remember the last time that the wind had blown from the east. Even Mike was put off by the strange event. His smile dimmed, and he immediately looked to her. He wanted an answer to the wind.

She breathed the wind in and exhaled, saying, "We didn't expect this to be easy." It was all the interpretation that was needed for him and he shrugged, smiling at her because he couldn't seem to help it. She smiled back for the same reason before heading to the roof of the prison with a hundred others to watch the Guardians struggle through the narrow opening in the bridge defenses. The small fleet then began to tack laboriously through the bay, a process which took some hours and it was late in the evening before they were able to dock.

Jenn purposely waited in her office and she waited alone, despite the advice of just about everyone. The problem was that each of the people closest to her had a different set of ideas when it came to the Guardians and they couldn't stop arguing the same points over and over again.

"We will wait to see what they offer," Jenn told them, putting off choosing a side.

The official delegation of the Guardians was made up of Bishop Wojdan, who was dressed in a simple black cassock with a purple sash, Faith Checkamian who was in a mousy grey pantsuit, and Commander Christian Walker, who proudly wore his armor and carried a shining spear twice his height.

Mike wanted to disarm him before he entered Jenn's office, but she wisely chose to trust the knight.

After Donna provided introductions, all the while shooting covetous looks at Commander Walker, she left and Jenn took a seat behind what was a rather mundane desk of chipped mahogany that had been on the island for decades. The Bishop sat directly across from her and for over a minute he only smiled, a dimple showing in one cheek.

"My, you are young," he said eventually.

"Yes," she answered, not knowing what else to say. She had met a few Guardians in her time and they were always judgmental, and it seemed as though the Bishop was no different, despite his smile. He was sizing her up, perhaps concluding that she was in some way unworthy.

Her only solace was that he had probably done the same with Jillybean, and Jenn was sure that *she*, at least, had surprised him. Jenn gave the Bishop an open but enduring look that suggested she could wait all night for him to come to the point of his visit.

When the Bishop didn't get more of an answer than the one word, his smile dimmed as did the dimple. "I want to start off by saying I don't blame you or the Bay Peoples. We have both been wronged by the old queen."

"I don't feel we have," Jenn replied. "Neither of us. Jillybean opened our eyes to a coming storm that we weren't prepared for. My only regret is not believing her right from the start. We may not be in this situation if I had trusted her fully." Her eyes shifted away and after a breath, she went on to explain what had occurred in Grays Harbor.

The stern lines that made up Faith's face seemed to wilt, while next to her Commander Walker shifted uncomfortably and shocked Jenn by rolling his eyes.

"We expected that," the Bishop said with a sigh.

"Really? You expected one of the Captain's spies to kidnap me? Or did you expect the Queen to give her life for mine?" She had been sharp and didn't apologize. "If these things hadn't happened, there was no way Leney would have turned traitor and she would have won."

Wojdan bowed his head and spread his soft hands. "Leney was always a traitor; the Queen was simply blind to the fact."

Jenn's anxiety was gone, and anger burned in its place. "She knew exactly who and what they were. Where she failed was being able to count on friends and those who should have been her allies."

This silenced the room for another minute. The Bishop slowly unfolded his hands and laid them on the desk. "I think we may have to agree to disagree on the Queen. For better or worse the subject is water under the bridge, as they say. What should concern both of us is the future. We both find ourselves in indefensible positions. Our wall is destroyed, and we have seen the state of your defenses which, according to Commander Walker, are abysmal."

"The word I used is pathetic," Walker said. "There's no need to pull punches. You are one raid away from being reduced to Corsair slaves."

"And your solution?" Jenn asked.

Walker glanced at the Bishop, who said nothing, letting his commander drop his bomb. "The smart route to take for everyone involved would be for the Guardians to transfer our base of operations here. Under our leadership, we all have a chance of defending ourselves against a possible Corsair attack."

"Possible attack?" Jenn asked. "That's being a little optimistic, don't you think?"

361

The Bishop fielded this question. "We plan on opening a line of communications with the Corsairs. I think we'll be able to convince them that both sides can gain from a period of de-escalation."

"De-escalation?" After dealing with Jillybean for so long, Jenn was no longer made nervous by fancy words. "You're talking peace with the Corsairs. Sorry, but I just can't see that happening. They have the upper hand, militarily. They'll never go for it."

Walker looked pained as the Bishop explained, "It will take a little flexibility on our part." When Jenn only looked confused, he added, "Concessions. We'll need to make certain concessions to the Captain, probably in the form of food or maybe ammo."

Jenn sat back in shock, her mouth falling open. "Are you suggesting offering them a bribe, so they don't enslave us?"

"I am," Wojdan replied. "It's not a good choice, but we are out of options. Even if we join forces, I don't believe we stand a chance. Our ammo situation is…not good, while you clearly lack core fighters. And it'll only be for a few years until we can figure out a better plan. Peace is the proper route."

She couldn't believe what she was hearing. The Guardians had been her people's one great hope and now he was suggesting they accept some sort of modified servitude? Next to Jenn's right hand was a ring left by some long-destroyed coffee mug. She traced it, the tip of her finger going round and round. Twenty times she traced it before she said, "No. You don't know the Corsairs like we do. Like *I* do. I have been in Hoquiam and I know just how evil they are. They'll use the bribes to cripple us, always demanding more and more until we have nothing left to give. And then what? We'll be in the same position as we are now. So, why wait? I say we fight now."

Walker grunted but what he meant by it, she didn't know. The Bishop's response was far clearer. "If this is about your position as queen, I have to say that you can't let selfishness get in the way of the safety of your people."

She stood up behind the desk. "The truth is that I don't want to be queen. I've never wanted to be queen. At the same time, I don't want to be a slave. Given the choice, I'll stay queen, thank you."

Bishop Wojdan looked stunned. "This is a one-time offer. If you turn us down, we'll have to make other arrangements that won't include you or your people. You'll be on your own."

It shook the sixteen-year-old to hear that and for a moment she wavered, wondering whether she was doing the right thing. Her people were weak, outgunned and unprepared. She was no wartime leader and there was no great general among them. To put it bluntly, they were the leftovers.

And yet they were the same leftovers that Jillybean had won three great battles with. A grin appeared on her face as she went to the door. Opening it, she waved the Bishop through, saying, "We've lived as free people. We're prepared to die that way, too." She waited until all three were in the reception room before adding, "I'll expect you off the island within the hour. Good luck dealing with the devil." She then shut the door on them.

They were now on their own.

B—Hoquiam

Stu Currans put the key to Jillybean's cell in his coat pocket. He checked that his M4 was fully loaded and that the safe was on before he pushed through the crowd around the police station. The Corsairs were buzzing about the "crazy Queen."

"She nearly escaped again!"

"I heard she killed The Cadaver and the weird gimp that hangs around him."

"Was it bombs again or that nerve gas of hers?"

The idea of nerve gas kept everyone back a little and Stu was able to head right to the front doors, his boots gritting on the broken glass that had been lying there since Emily's escape days before. A small, whey-faced man stopped him at the door. It was Dean Bridge, the Captain's head of security.

"Hold up, junior. No one goes in or out."

"Snawder sent me to get the key to the Queen's cell," Stu answered, trying to look past the man. "That was like twenty minutes ago. Is it true she killed him? That's what those guys back there were saying."

Dean shook his head in disbelief. "Yawp. They said she killed them without even blinking. She's a cold one, and that's the god's honest truth. Hand over that key, will ya?" There were four other guards with him and an entire slew of them further inside.

Stu smiled easily and fished out the key with numb hands. He was numb all over and yet he shivered with the cold. It didn't make sense, but it didn't have to. The only thing that made sense was putting a bullet in The Black Captain and telling Jillybean that he loved her. If he could do those two things, he would die a happy man.

First, he had to get close enough to the Captain not to waste his life. He was just about to try his luck with the backdoor when the whey-faced man turned back. "You were here twenty minutes ago? You see anything? They say there was some sort of mutant zombie hybrid with them."

"When I was leaving, I saw something weird. This little guy with a messed-up face. I just thought it was shadows, but you're saying that was real?"

"Hey, come on with me. The Captain will want to hear this."

"Sure," Stu said, easily. Fate was guiding him now and he went with the flow. He followed the man through the crowd of vile men and realized that he fit right in. After days of fighting and running and scraping to survive, he was ugly and dirty. His beard was crawling up his cheeks and down his throat, and his hair was long and dirty.

He was one of them. Even his job—assassin—was fit for the likes of them. No one blinked at the tall, rangy man strolling among them, the strap of his M4 sliding easily off his shoulder. He carried it by the hand guard; just one of the boys. The station was loud and crowded, and yet he floated right through it, passing through groups of men as if they were air.

In no time, he was through the doors that led to the holding cells and there on his left was the guard Neil had shot through the wrist. The man looked Stu right in the eye and didn't blink. The other guard was there as well, looking past Stu as if he were invisible.

Colleen had not been released from her cell. She was yammering to someone about how she was trying to capture the infiltrators and that: "None of this was my fault, damn it!"

Stu ignored her. His eyes slipped right past her and settled on his queen. She was standing at the back of her cell, her arms holding the threadbare blanket to her shoulders. She seemed afraid to look up as if she knew she would see him and knew that what he had to do was too important to stop. It was also too late. There'd be no walking out of that room again no matter what happened next.

The Black Captain was hidden by the crowd at first and then Dean called to him and, as if by magic, the crowd parted and Stu was staring across fifteen feet of cement at a living horror. His face was velvet darkness; his smile white and perfect; his eyes dark as night. He was surprisingly handsome.

"He saw them, Captain," Dean said in a carrying whisper. "With his own eyes, is what he said, and they do got some freak with 'em!"

Stu should have brought that gun up and pulled the trigger right then, but he felt it when Jillybean suddenly looked up. Her magnificent blue eyes were like searchlights and they were on him now. He should have shot, but instead he looked at her and their gaze locked. A thousand words of sorrow past through that look and yet neither wanted to waste the moment on grief; they would have time for that later.

She drew her full lips into the tiniest of secret smiles and ten thousand words of endless love and the hunger for joy were spoken by the curve of those lips. Stu felt his doubts leave him and his heart swelled, and he couldn't help the silly kid smirk or the wink he gave her

In that sea of people around them, he was a ghost; however, the Queen's long, lingering look was noticed by at least eleven people. Its meaning was lost on the Corsairs, but Colleen White had seen it and knew that any man would kill for a woman who looked at him the way she was looking. She followed the Queen's gaze and what she saw sent a stab of the bitterest jealousy into her heart.

Fire seemed to ignite inside her. She screamed, "That's one of them," and pointed a damning finger.

A spell, woven by love, had slowed time for the pair, but now it was broken and destiny rushed down with stunning speed.

The scream unleashed chaos and Stu reacted automatically, yanking the gun up, his hand fumbling for the right position, his finger digging for the trigger. After what felt like eons, his right index finger found it and pulled; there were explosions and two rounds burned through the air just over everyone's head. Someone had grabbed the barrel, while someone else was just landing a punch on the side of his head. In the next second, he was pummeled to the ground and stomped and punched until he snarled blood as well as curses.

The room was in an uproar with everyone going crazy—all save two people: the Queen and the Captain. She was calmly broken, dying slowly from the inside out, while he was in a perfectly disguised fury. He had just been saved by a girl; the same air-headed nitwit who had managed to turn "The Cadaver" into "a cadaver."

Am I losing it? he wondered. In the old days he would have been too fast, too slick, too...something for a clay-footed Hillman to get the drop on him. He should have put a slug into him the second he walked through the door.

But he hadn't even touched either of his twin .44 caliber Colt Anaconda revolvers.

He was getting slow, like some old man. In his world, slow meant weak. "For the Lord will judge both the quick and the dead," he misquoted in a whisper, pushing through the crowd. Fate or luck, or what have you, had saved him once more, and yet he wasn't happy. His luck had been wonky and no one knew what their ultimate fate would be. The only thing the Captain could really trust was himself.

"You want to kill me?" he asked of the bloody man glaring up at him.

"Yeah," Stu answered, simply. There was no need to go on a tirade. The Captain knew his crimes.

Unbelievably, the Captain unbuckled one of his holsters and held it out. "Here's your chance to kill me like a real man. Face to face. No tricks." He nodded to his Corsairs, who were staring at him in awe and wonder. His instincts had always been spot on and this was exactly what he and his people needed. Everyone needed to see the Black Captain back in all his glory.

A white grin spread across his face as he backed away, his hands just below shoulder height. "It'll be an old west duel. You know what that is, boy?"

Stu was being yanked to his feet and turned away from the Captain. "Yeah," he answered again, his mind so warped by what was happening that he was having trouble focusing. *An old west duel?* He had a vague memory of seeing a movie with a gunfight as a kid. It seemed crazy that this was actually happening.

Two men held his arms, while a third buckled the holster to his slim hips. When it was in place, Dean held up the .44 for Stu to see that it had a full load. He then spun the cylinder before slapping it closed and shoving it heavily into the holster.

"Now what?" Stu asked, looking over his shoulder. The Captain looked so calm as to be serene. Only his right hand, slowly clenching and unclenching, held out from his side, suggested that he was ready to shoot a man...or be shot in return.

"You turn with your hands out and from there it's whoever's fastest. It's pretty simple stuff. You afraid?"

Stu had only one fear and that was of dying badly in front of Jillybean. He could feel her eyes on him and had to fight the desire to look her way. It was a fight he lost and again time was elongated, making that fleeting glimpse stretch further than possible. She was afraid for him.

"I'm not afraid," he said, speaking to both of them at once.

"Then turn around." The Captain spoke with the silky tongue of the devil. It compelled Stu, who dragged his eyes from his queen and turned. The Black Captain stood alone; his followers were pressed back into the walls leaving a lane through the long room. With aching slowness, the Captain brought his right hand down to hover over the ivory butt of his Colt.

Stu did the same. The one thing about the western he had seen as a child that he didn't understand was why the gunfighters waited to shoot. It seemed logical to draw right away and get to shooting before fear set in. Logic had nothing to do with this. His mind was too spun for logic. Twenty minutes ago, he was trying for a jailbreak; two minutes ago, he was looking to assassinate a man; now he was in the middle of an old west duel.

He couldn't feel his right hand. Nor could he feel the weight of the gun on his hip. Had someone taken it? Was he about to reach for nothing and get shot in the process? And even if it was there, would his hand come down on the butt or would he miss...

"It'll be okay, Stu," Jillybean whispered. She had seen the shock of the moment hit him. She saw him stiffen and his face go white beneath his beard. He had no chance like this. But at her soft words the shock faded and he found his body finding that sweet spot between tense and limp. He nodded without taking his eyes from the Black Captain, who's lips drew up on the left in a smirk.

"You ready?"

Stu didn't answer him and he didn't wait. There was no need to, now. He drew the gun faster than any striking snake and fired from the hip just as he had seen in the movie. There were two explosions coming one on top of the other. Both were muffled, sounding distant. Stu tried to see where he had hit the Captain, only his eyes wouldn't focus; they tracked upward along the back wall and then across the length of the ceiling until he found himself staring straight up.

A great weight had settled onto his chest. It was an invisible force crushing down on him, keeping him from breathing and smothering his heart. Stu could no longer feel its beat. In its place was a slow, gravely crunching sound and then Captain was staring down at him; he looked ten feet tall.

"You were good. Just not good enough." The Captain folded his knees and bent over him. He retrieved his pistol and as he did, he whispered, "And now she's mine. Sorry, boy."

Stu's eyesight began to grow dim, but before it could fade altogether, he forced his head to the side so that he could see Jillybean holding onto the bars of her cage. She was losing strength as fast as he was and her legs could no longer hold her up. Slowly she slid down the bars and, to Stu, who was sinking down into the darkness, it seemed like she was following him down, down, down into nothingness.

He tried to cry out to her, not from fear or sadness, but for love; however the only sound that came from his parted lips was a long warm breath that washed gently over her outstretched fingers.

C—The Sound

Emily Grey paddled fiercely, digging at the water with all her might. It didn't matter to her that the boat corkscrewed back and forth. The only thing that mattered was getting to Gunner before it was too late.

"I…can…fix…him," she huffed, almost out of breath. Sweat ran down out of her sagging golden hair. Her arms trembled, feeling as though they were filled with lead, and long, pus-filled blisters began to form across her palms. When they popped her grip would go suddenly slick and each time, the oar would slip. She had nearly lost the damned thing twice already.

She tuned out the pain and rowed on, leaning over her knees and looking up every few strokes. There was nothing she could do about the exhaustion. It turned her epic charge into a dismal endless slog. She simply lacked Gunner's ability to will himself beyond his body's limited abilities.

The canoe went slower and slower; it was like paddling through dark molasses and with each stoke the oar grew heavier and heavier. Her arms begged to quit but with Gunner still fighting, she knew she couldn't give up.

When she was two hundred yards out, the tempo of the battle changed, and her body quit without permission. Sitting back, she stared up at the looming cliff-face and it slowly dawned on her that someone was shooting in her direction. The bullets were missing high, so high that there was no need to even consider ducking.

"Can they even see me?" she wondered. She certainly couldn't see them, not even as dark shapes. All she could see were little twinkles and, as far as she could tell, all of them were aimed in the general direction of where she had left Gunner. At least they had been. Now, they were aiming slightly to her right.

"At the stairs!" She had a sudden feeling of triumph, which faded quickly as she realized he would never be able to get down the stairs with them shooting above him, and that even if he could, she would have to get right below him to pull him to safety—she would be a sitting duck. Even in the dark, the little canoe fairly gleamed with silver.

As she was working up a sweat, she pulled off her coat and flung it over the front of the canoe. It was only then that she noticed a number of sealed green trash bags at the bottom of the boat. Quickly she peeked inside them, hoping she would find something she could use to help Gunner. There were only packages of dried meat, nuts and what may have been flour. There was also a lighter, a water purifier, some dark clothes and two blankets wrapped in plastic.

Frustrated at not finding a missile launcher, she shoved the bags aside and picked up the oar again. The brief rest might have helped her arms, but it didn't help her situation as a gusty breeze swept down off the forty-foot cliff and ran square into her face.

In agony, she bent back to paddling, and wondered if it was all for nothing. Gunner couldn't hold out much longer. His return fire had begun to sound rhythmic, as if he wasn't even aiming anymore. The sound of his gun changed as well; there was a crack to it that didn't make sense until Emily was close enough to see that he was now out onto the rickety stairs.

She was only a hundred yards away and when he turned and fired at her, the act was unmistakable. Again, the bullets missed high, but that didn't matter. He was still shooting at her! Was he trying to warn her away or…

"What the heck?" The oar froze in her hand as she saw him climb to his feet. He wasn't heading down and he wasn't shooting. He looked like he was pushing against the dark, wet cliff face. A long groan carried across the water. It was the wood making the sound. It suddenly occurred to her that he was trying to bring the entire thing down.

Her heart leapt into her throat, choking off her scream. She began praying: "Please don't let it fall. Please don't let it fall," as she paddled. The wind seemed to be on Gunner's side and for every three feet she went forward, she went two back. She refused to stop, until she heard a large splash.

It wasn't Gunner. A twelve-foot-long section of railing had come tumbling down and the rest wasn't going to be far behind. Gunner was thrusting with his rifle as the rickety stairs swayed further and further from the cliff face—until they went a foot too far. Now the entire thing seemed to be trembling. Gunner dropped to the platform, finally overcome by his exertions and blood loss. The sudden shift in his weight was the final straw that sent the top platform crashing down onto the next landing, which collapsed onto the next, and the next until all five flights went plummeting into the dark water.

Emily jumped to her feet, desperate to see if Gunner had somehow managed to dive to safety, but as she stood, the oar knocked against the side of the canoe and fell into the water. Her initial, electric fear was that it would sink, leaving her stranded. Thankfully, it floated and as she scrambled to reach for it, the wind turned the canoe side on to the cliff.

Out of the corner of her eye, Emily saw why Gunner had acted the way he had, and why he had fired at her and why he had purposely caused the stairs to collapse. He hadn't been worried about the Corsairs on the land with him. No, he had been afraid of the Corsairs in the water.

Seventy yards away and tacking right for her was a dead black boat with huge black storm sails.

Gunner had given his life to save her and she had thrown his gift away.

D- Bainbridge

It was just after midnight before Deanna returned once more to her nearly empty mansion. Only her assistant Shelley Deuso was home, probably snoring away in the third-floor guest room or so Deanna guessed.

The day had been long and difficult. Her people were frightened. So many murders in so short a time had undermined their confidence in all things except the wall. "At least we still have the wall," was the constant refrain Deanna had heard. She made sure to keep her smile fixed when she heard it. As far as she was concerned, the wall had been a failure. The Black Captain had proven that.

With ease he had reached through it to take her daughter, to kill Gina Sanders to keep her from talking, and to assassinate Norris Barnes. He hadn't been murdered, he had been assassinated and Deanna knew perfectly well why. The Captain had his hooks set deep into Deanna's flesh. He had her limbs strung up by wire and could, at any time he chose, make her dance.

Deanna had been expecting the first tug to come at any time. She had gone to her meetings that morning thinking she'd find a letter and a picture of her daughter. She had given half a dozen speeches after lunch and every time she had pulled out her notes, she just knew that there'd be some demand scrawled on a napkin or something similar mixed in with the pages. And that evening as she presided hour after hour over Norris at his wake, she kept fearing to look in the casket, sure that stuffed in the breast pocket of his suit would be that first demand.

The interminable wake passed without so much as a fortune from a cookie being discovered.

The population of the entire island passed through the parlor doors that night, ostensibly to pay their respects. The true reason they had come was because assassinations were a rarity and they wanted to see which of the wild rumors about his death were true. Thankfully, Deberha Perkins had dressed him and, although she went a touch heavy on the rouge, she did an otherwise fine job of bringing him back to life—so to speak.

Now, hours later, Deanna kicked off her heels and headed upstairs, exhausted, but not expecting to get more than two or three hours' worth of fractured sleep. She had been running on fumes for days. She opened her bedroom door and reached for the light only to find something covering it. Confused, she let her hand explore the soft, plastic-like substance… "It's tape. Who's here?"

She expected to find someone sitting in the chair that faced the window. In her mind he resembled some sort of Bond villain, instead as she stared around at the shadows of her room, something hard thunked into the back of her head and she caught a whiff of gunpowder.

"Inside," said a strange, metallic voice. The word sounded like it had come out of a machine. Out of habit, she tried to look back and caught the end of a sawed-off shotgun on the side of her face. "Inside and face the wall."

"Okay. There's no reason to be like this. It's not like I plan on doing anything to you. The Captain still has my daughter, correct?"

"He has more than that," the grating metal voice answered. Deanna was pushed against the wall and stiffened as a hand ran up and down her body looking for a weapon and finding the nine-millimeter Taurus that she had been carrying around for days.

Once it was taken, Deanna began to turn around. "No!" The Corsair ground the gun into her spine. "You will face the wall and listen. From here on, you will do as you're told or the Captain will start sending pieces of Emily to you in little boxes. Do you understand?"

"Yes," Deanna answered with surprising strength. She had been dreading those words and thought that she would fold into a ball and start to whine and beg when she heard them. But they had come out too coldly, almost as if the person had rehearsed the line. And the words had been almost the very same ones that had been playing in her head. All in all, it made the horror of what might happen less intangible and more human, and Deanna was skilled at dealing with humanity.

"Good," the person said, easing the barrel of the gun back slightly. "You better understand because your situation isn't good. You have no allies. The Captain has crushed the revolt and has separated his foes. He holds the Queen captive and has slain all who have dared to go up against him, including your little friends."

The sinking feeling she had expected early began and Deanna swallowed loudly. "You mean Neil?" Once again, she started to look back.

The gun pinned her to the wall. "Yes. And others. Many others. McCarrt, Steinmeyer, Powers, Currans, Gunner, all of them. Bainbridge stands alone and its fate is guaranteed and do you know why? It's because you are weak. You've always been weak."

"I'm not the one hiding behind a mask," Deanna spat, suddenly furious. Neil had been as innocent as Emily and his death filled her with acid.

"No, you're just hiding behind these walls. You and all the rest are hiding like rats. But what would happen if the Captain decides to tear down these walls? What would you do then? I think you'd get down on your knees and beg to be his slave if you were faced with the kind of death he could give you."

Deanna was slow to reply. This person seemed to have a real animus against her and the people of Bainbridge—almost as if it was personal. *What if I make it more personal?* she wondered. Ignoring the gun grinding her spine, she looked back and said, "I really don't care what you think, and you know what? Neither does the Captain. You're nothing but a go-between. You're nothing but a servant and isn't that something very much like a slave?"

The gun dug into her back, but she was no longer afraid of it. "Listen, slave, get that thing away from me." Deanna turned, knowing now that she wouldn't be shot. She gazed with hard eyes at the dark figure standing in front of her. He—or she, as Deanna suspected—was an inch shorter than her. "You won't shoot me because then where would you be? You'd be on the Captain's naughty list and we all know what happens to people on that particular list."

"You're on that list," the person growled.

Deanna smiled, showing off her fabulous white teeth. Being told she was on the Captain's kill list was not a revelation, and yet it had been a mistake. It made all subsequent threats a little less threatening if the end game was going to be the same no matter what.

"Do I look scared?" Deanna asked, halfway to yanking back the black cowl covering the spy. "You've given your little speech, now let's get to the point. Tell me what the Captain wants."

"He wants Bainbridge. All of it, including its people, and you'll be the one to hand it over. There's a way onto the island— a secret way—and if you set things up correctly, the Captain will release Emily to you and let you both go free. If not, Emily dies slowly in dreadful pain. And your people will suffer as well. The Captain will starve you out. We control the sea and the Sound. Even now we have ships in these waters and soon the island will be ringed with men. Nothing will get on or off the island."

Once more, Deanna wasn't surprised. Obviously, Joslyn had known about Jillybean's secret way off the island and had spilled it to the Captain. The secret tunnel was small, yet a hundred men could get through it every two minutes. Under the right circumstances, Bainbridge could be overwhelmed in no time. Deanna had already considered this and had plans to block up the tunnel.

And the idea of being starved into submission wasn't a new concept either. A few years before, Jillybean, without being asked, had drawn up six attack plans that were the most likely to succeed against the island. Slow starvation had been the first on the list.

"Well, this is a lot to take in," Deanna said. Without asking, she went to the chair and dropped down into it. She drummed her fingers on the armrest as if thinking. She wasn't, however. Her mind was made up. She knew the truth. As hard as it was to face, the Captain would never let her go and so, Emily's fate would hinge on her coming up with a different plan.

Almost as an afterthought, Deanna asked, "And what guarantees do I have that Emily and I will be safe?"

"None. Then again, why would he lie? If he keeps his word in these sorts of matters, it'll make the next set of negotiations that much easier. It behooves him to keep his word."

Deanna slowly shook her head. "You'd think so and yet I can't recall a single time he has kept his word about anything. Can you?"

Taken by surprise by the question, the dark figure was quiet for a moment before answering, "This isn't about the Captain. This is about you and what you're willing to do to save your daughter."

She smiled because that was exactly what she had been asking herself. Giving in to the Captain's demands would be as easy as it would be useless. Deanna would have to do the hardest thing imaginable and that was to turn the tables on the man who held her daughter. She had to put him to the test and back up her words with actions.

Standing, she faced the person as if the gun was nothing but a toy. "Let me tell you what I'm willing to do to save my daughter. I'm willing to arm every single person on this island and march to Hoquiam and kill every damned Corsair who gets in my way." The words were spoken softly but icily cold.

The person wavered and Deanna's eyes blazed, feeling that she had just pried an edge off a safe. "Here's what I want you to tell your master, slave." Deanna leaned in close and jabbed the woman in her soft chest. "Tell him that he will give me back Emily, unharmed, or by God I will destroy him, piece by fucking piece. I guarantee that. Those are the only terms I will accept."

The woman in black leaned back and when she swallowed, it was amplified. She began shaking her head. "Okay, sure. I'll tell him exactly that, but he won't believe you. He knows exactly how soft your people are. They'll never come out of their little holes to fight."

Now, it was Deanna's turn to nod in agreement. "You're right, but that's why I plan to unleash *Operation Otter Pop*."

"And what the hell is that? It doesn't sound all that bad."

"No, it doesn't. Ask Jillybean what it is." The person looked uncertain and Deanna snapped her fingers. "Go. Now! Tell the Captain he has one week to bring me my daughter or face my wrath." Deanna even pushed the spy out of her room. She then put her ear to the door and listened as the steps retreated down the hall.

When the front door clicked shut, she began pacing, her mind in a storm, wondering how she could pull off the most dangerous and insane of Jillybean's defensive plans. *Operation Otter Pop* was simple. Jillybean had explained the plan four years before in that very room. "As good as our defenses are, they are passive. We have to wait and react. In the end it's a losing strategy. In truth, the best defense is a good offense."

"But we don't have an offense," Deanna answered, looking over at Neil as if she had missed something.

"Exactly," Neil said. "And we will never be an offensive force because of the walls."

"So, what would happen if we were to remove them?" Jillybean asked, that terrible sly grin of hers showing.

375

Deanna had laughed. "Are you suggesting that we destroy our own walls? Because that's crazy, under any circumstances."

And yet, here she was, not only contemplating destroying the walls she had helped to build but also planning the best way to take them down. The Captain wanted to know what she was willing to do to save her daughter and he was going to find out.

The End.

Author's Note:

Before you ask, yes the Generation Z story continues! Luckily, there is a way for you to read Book 6, chapter by chapter, before anyone else! All you have to do is go to my Patreon page (**Here**) and support my writing. The tier levels are exceedingly generous with freebies running from autographed books, video podcasts, free Audible books, signed T-shirts, and swag of all sorts. At a high enough tier you will even get to meet me in person as I take you and three friends out to dinner.

Patreon a great way to help support me so I don't have to go back into the coal mines...back into the dark.

Another way is to write a review of this book on Amazon and/or on your own Facebook page. The review is the most practical and inexpensive form of advertisement an independent author has available to get his work known. I would greatly appreciate it.

Now, that you've gone to my Patreon page and left your review—thank you very much—I would love for you to take a look at another series of mine: **The Apocalypse Crusade**. I am currently finishing the series with Day 5:

Forget what you think you know about zombies...

Forget the poorly acted movies and the comic books. Forget the endless debates over fast and slow walkers. From this day on, all that crap will fade away to nothing. America is on the precipice of hell and not for a moment do you believe it. You have your cable and your smartphone and your take-out twice a week and your vacation to Disney Land all planned, and you tell yourself you'll drop those ten pounds before you go.

But you aren't going anywhere.

In one horrible day your world collapses into nothing but a spitting, cursing, bleeding fight for survival. For some the descent into hell is a long, slow, painful process of going at it tooth and nail, while for others it's over in a scream that's choked off when the blood pours down their windpipe. Those are the lucky ones.

But you will live, somehow, and you'll remember day one of the apocalypse where there was a chance, in fact there were plenty of chances for someone to stop it in its tracks and you'll wonder why the hell nobody did anything.

At first light on that first morning, Dr. Lee steps into the Walton facility on the initial day of human trials for the cure she's devoted her life to; she can barely contain her excitement. The labs are brand spanking new and everything is sharp and clean. They've been built to her specifications and are, without a doubt, a scientist's dream. Yet even better than the gleaming instruments is the fact that Walton is where cancer is going to be cured once and for all. It's where Dr. Lee is going to become world famous...only she doesn't realize what she's going to be famous for.

By midnight of that first day, Walton is a place of fire, of blood and of death, a death that, like the Apocalypse, is just the beginning.

What readers say about The Apocalypse Crusades:

"DO NOT pick this up until you are ready to commit to an all-night sleep-defying read!"

"WAY OUT WICKED"

"...full of suspense and intrigue, love, both innocent and romantic, hate, both blinding and unnatural, non-stop action, and a very real gripping and palpable fear."

PS If you are interested in autographed copies of my books, souvenir posters of the covers, Apocalypse T-shirts and other awesome Swag, please visit my website at **https:// www.petemeredith1.com**

PPS: I need to thank a number of people for their help in bringing you this book. My beta readers Joanna Niederer, Jenn Lockhart, KariAnn Morgan, Kari-Lyn Rakestraw, Doni Battenburg, Brenda Nord, Monica Turner, S.D. Buhl, Michelle Heeder, Wendy Boughton, Mindy Wilkinson, Nikki Johnson-Tyner, Amber Carrol—Thanks so much!

Fictional works by Peter Meredith:

A Perfect America

Infinite Reality: Daggerland Online Novel 1

Infinite Assassins: Daggerland Online Novel 2

Generation Z

Generation Z: The Queen of the Dead

Generation Z: The Queen of War

Generation Z: The Queen Unthroned

Generation Z: The Queen Enslaved

The Sacrificial Daughter

The Apocalypse Crusade War of the Undead: Day One

The Apocalypse Crusade War of the Undead: Day Two

The Apocalypse Crusade War of the Undead Day Three

The Apocalypse Crusade War of the Undead Day Four

The Horror of the Shade: Trilogy of the Void 1

An Illusion of Hell: Trilogy of the Void 2

Hell Blade: Trilogy of the Void 3

The Punished

Sprite

The Blood Lure The Hidden Land Novel 1

The King's Trap The Hidden Land Novel 2

To Ensnare a Queen The Hidden Land Novel 3

The Apocalypse: The Undead World Novel 1

The Apocalypse Survivors: The Undead World Novel 2

The Apocalypse Outcasts: The Undead World Novel 3

The Apocalypse Fugitives: The Undead World Novel 4

The Apocalypse Renegades: The Undead World Novel 5

The Apocalypse Exile: The Undead World Novel 6

The Apocalypse War: The Undead World Novel 7

The Apocalypse Executioner: The Undead World Novel 8

The Apocalypse Revenge: The Undead World Novel 9

The Apocalypse Sacrifice: The Undead World 10

The Edge of Hell: Gods of the Undead Book One

The Edge of Temptation: Gods of the Undead Book Two

The Witch: Jillybean in the Undead World

Jillybean's First Adventure: An Undead World Expansion

Tales from the Butcher's Block

40382212R00211

Made in the USA
San Bernardino, CA
26 June 2019